THE MAP AND THE TERRITORY

MICHEL HOUELLEBECQ

Translated from the French by Gavin Bowd

WILLIAM HEINEMANN: LONDON

Published by William Heinemann 2011

2 4 6 8 10 9 7 5 3 1

Translated from the original French edition
LA CARTE ET LE TERRITOIRE © Michel Houellebecq et Flammarion 2010

First published in Great Britain in 2011 by
William Heinemann
Random House, 20 Vauxhall Bridge Road,
London SW1V 2SA

www.randomhouse.co.uk

Addresses for companies within The Random House Group Limited
can be found at: www.randomhouse.co.uk/offices.htm

The Random House Group Limited Reg. No. 954009

A CIP catalogue record for this book
is available from the British Library

ISBN 9780434021406 (Hardback)
ISBN 9780434021413 (Trade paperback)

MIX
Paper from
responsible sources
FSC® C018575

The Random House Group Limited supports The Forest Stewardship Council
(FSC®), the leading international forest certification organisation. Our books carrying the FSC
label are printed on FSC® certified paper. FSC is the only forest certification scheme endorsed by
the leading environmental organisations, including Greenpeace. Our paper procurement policy
can be found at www.randomhouse.co.uk/environment

Typeset in Dante MT by Palimpsest Book Production Limited,
Falkirk, Stirlingshire

Printed and bound in Great Britain by
Clays Ltd, St Ives plc

Also by Michel Houellebecq

H. P. Lovecraft: Against the World, Against Life
Whatever
Atomised
Platform
Lanzarote
The Possibility of an Island
Public Enemies (with Bernard-Henri Lévy)

THE MAP AND THE TERRITORY

Michel Houellebecq is a poet, essayist and novelist. He is the author of five novels, *Whatever*, *Atomised*, *Platform*, *The Possibility of an Island* and *The Map and the Territory*, which won the prestigious literary prize, the Prix Goncourt. He lives in Ireland.

This book is supported by the French Ministry of Foreign Affairs, as part of the Burgess programme run by the Cultural Department of the French Embassy in London. www.frenchbooknews.com

Liberté • Égalité • Fraternité
RÉPUBLIQUE FRANÇAISE

'The world is weary of me,
And I am weary of it.'

Charles d'Orléans

Jeff Koons had just got up from his chair, enthusiastically throwing his arms out in front of him. Sitting opposite him, on a white leather sofa partly draped with silks and slightly hunched up, Damien Hirst seemed to be about to express an objection; his face was flushed, morose. Both of them were wearing black suits – Koons's had fine pinstripes – white shirts and black ties. Between them, on the coffee table, was a basket of candied fruits that neither paid any attention to. Hirst was drinking a Budweiser Light.

Behind them, a bay window opened onto a landscape of tall buildings that formed a Babylonian tangle of gigantic polygons reaching the horizon. The night was bright, the air absolutely clear. They could have been in Qatar, or Dubai; the decoration of the room was, in reality, inspired by an advertisement photograph, taken from a German luxury publication, of the Emirates Hotel in Abu Dhabi.

Koons's forehead was slightly shiny. Jed shaded it off with his brush and stepped back three paces. There was certainly a problem with Koons. Hirst was basically easy to capture: you could make him brutal, cynical in an 'I shit on you from the top of my pile of dosh' kind of way; you could also make him a *rebel artist* (but rich all the same) pursuing an *anguished work on death*; finally, there was in his face something ruddy and heavy, typically English, which made him look like a rank-and-file Arsenal supporter. In short, there were various aspects, but all of them could be combined in the coherent, representable portrait of a British artist typical of his generation. Koons, on the other hand, seemed to carry in him something dual, like an insurmountable contradiction between the basic cunning of the technical sales rep and the exaltation of the ascetic. It was already three weeks now that Jed had been retouching Koon's expression as he stood up from his chair,

throwing his arms out in front of him as if he was trying to convince
Hirst about something. It was as difficult as painting a Mormon
pornographer.

He had photographs of Koons on his own, in the company of
Roman Abramovich, Madonna, Barack Obama, Bono, Warren
Buffett, Bill Gates . . . Not one of them managed to express nearly
as much personality, to go beyond the appearance of a Chevrolet
convertible salesman that Koons had decided to display to the world,
and this was exasperating. In fact, for a long time photographers
had exasperated Jed, especially the *great photographers*, with their
claim to reveal in their snapshots the *truth* of their models; they
didn't reveal anything at all, they just placed themselves in front
of you and switched on the motor of their camera to take at
random hundreds of snapshots while chuckling, and later chose
the least bad of the lot; that's how they proceeded, without exception, all those so-called *great photographers*. Jed knew some of them
personally and had nothing but contempt for them; he considered
them all about as creative as a Photomaton.

In the kitchen, a few steps behind him, the boiler uttered a succession of loud banging noises. It went rigid, paralysed. It was already
15 December.

One year before, on almost the same date, his boiler had uttered
the same succession of banging noises before stopping completely.
In a few hours, the temperature in the studio had fallen to 3°C.
He had managed to sleep a little, or rather doze off, for brief
periods. Around six in the morning, he had emptied the hot-water
tank to quickly wash himself, then had brewed coffee while waiting
for the man from Plumbing in General, who had promised to send
someone in the early hours of the morning.

On its website, Plumbing in General offered to 'make plumbing
enter the third millennium'; they could at least start by turning up
on time, grumbled Jed at about eleven, pacing around his studio
in a vain attempt to warm himself up. He was then working on a

painting of his father, which he was going to entitle *The Architect Jean-Pierre Martin Leaving the Management of his Business*; inevitably, the fall in temperature meant that the last layer of paint would take an age to dry. He had agreed, as he did every year, to dine with his father on Christmas Eve, two weeks hence, and hoped to have finished it by then; if a plumber didn't intervene quickly, his plan risked being compromised. To tell the truth, in absolute terms, it wasn't that important: he didn't intend to offer this painting to his father as a gift, he wanted simply to *show* it to him. Why, then, was he suddenly attaching so much importance to it? He was certainly at the end of his tether; he was working too hard and had started six paintings simultaneously. For a few months he hadn't stopped. It wasn't sensible.

At around three in the afternoon, he decided to call Plumbing in General again, but the line was constantly engaged. He managed to get through to them just after five, when the customer services secretary explained that there had been an exceptional workload due to the frigid weather, but promised that someone would certainly come the following morning. Jed hung up, then reserved a room in the Mercure Hotel on the boulevard Auguste-Blanqui.

The following day, he again waited all day for the arrival of Plumbing in General, but also for Simply Plumbers, whom he had managed to contact in the meantime. While Simply Plumbers promised to respect the craft traditions of 'higher plumbing', they showed themselves to be no more capable of turning up on time.

In the painting he had made of him, Jed's father, standing on a podium in the middle of the group of about fifty employees that made up his business, was lifting his glass with a sorrowful smile. The farewell drinks party took place in the open space of his architectural practice, a large room thirty metres by twenty with white walls, and a skylight under which computer design posts alternated with trestle tables carrying the scale models of current projects. Most of those present were nerdy-looking young people – the 3D designers. Standing at the foot of the podium, three forty-something architects surrounded his father. In accordance with a configuration borrowed from a minor painting by Lorenzo Lotto, each of them avoided the eyes of the others, while trying to catch those of his father; each of them, you understood right away, nurtured the hope of succeeding him as the head of the business. His father's eyes, staring just above those present, expressed the desire to gather his team around him for one last time, a reasonable confidence in the future, but also an absolute sadness. Sadness at leaving the business he had founded, to which he had given all his strength, and sadness at the inevitable: you were quite obviously dealing with a finished man.

In the middle of the afternoon, Jed tried in vain, a dozen times, to get through to Ze Plumb, which used Skyrock radio as its on-hold music, while Simply Plumbing had opted for the radio station Laughter and Songs.

At about five, he returned to the Mercure Hotel. Night was falling on the boulevard Auguste-Blanqui; some homeless people had lit a fire on one side of the street.

The following days passed more or less in the same way: dialling numbers of plumbing businesses, being redirected almost instantaneously to on-hold music, waiting, as it got colder and colder, next to his painting, which refused to dry.

A solution came on the morning of 24 December, in the form of a Croatian workman who lived nearby on the avenue Stephen-Pinchon; Jed had noticed the sign by accident while returning from the Mercure Hotel. He was available, yes, immediately. He was a small man with black hair and a pale complexion, harmonious and fine features, and a rather belle époque moustache; in fact, he looked a bit like Jed – apart from the moustache.

Immediately after entering the flat, he examined the boiler for a long time, dismantling the control panel, running his slender fingers along the complex trail of pipes. He spoke of valves and siphons. He gave the impression of knowing a lot about life in general.

After a quarter of an hour, his diagnosis was the following: he could repair, yes, he could do *a sort of repair*, that would come to fifty euros, no more. But it would be less than a genuine repair job, only a makeshift one, really, that would do the trick for a few months, even a few years in the best-case scenario, but he refused to give any long-term guarantee; more generally, it was unseemly to make a long-term bet on this boiler.

Jed sighed and confessed he had half expected it. He remembered very well the day when he had decided to buy this flat; he could still see the estate agent, stocky and self-satisfied, boasting of the exceptional light, but not hiding the need for certain 'improvements'. He had then told himself that he should have become an estate agent, or a gynaecologist.

Barely amiable in the first few minutes, the stocky estate agent went into a lyrical trance when he learned that Jed was an artist. It was the first time, he exclaimed, that he'd had the opportunity to sell an *artist's studio* to an *artist*! Jed feared for a moment that he would declare his solidarity with authentic artists against the bourgeois bohemians and other such philistines who inflated prices, thus making artists' studios inaccessible to artists, but what can you do. I can't go against the truth of the market, it's not my role. But fortunately this did not happen. The stocky estate agent just offered him a ten per cent discount – which he had probably already foreseen offering after a mini-negotiation.

'Artist's studio' really meant an attic with a skylight – a very nice one, it must be said – and a few dark adjoining spaces, scarcely insufficient for someone like Jed, who had very limited hygienic needs. But the view was, indeed, splendid: beyond the place des Alpes it extended as far as the boulevard Vincent-Auriol and the overground Métro, and further on to those quadrangular buildings built in the mid-seventies in complete opposition to the rest of the Parisian aesthetic landscape, and which were what Jed preferred in Paris, by far, in terms of architecture.

The Croat did the repair job and pocketed the fifty euros. He didn't offer an invoice, and neither had Jed expected one. The door had just closed behind him when he knocked again very gently. Jed opened the door slightly.

'By the way, monsieur,' said the man. 'Merry Christmas. I wanted to say to you: Merry Christmas.'

'Yes, I'd forgotten,' said Jed, embarrassed. 'Merry Christmas to you too.'

It was then that he became aware of the problem of the taxi. As expected, ToAnywhere refused point-blank to drive him to Raincy, and Speedtax agreed to take him to the railway station, and at a pinch as far as the town hall, but certainly not near the Cicadas housing scheme. 'Security reasons, monsieur,' whispered the employee with a slight reproach in his voice. 'We only serve completely safe zones, monsieur,' said the receptionist for Fernand Garcin Cars with smooth self-importance. Jed felt more and more guilty about wanting to spend Christmas Eve in such an incongruous place, and, as happened every year, began to get angry with his father, who obstinately refused to quit that bourgeois house, surrounded by a vast park, that population movements had gradually relegated to the heart of a zone that grew ever more dangerous, and had recently fallen under the complete control of gangs.

Firstly, the perimeter wall had needed to be reinforced and topped with an electrified fence, then a CCTV system linked to the police station was installed, all so his father could wander alone in twelve rooms that were impossible to heat and where no one came except Jed, every Christmas Eve. The nearby shops had long since closed, and it was impossible to walk around the neighbouring streets since even attacks on cars at the traffic lights were not unheard of. Raincy council had given him a home help – a cantankerous and nasty Senegalese woman called Fatty who had disliked him from the start, refused to change the sheets more than once a month, and most probably stole from the shopping allowance.

Be that as it may, the temperature was rising slowly in the room. Jed took a photo of the painting in progress, which would at least give him something to show his father. He took off his trousers and his pullover, sat down cross-legged on the narrow mattress on the floor that served as his bed, and wrapped himself in a blanket. Gradually, he slowed the rhythm of his breathing. He visualised waves rolling slowly, lazily, beneath a matt twilight. He tried to lead his mind to a place of calm; and prepare himself as best he could for another Christmas Eve with his father.

This mental preparation bore fruit, and the evening was a zone of neutral time, even semi-convivial; he had hoped for nothing more.

The following morning, at about seven, assuming that the gangs too had *celebrated Christmas*, Jed walked to Raincy station and got back to Gare de l'Est without a hitch.

One year on, the repair had held, and this was the first time that the boiler had shown signs of weakness. *The Architect Jean-Pierre Martin Leaving the Management of his Business* had been finished for some time and put into storage by Jed's gallerist in anticipation of a personal exhibition that was taking a while to organise. Jean-Pierre Martin himself – to the surprise of his son, who he had long since given up talking to about it – had decided to leave the house in Raincy and move into a nursing home in Boulogne. Their annual meal would this time take place in a brasserie on the avenue Bosquet called Chez Papa. Jed had chosen it in *Pariscope* on the strength of an advert promising traditional quality, *à l'ancienne*, and this promise was, on the whole, kept. Some Father Christmases and trees decorated with tinsel sprinkled the half-empty room, essentially occupied by small groups of old people, some very old, who chewed carefully, consciously and even ferociously on dishes of traditional cuisine. There was wild boar, suckling pig and turkey; for dessert, of course, a patisserie yule log *à l'ancienne* was proposed by the house, whose polite and discreet waiters operated in silence, as if in a burns unit. Jed was a bit stupid, he realised, to offer his father such a meal. This dry, serious man, with a long and austere face, never seemed to have been taken by the pleasures of the table, and the rare times Jed had dined out with him, when he had needed to see him near his place of work, his father had chosen a sushi restaurant – always the same one. It was pathetic and vain to want to establish a gastronomical conviviality that had no *raison d'être*, and which had not even conceivably ever had one – his wife, while she was alive, had always hated cooking. But it was Christmas, and what else could you do? His father didn't seem interested in much anymore; he read less and less, and was utterly indifferent to questions of dress. He was, according to the director of the nursing home, 'reasonably integrated', which probably meant that he hardly said a word to anyone. For the time being, he chewed laboriously on his suckling pig, with about the same expression as if it were a piece of rubber; nothing indicated that he wanted to break the lengthening silence, and Jed, being nervous (he should never have taken Gewürztraminer with the oysters – he had realised that from the moment he had ordered, white wine always made his mind fuzzy), looked frenetically for some subject that might lend itself to conversation. If he had been married, or at least had a girlfriend, *well, some kind of woman*, things would have happened very differently. Women are generally more at ease with these family affairs, it's sort of their basic speciality; even in the absence of real children, they are there, potentially, on the edge of the conversation, and it is a known fact that old people are interested in their grandchildren, whom they link to natural cycles or something. Well, there's a sort of emotion that manages to be born in their old heads: the son is the death of the father, certainly, but for the grandfather the grandson is a sort of rebirth or revenge, and that can be largely sufficient, at least for the duration of a Christmas dinner. Jed sometimes thought that he should hire an escort for these Christmas Eves, create a sort of mini-fiction; it would be enough to brief the girl a couple of hours beforehand; his father wasn't very curious about the details of the lives of others, no more than men in general.

In Latin countries, politics is enough for the conversational needs of middle- or old-aged males; it is sometimes replaced in the lower classes by sport. Among people particularly influenced by Anglo-Saxon values, politics is supplanted by economics and finance; literature can provide backup. But neither Jed nor his father had any real interest in economics, or politics for that matter. Jean-Pierre Martin approved overall of the way in which the country was led, and his son didn't have an opinion; however, by reviewing each ministry in turn they at least managed to keep the conversation going until the cheese trolley arrived.

Over the cheese course, Jed's father got slightly animated and asked him about his projects. Unfortunately, this time it was Jed who risked spoiling the atmosphere, because since his last painting, *Damien Hirst and Jeff Koons Dividing Up the Art Market*, he no longer felt much about art. He was going nowhere. There was a sort of force that had carried him for a year or two but was now dissipating, crumbling, but what was the point of saying all that to his father, who could do nothing about it. To tell the truth no one could; when faced with such a confession, people could only be slightly sad. They really don't amount to much, anyway, human relationships.

'I'm preparing a solo exhibition in the spring,' he finally announced. 'Well, in fact it's dragging on a bit. Franz, my gallerist, wants a writer for the catalogue. He thought of Houellebecq.'

'Michel Houellebecq?'

'Do you know him?' asked Jed, surprised. He would never have suspected that his father could still be interested in anything cultural.

'There's a small library in the nursing home; I've read two of his novels. He's a good author, it seems to me. He's pleasant to read, and he has quite an accurate view of society. Has he replied to you?'

'No, not yet . . .' Jed was now thinking as fast as he could. If someone as deeply paralysed in such a hopeless and mortal routine, someone as far down the path of darkness, down the Valley of the Shadow of Death, as his father was had noticed Houellebecq's existence, it was because there had to be something compelling about this author. He then remembered that he had failed to get in touch with Houellebecq by email, as Franz had asked him to several times already. And yet time was pressing. Given the date of Art Basel and the Frieze Art Fair, the exhibition had to be organised by April, or May at the latest, and you could hardly ask Houellebecq to write a catalogue text in a fortnight. He was a famous writer, world-famous even, at least according to Franz.

His father's excitement had subsided, and he was chewing his Saint-Nectaire with as little enthusiasm as he had the suckling pig. It's no doubt through compassion that we imagine old people have a particularly good appetite, because we like to think that at least they have that left, when in the majority of cases the enjoyment of taste disappears irredeemably, along with the rest. Digestive problems and prostate cancer remain.

A few metres to their left, three octogenarian women seemed to be praying over their fruit salad – perhaps in homage to their dead husbands. One of them reached out towards her glass of champagne, then her hand fell onto the table; her chest was palpitating. After a few seconds she tried again, her hand shaking terribly, her face screwed up in concentration. Jed restrained himself from intervening, being in no position to help. Neither was the waiter himself, on duty only steps away, who was watching the operation carefully. This woman was now in direct contact with God. She was probably closer to ninety than eighty.

To go through all the motions, desserts were then served in turn. With resignation, Jed's father attacked his traditional yule log. There wasn't much longer to go now. Time passed bizarrely between them: although nothing was said, and the silence now permanently established over the table should have given the sensation of total gravity, it seemed that the seconds, and even the minutes, flowed with astonishing speed. Half an hour later, without even a thought really crossing his mind, Jed accompanied his father back to the taxi rank. It was only ten, but Jed knew that the other residents of the retirement home already deemed his father lucky: to have someone, for a few hours, to celebrate Christmas with. 'You have a good son . . .' This had already been pointed out to him, several times. On entering the nursing home, the former head of the family – now, irrefutably, an old man – feels a bit like a child at boarding school. Sometimes, he receives visits: then it's happiness, he can discover the world, eat some Pepitos and meet Ronald McDonald. But, more often, he doesn't receive any: he then wanders around sadly, between the handball goalposts, on the bitumous ground of the deserted boarding school. He waits for liberation, an escape from all of it.

Back in his studio, Jed noticed that the boiler was still working, the temperature normal, even warm. He got partly undressed before stretching out on his mattress and falling asleep immediately, his brain completely empty.

He awoke suddenly in the middle of the night; the clock said 4:43. The room was hot, suffocatingly so. It was the noise of the boiler that had woken him, but not the usual banging noises; the machine now gave out a prolonged, low-pitched, almost infrasonic roar. He threw open the kitchen window, which was covered in frost, and the freezing air filled the room. Six storeys below, some piglike grunts troubled the Christmas night. He shut the window immediately. Most probably some tramps had got into the courtyard; the following day they would take advantage of the Christmas leftovers in the block's dustbins. None of the tenants would dare call the police to get rid of them – not on Christmas Day. It was generally the tenant on the first floor who ended up taking care of it – a woman aged about sixty, with hennaed hair, who wore garishly coloured pullovers, and whom Jed guessed was a retired psychoanalyst. But he hadn't seen her in the last few days. She was probably on holiday – unless she'd died suddenly. The tramps were going to stay for several days; the smell of their defecations would fill the courtyard, preventing anyone from opening the windows. To the tenants they came across as polite, even obsequious, but the fights between them were ferocious, and generally ended with screams of agony rising to the night sky; someone would call an ambulance and a guy would be found bathed in blood, with an ear half ripped off.

Jed approached the boiler, which had gone silent, and carefully raised the flap over the control panel; immediately the machine uttered a brief roar, as if it felt threatened by the intrusion. An incomprehensible yellow light was flickering rapidly. Gently, millimetre by millimetre, Jed turned the intensity control leftwards. If things got worse, he still had the Croat's phone number; but was it still in service? He didn't want to 'stagnate in plumbing', he'd confessed candidly to Jed. His ambition, once he had 'made his pile', was to return home, to Croatia, more precisely the island of Hvar, to open a business renting out sea scooters. Incidentally, one of the last projects that his father had dealt with before retirement concerned an invitation to bid on the construction of a prestigious marina in Stari Grad, on Hvar, which was indeed beginning to become a celebrated destination; only last year Sean Penn and Angelina Jolie had been seen there, and Jed felt an obscure sense of human disappointment at the idea of this man abandoning plumbing, a noble craft, to rent out noisy and stupid machines to stuck-up rich kids living in the rue de la Faisanderie.

'But what is this place notable for?' asked the Internet portal of the isle of Hvar, before replying thus: 'There are meadows of lavender, old olive trees and vines in a unique harmony, and so the visitor who wants to get close to nature will first visit the small *konoba* (tavern) of Hvar instead of going to the most luxurious hotel, he will taste the local wine instead of champagne, he will sing an old folk song of the island and he will forget his daily routine.' That's probably what had seduced Sean Penn, and Jed imagined the dead season, the still mild October months, the ex-plumber sitting peacefully over his seafood risotto; obviously this choice could be understood, even excused.

A little despite himself, he approached *Damien Hirst and Jeff Koons Dividing Up the Art Market*, which was standing on his easel in the middle of the studio, and dissatisfaction seized him again, still more bitterly. He realised he was hungry, which wasn't normal after the complete Christmas dinner he'd had with his father – starter, main course, cheese and dessert, nothing had been left out – but he felt hungry and so hot he could no longer breathe. He returned to the kitchen, opened a tin of cannelloni in sauce and ate them one by one, while looking morosely at his failed painting. Koons was undoubtedly not light enough, not ethereal enough – it would perhaps have been necessary to give him wings, like the god Mercury, he thought stupidly; there, with his pinstriped suit and salesman's smile, he reminded you a bit of Silvio Berlusconi.

On the ArtPrice ranking of the richest artists, Koons was world number 2; for a few years now, Hirst, ten years his junior, had taken his place at number 1. As for Jed, he had reached 593 ten years ago – but 17 in France. He had then, as the Tour de France commentators say, 'dropped to the bottom of the *classement*', before disappearing from it altogether. He finished the tin of cannelloni and opened an almost empty bottle of cognac. Lighting his ramp of halogen lamps to the maximum, he trained them on the centre of the canvas. On closer inspection, the night itself wasn't right: it didn't have that sumptuousness, that mystery we associate with nights on the Arabian peninsula; he should have used a deep blue, not ultramarine. He was making a truly shit painting. He seized a palette knife, cut open Damien Hirst's eye, and forced the gash wider; it was a canvas of tight linen fibres, and therefore very tough. Catching the sticky canvas with one hand, he tore it in one blow, tipping the easel over onto the floor. Slightly calmed, he stopped, looked at his hands, sticky with paint, and finished the cognac before jumping feet first onto his painting, stamping on it and rubbing it against the floor until it became slippery. He ended up losing his balance and fell, the back of his head hitting the frame of the easel violently. He belched and vomited, and suddenly felt better, the fresh night air circulating freely on his face, and he closed his eyes contentedly: he had visibly reached the end of a cycle.

Part One

1

Jed no longer remembered when he had first begun to draw. No doubt all children draw, more or less, but as he didn't know any children, he wasn't sure. His only certainty was that he had begun by drawing flowers – in small jotters, with coloured pencils.

On Wednesday afternoons generally, and occasionally on Sundays, he had known moments of ecstasy, alone in the sunlit garden, while the babysitter telephoned her boyfriend of the moment. Vanessa was eighteen and in her first year studying economics at the University of Saint-Denis/Villetaneuse, and for a long time was the only witness to his first artistic endeavours. She found his drawings pretty, she told him sincerely, but she occasionally gave him a perplexed look. Little boys draw bloodthirsty monsters, Nazi insignia, and fighter planes (or, for the most advanced among them, cunts and cocks), rarely flowers.

Jed did not realise it then, nor did Vanessa, but flowers are only sexual organs, brightly coloured vaginas decorating the surface of the world, open to the lubricity of insects. Insects and men, and other animals too, seem to pursue a goal, their movements rapid and orientated, while flowers remain in the light, dazzling and fixed. The beauty of flowers is sad because they are fragile and destined for death, like anything on earth of course, but flowers are particularly fragile, and like animals their corpse is only a grotesque parody of their vital being, and their corpse, like that of an animal, stinks. You understand all of this once you have lived through the passing of the seasons, and as for the withering of flowers, Jed had understood it himself from the age of five, and maybe before, as there were lots of flowers in the park surrounding the house in Raincy. A lot of trees too, and the branches of the trees shaken by the wind were perhaps one of the first things he'd noticed when he was pushed around in his pram by an adult woman (his mother?), apart from the clouds and the sky. The animalistic will to live manifests itself in rapid transformations – a moistening of the hole, a stiffness of the stem, and the emission of seminal liquid – but he would only discover that later, on a balcony in Port-Grimaud, via Marthe Taillefer. The flower's will to live manifests itself in the dazzling spots of colour that break the greenish banality of the natural landscape, as well as the generally transparent banality of the urban landscape – or at least in municipalities in bloom.

In the evening, Jed's father would come home. He was called 'Jean-Pierre', or that's what his friends called him. Jed called him 'Dad'. He was a good father, and was considered as such by his friends and associates; a widower needs a lot of courage to bring up a child alone. Jean-Pierre had been a good father at first, but was less so now; he paid for a babysitter more often, and frequently ate out (most often with clients, sometimes with associates, and more and more rarely with friends, for the time of friendship was beginning to decline for him; he no longer believed that you could have friends, that these friendly relationships could really count in the life of a man, or change his destiny). He returned home late and didn't even try to sleep with the babysitter, unlike most men; he would listen to the day's events, smile at his son, and pay the sum requested. He was the head of a broken family, and had no plans to mend it. He earned a lot of money: chief executive of a construction business, he had specialised in the creation of all-inclusive seaside resorts; he had clients in Portugal, the Maldives, and on San Domingo.

From this period Jed had kept his jotters, which contained all of his drawings. They were all dying gently, unhurriedly (the paper was not of very good quality, nor were the pencils). They might last two or three centuries more: things and beings have a lifespan.

Probably dating back to Jed's early adolescence was a gouache entitled *Haymaking in Germany* (quite mysteriously, for Jed didn't know Germany, and had never attended *a fortiori* or participated in 'haymaking'). Although the light obviously evoked high summer, snow-clad mountains closed the scene; the peasants loading hay with their pitchforks and the donkeys harnessed to their carts were treated with bright solid colours; it was as beautiful as a Cézanne, or indeed anything. The question of beauty is secondary in painting: the great painters of the past were considered such when they had developed a world view that was both coherent and innovative, which means that they always painted in the same way, using the same methods and operating procedures to transform the objects of the world into pictorial ones, in a matter that was specific to them and had never been used before. Such was the classical vision of painting, the one to which Jed had been initiated during his high-school studies, and which was based on the concept of *figuration* – to which Jed, during a few years of his career, would return, and which, even more bizarrely, finally brought him fortune and fame.

Jed devoted his life (or at least his professional life, which quite quickly became *the whole of his life*) to *art*, to the production of representations of the world, in which people were never meant to live. He could thus produce critical representations – critical to a certain extent, for the general movement of art as of society as a whole led in Jed's youth to an acceptance of the world that was occasionally enthusiastic, but most often nuanced with irony. His father in no way had this freedom of choice; he had to produce inhabitable configurations, in an absolutely unironic way, where people were destined to live, and have the possibility of finding pleasure, at least during their holidays. He was held responsible for any grave malfunctioning of the machine for living – if a lift collapsed, or the toilets were blocked, for example. He was not responsible for an invasion of the residence by a brutal, violent population uncontrolled by the police and established authorities; his responsibility was mitigated in the case of an earthquake.

The father of his father had been a photographer – his own origins being lost in a sort of unsavoury sociological pond, stagnating since time immemorial, essentially made up of farmworkers and poor peasants. What had brought this man from a miserable background face to face with the first techniques of photography? Jed had no idea, nor did his father; but he had been the first of a long line to get out of the pure and simple reproduction of the same. Mostly he had earned his living by photographing weddings, occasionally communions, or the end-of-year fetes of village schools. Living in that long-since abandoned and marginalised area that is the Creuse, he had had almost no opportunity to photograph any openings of buildings, or visits by national politicians. It was a mediocre craft, that paid badly, and his son's access to the architectural profession was already a serious social promotion – without mentioning his later successes as an entrepreneur.

By the time he entered the Beaux-Arts de Paris, Jed had given up drawing for photography. Two years earlier, he had discovered in his grandfather's attic a large-format camera, a Linhof Master Technika Classic; he'd no longer been using it when he retired, but it was in perfect working condition. He had been fascinated by this object, which was strange, heavy and prehistoric, but with an exceptional production quality. Slightly groping in the dark, he had finally learned to master tilt and shift, as well as the Scheimpflug principle, before launching himself into what was to take up almost all his artistic studies: the systematic photography of the world's manufactured objects. He carried out his work in his bedroom, generally with natural lighting. Suspension files, handguns, diaries, printer cartridges, forks: nothing escaped his encyclopedic ambition, which was to constitute an exhaustive catalogue of the objects of human manufacturing in the industrial age.

If, by its grandiose and maniacal, in fact demented, character, this project won him the respect of his teachers, it did not enable him in any way to join any of the groups that formed around him on the basis of a common aesthetic ambition, or more prosaically an attempt at collectively entering the art market. However, he made a few friendships, although not very deep ones, without realising at what point they would prove ephemeral. He also had a few love affairs, none of which lasted long. The day after he graduated, he understood that he was now going to be quite alone. His six years of work had produced more than eleven thousand photos. Stored in TIFF format, with a lowest-resolution JPEG, they were easily held on a Western Digital 640 GB hard disk, which weighed a little under 200 grams. He carefully put away his large-format camera and his lenses (he had at his disposal a Rodenstock Apo-Sironar of 105 mm, which opened to 5.6, and a Fujinon of 180 mm, which also opened to 5.6), then considered the remainder of his possessions. There was his laptop, his iPod, a few clothes, a few books: not a lot, in fact; it would easily fit into two suitcases. The weather was fine in Paris. He hadn't been unhappy in this bedroom or very happy, either. His lease ran out in a week's time. Hesitating to leave, he made one last walk around the area, on the banks of the lake by l'Arsenal, then called his father for help in moving out.

Their cohabitation in the house in Raincy, for the first time in a very long time, for the first time really since Jed's childhood, apart from some school holidays, immediately turned out to be both easy and empty. His father still worked a lot and was far from letting go of his business; it was rare for him to come home before nine, even ten; he collapsed in front of the television while Jed heated up one of the meals he'd bought a few weeks before, filling the boot of the Mercedes, from the Carrefour in Aulnay-sous-Bois. Trying to vary things, and maintain a nutritional balance, he also bought cheese and fruit. Anyway, his father paid little attention to food; he listlessly switched channels, generally settling on one of those tedious economic debates on LCI. He went to bed almost immediately after their dinner; in the morning, he had left even before Jed got up. The days were bright and uniformly hot. Jed would stroll between the trees in the park and sit down beneath a tall lime tree, holding a book of philosophy, which he generally didn't open. Some childhood memories came back, but very few;

then he would return home to watch the coverage of the Tour de France. He loved those boring long shots, taken by helicopter, that followed the peloton as it advanced lazily through the French countryside.

Anne, Jed's mother, was from a lower-middle-class Jewish family – her father the local jeweller. At twenty-five she married Jean-Pierre Martin, then a young architect. It was a marriage of love, and a few years later she gave birth to a son they named Jed in homage to her uncle, whom she had loved. Then, a few days before her son's seventh birthday, she had committed suicide – Jed only learned about this many years later, through the indiscretion of his paternal grandmother. Anne was forty, her husband forty-seven.

Jed had almost no memory of his mother, and her suicide was hardly a subject he could broach during this sojourn in the house in Raincy. He knew that he had to wait for his father to talk about it himself – all the while knowing that this would doubtless never happen, that he would avoid it, like all the others, to the very end.

One point, however, had to be clarified, and it was his father who dealt with it one Sunday afternoon, after they'd just watched a short stage – the Bordeaux time trial – that hadn't marked any decisive change in the general *classement*. They were in the library, by far the most beautiful room in the house, with an oak-panelled floor, left in a half-light by stained-glass windows, with English leather furniture; the surrounding bookshelves which contained almost six thousand volumes, mainly scientific treatises published in the nineteenth century. Jean-Pierre Martin had bought the house at a very good price, forty years before, from an owner who urgently needed liquidity. This was a safe and elegant residential area at the time, and he imagined a happy family life; in any case, the house would have enabled him to have a large family and frequently receive friends – but none of that had ultimately happened.

At the moment when the broadcast returned to the smiling and predictable face of presenter Michel Drucker, he switched off the sound and turned to his son. 'Do you plan to pursue an artistic career?' he asked; Jed replied in the affirmative. 'And, for the moment, you can't earn a living?' He nuanced his reply. To his own surprise he had, in the course of the previous year, been contacted by two photography agencies. The first specialised in the photography of objects, had clients for catalogues that included CAMIF and La Redoute, and sometimes sold its pictures to advertising agencies. The second specialised in culinary work for magazines like *Notre Temps* and *Femme Actuelle* that regularly called on its services. Unprestigious, neither field offered much money: taking a photograph of a mountain bike, or a soft cheese tartiflette, earned much less than a snapshot of Kate Moss, or even George Clooney; but the demand was constant, sustained, and could guarantee a decent income. Therefore Jed was not, if he could be bothered, absolutely without means of support; what's more, he felt it desirable to maintain a certain style of pure photography. He contented himself with delivering large-format negatives, precisely defined and exposed, that the agencies scanned and modified as they saw fit; he preferred not to get involved with the retouching of images, presumably subject to different commercial or advertising imperatives, and simply delivered pictures that were technically perfect, but entirely neutral.

'I'm happy you're autonomous,' his father replied. 'I've known several guys in my life who wanted to become artists, and were supported by their parents; not one of them managed to break through. It's curious, you might think that the need to express yourself, to leave a trace in the world, is a powerful force, yet in general that's not enough. What works best, what pushes people most violently to surpass themselves, is still the pure and simple need for money.

'I'm going to help you to buy a flat in Paris, all the same,' he went on. 'You're going to need to see people, make contacts. What's more, you could say it's an investment: the market is rather depressed at the moment.'

The television screen now featured a comedian who Jed almost managed to identify. Then there was a close-up of Michel Drucker laughing blissfully. Jed suddenly thought that his father maybe just wanted to be alone; true contact between them had never been re-established.

Two weeks later, Jed bought the flat he still occupied, on the boulevard de l'Hôpital, in the north of the 13th arrondissement. That most of the neighbouring streets were named after painters – Rubens, Watteau, Veronese, Philippe de Champaigne – could be considered a good omen. More prosaically, he was not far from the new galleries that were opening around the Très Grande Bibliothèque quarter. He hadn't really negotiated but had gathered enough information to know that everywhere in France prices were collapsing, especially in the urban areas. Properties remained empty, never finding a buyer.

2

Jed's memory held almost no image of his mother, but of course he had seen photos. She was a pretty woman with pale skin, long black hair, and in certain pictures you could even say she was beautiful; she looked a bit like the portrait of Agatha von Astighwelt in the museum of Dijon. She rarely smiled in these pictures, and even her smile seemed to hide an anxiety. No doubt this impression was influenced by the fact of her suicide; but even when trying to cut yourself off from that there was something in her that was a bit unreal, or in any case timeless; you could easily imagine her in a painting from the Middle Ages or the early Renaissance; on the other hand, it seemed implausible that she could have passed her teens in the 1960s, that she ever owned a *transistor* or gone to *rock concerts*.

During the first few years following her death, Jean-Pierre had tried to follow his son's schoolwork, and had scheduled activities for the weekend at McDonald's or the museum. Then, almost inevitably, the demands of his business had eclipsed them; his first contract in the domain of all-inclusive seaside resorts had been a stunning success. Not only had the deadlines and initial estimates been met – which was in itself relatively rare – but the construction also had been unanimously praised for its balance and respect for the environment. He had received ecstatic articles in the regional press as well as in the national architectural reviews, and even a full page in the 'Styles' section of *Libération*. At Port-Ambarès, it was written, he had managed to capture 'the essence of the Mediterranean habitat'. In his view he had only lined up cubes of variable size, in uniform matt white, directly copied from traditional Moroccan buildings, then separating them with beds of oleanders. All the same, after this initial success, the orders had flooded in, and more and more often he was required to go abroad. When Jed reached the first year of secondary school, he decided to send him to board.

He opted for the college at Rumilly, in the Oise, run by Jesuits. It was a private institution, but not one of those reserved solely for the elite: the fees remained reasonable, the teaching was not bilingual, and the sports facilities were nothing extravagant. The parents were not ultra-rich but rather conservative people from the old bourgeoisie (many were diplomats in the military), though not fundamentalist Catholics; most of the time, the child had been put in boarding school after a divorce turned ugly.

Although austere and unattractive, the buildings were reasonably comfortable; two to a room in the first years, the pupils had a private room once they reached fourth year. The strength of the establishment, the major plus in its portfolio, was the pedagogical support it offered each of its pupils. The rate of success at the baccalaureate had, since the establishment's creation, always stayed above 95 per cent.

It was within these walls, and under the extremely dark cover of avenues of pine trees in the park during long walks, that Jed spent his studious and sad teenage years. He didn't complain about his lot, and couldn't imagine any other. The fights between pupils were sometimes violent, the relations of humiliation brutal and cruel, and Jed, being delicate and slight, would have been incapable of defending himself; but word spread that he was motherless, and such suffering, which none of them could claim to know, intimidated his schoolmates; thus there was around him a sort of halo of fearful respect. He didn't have a single close friend, and didn't seek the friendship of others. Instead, he spent afternoons in the library, and at the age of eighteen, having passed the baccalaureate, he had an extensive knowledge, unusual among the young people of his generation, of the literary heritage of mankind. He had read Plato, Aeschylus and Sophocles; he had read Racine, Molière and Hugo; he knew Balzac, Dickens, Flaubert, the German Romantics and the Russian novelists. Even more surprisingly, he was familiar with the main dogmas of the Catholic faith, whose mark on Western culture had been so profound – while his contemporaries generally knew more about the life of Spider-Man than that of Jesus.

This sense of a slightly old-fashioned seriousness was going to make a favourable impression on the teachers who had to examine his application for admission to the Beaux-Arts; they were obviously dealing with a candidate who was original, cultivated, serious and probably hard-working. The application itself, entitled 'Three Hundred Photos of Hardware', displayed a surprising aesthetic maturity. Avoiding emphasis on the shininess of the metals and the menacing nature of the forms, Jed had used a neutral lighting, with few contrasts, and photographed articles of hardware against a background of mid-grey velvet. Nuts, bolts and adjusting knobs appeared like so many jewels, gleaming discreetly.

He had, however, great trouble (and this difficulty would stay with him all his life) in writing the introduction to his photos. After various attempts at justifying his subject he took refuge in the purely factual, restricting himself to emphasising that the most rudimentary pieces of hardware, made of steel, already had a machine precision within 1/10 of a millimetre. Closer to precision engineering in the strictest sense, the pieces used in quality photographic cameras, or Formula One engines, were generally made of aluminium or a light alloy and machined to 1/100 of a millimetre. Finally, high-precision engineering, for example in watchmaking or dental surgery, made use of titanium; the tolerance was then within microns. In short, as Jed concluded in an abrupt and approximate way, the history of mankind could in large part be linked to the history of the use of metals – the still recent age of polymers and plastics not having had the time, in his view, to produce any real mental transformation.

Some art historians, more versed in the manipulation of language, noted later that this first real creation of Jed's already presented itself, just as in a way did all his subsequent creations, and this despite the variety of their supports, as a *homage to human labour*.

* * *

Thus, Jed launched himself into an artistic career whose sole project was to give an objective description of the world – a goal whose illusory nature he rarely sensed. Despite his classical background, he was in no way – contrary to what has often been written since – filled with a religious respect for the old masters; to Rembrandt and Velazquez he much preferred, from that time onwards, Mondrian and Klee.

During the first months following his move to the 13th arrondissement he did almost nothing, except fulfilling the numerous orders he received for photographs of objects. And then one day, while unwrapping a Western Digital multimedia hard disk that had just been delivered by courier, and which he had to shoot from different angles by the following day, he understood that he had finished with the photography of objects – at least on the artistic level. As if the fact that he had come to photograph these objects for a purely professional and commercial aim invalidated any possibility of using them in a creative project.

This realistion, as brutal as it was unexpected, plunged him into a period of low-intensity depression, during which his main daily distraction became watching *Questions for a Champion*, a programme presented by Julien Lepers. By dint of his sheer determination and a terrifying capacity for work, this initially ungifted presenter – he was a bit stupid, with the face and the appetite of a ram, who had first imagined, at the start, a career as a variety singer, for which he no doubt nursed a secret nostalgia – had gradually become a central figure in the French media landscape. People saw themselves in him: students in their first year at the École Polytechnique as well as retired primary-school teachers in the Pas-de-Calais, bikers from Limousin as well as restaurant owners in the Var. Neither impressive nor distant, he exuded an average, and even sympathetic, image of France in the 2010s. A fan of Jean-Pierre Foucault's, of his humanity and sly straightforwardness, Jed nevertheless had to admit that increasingly he was seduced by Julien Lepers.

★   ★   ★

At the beginning of October he received a phone call from his father, informing him that his grandmother had just died; Jean-Pierre's voice was slow, a bit downcast, but scarcely more than usual. Jed's grandmother had, he knew, never got over the death of her husband, whom she had loved passionately, which was surprising in a poor rural milieu that normally didn't lend itself to romantic outpourings. After his death nothing, not even her grandson, had managed to rescue her from a spiralling sadness that gradually made her give up all activity, from breeding rabbits to making jam, and finally abandon even the garden.

Jed's father had to go to the Creuse the following day for the funeral, then for the house and inheritance issues. He wanted his son to accompany him. In fact he would like him to stay a little longer to take care of all the formalities; he had a lot of work at the firm. Jed accepted immediately.

The following day, his father fetched him in his Mercedes. Around eleven they got on to the A20, one of the most beautiful motorways in France, one of those that cross the most harmonious rural landscapes; the air was clear and mild, with a little mist on the horizon. At three, they stopped at a service station just before La Souterraine; at his father's request, while he filled the tank, Jed bought a 'Michelin Departments' road map of the Creuse and Haute-Vienne. It was then, unfolding the map, while standing by the cellophane-wrapped sandwiches, that he had his second great aesthetic revelation. This map was sublime. Overcome, he began to tremble in front of the food display. Never had he contemplated an object as magnificent, as rich in emotion and meaning as this 1/150, 000-scale Michelin map of the Creuse and Haute-Vienne. The essence of modernity, of scientific and technical apprehension of the world, was here combined with the essence of animal life. The drawing was complex and beautiful, absolutely clear, using only a small palette of colours. But in each of the hamlets and villages, represented according to their importance, you felt the thrill, the appeal, of human lives, of dozens and hundreds of souls – some destined for damnation, others for eternal life.

His grandmother's body was already resting in an oak coffin. She wore a dark dress, her eyes closed and her hands joined; the employees of the funeral parlour were simply waiting for Jed and his father to close the lid. They left them alone, for about ten minutes, in the bedroom. 'It's better for her,' said his father after some silence. Yes, probably, thought Jed. 'She believed in God, you know,' his father added timidly.

The following day, during the funeral Mass, which the whole village attended, and then again in front of the church, as they received condolences, Jed told himself that he and his father were remarkably adapted to this sort of circumstance. Pale and weary, both dressed in sombre suits, they had no difficulty in expressing the required seriousness and resigned sadness; they even appreciated, without being able to believe in it, the note of discreet hope struck by the priest – a priest who himself was old, an *old hand* at funerals, which had to be, given the average age of the population, far and away his main activity.

After returning to the house, where they were served the *vin d'honneur*, Jed realised that this was the first time that he had attended a serious funeral, *à l'ancienne*, a funeral which didn't attempt to dodge the reality of death. Several times in Paris, he had attended cremations. The last one was of a fellow student at the Beaux-Arts who had been killed in a plane crash during his holidays in Lombok; he had been shocked that some of those present hadn't bothered to switch off their mobiles before the moment of the cremation.

His father left just afterwards: he had a business meeting the following morning in Paris. Jed went out into the garden. The sun was setting as the rear lights of the Mercedes disappeared in the direction of the motorway, and he thought again of Geneviève. They had been lovers for a few years, while he was studying at the

Beaux-Arts; it was with her, in fact, that he had lost his virginity. Geneviève was Malagasy, and had explained to him the curious exhumation customs practised in her country. One week after the death, the corpse was dug up, the shroud was undone, and a meal was eaten in its presence, in the family's dining room; then it was buried again. This was repeated after a month, then after three; he no longer could remember the details very well, but it seemed there were no less than seven exhumations in all, the last one taking place a year after the death, before the deceased was definitively considered dead, and capable of achieving eternal rest. This system of accepting death, and the physical reality of the corpse, went precisely against the modern Western sensibility, Jed thought, and fleetingly he regretted having let Geneviève leave his life. She was sweet and gentle; at the time he suffered from terrible ophthalmic migraines, and she would happily spend hours at his bedside, cooking him food, bringing him water and medication. Temperamentally, she was also rather *hot*, and on the sexual level she had taught him everything. Jed liked her drawings, which borrowed a little from *graff*, but distinguished themselves by the childlike and joyful character of the figures, by something rounded about the writing, and the palette she used – lots of cadmium red, Indian yellow, and raw or burnt sienna.

To finance her studies, Geneviève *cashed in on her charms*, as it was once described; Jed found this outmoded expression suited her better than the Anglo-Saxon term *escort*. She charged two hundred and fifty euros an hour, with a supplement of one hundred euros for anal sex. He had no objection to this activity, and even offered to take erotic photos to improve the presentation of her website. As much as men are often jealous, and sometimes horribly jealous, of their girlfriend's former lovers, and as much as they ask themselves anxiously for years, and sometimes until death, if it hadn't been *better* with the other one, if the other hadn't given them *more pleasure*, they easily accept, without the slightest effort, everthing their women might have done in the past as a prostitute. As soon as it is concluded by a financial transaction, any sexual activity is excused, rendered inoffensive, and in some way sanctified by the ancient curse of work. Depending on the month, Geneviève earned between five and ten thousand euros without devoting more than a few hours to it per week. She made him take advantage by inciting him not to 'make a thing of it', and several times they took winter holidays together in Mauritius or in the Maldives, which she paid for entirely. She was so natural, so cheerful, that he never felt the slightest unease at being in the skin of a *pimp*.

That said, he felt real sadness when she informed him that she was going to move in with one of her regular clients – a thirty-five-year-old lawyer, whose life exactly resembled, according to what she had told Jed, those of the corporate lawyers described in business thrillers – generally written by Americans. He knew that she would keep her word and that she would remain faithful to her husband, and, in short, when he went through the door of her studio flat for the last time, he knew that he undoubtedly would never see her again. Fifteen years had passed since then; her husband was presumably fulfilled, and she a happy mother; her children were, he was sure without knowing them, polite and well educated, and received excellent marks at school. Was the income of her husband, the corporate lawyer, now higher than that of Jed as an artist? It was a difficult question to answer, but perhaps the only one worth posing. 'You have the vocation of an artist, you truly want it . . .' she had told him during their last encounter. 'You're small, cute and slender, but you have the will to do something, you have enormous ambition. I saw it straight away in your eyes. Me, I do that just –' she vaguely pointed around at the charcoal drawings on the wall –, 'for fun.'

Jed had kept some of Geneviève's drawings, and he continued to find real value in them. Art should perhaps be like that, he occasionally told himself, an innocent and joyful, almost animalistic pastime; there had been opinions like that, 'stupid like a painter' or 'he paints like the bird sings', and so on; perhaps that's how art would be once man had got beyond the question of death, or maybe it had already been that way, in certain periods, for example, in the work of Fra Angelico, so close to paradise, so full of the idea that one's time on earth was just a temporary and obscure preparation for eternal life by the side of Jesus the Lord. *And now I am with you, every day, until the end of the world.*

On the day after the funeral, he was visited by the lawyer. He hadn't talked about this with his father – he realised they hadn't even broached the subject, yet it was the principal motive for him being there – but it appeared immediately obvious to him that there was no question of selling the house, and he didn't even feel the need to phone his father to discuss the matter. He felt good in this house, and from the start. It was a place where you could live. He liked the clumsy juxtaposition of the renovated wing, whose walls were covered with white insulation, and the old part, with walls made of unevenly joined stones. He liked the swing door, which was impossible to shut fully, that opened onto the road to Guéret, and the enormous stove in the kitchen, which you could feed with wood, coal and no doubt any sort of fuel. He was tempted in this house to believe in things like love, the reciprocal love of the couple that irradiates the walls with a certain warmth, a gentle warmth that passes on to future occupants, bringing peace to their soul. At this rate, he could well have believed in ghosts, or indeed in anything.

Anyway, the lawyer was in no mood to encourage him to sell; he would have reacted differently, he confessed, only two or three years ago. At that time English bankers, retired young-old English bankers, after having already taken over the Dordogne, were fanning out towards Bordelais and the Massif Central, progressing rapidly by using captured positions as bases, were now taking over central Limousin; very soon you could expect their arrival in the Creuse and a concomitant increase in property prices. But the crash on the London Stock Exchange, the subprime crisis and the collapse of speculative values had greatly changed the situation: far from dreaming of doing up charming rural residences, the young-old English bankers now suddenly had difficulty paying the mortgage on their houses in Kensington; they dreamed instead, more and more often, of *selling up*, and if the truth were told prices had collapsed completely. You would now have to wait, at least according to the lawyer's forecast, for the arrival of a new generation of rich people, whose wealth was more solid, based on some form of industrial production; they could be Chinese or Vietnamese, who knows, but anyway it seemed to him at the moment that the best course was to wait, to keep the house in good condition, and possibly make a few improvements that respected the traditions of local artisans. On the other hand, it was useless to invest in such luxuries as a swimming pool, a jacuzzi or a high-speed Internet connection; the nouveau riche, once they had bought the house, always preferred to deal with that themselves. He was completely categorical on this point; it was experience talking, and he had forty years as a lawyer behind him.

When his father came back to fetch him the following weekend, everything had been settled, the business sorted and tied up, the small legacies in the will distributed to the neighbours. They had the feeling that their mother and grandmother could *rest in peace*, as they say. Jed relaxed in the nappa-leather seat as the class S joined the motorway with a purr of mechanical satisfaction. For two hours, they crossed a landscape of autumn colours at moderate speed; they spoke little but Jed had the impression that a sort of entente had been established between them, an agreement on the general way of going about life. When they approached the Melun-Centre interchange, he understood that he had, during that week, experienced a peaceful interlude.

3

Jed Martin's work has often been presented as the product of a cold, detached reflection on the state of the world, and he has been made into a sort of descendant of the great conceptual artists of the previous century. It was, however, in a state of nervous frenzy that, on his return to Paris, he bought all the Michelin maps he could find – just over a hundred and fifty of them. He soon realised that the most interesting ones belonged to the 'Michelin Regions' series, which covered most of Europe, and 'Michelin Departments', limited to France. Turning away from purely moneymaking photography, he acquired a Betterlight 6000-HS digital back, which enabled the capture of 48 bits RGB files in a 6000 x 8000 pixels format.

For almost six months he seldom went out, except for a daily walk that took him to the Casino hypermarket on the boulevard Vincent-Auriol. His contact with the other students from the Beaux-Arts, already rare while he was there, became rarer until it disappeared completely, and it was with surprise that he received, at the beginning of March, an email inviting him to take part in a collective exhibition, *Let's Remain Courteous*, which was to be organised in May by the Ricard foundation. He accepted immediately, without understanding that it was precisely his almost ostentatious detachment that had created around him an aura of mystery, and that many of his former classmates wanted to know what he was up to.

On the morning of the *vernissage*, he realised that he hadn't said a word for almost a month, except the 'No' he repeated every day to the cashier (rarely the same one, it has to be said) who asked him if he had the Club Casino loyalty card; nevertheless he made his way, at the agreed hour, to the rue Boissy d'Anglas. There were perhaps a hundred people (well, he had never known how to calculate that sort of thing; in any case, the guests numbered in tens), and he was worried at first when he noticed that he didn't recognise any of them. For a moment he feared that he'd got the wrong day or exhibition, but his photo prints were there, hung on a wall at the back and lit correctly. After serving himself a glass of whisky, he went round the hall several times, following an ellipsoidal trajectory, more or less pretending to be absorbed in his thoughts while his brain managed to formulate no thoughts whatsoever except the surprise that his former classmates had completely disappeared from his memory, was effaced, and radically so, which made him wonder if he belonged to the human race. He would have recognised Geneviève, at least. Yes, it was certain that he would have recognised his former lover. That was a certainty he could cling to.

At the end of his third walk around, Jed saw a young woman staring intently at his photographs. It would have been difficult not to notice her: she was not only by far the most beautiful woman at the gathering but also without doubt the most beautiful woman he had ever seen. With a very pale, almost translucent complexion, platinum-blonde hair, and prominent cheekbones, she corresponded perfectly to the image of Slavic beauty as popularised by modelling agencies since the fall of the USSR.

When he walked around again, she was no longer there; but he caught sight of her halfway through his sixth circuit, smiling with a glass of champagne in her hand, in the middle of a small group. The men were staring at her with a lust that they didn't even try to hide; the jaw on one of them was half dislocated.

When he passed by his photos once more, she was standing there, alone. He had a second's hesitation, then sidled over and stood in front of the image, which he looked at and nodded.

She turned to study him pensively for a few seconds, then asked: 'Are you the artist?'

'Yes.'

She looked at him again, more intently, for at least five seconds, before saying: 'I find it very beautiful.'

She had said that simply, calmly, but with real conviction. Incapable of finding an appropriate reply, Jed turned back towards the image. He had to agree that he was, in fact, quite happy with it himself. For the exhibition he had chosen a part of the Michelin map of the Creuse, which contained his grandmother's village. He had used a very low camera angle, at thirty degrees from the horizontal, while setting the tilt to the maximum in order to obtain a very high depth of field. It was then, by using Photoshop layers that he had introduced the background blurring and the bluish effect on the horizon. In the foreground were the pond at Breuil and the village of Châtelus-le-Marcheix. Further away, the roads winding through the forest between the villages of Saint-Goussaud, Laurière and Jabreilles-les-Bordes appeared like a dream territory, fairy-like and inviolable. In the back-left corner of the image, as if merging from a bank of mist, the white-and-red ribbon of the A20 motorway could still be made out clearly.

'Do you often take photos of road maps?'

'Yes . . . Yes, quite often.'

'Always Michelin?'

'Yes.'

She pondered this before asking him: 'Have you made many photos like this?'

'Just over eight hundred.'

This time she stared at him, frankly taken aback, for at least twenty seconds, before continuing: 'We must talk about it. We must meet to talk about it. This may surprise you, but . . . I work for Michelin.'

Out of her tiny Prada bag she took a business card, which he looked at stupidly before putting it in his pocket: *Olga Sheremoyova, Public Relations, Michelin France.*

He called the following morning, and Olga proposed they dine together that very evening.

'I don't eat out much . . .' he objected. 'Well, I mean, not really in restaurants. I probably don't even know any restaurants in Paris.'

'I know lots of them,' she replied firmly. 'I could even say that . . . in some way it's my job.'

They met at Chez Anthony et Georges, a tiny restaurant with a dozen tables situated on the rue d'Arras. Everything in the room, the crockery as well as the furniture, had been bargain-hunted in antiques shops and formed a pretty but disparate mixture of tables and chairs copied from the eighteenth century, art nouveau knick-knacks, and English china and porcelain. The place was filled with tourists, especially Americans and Chinese; there was also a table of Russians. Olga was welcomed as a regular by Georges, a thin, bald, and vaguely worrying man who looked a bit like a former leather queen. Anthony, in the kitchen, was an understated *bear* who probably had to pay attention to his weight, since his menu betrayed a veritable obsession with foie gras. Jed catalogued them as semi-modern queers who were careful to avoid the excesses and errors in taste classically associated with their community, but who all the same, let themselves go a bit from time to time. The moment Olga arrived, Georges asked her: 'Can I take your coat, *ma chérie?*' insisting on the *ma chérie* in a very camp tone of voice. She was wearing a fur coat, a curious choice for the season, but underneath had on a very short miniskirt and a white-satin bandeau top, adorned with Swarovski crystals; she was truly magnificent.

'How are you, sweetie?' said Anthony, mincing in his apron in front of them. 'Do you like chicken with crayfish? We've received some crayfish from Limousin, that are sublime, absolutely sublime. Hello, monsieur,' he added, glancing at Jed.

'Does that tempt you?' Olga asked Jed once he left.

'I . . . yes. It's typical. I mean, you have the impression it's typical, but you're not very sure of what. Is it in the guide?' He had the impression this was the question to ask.

'Not yet. We're going to add it in next year's edition. There's been an article in *Condé Nast Traveller*, and the Chinese edition of *Elle.*'

Though currently she was working in Michelin's Paris office, Olga was in fact on secondment to the holding company Michelin

Finance, based in Switzerland. In a quite logical attempt at diver-
sification, the firm had recently bought back shares in the chain
Relais & Châteaux and even more French Touch, which had been
rapidly growing in importance for a few years – all the while maintaining, for deontological reasons, the strict editorial independence
in relation of the various guides. Michelin had soon become aware
that the French, on the whole, could no longer afford holidays in
France, and in any case certainly not in the hotels proposed by the
chains. A questionnaire distributed in the French Touch hotels the
year before had shown that 75 per cent of the clientele came from
China, India and Russia – the percentage rising to 90 per cent for
the '*résidences d'exception*', the most prestigious establishments. Olga
had been taken on to overhaul the marketing strategy and adapt
it to the expectations of this new customer base.

Patronage in the domain of contemporary art was not really
part of Michelin's traditional culture, she went on. A multinational,
based in Clermont-Ferrand since the beginning, and whose board
of directors always included a descendant of the founders, it had
the reputation of being a rather conservative, if not paternalistic,
business. The notion of opening a Michelin space in Paris dedicated
to contemporary art had a difficult time getting past the ruling
authorities, when in fact it would translate, she was sure, into a
big upmarket rise of the company's image in Russia and China.

'Am I boring you?' she said suddenly. 'I'm sorry, I only talk about
business, while you're an artist . . .'

'Not at all,' replied Jed sincerely. 'Not at all, I'm fascinated. Look,
I haven't even touched my foie gras.'

He was, in fact, fascinated, but rather by her eyes, by the movement of her lips when she spoke – her light pink, slightly pearly
lipstick went very well with her eyes.

They then looked at one another, for a few seconds, speechless,
and Jed had no doubt: the look she plunged into his own was
well and truly one of *desire*. And from his expression, she could
tell immediately that he knew this.

'In short,' Olga continued, slightly flustered, 'in short, for me it's unhoped-for to find an artist who takes Michelin maps as the subject of his work.'

'But, you know, I find these maps very beautiful.'

'That's obvious. That's obvious in your photos.'

It was only too easy to invite her to his place to show her more pictures. When the taxi entered the avenue des Gobelins, however, he was filled with unease.

'I'm afraid the flat is a bit untidy,' he said.

Obviously she replied that it wasn't a problem, but while they climbed the stairs his malaise got worse, and on opening the door he looked at her briefly: she had winced a bit all the same. *Untidy* was truly an understatement. Around the trestle table on which he had installed his Linhof camera, the entire floor was covered in prints, sometimes several layers of them, probably thousands in all. There was only a narrow passageway between the trestle table and the mattress on the floor. And not only was the flat untidy, it was *dirty*, the sheets were almost brown and spattered with organic stains.

'Yes, it's a bachelor pad,' said Olga light-heartedly, then she advanced into the room and knelt down to examine a print. Her miniskirt ran far up her thighs. Her legs were incredibly long and slender. How could she have legs so long and slender? Jed had never had such an erection, it was truly sore. He was trembling on the spot and had the impression that he would soon pass out.

'I . . .' he croaked. Olga turned around and noticed it was serious: she immediately recognised that blinded, panicked look of a man who can no longer withstand his desire. She made a few steps towards him, enveloped him with her voluptuous body, and kissed him on the lips.

4

It was best, however, to go to her place. Obviously, it was completely different there: a ravishing two-room flat, on the rue Guynemer, overlooking the Jardin du Luxembourg. Olga was one of those endearing Russians who have learned in the course of their formative years to admire a certain image of France – gallantry, gastronomy, literature and so on – and who are then regularly upset that the real country corresponds so badly to their expectations. It is often believed that the Russians made the great revolution to get rid of Communism with the unique aim of consuming McDonald's fare and films starring Tom Cruise; this is partly true, but a minority of them also had the desire to taste Pouilly-Fuissé or visit the Sainte-Chapelle. By her level of studies and her general knowledge, Olga belonged to this elite. Her father, a biologist at Moscow University, was a specialist in insects – a Siberian lepidoptera even bore his name. Neither he nor his family had really benefited from the great carving up that had taken place when the empire fell, but nor had they sunk into poverty; the university where he taught had retained a decent level of funding, and after a few uncertain years they had settled at a status that was reasonably *middle class*. And while Olga could live the high life in Paris, renting a flat in the rue Guynemer and dressing in designer clothes, she owed it exclusively to her salary from Michelin.

After they become lovers, a rhythm was quickly established. In the morning, Jed left the flat with her. She went up in her Mini Park Lane to work in the avenue de la Grande Armée, and he took the Métro to his studio in the boulevard de l'Hôpital. He came back in the evening, generally a little before her.

They went out a lot. In the two years since her arrival in Paris, she had had no problem creating a dense network of social relations. Her professional activity led her to frequent the press and the media – or rather the frankly *unglamorous* sectors of travel and food journalism. But, anyway, a girl of her beauty would have had an entrée anywhere and been admitted to any circle. It was surprising that when she met Jed she did not have a lover; it was even more suprising that she had set her heart on him. Certainly, he was quite a *pretty boy*, but of a small and slim kind not generally sought out by women. The image of the virile brute who *is good in bed* had been coming back in force recently, and it was indeed much more than a simple change of fashion; it was the return to the *fundamentals* of nature, of sexual attraction in its most elemental and brutal form. Just as the era of anorexic models was well and truly over, and exaggeratedly curvy women no longer interested anyone except some Africans and perverts, in every domain the early third millennium was returning, after various oscillations whose importance had never in fact been very great, to the adoration of a simple tried and tested type: beauty expressed in plenitude in the woman, physical power in the man. Such a situation did not really put Jed at an advantage. His artistic career was nothing impressive either; he wasn't even an *artist*, to tell the truth, having never exhibited solo or had an article written about his work and explaining its importance to the world. He was almost completely unknown at the time. Yes, Olga's choice was astonishing, and Jed certainly would've been astonished if his nature had allowed him to be astonished by this sort of thing, or even to notice it.

Anyway, in the space of a few weeks, he was invited to more *vernissages*, premieres and literary cocktail parties than he had ever been to during all his years at the Beaux-Arts. He rapidly assimilated the appropriate behaviour. It wasn't obligatory to be brilliant, and was actually best most often to say nothing at all, even if it was indispensable to listen to your interlocutor with seriousness and empathy, relaunching the conversation with a 'Really?' meant to register interest and surprise, or a 'That's for sure,' coloured with understanding and approval. What's more, Jed's small size facilitated a posture of submission generally appreciated by cultural figures – just as it is, if truth be told, by anyone. In short, it was an easy milieu to enter, like all milieux no doubt, and Jed's courteous neutrality, his silence about his own work, served him greatly by giving the then-justified impression that he was a serious artist, an artist *who really worked*. Floating among the others with polite disinterest, Jed adopted, without knowing it, the *groove* attitude which had made Andy Warhol successful in his time, while adding to it a nuance of seriousness – immediately interpreted as a concerned seriousness, a *citizen's* seriousness – which had become indispensable fifty years on. One November evening, at some literary prize ceremony, he was even introduced to Frédéric Beigbeder, then at the height of his media fame. The writer and publicist, after having kissed Olga several times on the cheek (but so ostentatiously, so theatrically that it became innocent through the all-too-clear indication of *playful intent*), turned towards Jed with a intrigued look, before being distracted by an acclaimed porn actress who'd just published a book of interviews with a Tibetan religious leader. Nodding regularly to what the ex-hardcore star was saying, Beigbeder flashed looks at Jed out of the corner of his eye as if asking him not to get lost in the crowd, which became denser and denser as the petits fours disappeared. Having lost a lot of weight, the author of *SOS Forgiveness* had at that time a thin beard, with the obvious aim of looking like the hero of a Russian novel. At last, the girl was taken aside by a tall, rather flabby man, with medium-length hair, who seemed to have editorial responsibilities at Grasset, and Beigbeder was able to free himself. Olga was a few metres away, surrounded by her usual swarm of male admirers.

'So it's you?' he finally asked Jed, looking him straight in the eyes with worrying intensity – and then he really did look like the hero of a Russian novel, though the gleam in his eyes no doubt owed more to cocaine than to religious fervour. But was there really any difference, Jed wondered. 'It's you who's having her?' Beigbeder asked again with increasing intensity. Not knowing what to say, Jed remained silent.

'You know that you're with one of the five most beautiful women in Paris?' His tone had returned to being serious, professional; he visibly knew the other four. Jed had no reply to that either. What can you reply, in general, to human questions?

Beigbeder sighed, suddenly appearing very weary, and Jed thought that the conversation was finally going to become easy again; that he was going to be able, as usual, to listen and implicitly approve the conceptions and anecdotes developed by his interlocutor; but there was none of it. Beigbeder was interested in *him*, and wanted to know more about him. That in itself was extraordinary, as Beigbeder was one of the most courted celebrities in Paris, and the people around them were astonished, probably drawing conclusions, and turning their eyes towards them. Jed coped at first by saying that he did photography, but Beigbeder wanted to know more: what *kind* of photography? The reply left him flustered: he knew publicity photographers, fashion photographers, and even a few war photographers – although he'd met them doing the work of paparazzi, which they did while more or less hiding it, since it was generally considered less noble *in the profession* to photograph Pamela Anderson's breasts than the scattered remains of a Lebanese suicide bomber; the lenses used are, however, generally the same, and the physical requirements almost similar; it is difficult to avoid the hand trembling when you shoot, and the maximum apertures can only make the best of already bright light, such are the problems you meet with telephoto lenses with very high magnification. On the other hand, people who photographed road maps, no, that was new to him. Becoming a bit confused, Jed ended up saying that yes, in a certain sense, you could say he was an artist.

'Ha ha haaa!' The writer gave an exaggerated laugh, making a dozen people turn round, including Olga. 'But yes, of course, you have to be an *artist*! Literature, as a plan, is completely old hat! To sleep with the most beautiful women today, you have to be an *artist*! I too want to become *an ar-tist*!

And in a surprising manner, stretching his arms out wide, he intoned, very loudly and almost without a false note, the 'Blues of the Businessman':

> I would have liked to be an artiiiist
> To reinvent the world
> To be an anarchiiiist
> And live like a millionaire!

His glass of vodka was trembling in his hands. Half the room was now looking at them. He dropped his arms, and added, in a bewildered voice, 'Words by Luc Plamondon, music by Michel Berger', and burst out sobbing.

'That went well . . . with Frédéric,' Olga told him as they walked home, along the boulevard Saint-Germain. 'Yes . . .' replied Jed, perplexed. Among his readings as an adolescent, at his Jesuits' college, there had been those realist novels of the French nineteenth century where it happens that ambitious young men *succeed through women*; but he was surprised to find himself in a similar situation, and in truth he had rather forgotten those realist novels of the French nineteenth century. For a few years he had only been able to read Agatha Christie, and even more specifically, only those involving Hercule Poirot, which could hardly help him in the present circumstances.

At least he was *launched*, and it was nearly with ease that Olga convinced her director to organise Jed's first solo exhibition, in the firm's premises on the avenue de Breteuil. He visited the space, which was vast but quite sad, with walls and a floor of grey concrete; this bareness seemed to him rather a good thing. He suggested no modification, requesting only the installation at the entrance of a big supplementary panel. However, he gave very precise instructions for the lighting and spent the weeks leading up to the exhibition making sure that they were followed to the letter.

The date of the *vernissage* had been fixed for the 28 January, which was quite clever; it left the critics time to return from their winter holidays, then organise their schedule. The budget allocated for the buffet was very decent. The first real surprise for Jed was the press officer: filled with preconceived ideas, he had always imagined press officers to be *absolute stunners*, and was shocked to find himself standing before a small sickly thing, thin and almost hunchbacked, inappropriately called Marylin, who was probably neurotic as well. Throughout their first conversation she anxiously twisted her long and flat black hair, gradually composing knots impossible to untie and then abruptly tearing out the offending lock of hair. Her nose constantly dripped, and in her enormous handbag, which was more like a shopping bag, she carried about fifteen packs of disposable hankies – almost her entire daily consumption. They met in Olga's office, and it was troubling to see side by side this sumptuous creature, with indefinitely desirable forms, and this poor little runt of a woman, with her unexplored vagina; Jed wondered for a moment if Olga had not chosen her precisely for her ugliness, to avoid having any female competition around her. But no, certainly not, she was far too conscious of her own beauty, and too objective as well to feel competitive when her supremacy wasn't objectively threatened – and this had never happened in her real life, even if she had had occasion to fleetingly envy Kate Moss's cheekbones or the arse of Naomi Campbell, during a fashion show broadcast on M6. If Olga had chosen Marylin, it was because she had the reputation of being an excellent press officer, undoubtedly the best in the field of contemporary art, at least in the French market.

'I'm very happy to work on this project . . .' announced Marylin in a whiny voice. 'Deeply happy.'

Olga, bending down to try and match her height, felt atrociously uncomfortable and ended up indicating to them a small conference room next to her office. 'I'll let you get on with your work,' she said before leaving with relief. Marylin took out an oversize diary and two packs of paper hankies before continuing.

'First of all, I studied geography. Then I turned towards human geography. And now I am exclusively into the humans. Well, if you can call them human beings,' she added.

She initially wanted to know if he had any 'pet media' as far as the written press was concerned. This certainly wasn't the case; in fact, Jed couldn't remember ever buying a newspaper or a magazine. He liked television, especially in the morning. You could comfortably jump from cartoons to news from the stock exchange; occasionally, when a subject particularly interested him, he connected to the Internet. But the printed press seemed a strange remnant, probably doomed in the short term, and whose interest in any case escaped him.

'OK . . .' commented Marylin politely. 'So, I suppose I have more or less carte blanche.'

5

She did indeed have carte blanche, and used it to the best of her ability. When they went into the hall in the avenue de Breteuil on the evening of the *vernissage*, Olga was shocked. 'There's a lot of people,' she finally said, impressed. 'Yes, people have come along,' confirmed Marylin with a muted satisfaction that seemed bizarrely mixed with rancour. There were about a hundred people, but what she meant was that there were some important people, and how could you know that? The only person Jed knew by sight was Patrick Forestier, Olga's immediate superior, the director of communications for Michelin France, a typical product of the École Polytechnique who had spent three hours trying to dress *artistically*, going through his entire wardrobe before opting for one of his usual grey suits – worn without a tie.

The entrance to the hall was barred by a big panel, leaving two metres wide passageways at either side that were, in which Jed had displayed a satellite photo taken around the mountain of Guebwiller next to an enlargement of a 'Michelin Departments' map of the same zone. The contrast was striking: while the photograph showed only a soup of more or less uniform green sprinkled with vague blue spots, the map developed a fascinating maze of departmental and scenic roads, *viewpoints*, forests, lakes and cols. Above the two enlargements, in black capital letters, was the title of the exhibition: THE MAP IS MORE INTERESTING THAN THE TERRITORY.

In the hall itself, on big movable walls, Jed had hung about thirty photographic enlargements – all borrowed from 'Michelin Departments' maps, but choosing the most varied geographical zones, from the high mountains to the Breton coast, from the bocage of the Manche to the cereal-growing plains of Eure-et-Loir. Flanked by Olga and Jed, Marylin stopped on the threshold to observe the crowd of journalists, personalities and critics like a predator surveys the herd of antelope at a watering hole.

'Pépita Bourguignon is there,' she finally said with a dry sneer.

'Bourguignon?' asked Jed.

'The art critic for *Le Monde*.'

He almost stupidly repeated 'of the world?' before remembering that it was an evening newspaper, and resolved to shut up, as much as possible, for the rest of the soirée. Once separated from Marylin, he had no problem walking peacefully among his photos, without anyone recognising him as *the artist*, and without even attempting to listen in on the conversations. It seemed to him, in relation to other *vernissages*, that the hubbub was rather less loud; the atmosphere was concentrated, almost reverential, and many people were looking at his work – this was probably a good sign. Patrick Forestier was one of the few exuberant guests; with a glass of champagne in his hand, he was turning around to widen his audence while congratulating himself loudly on the 'end of the misunderstanding between Michelin and the art world'.

Three days later, Marylin burst into the conference room where Jed had taken a seat, near Olga's office to wait for the press reviews. She took out of her shopping bag a pack of paper hankies and that day's *Le Monde*.

'Have you not read it?' she exclaimed with what, for her, was overexcitement. 'Well, it's just as well I came.'

Written by Patrick Kéchichian, the article – a full page, with a very beautiful colour reproduction of his photograph of the map of Dordogne and the Lot – was ecstatic in its praise. From the very first lines, he likened the point of view of the map – or of the satellite image – to that of God. 'With that profound tranquillity of the great revolutionaries,' he wrote, 'the artist – a man of tender age – moves away, starting with the inaugural piece by which he makes us enter his world, from that naturalist and neo-pagan vision by which our contemporaries exhaust themselves in an attempt to retrieve the image of the Absent One. Not without gallant audacity, he adopts the point of view of a God co-participating, alongside man, in the (re)construction of the world.' He then wrote, at length, about the works, displaying a surprising knowledge of photographic technique, before concluding: 'Between mystical union with the world and rational theology, Jed Martin has made a choice. The first perhaps in Western art since the great figures of the Renaissance, he has, to the nocturnal seductions of Hildegard of Bingen, preferred the difficult and clear constructions of the "silent bull", as his fellow students at the University of Cologne had the habit of nicknaming the Aquinite. If this choice is of course questionable, the loftiness of vision it implies is scarcely that. Here is an artistic year that begins under the most promising of auspices.'

'It's not stupid, what he's saying,' Jed commented.

She looked at him indignantly. 'This article is enormous!' she replied severely. 'OK, it's quite surprising that Kéchichian did it; usually he only deals with books. After all, Pépita Bourguignon was there . . .' She was perplexed for a few seconds before concluding, firmly: 'Well, let's say I prefer a full page by Kéchichian to a tiny note by Bourguignon.'

'And now what's going to happen?'

'They're going to come. The articles are going to come, more and more of them.'

They celebrated the event that very evening at Chez Anthony et Georges. 'They're talking a lot about you,' Georges slipped to him while helping Olga take off her coat. Restaurateurs like celebs; it's with the utmost attention that they follow cultural and high-society news, and they know that the presence of celebs in their establishment can have a real draw on the stupidly rich segment of the population that they want above all as their clientele. And the celebs, in general, love restaurants; it's a sort of symbiosis that is established, naturally, between restaurants and celebs. As a very young mini-celeb, Jed adopted without difficulty that attitude of modest detachment which suited his new status, for which

Georges, an expert in intermediary celebrity, showed his apprecia-
tion. There weren't many people that evening in the restaurant,
just a Korean couple who left quickly. Olga opted for a *gazpacho
à l'arugula* and semi-cooked lobster with its yam mash, Jed for
pan-seared scallops and a baby turbot and caraway soufflé with its
Passe Crassane pear emulsion. Anthony came to join them for
dessert, wearing his kitchen apron, and brandishing a bottle of
Bas-Armagnac Casterède 1905. 'On the house,' he said, out of
breath, before filling the glasses. According to Rothenstein and
Bowles, this *millésimé* enchanted by its amplitude, nobility and
panache. The finale of prune and rancio was the typical example
of a mature eau-de-vie, long on the finish, with a note of fine old
leather at the last. Anthony had put on a bit of weight since their
last visit, as was no doubt inevitable; the secretion of testosterone
diminishes with age, the level of fat increases; he was reaching
the critical age.

Olga breathed in at length, and with delectation, the bouquet
of the Armagnac, before wetting her lips: she was adapting marvellously well to France, it was difficult to believe that she had spent
her childhood in a block of flats in the Moscow suburbs.

'How is it that the new chefs,' she asked after her first sip, 'I mean
the chefs who get talked about, are almost all homosexuals?'

'Hah!' Anthony stretched out voluptuously in his seat, casting a
delighted look around the restaurant. 'Well, there, *ma chérie*, lies
the big secret, because homosexuals have always *a-dored* cooking,
right from the start, but *nobody* said it, absolutely *no-body*. What
helped a lot, I think, was the three stars given to Frank Pichon.
That a transsexual cook could get three Michelin stars, now that,
that was really a strong signal . . .' He took a sip, and seemed to
plunge back into the past. 'And then, obviously,' he continued with
extraordinary excitement, 'obviously what triggered everything, the
atomic bomb, was the outing of Jean-Pierre Pernaut!'

'Yes, it's sure that the outing of Jean-Pierre Pernaut was huge
. . .' agreed Georges with bad grace. 'But you know, Tony,' he
continued in a hissing and querulous tone, 'basically it's not society

which refused to accept homosexual chefs, it was homosexuals who refused to accept themselves as chefs. Look, we've never had an article in *Têtu*, nothing; it was *Le Parisien* who spoke about the restaurant first. In the traditional gay scene, they didn't find it glamorous enough to go into cuisine. For them it was *homey*, it was too *homey*, precisely that!' Jed suddenly intuited that Georges was also addressing Anthony's emerging rolls of fat, that he was beginning to miss an obscure, pre-culinary *leather and chains* past, that it would be best to change the subject. Jed then skilfully returned to the outing of Jean-Pierre Pernaut, an obvious and outrageous subject: he himself as a television viewer had been overwhelmed. Pernaut's 'Yes, it's true, I love David' live before the cameras of France 2 would remain in his view as one of the pivotal moments of television in the 2010s. A consensus was quickly reached on this subject and Anthony poured another round of Bas-Armagnac. 'As for me, I define myself, above all, as a television viewer!' exclaimed Jed with a passionate exaltation that earned him a surprised look from Olga.

6

A month later Marylin came into the office, her bag even more stuffed than usual. After having blown her nose three times, she placed in front of Jed a fat dossier, held together with elastic bands.

'It's the press,' she added, as if he wasn't reacting.

He looked blankly at the cardboard cover. 'How is it?' he asked.

'Excellent. We've got everyone.' She didn't seem particularly pleased. Behind her snivelling facade, this little woman was a warrior, a specialist in *commando operations*. What got her juices flowing was unleashing the movement, getting the first big article; then, when things started going by themselves, she would fall back into her nauseous apathy. She spoke more and more softly, and Jed hardly heard her add: 'There's just Pépita Bourguignon who's done nothing.

'Oh, well,' she concluded sadly, 'it was nice working with you.'

'We'll never meet again?'

'If you need me, yes, of course. You have my mobile number.'

Then she took her leave, going off to an uncertain fate – you had the impression, in fact, that she would go back to bed immediately and make herself a tisane. While passing through the doorway, she turned around one last time and added in a lifeless voice, 'I think it was the biggest success of my life.'

The critics were, Jed realised on browsing through the dossier, exceptionally unanimous in their praise. It happens in contemporary societies, despite the determination with which journalists hunt and identify fashions in formation, and if possible create them, that some develop in a wild, anarchic fashion and prosper before being named – in fact, this happens more and more often, since the massive spread of the Internet and the accompanying collapse of printed media. The growing popularity, across all of France, of cookery classes, the recent appearance of local competitions rewarding new creations in charcuterie or cheese-making, the massive and inexorable spread of hiking, and even the outing of Jean-Pierre Pernaut, combined to bring about this new sociological fact: for the first time in France since Jean-Jacques Rousseau, the countryside had become *trendy* again. French society seemed to suddenly become aware of this through its major dailies and magazines, in the few weeks which followed Jed's *vernissage*. And the Michelin map, an utterly unnoticed utilitarian object, became in the space of those very weeks the privileged vehicle for initiation into what *Libération* was to shamelessly call the 'magic of the *terroir*'.

Patrick Forestier's office, whose windows offered a view of the Arc de Triomphe, was ingeniously modular: by moving certain elements you could organise a conference, project images or have a brunch, all confined in a space of seventy square metres; a microwave enabled you to heat up food; you could also sleep there. To receive Jed, Forestier had chosen the 'working breakfast' option: fruit juice, pastries and coffee waited on the table.

He opened his arms wide to greet him; it was an understatement to say he was beaming. 'I was confident . . . I've always been confident!' he exclaimed, something which, according to Olga, who had briefed Jed before the meeting, was at the very least exaggerated. 'Now we must convert the try!' (His arms made rapid horizontal movements that were, Jed understood immediately, an imitation of rugby passes.) 'Please sit down.' They took their places on the sofas surrounding the table; Jed poured himself coffee. '*We are a team,*' added Forestier in English, rather unnecessarily.

'Our map sales have grown by 17 per cent in the past month,' he continued. 'We could, and others would do it, raise the prices; we won't.'

He left Jed the time to appreciate the lofty considerations behind this commercial decision before adding: 'What is most unexpected is that there are even buyers for the old Michelin maps, which we have seen auctioned on the Internet. And until a few weeks ago, we were happy to pulp these old maps,' he said funereally. 'We squandered a heritage whose value no one in-house suspected . . . until your magnificent photos.' He seemed to sink into a depressed meditation on this money lost so stupidly, or perhaps more generally on the destruction of value, but he pulled himself together. 'Concerning your . . .' – he sought the appropriate word –, 'concerning your *works*, we must strike very hard!' Suddenly he sat up on his sofa. Fleetingly, Jed had the impression that he was going to jump straight onto the table and beat his chest in a Tarzan impersonation; he creased his eyes to get rid of the vision.

'I had a long conversation with Mademoiselle Sheremoyova, with whom I believe . . .' again he searched for the right words, which is a disadvantage with former pupils of the Polytechnique; they're a bit cheaper to hire than those of the École Nationale d'Administration, but they take more time finding their words; finally, he noticed that he was off subject. 'In short, we've concluded that marketing them directly through our networks is unthinkable. It's out of the question for us to appear to take away your artistic independence. I believe,' he continued uncertainly, 'that usually the trade in artworks happens via *galleries* . . .'

'I don't have a gallerist.'

'That's what I understood. So, I thought of the following arrangement. We could look after the designing of an Internet site where you would present your works, and put them directly on sale. Naturally the site would be in your name – Michelin would be mentioned nowhere. I believe it's best that you personally oversee the making of the prints. That said, we can completely handle the logistics and the shipping.'

'I agree.'

'That's perfect, perfect. This time, I believe we're genuinely in a win-win situation!' he enthused. 'I have formalised all that in a draft contract, which of course I will leave for you to study.'

Jed went out into a very bright long corridor; in the distance a bay window looked out onto the arches of La Défense; the sky was a splendid winter blue, which appeared almost artificial – a phthalo blue, Jed fleetingly thought. He was walking slowly, hesitantly, as if he were crossing cotton wool; he knew that he had just reached a new turning point in his life. The door of Olga's office was open and she smiled at him.

'Well, it's exactly as you told me.'

7

Jed's studies had been purely literary and artistic, and he had never had the occasion to meditate on the capitalist mystery par excellence: that of *price formation*. He had opted for Hahnemühle FineArt Canvas, which offered an excellent saturation of colours and very good performance over time. But with this paper the correct calibration of colours was difficult to achieve and very unstable. The Epson driver wasn't quite right either, so he decided to limit himself to twenty enlargements per photo. A print cost him about thirty euros; he thought he would offer them at two hundred euros on the site.

When he put the first photograph online, an enlargement of the Hazebrouck region, the series was sold out in a little under three hours. Obviously, the price wasn't quite right. After a few tentative weeks it stabilised at around two thousand euros for a 40 x 60 format print. There, that was now sorted out: he knew his *market price*.

Spring was settling over Paris, and without having planned it, he was becoming comfortably well off. In April, they noticed with surprise that his monthly income had just overtaken Olga's. That year, the long weekends in May were exceptional: May Day fell on a Thursday, as did VE Day – then there was Ascension Day, and it all ended with the long weekend of Pentecost. The new French Touch catalogue had just come out. Olga had supervised its production, occasionally correcting the texts proposed by the hoteliers, choosing the photos, and having them retaken if those proposed by the establishments didn't seem sufficiently attractive.

Evening was falling on the Jardin du Luxembourg. They sat out on the balcony in the mild air; the last cries of children were disappearing in the distance, and the gates would soon be closed for the night. Of France Olga basically knew only Paris, Jed thought as he flicked through the French Touch guide; and he, in truth, hardly knew more. Throughout the guide, France appeared as an enchanted land, a mosaic of superb *terroirs* spangled with châteaux and manors, of an astonishing variety but in which, everywhere, *life was good*.

'Would you like to go away this weekend?' he proposed as he put down the volume. 'In one of the hotels described in your guide?'

'Yes, that's a good idea.' She thought for a few seconds. 'But incognito. Without saying I work for Michelin.'

Even in these conditions, thought Jed, they could expect from the hoteliers a special welcome: a rich young urban couple without children, aesthetically very decorative, still in the first phase of their love affair – and for this reason quick to marvel at everything, in the hope of building up a store of *beautiful memories* that would come in handy when they reached the difficult years, perhaps enabling them to overcome a *crisis in their relationship*. They represented, for any professional in the hotel-restaurant trade, the archetype of ideal clients.

'Where would you like to go first?'

On reflection, Jed noticed that the question was far from simple. Many regions, as far as he knew, were of real interest. It was conceivably true, he thought, that France was a marvellous country – at least from the tourist's point of view.

'We'll start with the Massif Central,' he finally decided. 'For you, it's perfect. It's perhaps not the best, but I think it's very French; I mean, it could only be in France.'

It was Olga's turn to flick through the guide, and she pointed a hotel out to him. Jed frowned. 'The shutters are badly chosen. On grey stone I would've put brown or red shutters, green at a pinch, but certainly not blue.' He looked further at the introduction, and his perplexity increased. 'What is this gibberish? "In the heart of a Cantal crossed with the Midi where tradition rhymes with relaxation and freedom with respect . . ." Freedom and respect – that doesn't even rhyme!'

Olga took the guide from him, and read the text closely. 'Ah yes, I see now . . . "Martine and Omar make us discover the authenticity of the food and wine." She married an Arab: that's why respect's there.'

'That could be all right, especially if he's Moroccan. It's bloody good, Moroccan cuisine. Maybe they do Franco-Moroccan fusion food, foie gras pastilla and the like.'

'Yes,' said Olga, unconvinced. 'But I'm a tourist. I want something Franco-French. A Franco-Moroccan or Franco-Vietnamese thing can work for a trendy restaurant on the canal Saint-Martin; certainly not for a *hôtel de charme* in the Cantal. I'm maybe going to remove it from the guide, this hotel.'

She did nothing of the sort, but this conversation gave her food for thought, and a few days later she proposed to the management that they organise a statistical survey of the dishes actually consumed in the hotels. The results were only known six months later, but they largely validated her first intuition. Creative cuisine, as well as Asian cuisine, was unanimously rejected. North African cuisine was only appreciated in the far south and on Corsica. Whatever the region, the restaurants boasting a 'traditional' or '*à l'ancienne*' image registered bills 63 per cent higher than the average. Pork products and cheeses were a safe bet, but above all the dishes based on bizarre animals, with not only a French but also a regional connotation, such as wood pigeon, snails and lamprey, achieved exceptional scores. The director of the segment 'Food, Luxury and Intermediary', who authored the summary accompanying the report, concluded categorically:

We were probably wrong to concentrate on the tastes of an Anglo-Saxon clientele in search of a *light* gastronomic experience, combining flavours with health and safety, and concerned with pasteurisation and respect for the cold chain. This clientele, in reality, does not exist: American tourists have never been numerous in France, and the English are in constant decline; the Anglo-Saxon world as a whole now represents only 4.3% of our turnover. Our new clients, our real clients, from younger and rougher countries, with health norms that are recent and, anyway, seldom enforced, are on the contrary, when they stay in France, in search of a *vintage*, even *hard-core* gastronomic experience; only restaurants capable of adapting to this new situation should deserve, in the future, to figure in our guide.

8

They had several happy weeks. It was not, it couldn't be, the exacer-
bated, feverish happiness of young people, and it was no longer a
question for them in the course of a weekend to get *plastered* or
totally shit-faced; it was already – but they were still young enough
to laugh about it – the preparation for that epicurean, peaceful,
refined but unsnobbish happiness that Western society offered the
representatives of its middle-to-upper classes in middle age. They
got used to the theatrical tone adopted by waiters in high-star establishments as they announced the composition of the *amuse-bouches*
and other 'appetisers'; used also to that elastic and declamatory way
in which they exclaimed: '*Excellente continuation, messieurs dames!*'
each time they brought the next course, and which each time
reminded Jed of the '*Bonne célébration!*' that a flabby and probably
socialist young priest had said to him when he and Geneviève, on
an irrational whim, had entered the church of Notre-Dame-des-
Champs, at Sunday-morning Mass, just after making love in the
studio flat she then had in the boulevard Montparnasse. Several
times afterwards he'd thought of this priest: physically he looked a
bit like François Hollande, but unlike the political leader he had
made himself a eunuch for God. Many years later, after he had started
the 'Series of Simple Professions', Jed had sometimes envisioned
doing a portrait of one of those men who, chaste and devoted, less
and less numerous, criss-crossed the big cities to bring the comfort
of their faith. But he had failed, and hadn't even managed to compre-
hend the subject. Inheritors of a millennia-old spiritual tradition that
nobody really understood anymore, once placed in the front rank
of society, priests were today reduced, at the end of terrifyingly
long and difficult studies that involved mastering Latin, canon law,
rational theology and other almost incomprehensible subjects, to
surviving in miserable material conditions. They took the Métro

alongside other men, going from a Gospels reading group to a literacy workshop, saying Mass every morning for a thin and ageing audience, being forbidden all sensual joy or even the elementary pleasures of family life, yet obliged by their function to display day after day an unwavering optimism. Almost all of Jed Martin's paintings, art historians would later note, represent men and women practising their profession in a spirit of *goodwill*, but what was expressed there was a sensible goodwill, where submission to professional imperatives guaranteed in return, in variable proportions, a mixture of financial satisfaction and the gratification of self-esteem. Humble and penniless, sneered at by everyone, subjected to all the problems of urban life without having access to any of its pleasures, young urban priests constituted, for those who did not share their faith, a puzzling and inaccessible subject.

The French Touch guide, on the other hand, proposed a range of limited but attestable pleasures. You could share the satisfaction of the owner of the Laughing Marmot when he concluded his introduction with this serene and assured sentence: 'Spacious bedrooms with a terrace and jacuzzi bathtubs, *menus séduction*, ten home-made jams at breakfast: you are well and truly in a *hôtel de charme*.' You could let yourself be carried away by the poetic prose of the manager of the Carpe Diem when he presented a visit to his establishment in the following terms: 'A smile will lead you from the garden (Mediterranean species) to your suite, a place which will stimulate your senses. Then you will need only close your eyes to remember the scents of paradise, the fountain murmuring in the white marble Turkish bath which lets one simple truth filter through: "Here, life is beautiful."' In the grandiose setting of the Château de Bourbon-Busset, whose descendants elegantly perpetuated the art of hospitality, you could contemplate deeply moving souvenirs (moving for the Bourbon-Busset family, probably) that went back to the Crusades; some bedrooms were fitted with waterbeds. This juxtaposition of *Old France* or *terroir* elements with contemporary hedonistic facilities sometimes had a strange effect, almost that of an error of taste; but it was perhaps this improbable mixture, Jed thought, that was sought by the chain's clientele, or at least its *core target*. The factual promises in the presentation were kept all the same. The park of the Château des Gorges du Haut-Cézallier was supposed to be home to does, roe deer and a little donkey; there was, indeed, a little donkey. While strolling in the gardens of the Vertical Inn, you were supposed to catch sight of Miguel Santamayor, an *intuitive chef* who carried out an 'extraordinary synthesis of tradition and futurism'; in fact, you saw a guy who vaguely looked like a guru busying himself in the kitchen, until at the end of his 'symphony of vegetables and seasoning' he personally came to offer you one of his *favourite havanas*.

They spent their last weekend, over Pentecost, in the Château du Vault-de-Lugny, a *résidence d'exception* whose sumptuous bedrooms opened onto a park of forty hectares whose original layout was attributed to Le Nôtre. The cuisine, according to the guide, 'lifted to sublime heights a *terroir* of infinite wealth'; you were in the presence of 'one of the most beautiful compendiums of France'. It was there, on the Monday of Pentecost, that Olga announced to Jed that she was returning to Russia at the end of the month. At that moment she was tasting a wild-strawberry jam, and some birds indifferent to any human drama were twittering in the park originally designed by Le Nôtre. A few metres away, a Chinese family were stuffing their faces with Belgian waffles and sausages. The sausages at breakfast had originally been introduced at the Château du Vault-de-Lugny to appeal to the desires of a traditionalist Anglo-Saxon clientele, who were attached to a fatty high protein breakfast; they had been put under discussion, in the course of a brief but decisive business meeting; the tastes of this new Chinese clientele, which were still uncertain and clumsily formulated, but apparently drawn to sausages, had led to this food line being preserved on the menu. Other *hôtels de charme* in Burgundy, during those same years, reached an identical conclusion, and it was thus that the Martenot Sausage and Salted Meat Company, operating in the region since 1927, escaped bankruptcy, and the 'Social Affairs' section of the regional news programme on FR3.

Olga, however, a girl in any case *not very taken with protein*, preferred the wild-strawberry jam, and she began to feel really nervous because she understood that her life was going to be decided there, in the next few minutes, and men were so difficult to work out these days, not so much at the start, when miniskirts always worked – but then they became more and more bizarre. Michelin's big ambition was to strengthen its presence in Russia, one of its priority areas for expansion; her salary was going to be trebled, and she would have about fifty people working under her. It was a transfer that she could in no way refuse: in the eyes of top management, a refusal would have been not only incomprehensible but even criminal. A manager of a certain level has obligations not only in relation to the company but also to himself. He must look after and cherish his career like Christ does for the Church, or the wife for her husband. He at least owes it to himself to give the demands of his career that minimum of attention without which he proves to his dismayed superior that he is unworthy of rising above a subaltern position.

Jed kept stubbornly silent, turning his spoon in a boiled egg, glancing up at Olga like a punished child.

'You can come to Russia,' she said. 'You can come whenever you like.'

She was young, or more precisely she was *still young*, she still imagined that life offered various possibilities, that a human relationship could go through successive and contradictory developments.

A breeze rustled the curtains of the French windows opening onto the park. The twittering of the birds suddenly became louder, then stopped. The table of Chinese had disappeared without any warning; they had in some way dematerialised. Jed was still silent, and then he put down his spoon.

'You are taking time to reply,' she said. 'Little Frenchman,' she added with gentle reproach. 'Little indecisive Frenchman . . .'

9

On Sunday 28 June, mid-afternoon, Jed accompanied Olga to Roissy
airport. It was sad: something inside him understood that they
were living a moment of mortal sadness. The fine, calm weather
did not favour the expression of the appropriate feelings. He could
have interrupted the process of breaking up, thrown himself at her
feet, begged her not to take this plane; she probably would have
listened to him. But what would she do next? Look for a new flat
(the lease on the rue de Guynemer expired at the end of the month)?
Cancel the movers scheduled for the following day? It was possible;
the technical difficulties were not enormous.

Jed wasn't young – strictly speaking he never had been – but
he was a relatively inexperienced man. In terms of human beings he
only knew his father, and still not very well. This could not
encourage in him any great optimism about human relations. From
what he had been able to observe, the existence of men was organised around *work*, which occupied most of life, and took place in
organisations of variable dimension. At the end of the years of
work opened a briefer period, marked by the development of
various pathologies. Moreover, some human beings, during the
most active period of their lives, tried to associate in micro-groups
called *families*, with the aim of reproducing the species; but these
attempts, most often, came to a sudden end, for reasons linked to
the 'nature of the times', he thought vaguely while sharing an
espresso with his lover (they were alone at the counter of the
Segafredo bar, and, more generally, there was little activity in the
airport, the hubbub of the inevitable conversations muffled by a
silence that seemed consubstantial to the place, as in certain private
clinics). But this was only an illusion. The general transport system
of human beings, which played such an important role today in
the accomplishment of human destinies, simply marked a short

pause before starting a sequence of functioning at full capacity, during the period of the first holiday departures. It was, however, tempting to see in it a homage, a discreet homage from the social machinery to their love which had been so quickly interrupted.

Jed did not react when Olga, after one last kiss, walked towards passport control, and it was only on returning home, in the boulevard de l'Hôpital, that he realised that he had just, almost unknowingly, entered a new stage in the course of his life. He understood this because everything that, a few days previously, had constituted his world suddenly seemed completely empty to him. Road maps and photographic prints were spread out by the hundreds on the floor, and not a single one of them meant anything anymore. In resignation, he went out and bought two rolls of 'garden waste' bags at the Casino hypermarket in the boulevard Vincent-Auriol, then went home and began to fill them. Paper's heavy, he thought. He would need to make several trips to take the bags down. It was months, or rather years of work that he was in the process of destroying; and yet he didn't hesitate for one moment. Many years later, when he had become famous – extremely famous, if the truth be told – Jed would be asked numerous times what it meant, in his eyes, to be an *artist*. He would find nothing very interesting or original to say, except one thing, which he would consequently repeat in each interview: to be an artist, in his view, was above all to be someone *submissive*. Someone who submitted himself to mysterious, unpredictable messages, that you would be led, for want of a better word and in the absence of any religious belief, to describe as *intuitions*, messages which nonetheless commanded you in an imperious and categorical manner, without leaving the slightest possibility of escape – except by losing any notion of integrity and self-respect. These messages could involve destroying a work, or even an entire body of work, to set off in a radically new direction, or even occasionally no direction at all, without having any project at all, or the slightest hope of continuing. It was thus, and only thus, that the artist's condition could, sometimes, be described as *difficult*. It was also thus, and only thus, that it distinguished itself from other professions or trades, to which he would pay homage in the second part of his career, the one which would earn him worldwide renown.

The following day, he took down the first refuse bags, then slowly, meticulously, dismantled his photographic camera before putting away the bellows, the ground glasses, the lenses, the digital back and the body of the apparatus in their travelling cases. The weather in Paris remained fine. In the middle of the afternoon he switched on his television to follow the prologue of the Tour de France, which was won by an unknown Ukrainian rider. Once he had switched it off, he told himself he should probably phone Patrick Forestier.

The director of communications of the Michelin France group greeted the news without real emotion. If Jed was deciding to stop making photos of Michelin maps, nothing could force him to continue; he could stop at any moment, as was spelled out in the contract. In fact he almost gave the impression that he didn't care, and Jed was rather surprised when he proposed a meeting for the next morning.

Not long after his arrival at the office in the avenue de la Grande Armée, he understood that what Forestier really wanted was to hold forth, to air his professional concerns to a sympathetic listener. With Olga's transfer, he had just lost an intelligent, devoted, and polyglot colleague; and, almost unbelievably, for the moment no one was offering him a replacement. In his bitter terms, he had been 'completely fucked over' by the general management. Obviously she was leaving for Russia, obviously it was her country, obviously those fucking Russians were buying billions of tyres, with their fucking potholed roads and fucking awful climate; nevertheless, Michelin remained a French company, and things would not have turned out this way even a few years ago. Until very recently, the desiderata of the French branch had been orders, or at least they were given special attention, but ever since the foreign institutional investors had taken the majority of capital in the group all that was well and truly over. Yes, things had truly changed, he repeated with morose delectation, obviously the interests of Michelin France no longer counted for much by comparison to Russia, not to mention China, but if that was to continue you had to wonder if he wasn't to return to Bridgestone, or even Goodyear. I mean, that's between you and me, he said, suddenly afraid.

Jed assured him he would be completely discreet, and tried to redirect the conversation back to his own case. 'Ah yes, the Internet site . . .' Forestier seemed only just then to remember it. 'Ah well, we're going to add a message indicating that you consider this series of works over. The previous prints will remain on sale. Do you have any objection?' Jed saw none. 'Besides, there's not many left, they've sold very well,' Forestier continued in a voice that conveyed a touch of revived optimism. 'We will also continue to state in our publicity that the Michelin maps have been the basis of an artistic work unanimously praised by the critics. That doesn't bother you either?' It in no way bothered Jed.

Forestier felt much brighter when he accompanied him to the door of his office, and while warmly shaking his hand, he concluded: 'I've been very happy to know you. It was win-win between us, absolutely win-win.'

10

Nothing, or almost nothing, happened for several weeks; and then one morning, when coming back from shopping, Jed saw a man of about fifty, dressed in jeans and an old leather jacket, who was waiting in front of the entrance to his block of flats; he seemed to have been there for a long time.

'Hello,' he said. 'I'm sorry to approach you like this, but I haven't found any other way. I've seen you in the neighbourhood several times already. Am I right in thinking you're Jed Martin?'

Jed nodded. The voice of his interlocutor was that of an educated man who was accustomed to speaking; he looked like a Belgian situationist, or a proletarian intellectual – from his strong, worn hands, you guessed that he had indeed done manual labour.

'I'm familiar with your work using road maps, and I've followed it almost from the start. I'm also from around here.' He held out his hand. 'I'm Franz Teller. I own a gallery.'

On the way to his gallery in the rue de Domrémy (he had bought the premises just before the area became more or less fashionable; it had been, he said, one of the few good ideas in his life), they stopped to drink something at Chez Claude, in the rue du Château-des-Rentiers, which would later become their habitual cafe, and give Jed the subject for his second painting in the 'Series of Simple Professions'. The establishment persisted in serving glasses of cheap red wine and pâté and gherkin sandwiches for the last 'working-class' pensioners of the 13th arrondissement. They were dying one by one, without being replaced by new customers.

'I read in an article that, since the end of the Second World War, 80 per cent of the cafes have disappeared in France,' remarked Franz while looking around the place. Not far from them, four pensioners were silently pushing cards around on the Formica table, according to incomprehensible rules that seemed to belong to the prehistory of card games (*belote, piquet?*). Further away, a fat woman with broken veins on her face downed her pastis in a single gulp. 'People have begun to spend half an hour over lunch, to drink less alcohol as well; and then the *coup de grâce* was the smoking ban.'

'I think it'll come back, in different forms,' Jed said. 'There has been a long historical phase of increased productivity, which is reaching an end, at least in the West.'

'You have a really strange way of seeing things . . .' Franz said after taking a long look at him. 'It had interested me, your work on Michelin maps, really interested me; however, I wouldn't have taken you in my gallery. You were, I would say, too sure of yourself; that didn't seem to me completely normal for someone so young. And then, when I read on the Internet that you had decided to stop the map series, I decided to come and see you. To propose that you be one of the artists I represent.'

'But I'm not at all sure what I'm going to do. I don't even know if I want to continue with art at all.'

'You don't understand,' Franz said patiently. 'It's not a particular art form, or *manner*, that interests me, it's a personality, a view of the artistic gesture, of its situation in society. If you came here tomorrow with a simple sheet of paper, torn from a spiral note-book, on which you'd written *"I don't even know if I want to continue with art at all"*, I would exhibit this sheet without hesitation. Yet I'm not an intellectual. But you interest me.

'No, no, I'm not an intellectual,' he insisted. 'I try to look more or less like an intellectual from the fashionable side of town, because it's useful in my milieu, but I'm not one, I never even got past the baccalaureate. I started by putting on and taking down exhibitions, and then I bought this little premises, and I had a few strokes of luck with artists. But I've always made my choices intuitively, uniquely so.'

They then visited the gallery, which was bigger than Jed had imag-ined, with a high ceiling and concrete walls supported by metal girders. 'It was a mechanical construction factory,' Franz told him. 'They went bust in the mid-eighties, then it stayed empty for quite a long time, until I bought it. There was a lot of cleaning work to be done, but it was worth it. It's a beautiful space, I find.'

Jed nodded. The movable dividing walls had been put away to the side, so that the exhibition space was at its maximum dimensions – thirty metres by twenty and the moment was occupied by big sculptures made of dark metal. They could have been inspired by traditional African statuary, but their subjects clearly recalled contemporary Africa: all the figures were in agony, or were massacring one another with machetes and Kalashnikovs. This juxtaposition of the violent actions with the fixed expressions of the figures produced a particularly sinister effect.

'For storage,' Franz continued, 'I've got a hangar in the Eure-et-Loir. The hygrometrical conditions aren't great, and security's non-existent – in short they're very bad storage conditions; but, so far, I haven't had any problems.'

They said goodbye a few minutes later, leaving Jed extremely troubled. He wandered for a long time across Paris, getting lost twice, before returning home. And in the following weeks it was the same: he went out, walked aimlessly in the streets of this city that in the end he barely knew. From time to time he stopped to ask for directions at a brasserie. More often he needed the help of a map.

One October afternoon, returning up the rue des Martyrs, he was suddenly seized by a vague feeling of familiarity. Further up, he remembered, there was the boulevard de Clichy, with its sex shops and boutiques of erotic lingerie. Both Geneviève and Olga had liked, from time to time, to buy erotic outfits there in his company, but generally they went to Rebecca Ribs, much further down the boulevard. No, there was something else.

He stopped at the corner of the avenue Trudaine, looked right – and then he knew. A few dozen metres away were the offices where his father, now at the end of his career, worked. Jed had only gone there once, right after the death of his grandmother. The practice had just then moved into its new premises. After the contract for the cultural centre in Port-Ambonne, they had felt the necessity of *going upmarket*, and the headquarters now had to be in a *town house*, preferably in a *cobbled square*, or at least in an *avenue lined with trees*. And the avenue Trudaine, which was wide, with an almost provincial calm thanks to its rows of plane trees, suited perfectly an architectural practice of some renown.

Jean-Pierre Martin was in meetings all afternoon, the receptionist told him. 'I'm his son,' Jed gently insisted. She hesitated, then picked up her phone.

His father burst into the hallway a few minutes later, in shirt-sleeves, his tie undone, holding a thin dossier. He was breathing heavily, under the effect of a violent emotion.

'What's happening? Has there been an accident?'

'No, nothing. I was just passing through the area.'

'I'm a bit busy, but . . . wait. We'll go out and have a coffee.'

The company was going through a difficult period, he explained to Jed. The new headquarters cost a lot, and they had failed to land a big contract for the renovation of a tourist resort on the Black Sea coast; he'd just had a violent shouting match with one of his associates. He was breathing more normally, though, and was gradually calming down.

'Why don't you stop?' asked Jed. His father looked at him without reacting, with an expression of total incomprehension.

'I mean, you've made a lot of money. You could certainly retire, and take advantage of life.' His father was still staring at him, as if the words weren't registering, or he was not managing to give them a meaning. Then, after a minute, he asked, 'But what would I do?' and his voice was that of a lost child.

Springtime in Paris is often simply a continuation of winter – rainy, cold, muddy, and dirty. Summer there is unpleasant more often than not: the city is noisy and dusty, the hot seasons never last long and end after two or three days with a storm, followed by a sharp drop in temperature. It is only in autumn that Paris is truly a pleasant city, offering short sunny days, where the dry and clear air leaves an invigorating sensation of freshness. During the whole of October Jed continued his long strolls, if that's what you would call an almost robotic walking during which no external impressions reached his brain, and no meditation or project came, either, to fill it, and whose only aim was to bring him each evening to a sufficient state of fatigue.

One afternoon in early November, at about five, he found himself in front of Olga's old flat in the rue Guynemer. That had to happen, he thought: trapped by his automatisms, he had followed, almost to the very second, the path he had taken every day for months. Speechless, he turned back to the Jardin du Luxembourg and collapsed on the first bench he could find. He was just next to that curious red-brick pavilion, adorned with mosaics, which occupies one of the corners of the garden, at the corner of the rue Guynemer and the rue d'Assas. In the distance, the setting sun bathed the chestnut trees with an extraordinary orangey and warm shade – almost an Indian yellow, thought Jed, and effortlessly the words of 'Jardin du Luxembourg' came back in his memory:

> Another day
> Without love
> Another day
> Of my life
> The Luxembourg
> Has aged
> Is it the gardens?
> Is it me?
> I don't know.

Like many Russians, Olga adored Joe Dassin, especially the songs on his last album, with their resigned, lucid melancholy. Jed shivered, feeling an irrepressible crisis coming on, and when he remembered the words of 'Hello Lovers', he began to cry.

We loved like we leave each other
Simply, with no thought of tomorrow,
Tomorrow that comes a little too fast,
Of farewells that come a little too easy.

In the cafe on the corner of the rue Vavin he ordered a bourbon, and immediately noticed his mistake. After the comfort of the burning sensation in his throat, he was again engulfed by sadness, and tears streamed down his face. He looked around worriedly, but fortunately no one was paying him any attention; all the tables were taken by law students who were talking about rave parties or 'junior associates', in other words those things which interest law students. He could cry in peace.

Once he had left he took a wrong turn, then wandered for a few minutes in a state of numb semi-consciousness and found himself standing in front of the Sennelier Frères shop in the rue de la Grande-Chaumière. In the window were displayed brushes, current-format canvases, pastels, and tubes of colour. He went in, and, without thinking, bought a basic 'oil painting' box. Rectangular, made of beechwood, and divided into compartments, it contained twelve tubes of Sennelier extra-fine oil, an assortment of brushes and a flask of thinner.

These were the circumstances that began his 'return to painting', which would become the subject of so much comment.

11

Jed was not to remain faithful to the Sennelier brand, and his mature paintings are almost entirely made with Mussini oils by Schmincke. There are exceptions, and certain greens, particularly the cinnabar greens that give such a magical glow to the forests of California pine descending towards the sea in *Bill Gates and Steve Jobs Discussing the Future of Information Technology*, are borrowed from the Rembrandt range of oils by the firm Royal Talens. And for the whites he almost always used Old Holland oils, whose opacity he appreciated.

Jed Martin's first paintings, art historians have later emphasised, could easily lead you down the wrong track. By devoting his first two canvases, *Ferdinand Desroches, Horse Butcher* then *Claude Vorilhon, Bar-Tabac Manager*, to professions in decline, Martin could give the impression of nostalgia for a past age, real or fantasised, in France. Nothing, and this is the conclusion that has ended up emerging about all his works, was more foreign to his real preoccupations; and if Martin began by looking at two washed-up professions, it was in no way because he wanted to encourage lamentations on their probable disappearance: it was simply that they were, indeed, going to disappear soon, and it was important to fix their images on canvas while there was still time. For his third painting in the series of professions, *Maya Dubois, Remote Maintenance Assistant*, he devoted himself to a profession that was in no way stricken or *old-fashioned*, a profession on the contrary emblematic of the policy of *just-in-time production* which had orientated the entire economic redeployment of Western Europe at the turn of the third millennium.

In the first monograph he devoted to Martin, Wong Fu Xin develops a curious analogy based on colorimetry. The colours of the objects in the world can be represented by a certain number of primary colours; the minimum number, to achieve an almost realistic representation, is three. But you can perfectly build a colorimetric chart on the basis of four, five, six, or even more primary colours; the spectrum of representation would in this way become more extensive and subtle.

In the same way, asserts the Chinese essayist, the productive conditions of a given society may be recreated by means of a number of typical professions, whose number according to him (it is a figure he gives without any empirical evidence) can be fixed at between ten and twenty. In the numerically most important part of the 'Professions' series, the one that art historians have taken the habit of entitling the 'Series of Simple Professions', Jed Martin portrays no less than forty-two typical professions, thus offering, for the study of the productive conditions of the society of his times, a spectrum of analysis that is particularly extensive and rich. The following twenty-two paintings, centred on confrontations and encounters, classically called the 'Series of Business Compositions', themselves aimed to give a relational and dialectical image of the functioning of the economy as a whole.

The 'Series of Simple Professions' took Jed Martin a little more than seven years to paint. During these years, he didn't meet many people, and formed no new relationship – whether sentimental or simply friendly. He had moments of sensory pleasure: an orgy of Italian pasta after a raid on the Casino hypermarket in the boulevard Vincent-Auriol; such-and-such an evening with a Lebanese escort girl whose sexual performances amply justified the ecstatic reviews she received on the site Niamodel.com. 'Layla, I love you, you are the sunshine of my days in the office, my little oriental star,' wrote some unfortunate fifty-somethings, while Layla for her part dreamed of muscular men, virile, poor and strong: this was the life, basically, as she saw it. Easily identified as a guy who was 'a bit bizarre but nice, not at all dangerous', Jed benefited with Layla from that kind of *exception of extra-territoriality* that has always been attributed to artists by the *girls*. It is maybe Layla, but more certainly Geneviève, his Malagasy ex-girlfriend, who is recalled in one of his most touching canvases, *Aimée, Escort Girl*, treated with an exceptionally warm palette based on umber, Indian orange and Naples yellow. At the opposite extreme from Toulouse-Lautrec's representation of a made-up, chlorotic and unhealthy prostitute, Jed Martin paints a fulfilled young woman, both sensual and intelligent, in a modern flat bathed in light. With her back to the window, which opens onto a public garden since identified as the square des Batignolles, and simply dressed in a tight white miniskirt, Aimée is finishing putting on a tiny orange-yellow top that only very partially covers her magnificent breasts.

Martin's only erotic painting, it is also the first where openly autobiographical echoes have been uncovered. The second one, *The Architect Jean-Pierre Martin Leaving the Management of his Business*, was painted two years later, and marks the beginning of a genuine period of creative frenzy that would last for a year and a half and end with *Bill Gates and Steve Jobs Discussing the Future of Information Technology*, subtitled *The Conversation at Palo Alto*, which many consider his masterpiece. It is astonishing to think that the twenty-two paintings of the 'Series of Business Compositions', often complex and in wide format, were made in just eighteen months. It is also surprising that Jed Martin finally hit a snag on a canvas, *Damien Hirst and Jeff Koons Dividing Up the Art Market*, which could have, in many regards, matched his Jobs-Gates composition. Analysing this failure, Wong Fu Xin sees in it the reason for his return, a year later, to the 'Series of Simple Professions' through his sixty-fifth and final painting. Here, the clarity of the Chinese essayist's thesis carries conviction: in his desire to give an exhaustive view of the productive sector of the society of his time, Jed Martin was inevitably, at one moment or another in his career, going to portray an artist.

Part Two

12

Jed woke up with a start at about eight, on the morning of the 25 December. Dawn was breaking on the place des Alpes. He found a towel in the kitchen, wiped up his vomit, then contemplated the sticky debris of *Damien Hirst and Jeff Koons Dividing Up the Art Market*. Franz was right: it was time to organise an exhibition. He had been going round in circles for a few months, and it was beginning to rub off on his mood. You can work alone for years, it's actually the only way to work if truth be told; but there always comes a moment when you feel the need to show your work to the world, less to receive its judgement than to reassure yourself about the existence of this work, or even of your own existence, for in a social species individuality is little more than a short piece of fiction.

Thinking again of Franz's exhortations, he wrote an email reminder to Houellebecq, then made some coffee. A few minutes later, he felt nauseous reading his words. 'In this festive period, which I imagine you are spending with your family . . .' What made him write such a load of rubbish? It was public knowledge that Houellebecq was a loner with strong misanthropic tendencies: it was rare for him even to say a word to his dog. 'I know that you are very much in demand. Therefore please forgive me for taking the liberty of stressing again how important, in my view and that of my gallerist, your participation in the catalogue of my future exhibition would be.' Yes, that was better: a dose of toadying does no harm. 'I attach a few photographs of my paintings, and I am at your complete disposal to present my work to you in a more complete manner, where and when you so wish. I am led to believe you live in Ireland; I am perfectly happy to come over if that is more convenient for you.' Good, that'll do the trick, he thought, and he clicked the Send button.

★   ★   ★

The square of the Olympiades shopping centre was deserted on this December morning, and the high quadrangular buildings looked like dead glaciers. As he entered the cold shadow cast by the Omega tower, Jed thought again of Frédéric Beigbeder. Beigbeder was a close friend of Houellebecq, or at least he had that reputation; maybe he could intervene. But Jed only had an old mobile number, and anyway Beigbeder surely wouldn't answer on Christmas Day.

He did, however, reply. 'I'm with my daughter,' he said angrily. 'But I'm taking her back to her mother in a minute,' he added, toning down the reproach.

'I've a favour to ask.'

'Ha ha ha!' scoffed Beigbeder with contrived gaiety. 'You know, you're a wonderful guy. You haven't called me for ten years. And then you call me, on Christmas Day, to ask a favour. You're probably a genius. Only a genius could be so egocentric, autistic even . . . OK, we'll see each other in the Flore at seven,' concluded, unexpectedly, the author of *A French Novel*.

Jed arrived five minutes late and immediately spotted the writer at a table at the back. The neighbouring tables were unoccupied, forming a sort of security perimeter of two metres radius. Some provincials entering the cafe, and even a few tourists, were nudging one another and pointing at him in wonderment. An acquaintance, penetrating the perimeter, kissed him before disappearing. There was certainly a bit of a financial shortfall for the establishment to make up (similarly, the illustrious Philippe Sollers had, it seems, a table reserved at the Closerie des Lilas that could be taken by no one else, whether or not he came to have lunch). This minimal loss of revenue was largely compensated for by the tourist attraction that the regular, attestable presence of the author of *99 Francs* represented – a presence, what's more, completely in keeping with the establishment's historical vocation. By his courageous stands in favour of legalising drugs and granting legal status to prostitutes of both sexes as well as the more consensual ones on illegal immigrants and the living conditions of prisoners, Frédéric Beigbeder had progressively become a sort of Sartre of the 2010s, and this to general surprise and even slightly to his own, the past predisposing him to play instead the role of a Jean-Edern Hallier, or even a Gonzague Saint-Bris. A demanding fellow traveller of Olivier Besancenot's New Anti-Capitalist Party, which, he pointed out to *Der Spiegel*, risked drifting towards anti-Semitism, he had succeeded in making people forget the half bourgeois, half aristocratic origins of his family, and even the presence of his brother in the top echelons of French business. Sartre himself, it's true, was hardly born destitute.

Sitting in front of a Mauresque cocktail, the author stared melancholically at an almost empty metal pill case that now contained only a few specks of cocaine. Catching sight of Jed, he beckoned him to sit down at his table. A waiter quickly approached to take the order.

'Uh, I don't know. A Viandox? Does that still exist?'

'A Viandox,' repeated Beigbeder pensively. 'You really are a strange guy.'

'I was surprised you remembered me.'

'Oh yes,' the author replied in a strangely sad voice. 'Oh yes, I remember you . . .'

Jed explained what it was about. At the name of Houellebecq, he noticed, Beigbeder suddenly became tense. 'I'm not asking you for his phone number,' Jed quickly added, 'I'm just asking if you can phone him to talk about my request.'

The waiter brought the Viandox. Beigbeder sat silently, deep in thought.

'OK,' he finally said. 'OK, I'm going to call him. With him, you never quite know how he'll react; but in the circumstances it might be useful for him as well.'

'You think he'll accept?'

'I have absolutely no idea.'

'Is there anything that could persuade him?'

'Well . . . This may surprise you, because he doesn't have this reputation at all: money. In principle he doesn't care about money, he lives on sweet fuck all; but his divorce has left him high and dry. What's more, he'd bought flats in Spain at the seaside that are going to be repossessed without compensation, because of a law protecting the coastline with retroactive effect – a crazy story. In reality, I think he's a bit hard up at the moment – it's unbelievable, no, with all that he could have earned? So, there you go: if you offer him a lot of money, I think you've got a good chance.'

He turned silent, finished his Mauresque in one go, ordered another, and looked at Jed with a mixture of reproach and melancholy. 'You know,' he finally said, 'Olga. She loved you.'

Jed shrunk slightly in his chair. 'I mean,' Beigbeder continued, 'she *truly* loved you.' He went silent and looked at him, nodding incredulously. 'And you let her go back to Russia . . . And you never gave her any news . . . Love . . . Love is *rare*. Didn't you know that? Have you never been told that?

'I'm speaking to you about this, although obviously it's none of my business,' he went on, 'because she's coming back to France soon. I still have a few friends in television, and I know that Michelin is going to create a new channel on TNT, Michelin TV, centred on gastronomy, the *terroir*, heritage, the French landscape, et cetera. It's Olga who'll run it. OK, on paper, the director general will be Jean-Pierre Pernaut; but, in practice, it's she who'll have all the say on the programming. So there you are,' he concluded in a tone that clearly indicated that the conversation was over, 'you came to ask me a small favour, and I've done you a big one.'

He gave Jed a sharp look as he got up to leave. 'Unless you think that the most important thing is your exhibition.' He nodded again and, mumbling in an almost inaudible voice, added with disgust: 'Fucking artists . . .'

13

The Sushi Warehouse in Roissy 2E offered an exceptional range of Norwegian mineral waters. Jed opted for the Husqvarna, a water from the centre of Norway, which sparkled discreetly. It was extremely pure – although, in reality, no more than the others. All these mineral waters distinguished themselves only by the sparkling, a slightly different texture in the mouth; none of them were salty or ferruginous; the basic point of Norwegian mineral waters seemed to be moderation. Subtle hedonists, these Norwegians, thought Jed as he bought his Husqvarna; it was pleasant, he thought again, that so many different forms of purity could exist.

The cloud ceiling arrived very quickly, and with it that nothingness that characterises a plane journey above the clouds. Briefly, around halfway, he saw the gigantic and wrinkled surface of the sea, like the skin of a terminally ill old man.

Shannon airport, however, enchanted Jed with its rectangular and clear forms, the height of its ceilings, the astonishing dimensions of its corridors. It was barely making it, and now served mostly low-cost airlines and American army troop transports, but it had visibly been planned for five times more traffic. With its structure of metal pillars and its short-piled carpet, it probably dated from the early 1960s or the end of the 1950s. Even more than Orly, it recalled that period of technological enthusiasm of which air travel was one of the most innovative and prestigious achievements. Yet from the early 1970s, with the first Palestinian terrorist attacks – later continued, in a more spectacular and professional manner by those of al-Qaeda – air travel had become an infantilising and concentration-camp-like experience you prayed would be over as soon as possible. But at the time, thought Jed as he waited for his suitcase in the immense arrivals hall – the metal baggage trolleys, square and massive, were probably also from that time – during that surprising period of the 'Thirty Glorious Years', air travel, a symbol of the modern technological adventure, was certainly something else. Still reserved for engineers and managers, for the builders of tomorrow's world, it was destined, and no one doubted this in the context of triumphant social democracy, to become more and more accessible to the lower classes as their purchasing power and free time developed (which, besides, finally happened, but after a detour via the ultra-liberalism appropriately symbolised by the low-cost airlines, and at the price of a total loss of the prestige previously associated with this method of travel).

A few minutes later, Jed found confirmation of his hypothesis about the age of the airport. The long exit corridor was decorated with photographs of eminent personalities who'd honoured the airport with a visit – essentially Presidents of the United States of America and popes. John Paul II, Jimmy Carter, John XXIII, George Bush I and II, Paul VI, Ronald Reagan . . . none of them were missing. On arriving at the end of the corridor, Jed was surprised to notice that the first of these illustrious visitors had been immortalised not by a photo, but by a *painting*.

Standing on the tarmac, John Fitzgerald Kennedy had left behind the small group of officials – among whom were two ecclesiastics; in the background, some men in gabardines probably belonged to the American security services. His arm stretched forward and upward – towards crowd massed behind the barriers, you imagined – and he smiled with that cretinous enthusiasm and optimism which is difficult for non-Americans to counterfeit. That said, his face seemed Botoxed. Turning back, Jed closely examined all the portraits of eminent personalities. Bill Clinton was as chubby and smooth as his more illustrious predecessor; you had to agree that, on the whole, American Democrat presidents resembled Botoxed leches.

Returning to the portrait of Kennedy, however, Jed was led to a conclusion of a different order. Botox did not exist at the time, and the control of puffiness and wrinkles, today achieved by transcutaneous injections, was then done by the indulgent brush of the artist. Thus, right at the end of the 1950s, and even at the very beginning of the 1960s, it was conceivable to entrust the task of illustrating and exalting the memorable moments of a reign to painters – or at least to the most mediocre among them. This was undoubtedly a daub – you only had to compare the treatment of the sky with what Turner or Constable would have done; even second-class English watercolourists could do better. All the same, there was in this painting a sort of human and symbolic truth about John Fitzgerald Kennedy that was achieved by none of the photos in the gallery – even that of John Paul II, although in good shape, taken on the steps of the plane as he opened his arms wide to salute one of the last Catholic populations in Europe.

The Oakwood Arms Hotel, too, borrowed its decor from those pioneering days of commercial aviation: period advertisements for Air France and Lufthansa, black-and-white photographs of Douglas DC-8s and Caravelles piercing the limpid atmosphere, of captains in full dress uniforms posing proudly in their cockpits. The town of Shannon, Jed had learned on the Internet, owed its birth to the airport. It had been built in the 1960s on a site where no human settlement, not even a village, had ever existed. Irish architecture, as far as he could see, had no specific character; it was a mixture of maisonettes in red brick, similar to those you might encounter in English suburbs, and vast white bungalows fronted by tarmacked parking spaces and bordered with lawns, American-style.

He more or less expected to have to leave a message on Houellebecq's voicemail: until then they had only communicated by email, and, most recently, by SMS; however, after it rang a few times, he answered.

'You'll easily recognise the house, it's the worst-kept lawn in the area,' Houellebecq had told him. At the time Jed had thought he was exaggerating, but the vegetation indeed was reaching phenomenal heights. He followed a flagstoned path that snaked for a dozen metres between clumps of nettles and thorns, up to the tarmacked pad on which a SUV Lexus RX 350 was parked. As you might expect, Houellebecq had taken the bungalow option: it was big and brand-new, with a tiled roof – a completely banal house, in fact, apart from the disgusting state of the lawn.

He rang the door bell, waited for about thirty seconds, and the author of *Atomised* came to open the door, wearing slippers, corduroy trousers, and a comfortable fleece of undyed wool. He looked long and pensively at Jed before turning his eyes to the lawn in a morose meditation that seemed habitual.

'I don't know how to use a lawnmower,' he concluded. 'I'm afraid of the blades cutting my fingers off; it seems to happen quite often. I could buy a sheep, but I don't like them. There's nothing more stupid than a sheep.'

Jed followed him through rooms that had tiled floors and were empty of furniture, with moving boxes here and there. The walls were covered with a uniform off-white paper; a light layer of dust covered the floor. The house was vast, and there must've been at least five bedrooms; it wasn't very warm, no more than sixteen degrees; Jed guessed that all the bedrooms, with the exception of the one where Houellebecq slept, had to be empty.

'Have you just moved in?'

'Yes. I mean, three years ago.'

They finally arrived in a room that was a little warmer, a sort of small square greenhouse, with glass walls on three sides, what the English call a *conservatory*. It was furnished with a sofa, a coffee table and an armchair; a cheap oriental carpet decorated the floor. Jed had brought two A3 portfolios; the first contained about forty photos retracing his previous career – essentially taken from his 'Hardware' series and his 'Road Maps' period. The second portfolio contained sixty-four photos of paintings, which represented the entirety of his pictorial production, from *Ferdinand Desroches, Horse Butcher* to *Bill Gates and Steve Jobs Discussing the Future of Information Technology*.

'Do you like charcuterie?' the writer asked.

'Yes . . . Let's say I have nothing against it.'

'I'll go make some coffee.'

He got up swiftly and returned about ten minutes later carrying two cups and an Italian cafetière.

'I've neither milk nor sugar,' he said.

'No problem. I don't take any.'

The coffee was good. The silence continued, absolute, for two or three minutes.

'I used to like charcuterie a lot,' Houellebecq finally said, 'but I've decided to do without it. You understand, I don't think it should be allowed for man to kill pigs. I've told you how much I don't like sheep, and I persist in my view. The cow itself, and on this point I am in disagreement with my friend Benoît Duteurtre, seems to me overrated. But the pig is an admirable animal, intelligent, sensitive, and capable of sincere and exclusive affection for its master. And its intelligence is really surprising – its limits aren't precisely known. Did you know they've been taught to master simple operations? Well, at least addition, and I believe subtraction among some very gifted specimens. Does man have the right to sacrifice an animal capable of rising to the basics of arithmetic? Frankly, I don't think so.'

Without waiting for a reply, he examined Jed's first portfolio closely. After rapidly observing the photos of nuts and bolts, he lingered, for what seemed to Jed an eternity, over the photos of road maps; from time to time, unpredictably, he turned a page. Jed looked discreetly at his watch: a bit more than an hour had passed since his arrival. The silence was total, then, in the distance, the cavernous purring of a fridge compressor could be heard.

'They're just old works,' Jed finally ventured. 'I just brought them to situate my work. The exhibition, well, it's uniquely about the content of the second folder.'

Houellebecq lifted a blank look towards Jed. He seemed to have forgotten what Jed was doing there, the reason for his presence. However, obediently, he opened the second folder. Half an hour passed again before he snapped it shut and lit a cigarette. Jed noticed then that he hadn't smoked all the time he was looking at his photographs.

'I'm going to accept,' he said. 'You know, I've never done this before, but I knew it would happen, at one moment or other in my life. Many writers, if you look closely, have written about painters, going back centuries. It's funny. There's one thing I ask myself while looking at your work: why did you give up photography? Why did you return to painting?'

Jed thought for a long time before replying. 'I'm not sure I know,' he finally confessed. 'But the problem of the visual arts, it seems to me,' he continued hesitantly, 'is the abundance of subjects. For example, I could readily consider this radiator as a valid subject for a picture.' Houellebecq turned round quickly to look suspiciously at the radiator, as if it were going to jump with joy at the idea of being painted; nothing of the sort happened.

'I don't know if you could do anything, on the literary level, with the radiator,' insisted Jed. 'Well, I guess you could. There's Robbe-Grillet, who simply would have described the radiator. But, I don't know, I don't find that particularly interesting . . .' He was getting bogged down, he had the feeling he was confused and maybe clumsy, he didn't know if Houellebecq liked Robbe-Grillet or not, but above all he asked himself with a sort of anguish, why he had turned to painting, which still, several years later, posed him insurmountable technical problems, while he had totally mastered the principles and the equipment of photography.

'Let's forget Robbe-Grillet,' Houellebecq interjected to Jed's great relief. 'If, sometime, with this radiator, something could be done . . . For example, I think I read on the Internet that your father was an architect.'

'Yes, it's true. I portrayed him in one of my paintings, the day he left his business.'

'People rarely buy this kind of radiator individually. Clients are generally construction companies, like the one your father ran, and they buy radiators by the dozen, even hundreds of them. You could easily imagine a thriller involving a big market for thousands of radiators – to equip, for example, all the classrooms of a country – and all the bribes, political interventions, the very sexy sales rep of a Romanian radiator firm. In this context, there could very well be a long description, over several pages, of this radiator, and competing models.'

He was speaking quickly now, lighting cigarette after cigarette; he gave the impression of smoking to calm himself, to slow down the functioning of his brain. Jed thought fleetingly that, given his firm's activities, his father had probably been in a position to make massive purchases of air conditioners; no doubt he had.

'These radiators are made of cast iron,' Houellebecq went on excitedly, 'probably in grey cast iron, with a high level of carbon, whose dangerousness has often been underlined in experts' reports. You might consider it scandalous that this recently built house has been equipped with such old radiators, low-cost radiators in a way, and in the case of an accident, for example the explosion of the radiators, I could conceivably turn against the manufacturers; I suppose that, in a case of this kind, the responsibility of your father would have been invoked?'

'Yes, undoubtedly.'

'That's a magnificent subject, fucking fascinating even, a *genuine human drama!*' the author of *Platform* enthused. 'A priori cast iron has a small nineteenth-century workers' aristocracy of the furnaces side to it, absolutely outmoded in other words, and yet cast iron is still manufactured, not in France obviously, but rather in countries like Poland and Malaysia. Today, you could very easily retrace in a novel the journey of the iron ore, the reductive fusion of iron and metallurgical coke, the machining of the material, and finally its marketing – all that could come at the beginning of the book, like a genealogy of the radiator.'

'In any case, it seems that you need characters.'

'Yes, that's true. Even if my real subject was industrial processes, without characters I could do nothing.'

'I think that's where the fundamental difference lies. As long as I was just portraying objects, photography suited me perfectly. But, when I decided to take as my subject human beings, I felt I had to return to painting; I couldn't tell you exactly why. Conversely, I can never manage to get interested in still lives; since the invention of photography, I find it no longer makes sense. Well, that's my personal point of view,' he concluded apologetically.

Evening was coming. Through the window, looking southwards, could be made out meadows descending to the Shannon estuary; in the distance, a bank of mist floated on the water, faintly refracting the rays of the setting sun.

'For example, this landscape,' continued Jed. 'OK, I know very well that there were very beautiful Impressionist watercolours in the nineteenth century; however, if I had to depict this landscape today, I would simply take a photo. If, however, there's a human being in the scene, even if it was just a peasant repairing his fences in the distance, then I would be tempted to have recourse to painting. I know that can sound absurd; some will tell you that the subject has no importance, that it's even ridiculous to want to make the treatment depend on the subject being treated, that the only thing that counts is the manner in which the painting or the photograph breaks down into figures, lines and colours.'

'Yes, the formalist point of view. That exists among writers too; but it's even more widespread in the visual arts, it seems.'

Houellebecq fell silent, dropped his head, then lifted his eyes to Jed; he suddenly seemed filled with sad thoughts. He got up and left for the kitchen. He came back a few minutes later, carrying a bottle of Argentinian red and two glasses.

'We'll have dinner together, if you like. The restaurant at the Oakwood Arms isn't bad. There are traditional Irish dishes – smoked salmon, Irish stew, pretty insipid and basic things, in fact; but there are also kebabs and tandooris, their chef's Pakistani.'

'It's not even six o'clock,' Jed said, astonished.

'Yes, I think it opens at half past six. You know, they eat early in this country; but it's never early enough for me. What I prefer, now, is the end of December; night falls at four o'clock. Then I can put on my pyjamas, take some sleeping pills and go to bed with a bottle of wine and a book. That's how I've been living, for years. The sun rises at nine; well, with the time it takes to wash and have some coffee, it's almost midday, so there are four hours left for me to hold out, and most of the time I manage without too much pain. But in spring it's unbearable. The sunsets are endless and magnificent, it's like some kind of fucking opera, there are constantly new colours, new flashes of light. I once tried to stay here the whole spring and summer and thought I would die. Every evening, I was on the brink of suicide, with this night that never fell. Since then, at the beginning of April, I go to Thailand and stay there until the end of August. Day starts at six and ends at six, it's simpler, equatorial and administrative. It's unbearably hot but the air conditioning works well and it's the dead season for tourists. The brothels are empty but they're still open and that suits me fine; the service remains excellent or very good.'

'Now I have the slight impression you're playing your own role . . .'

'Yes, that's true,' agreed Houellebecq with surprising spontaneity, 'these are things that don't interest me much any more. I'm soon going to stop anyway, I'm going to return to the Loiret; I spent my childhood in the Loiret, I made huts in the forest, so I think I can find some activity along the same lines. Coypu hunting?'

He drove his Lexus fast and smoothly, with obvious pleasure. 'All the same, they suck without a condom, and that, that's nice . . .' the author of *Atomised* murmured vaguely, as if in the memory of a dead dream, before stopping in the hotel car park. Then they entered the dining room, which was vast and well lit. As a starter he ordered the prawn cocktail, and Jed opted for smoked salmon. The Polish waiter put a bottle of lukewarm Chablis in front of them.

'They don't manage,' the novelist complained. 'They don't manage to serve white wine at the right temperature.'

'Are you interested in wine?'

'That gives me a certain distinction; it's very French. And you do have to be interested in something in life. I find it helps.'

'I'm a bit surprised,' Jed confessed. 'On meeting you, I expected something . . . well, let's say, more difficult. You have the reputation for being very depressed. I thought, for example, that you drank much more.'

'Yes,' replied the novelist, studying the wine list closely. 'If you take the gigot of lamb as a main course, we'll have to choose something: perhaps an Argentinian wine again? You know, it's the journalists who've given me the reputation for being a drunk; what's curious is that none of them ever realised that if I was drinking a lot in their presence, it was simply in order to put up with them. How could you bear to have a conversation with a twat like Jean-Paul Marsouin without being almost shit-faced? How could you meet someone who works for *Marianne* or *Le Parisien libéré* without wanting to throw up on the spot? Anyway, the press is unbearably stupid and conformist, don't you find?' he insisted.

'I don't know, really, I don't read it.'

'You've never opened a newspaper?'

'Yes, probably,' said Jed good naturedly, but in fact he had no memory of ever doing so. He managed to visualise piles of *Figaro Magazine* on a coffee table, in his dentist's waiting room; but his dental problems had been solved a long time ago. In any case he had never *felt the need* to buy a newspaper. In Paris the atmosphere is saturated with information. Whether you like it or not, you see the headlines in the kiosks, you hear conversations in the supermarket queues. When he went to the Creuse for his grandmother's funeral, he'd realised that the atmospheric density of information diminished considerably the further you got away from the capital; and that, more generally, human affairs lost their importance, and gradually everything disappeared, except plants.

'I'm going to write the catalogue for your exhibition,' Houellebecq went on. 'But are you sure it's a good idea for you? I'm really hated by the French media, you know, to an incredible degree; a week doesn't pass without someone talking shit about me in some kind of publication.'

'I know, I looked on the Internet before coming here.'

'By associating yourself with me, aren't you afraid you'll crash and burn?'

'I talked about it with my gallerist; he thinks it's not important. We're not really aiming at the French market with this exhibition. Anyway, there are almost no French buyers of contemporary art at the moment.'

'Who buys?'

'The Americans. It's been the novelty of the past two or three years; the Americans are starting to buy again, and the English a little bit as well. But above all it's the Chinese and the Russians.'

Houellebecq looked at him as if he was weighing up the pros and cons. 'So, it's the Chinese and Russians who count, you're maybe right . . .' he concluded. 'Excuse me,' he added, getting up quickly, 'I need a cigarette, I can't think without tobacco.'

He went outside and came back five minutes later, just as the waiter was bringing their dishes. He attacked his lamb biriyani with gusto, but looked suspiciously at Jed's course. 'I'm sure they've put mint sauce on your gigot,' he commented. 'You can't do anything about that, it's the English influence. Yet the English also colonised Pakistan. But here it's worse, they've become mixed with the natives.' His cigarette had obviously done him some good. 'It counts a lot, for you, this exhibition, no?' he continued.

'Yes, enormously. I've the impression that, since I began my series of professions, no one understands where I'm coming from any more. On the pretext that I practise painting on canvas, and even the particularly dated form that is oil painting, I'm always classified in a sort of movement that preaches for a return to painting, when in fact I don't know these people and I don't feel the slightest affinity with them.'

'Is there a return to painting at the moment?'

'More or less. Well, it's one of the trends. Return to painting, or to sculpture, well, let's say return to the object. But, in my view, it's above all for commercial reasons. An object is easier to store and resell than an installation or a performance. In truth, I've never done performance art, but I feel like I might have something in common with that. From one painting to another, I try to construct an artificial, symbolic space where I can depict situations that have a meaning for the group.'

'It's a bit like what theatre tries to do as well. Except that you're not obsessed with the body . . . I must admit I find that comes as a relief.'

'And anyway, it's a bit passé, this obsession with the body. Well, not yet at the theatre, but in the visual arts, yes. What I do, in any case, is situated entirely in the social.'

'OK, I see . . . I now almost see what I can do. You need the text for when?'

'The opening of the exhibition is scheduled for May; we'd need the text of the catalogue by the end of March. That gives you two months.'

'It's not much time.'

'It doesn't have to be very long. Five or ten pages, that would be very good. If you want to do more, you can, of course.'

'I'm going to try . . . Well, it's my fault, I should've replied to your emails before.'

'As remuneration, as I told you, we've budgeted for ten thousand euros. Franz, my gallerist, told me that I could, instead, offer you a painting, but I'm a bit uncomfortable with that, as it would be delicate for you to refuse. So, a priori, we'll say ten thousand euros; but if you prefer a painting, it's a deal.'

'A painting,' Houellebecq said pensively. 'Well, I have walls to hang it on. It's the only thing I really have, in my life: walls.'

14

At midday, Jed had to check out of his hotel, and his flight for Paris didn't leave until 7:10 that evening. Although it was a Sunday, the neighbouring shopping centre was open; he bought a bottle of local whiskey – the cashier was called Magda and asked him if he had the Dunnes Store loyalty card. He hung around for a few minutes in the sparklingly clean alleys, coming across groups of youths who were going to a fast-food restaurant or a video-games room. After an orange-kiwi-strawberry fruit juice at Ronnie's Rocket, he felt he knew enough about the Skycourt Shopping Centre and ordered a taxi for the airport; it was just after one o'clock.

The Estuary Cafe had the same qualities of sobriety and size that he'd noticed in the rest of the edifice: the rectangular tables, made of dark wood, were very spaced out, much more than in most luxury restaurants today; they had been designed so that six people could sit there comfortably. Jed then remembered that the 1950s had also been the time of the baby boom.

He ordered a low-fat coleslaw and a chicken korma, and sat down at one of the tables, accompanying his meal with small sips of whiskey while studying the schedule of flights departing from Shannon airport. No capitals of Western Europe were served, with the exception of Paris and London, respectively by Air France and British Airways. However, there were no fewer than six flights bound for Spain and the Canary Islands: Alicante, Girona, Fuerteventura, Malaga, Reus and Tenerife. All of these flights were with Ryanair. The low-cost company also served six destinations in Poland: Krakow, Gdansk, Katowice, Łódź, Warsaw and Wrocław. The previous evening, over dinner, Houellebecq had told him that there was an enormous number of Polish immigrants in Ireland. It was the country they preferred above all others, no doubt because of its reputation – long since weakened, it must be said – as a sanctuary of Catholicism. Thus, free-market economics redrew the geography of the world in terms of the expectations of the clientele, whether the latter moved to indulge in tourism or to earn a living. The flat, isometric surface of the map was substituted by an abnormal topography where Shannon was closer to Katowice than to Brussels, to Fuerteventura than to Madrid. For France, the two airports used by Ryanair were Beauvais and Carcassonne. Were they two particularly touristy destinations? Or did they become touristy for the simple reason that Ryanair had chosen them? Meditating on power and the topology of the world, Jed dozed off.

He was in the middle of a white, apparently limitless space. No horizon could be made out, the matt-white floor merging, very far away, with an identically coloured sky. On the surface of the floor could be seen, irregularly arranged, from place to place, blocks of text with black letters forming a slightly raised relief; each of the blocks could include about fifty words. Jed then realised that he was standing in a book, and wondered if this book told the story of his life. Looking down at the blocks he encountered as he walked, he had the impression this was the case: he recognised names like Olga and Geneviève; but no precise information could be drawn from any of them, most of the words having been erased or angrily crossed out, indecipherable, and new names appeared that meant nothing to him. No temporal direction could be defined either: progressing in a straight line, he encountered several times the name of Geneviève, reappearing after Olga's. While he was certain, absolutely certain, that he would never have occasion to see Geneviève again, Olga, perhaps, was still part of his future.

He was woken by the loudspeakers announcing boarding for the flight to Paris. On arriving in the boulevard de l'Hôpital, he telephoned Houellebecq – who again answered almost immediately.

'So there you are,' Jed said. 'I've had a think. Rather than offering you a painting I would like to do your portrait, and give it to you as a gift.'

Then he waited: at the end of the line, Houellebecq stayed silent. Jed creased his eyes: the lighting in the studio was brutal. In the centre of the room, the floor was still strewn with the ripped remains of *Damien Hirst and Jeff Koons Dividing Up the Art Market*. As the silence lengthened, he added: 'That wouldn't put into question your remuneration: that would come on top of the ten thousand euros. I really want to do your portrait. I've never painted a writer, so I feel I have to do it.'

Houellebecq was still saying nothing, and Jed began to worry; then finally, after at least three minutes' silence, in a voice terribly slurred by alcohol, he replied: 'I don't know. I don't feel capable of posing for hours.'

'Ah, but that's not important! Sittings are all in the past, no one agrees to them anymore. People are overbooked or imagine or pretend they are, I don't know, but I know absolutely no one who would agree to stay still for an hour. No, if I do your portrait I'll come back and visit you, and take photos. Lots of photos: general pictures but also of the place where you work, the tools of your trade. And also detailed shots of your hands, the grain of your skin. Then, I'll use all that back here.'

'OK,' the author replied unenthusiastically. 'It's a deal.'

'Is there a day or a particular week when you're free?'

'Not really. Most of the time I do nothing. Call me when you intend to come. Goodnight.'

The following morning, very early, Jed phoned Franz, who reacted enthusiastically and proposed that he come to the gallery straight away. Jed had rarely seen him so excited.

'Now we can really put on something . . . And I guarantee you that it'll make some noise. We can already choose the press officer. I'd thought of Marylin Prigent.'

'Marylin?'

'Do you know her?'

'Yes, she was the one who looked after my first exhibition. I remember her well.'

*   *   *

Curiously, Marylin had rather sorted herself out with age. She had slimmed down a bit, and had her hair cut very short – with dull and flat hair like hers, she said it was the only thing to do. She had ended up following the advice of women's magazines – she was dressed in very close-fitting trousers and a leather jacket; altogether she had the fake lesbian-intellectual look which might seduce boys with a rather passive temperament. In fact, she looked a bit like the novelist Christine Angot – but a bit nicer all the same. And then, above all, she had managed to get rid of the quasi-permanent sniffling that had characterised her.

'That took me years,' she said. 'I spent my holidays following cures in all the thermal resorts you can imagine, but I finally found a treatment. Once a week I do inhalations of sulphur, and that works; well, up to now it hasn't returned.'

Her voice itself was stronger, clearer, and she now spoke of her sex life with a candour that was astonishing to Jed. As Franz complimented her on her tan, she replied that she had just come back from her winter holidays in Jamaica. 'I fucked my brains out,' she added, 'Christ, those guys are superb.' He raised his eyebrows in surprise, but already changing the subject she had taken out of her handbag – an elegant bag now, an Hermès, in tawny leather – a big blue spiral-bound notebook.

'No, that's something that hasn't changed,' she told Jed with a smile. 'Still no PDA . . . But I've modernised a little all the same.' She took from her inside jacket pocket a memory stick. 'On there you have all the scanned articles on your Michelin exhibition. That'll help us a lot.' Franz nodded, giving her an impressed and incredulous look.

She sat back in her chair and stretched. 'I've tried to follow a little what you were doing,' she said to Jed, speaking familiarly with him now; this too, was new. 'I think you were right not to exhibit earlier, most of the critics would've had difficulty following your change in direction. I'm not even talking about Pépita Bourguignon, and anyway she's never understood your work.'

She lit a cigarillo – another novelty – before continuing. 'As you haven't exhibited, they haven't had to pronounce judgement. If they have to do a good review now, they won't give the impression they're going back on their opinions. But it's true, and there I'm in agreement with you, that we have to target the Anglo-Saxon magazines straight away; and it's there that Houellebecq's name can help us. What will the print run of the catalogue be?'

'Five hundred copies,' said Franz.

'That's not enough: print a thousand. I need three hundred just for the press office. And we'll authorise the reproduction of extracts, even long ones, almost everywhere; we'll have to check with Houellebecq or Samuelson, his agent, so they don't have any difficulties with it. Franz told me about the portrait of Houellebecq. It's a truly a great idea. What's more, at the time of the exhibition, it will be your most recent work; that's excellent, and it'll give extra impact to the whole thing, I'm sure of it.'

'She's a smooth talker, that girl,' Franz remarked after she left. 'I knew her by reputation, but I'd never worked with her.'

'She's changed a lot,' said Jed. 'I mean, on a personal level. Professionally, however, not a bit. It's impressive all the same to what extent people cut their lives into two parts that don't really communicate, that don't have any interaction at all. I'm amazed they manage it so well.'

'It's true you've been very interested in the work . . . in the professions that people do,' continued Franz once they'd got to Chez Claude. 'More than any other artist I know.'

'What defines a man? What's the question you first ask a man, when you want to find out about him? In some societies, you ask him first if he's married, if he has children; in our society, we ask first what his profession is. It's his place in the productive process, and not his status as reproducer, that above all defines Western man.'

Franz pensively emptied, with small sips, his glass of wine. 'I hope that Houellebecq's going to write a good text,' he finally said.

'It's a big gamble, you know. It's very difficult to make people accept an artistic development as radical as yours. And what's more, I think it's in the visual arts that we have the most favourable conditions. In literature and music, it's downright impossible to change direction, you're certain to get lynched. On the one hand, if you always do the same thing, you're accused of repeating yourself and being in decline, but if you change you're accused of being an incoherent dilettante. I know that, in your case, it makes sense to return to painting, and at the same time to the portrayal of human beings. I would be incapable of explaining exactly why, and probably so would you, but I know there's nothing gratuitous about it. But that's just an intuition, and to have some reviews isn't enough, you need to produce some kind of theoretical discourse. And I'm completely incapable of doing that; so are you.'

During the days that followed they tried to define a circuit, an order of presentation of the pieces, and they finally settled on a purely chronological order. The last painting was therefore *Bill Gates and Steve Jobs Discussing the Future of Information Technology*, with an open space for the planned Houellebecq portrait. At the end of the week, Jed tried to get hold of the writer, but this time he didn't answer his phone, and he didn't have a voicemail service. After a few attempts at various times, he sent him an email; then a second, then a third a few days later, still without any reply.

After two weeks, Jed began to get really worried. He sent more and more SMSs and emails. Houellebecq finally replied. His voice was so listless that he almost sounded dead. 'I'm sorry,' he said. 'I'm going through a few personal problems. Well, you can come and take your photos.'

15

The flight leaving Beauvais at 1:25 p.m. for Shannon the following day was offered, on Ryanair.com, at a price of €4.99, and Jed's first thought was that this was a mistake. Further into the booking process he noticed there were extra charges and taxes; the final price came to €28.01, which was still very modest.

A shuttle linked the Porte Maillot to Beauvais airport. On getting into the bus he noticed there were mainly young people, probably students, who were leaving on holiday, or were going home – it was the February holidays. There were also some pensioners, and a few Arab women accompanied by young children. In fact, there was almost every type except active, productive members of society. Jed also realised that he felt rather at home on this shuttle, which gave him the impression of going on holiday – while the last time, on the Air France flight, he'd felt like he was going to work.

Leaving the rough or residential suburbs to the north of Paris, the bus rapidly crossed fields of wheat and beetroot on an almost deserted motorway. Some isolated and enormous crows crossed the grey sky. No one was speaking around him, and gradually Jed felt touched by a sort of peace.

It was already ten years, he thought; ten years during which he had worked in an obscure, very solitary way. Working alone, without ever showing his paintings to anyone – except Franz, who he knew arranged discreet private showings, without ever giving him any feedback – and going to no openings, no debates, and almost no exhibitions. Jed had gradually let himself slip, in the course of the last few years, outside the status of professional artist. He had gradually, in the eyes of the world and even to some extent his own, turned into a *Sunday painter*. This exhibition was going to return him brutally to that milieu, the circuit, and he wondered if he really wanted this. No doubt no more than you want, at first, on the Breton coast, to plunge into a cold and rough sea – while knowing that after a few strokes you'll find the coolness of the waves delicious and invigorating.

While waiting on the little airport's benches for his flight's departure, Jed opened the instruction manual for the camera he'd bought the day before at the Fnac. The Nikon D3x he normally used for preparatory pictures had struck him as too imposing, too professional. Houellebecq had a reputation for harbouring a deeply ingrained hatred of photographers; he had felt that a more playful, family-friendly camera would be more appropriate.

From the outset, the Samsung firm congratulated him, not without a certain grandiloquence, on having chosen the ZRT-AV2. Neither Sony nor Nikon would have thought of congratulating him: those firms were too arrogant, too sure of their professionalism, unless it was the arrogance characteristic of the Japanese; anyway, those well-established Japanese companies were unbearable. The Germans tried to maintain the fiction of a sensible, loyal choice, and reading the owner's manual of a Mercedes remains a real pleasure; but, on the level of value for money, the magical fiction, the social democracy of gremlins could no longer stand the pace. There remained the Swiss and their policy of extreme prices, which might tempt some. Jed had, in certain circumstances, considered buying a Swiss product, generally an Alpa camera, and on another occasion a watch, but the price differential, from 1 to 5 in relation to a normal product, had quickly put him off. Undoubtedly, the best way for a consumer to *have a good time* in the 2010s was to turn to Korean products: for a car, Kia and Hyundai; for electronics, LG and Samsung.

The Samsung ZRT-AV2 combined, according to the manual introduction, the most ingenious technological innovations – such as, for example, the automatic detection of smiles – with the legendary easiness of use that had made the brand's reputation.

After this lyrical passage, the rest became more factual, and Jed flicked through it quickly, looking to identify just the essential information. It was clear that a reasoned, ample and unifying optimism had underscored the design of the product. Prevalent in modern technological objects, this tendency was not however a fatality. Instead of, for example, the programs FIREWORKS, BEACH, BABY1 and BABY2 proposed by the cameras in scene mode, you could just as well have encountered FUNERAL, RAINY DAY, OLDMAN1 and OLDMAN2.

Why BABY1 and BABY2? Jed wondered. By going to page 37 of the manual, he learned that this function enabled you to set the birthdays of two different babies, in order to enter their ages into the electronic settings linked to the pictures. Further information was given on page 38: these programs, the manual promised, were designed to reproduce the 'fresh and healthy' complexion of the babies. After all, their parents would probably have been disappointed if, on their birthday photos, BABY1 and BABY2 appeared with wrinkled and jaundiced faces; but Jed did not, personally, know any babies; nor would he have had the occasion to use the PET program, and hardly the PARTY one; at the end of the day, this camera was perhaps not made with him in mind.

Rain was falling steadily on Shannon, and the taxi driver was a malicious imbecile. 'Come for holidays?' he asked, as if rejoicing in advance at his bad luck. 'No, working,' replied Jed, who didn't want to give him this joy, though the other man obviously didn't believe him. 'What kind of job do you do?' he asked his tone clearly implying that he thought it improbable that he'd be given any kind of work. 'Photography,' Jed told him. The driver sniffed, admitting defeat.

He hammered on the door for at least two minutes, under a heavy downpour, before Houellebecq came to open it. The author of *Atomised* was wearing grey-striped pyjamas that made him vaguely resemble a prisoner in a television series; his hair was ruffled and dirty, his face red, almost with broken veins, and he stank a little. The inability to wash, Jed remembered, is one of the surest signs of depression.

'I'm sorry to bang on your door, I know you're not doing very well. But I'm impatient to start on my portrait of you,' he said, producing a smile which he hoped was *disarming*. *Disarming smile* is an expression you still encounter in certain novels, and therefore must correspond to some kind of reality. But unfortunately Jed for his part, didn't feel sufficiently naive to be able to be *disarmed* by a smile; and he suspected Houellebecq wasn't either. Nevertheless, the poet of *The Meaning of the Fight* stepped back a metre, just enough to allow Jed to take shelter from the rain, without, however, really giving him access inside.

'I've brought a bottle of wine. A good bottle!' Jed exclaimed with slightly fake enthusiasm, rather like how you offer sweets to children, as he took it out of his travel bag. It was a Château Ausone 1986, which had cost him four hundred euros – a dozen Paris–Shannon flights with Ryanair.

'Just one bottle?' asked the poet of *The Pursuit of Happiness* while stretching his neck towards the label. He stank a little, but less than a corpse; worse things could have happened, after all. Then he turned round without saying a word, and Jed interpreted this as an invitation.

The main room, the living room, had been empty the last time, as far as he remembered; it was now furnished with a bed and a television.

'Yes,' said Houellebecq, 'after your visit I realised you were the first visitor to enter this house, and that you would probably be the last. So I told myself, what's the point of maintaining the fiction of a reception room? Why not just have my bedroom in the main room? After all, I spend most of my days in bed; I most often eat in bed, watching cartoons on Fox TV; it's not as if I throw dinner parties.'

Indeed, bits of toast and scraps of mortadella were strewn on the sheets, which were stained with wine and cigarette burns in places.

'We'll go into the kitchen, all the same,' proposed the author of *Renaissance*.

'I came to take the photos.'

'Your camera doesn't work in kitchens?'

'I've relapsed . . . I've completely relapsed into charcuterie,' Houellebecq went on darkly. The table was covered with packages of chorizo, mortadella and pâté de campagne. He handed Jed a corkscrew, and once the bottle was open he downed a glass of wine in one long swallow, without even pretending to taste it. Jed took a dozen close-ups, trying to vary the angles.

'I'd like to have some photos of you in your office . . . the place where you work.'

The author groaned unenthusiastically, but got up and led him down a corridor. The removal boxes piled up along the walls had still not been opened. He'd put on some weight since the last time, but his neck and his arms were still just as spindly; he looked like a sick old turtle.

The office was a large rectangular room with bare walls, almost empty except for three garden tables in green plastic lined up against a wall. On the central table were a 24-inch iMac and a Samsung laser printer; sheets of paper, printed or handwritten, were scattered on the other tables. The only luxury was a black leather executive armchair with a tall back and fitted with casters.

Jed took a few photos of the room as a whole. As he saw Jed approach the tables, Houellebecq suddenly became nervous.

'Don't worry, I won't look at your manuscripts, I know you hate that. However . . .' he thought for a moment, 'I'd like to see what your annotations and corrections look like.'

'I'd rather you didn't.'

'I'm not looking at the content, not at all. It's just to have an idea of the geometry of it all. I promise you that in the painting no one will recognise the words.'

Reticently, Houellebecq took out a few sheets of paper. There were very few crossings-out, but numerous asterisks in the middle of the text, accompanied by arrows that led to new blocks of text, some in the margin, others on separate sheets. Inside these blocks, which were roughly rectangular, new asterisks led towards other blocks, forming a sort of tree diagram. The handwriting was slanting, almost illegible. Houellebecq didn't take his eyes off Jed all the time he was taking pictures, and sighed with visible relief when he moved away from the table. On leaving the room, he closed the door carefully behind him.

'It's not the text about you, I haven't yet started,' the author said while returning to the kitchen. 'It's a preface to a new edition of Jean-Louis Curtis with Omnibus – I have to submit it soon. You want a glass of wine?' He was speaking with exaggerated cheerfulness now, no doubt to make Jed forget the initial coolness of his welcome. The Château Ausone was almost finished. He extravagantly opened a cupboard, revealing about forty bottles.

'Argentina or Chile?'

'Chile, for a change.'

'Jean-Louis Curtis is totally forgotten today. He wrote about fifteen novels, novellas, an extraordinary collection of pastiches . . . *France Exhausts Me* contains, in my view, the best pastiches in French literature: his imitations of Saint-Simon and Chateaubriand are perfect; he also does Stendhal and Balzac very well. And yet today there's nothing left, no one reads him any more. It's unfair, he was rather a good author, in a slightly conservative and classical kind of way, but he tried to do his job honestly. *Quarantine* is a very well-written book, I find. There's a real nostalgia, a sensation of loss in the transition from traditional France to the modern world, and you can completely relive that moment by reading him; it's rarely caricatural, except occasionally with some characters who are left-wing priests. And then *A Young Couple* is a very surprising book. Tackling exactly the same subject as Georges Perec in *Things*, he manages not to be ridiculous in comparison, and that's already saying something. Obviously he doesn't have Perec's virtuosity, but who did, in his century? You might also be astonished to see him take the side of the young, the tribes of hippies who were apparently crossing Europe at the time, wearing backpacks and rejecting 'consumer society', as they called it then; his rejection of consumer society is, however, as strong as theirs, and rests on a much more solid basis, as subsequent events have shown all too clearly. Conversely, Georges Perec accepts the consumer society and he rightly considers it the only possible horizon; his observations on the happiness found in Orly airport are in my view completely convincing. It's quite wrongly that Jean-Louis Curtis has been classified as a *reactionary*. He's just a good author who's slightly sad, and convinced that mankind can hardly change, in one way or the other. A lover of Italy, he's fully conscious of the cruelty of the Latin view of the world. Well, I don't know why I'm telling you all this, you don't give a toss about Jean-Louis Curtis, but you're wrong not to. It should interest you, for I also sense in you a sort of nostalgia, but this time it's nostalgia for the modern world, for the time when France was an industrial country, or am I wrong?' He took out of the fridge some chorizo, sausage and brown bread.

'That's true,' replied Jed after a few moments' thought. 'I've always loved industrial products. I would never have imagined photographing, for example . . . a sausage.' He held his hand out towards the table, and then immediately apologised. 'Well it's very good, I don't mean that, I like eating it . . . But photographing it, no. There are those irregularities of organic origin, those venules of fat that vary from one slice to the next. It's a bit . . . off-putting.'

Houellebecq nodded, opening his arms as if he were entering a tantric trance; he was, more probably, drunk, and trying to keep his balance on the kitchen stool where he'd crouched. When he spoke again his voice was soft and deep, filled with naive emotion. 'In my life as a consumer,' he said, 'I've known three perfect products: Paraboot walking boots, the Canon Libris laptop-printer combination, and the Camel Legend parka. I loved those products, with a passion; I would've spent my life in their presence, buying regularly, with natural wastage, identical products. A perfect and faithful relationship had been established, making me a happy consumer. I wasn't completely happy in all aspects of life, but at least I had that: I could, at regular intervals, buy a pair of my favourite boots. It's not much but it's something, especially when you've quite a poor private life. Ah yes, that joy, that simple joy, has been denied me. My favourite products, after a few years, have disappeared from the shelves, their manufacture has stopped purely and simply – and in the case of my poor Camel Legend parka, no doubt the most beautiful parka ever made, it will have lived for only one season . . .' He slowly began to cry, big tears streaming down his face, and served himself another glass of wine. 'It's brutal, you know, it's terribly brutal. While the most insignificant animal species take thousands, sometimes millions of years to disappear, manufactured products are wiped off the surface of the globe in a few days; they're never given a second chance, they can only suffer, powerless, the irresponsible and fascistic diktat of product line managers who of course know better than anyone else what the customer wants, who claim to capture an *expectation of novelty* in the consumer, and who in reality just turns his life into one exhausting and desperate quest, an endless wandering between eternally modified product lines.'

'I understand what you mean,' Jed interjected. 'I know that a lot of people were heartbroken when they stopped manufacturing the double-lens Rolleiflex. But maybe then . . . maybe you'd have to reserve your trust and love for extremely expensive products that enjoy a mythical status. I can't imagine, for example, Rolex stopping production of the Oyster Perpetual Day-Date.'

'You're young . . . You're so terribly young . . . Rolex will do like all the others.' He then seized three slices of chorizo, put them on a bit of bread, gulped it down, and poured himself another glass of wine. 'You've just bought a new camera, you told me . . . Show me the manual.'

For two minutes he went through the user manual of the Samsung ZRT-AV2, nodding his head as if each of the lines confirmed his dark predictions. 'Ah yes,' he finally said, handing it back. 'It's a beautiful product, a modern product that you can love. But you must know that in a year, or two at most, it will be replaced by some new product with supposedly improved features.

'We too are products,' he went on, 'cultural products. We too will become obsolete. The functioning of the system is identical – with the difference that, in general, there is no obvious technical or functional improvement; all that remains is the demand for novelty in its pure state.

'But that's nothing, that's nothing,' he went on light-heartedly. He began to cut up a second sausage and then, with his knife in his hand, stopped to intone in a powerful voice: 'To love, laugh and sing!' His sweeping hand knocked over the bottle of wine, which shattered on the tiles.

'I'll tidy it up,' said Jed, springing up from his stool.

'No, leave it, it's not a problem.'

'Yes, it is, there're bits of broken glass, you could cut yourself. Do you have a mop?' He looked around him: Houellebecq was just nodding his head. In a corner, he saw a small brush and a plastic dustpan.

'I'm going to open another bottle,' said the writer. He stood up and crossed the kitchen, zigzagging past the shards of glass that Jed was doing his best to sweep up.

'We've already drunk a lot . . . I've done all my photos.'

'Come on, you're not going to leave now! The fun's just started,' he announced before gulping down a glass of Chilean wine. 'Foucra bouldou! Bistroye! Bistroye!' he added with conviction. For some time now, the famous writer had contracted this mania for using bizarre, outmoded or frankly inappropriate words, as if they weren't infantile neologisms worthy of Captain Haddock. His few remaining friends, like his publishers, allowed him this weakness, as you do almost anything from a tired old decadent.

'It's grandiose, this idea you've had of making my portrait, truly grandiose.'

'Really?' Jed asked, surprised. He finished tidying up the pieces of glass, and put it all in a special garden refuse bag (Houellebecq, apparently, didn't have any other kind), sat down again at the table and took a slice of sausage.

'You know,' he continued, unflustered, 'I really intend to do this painting well. These last ten years, I've tried to portray people belonging to all layers of society, from the horse butcher to the chief executive of a multinational. My only failure was when I tried to portray an artist – more precisely Jeff Koons, I don't know why. Well, I also failed in the case of a priest, I didn't know how to approach that subject either, but in the case of Jeff Koons it's worse. I'd started the painting, and I was obliged to destroy it. I don't want to end on this failure – and with you, I believe, I will succeed. There's something in your eyes, I don't know what, but I believe I can transcribe it . . .'

The word *passion* suddenly crossed Jed's mind, and all of a sudden he found himself ten years previously, during his last weekend with Olga. It was on the terrace of the Château de Vault-de-Lugny, on the Sunday of Pentecost. The terrace overlooked the immense park, whose trees swayed in a gentle breeze. Night was falling, and the temperature ideally mild. Olga seemed deep in contemplation of her pressed lobster. She had said nothing for at least a minute when she lifted her head, looked him straight in the eyes and asked: 'Do you know why you are attractive to women?'

He muttered an inaudible reply.

'I suppose you've had the opportunity to notice it. You're rather cute, but it's not that, beauty's almost a detail. No, it's something else.'

'Tell me.'

'It's very simple: it's because you have an intense look in your eyes. A passionate look. And it's that, above all, that women are looking for. If they can read in the eyes of a man an energy, a passion, then they find him attractive.'

Leaving him to meditate on this conclusion she took a sip of Meursault, and tasted her starter. 'Obviously,' she said a little later with a slight sadness, 'when this passion isn't addressed to them, but to an artistic work, women are incapable of noticing it. Well, at least at the beginning.'

Ten years later, observing Houellebecq, Jed became aware that there was also passion in his eyes, even something wild. He must have aroused passions in women, maybe violent ones. Yes, from everything Jed knew about women, it seemed probable that some of them might have fallen for this tortured wreck who was now gently nodding his head in front of him while devouring slices of pâté de campagne, and who had manifestly become indifferent to anything connected to a loving relationship, and most probably any kind of human relationship.

'It's true, I feel only a faint sense of solidarity with the human species . . .' said Houellebecq as if he'd read Jed's thoughts. 'I would say that my feeling of belonging diminishes a little more each day. Yet I like your last paintings, even if they portray human beings. They have something . . . general, I would say, which goes beyond the anecdotal. I mean, I don't want to anticipate my text, otherwise I'll write nothing. In fact, that doesn't bother you too much, does it, if I haven't finished it by the end of March? I'm really not well at the moment.'

'No problem. We'll delay the exhibition; we'll wait for as long as it takes. You know you've become important for me, and, what's more,' he exclaimed, 'that's happened so quickly! No human being has ever had this effect on me!

'What's curious, you know,' he went on more calmly, 'is that you expect a portrait painter to stress the singularity of the model, what makes him a unique human being. And that's what I do in a way, but from another point of view I have the impression that people resemble one another more than is normally said, especially when I do the planes or the jawbones, I have the impression I'm repeating the motifs of a puzzle. I know very well that human beings are the subject of the novel, of the *great Western novel*, and one of the great subjects of painting as well, but I can't help thinking that people are much less different than they generally think. That there are too many complications in society, too many distinctions and categories.'

'Yes, it's a bit *byzantinesque*,' the author of *Platform* agreed heartily. 'But I don't feel that you're really a portrait painter. Picasso's portrait of Dora Maar, who gives a fuck about that? Anyway, Picasso's ugly, and he paints a hideously deformed world because his soul is hideous, and that's all you can say about Picasso. There's no reason any more to support the exhibition of his works. He has nothing to contribute, and with him there's no light, no innovation in the organisation of colours or forms. I mean, in Picasso's work there's absolutely nothing that deserves attention, just an extreme stupidity and a priapic daubing that might attract a few sixty-somethings with big bank accounts. The portrait of Fuck-face, member of the Merchants' Guild, by Van Dyck, now that's something else; because it's not Fuck-face who interests Van Dyck, but the Merchants' Guild. I mean, that's what I understand in your paintings, but maybe I've got it completely wrong; anyway, if you don't like my text you can just chuck it in the bin. Sorry, I'm becoming aggressive, it's this damn athlete's foot.' Before Jed's terrified eyes, he began scratching his feet, furiously, until drops of blood began to appear. 'I've got athlete's foot, a bacterial infection, a generalised atopic eczema. I'm rotting on the spot and no one gives a damn, no one can do anything to help me. I've been shamefully abandoned by science, so what's left for me to do? Just scratch, scratch myself endlessly, that's what my life's now become, one endless scratching session . . .'

Then he stood up, slightly relieved. 'I'm a bit tired now, I think I'm going to have a rest,' he said, sounding like a man who had got out of a jam pretty well.

Houellebecq accompanied Jed to the door. At the last moment, just before he disappeared into the night, he told him: 'You know, I realise what you're doing, and I know the consequences. You're a good artist – without going into detail one could say that. The result is that while I've been photographed thousands of times, if there's an image of me, just one, that will last for the centuries to come, it will be your painting.' He suddenly made a smile that was juvenile and this time truly *disarming*. 'You see, I take painting seriously,' he said. Then he closed the door.

16

Jed stumbled into a buggy, only just regained his balance before the body scanner, then stepped back to retake his place in the queue. Apart from him there mostly families, each with two or three children. In front of him, a blond child aged about four was whining, demanding God knows what, then he suddenly threw himself on the floor screaming and trembling with rage; his mother exchanged an exhausted look with her husband, who tried to pick the vicious little bastard up again. It's impossible to write a novel, Houellebecq had told him the day before, for the same reason that it's impossible to live: due to accumulated inertia. And all the theories of freedom, from Gide to Sartre, are just immoralisms thought up by irresponsible bachelors. Like me, he'd added, attacking his third bottle of Chilean red.

There were no designated seats in the plane, and at boarding he tried to join a group of teenagers but was held back at the foot of the metal steps – his hand luggage was too big, he had to pass it to the flight crew – and found himself stuck between a five-year-old girl who was fidgeting in her seat, constantly demanding sweets, and an obese woman, with dull hair, holding in her lap a baby which began to scream just after take-off; half an hour later, she had to change its nappy.

At the exit from the airport of Beauvais-Tillé, he stopped, put down his travel bag, and breathed slowly before picking it up again. The families loaded with buggies and children were rushing onto the bus bound for the Porte Maillot. Just next to it was a small white van, with big side windows, bearing the logo of Beauvaisis Urban Transport. Jed approached and asked for information: it was the shuttle for Beauvais, the driver told him; the journey cost two euros. He bought a ticket; he was the only passenger.

'Shall I drop you at the station?' the driver asked a little later.

'No, in the centre.'

The driver looked at him in surprise; Beauvaisis tourism, apparently, hadn't benefitted much from the presence of the airport. However, an effort had been made, as in almost every town in France, to pedestrianise streets in the centre, with signs giving historical and cultural information. The first traces of settlement on the site of Beauvais could be dated from 65,000 BC. A camp fortified by the Romans, the town took the name of Caesaromagus, then of Bellovacum, before being destroyed in AD 275 by the barbarian invasions.

Standing at a crossroads of trade routes, surrounded by very rich wheat fields, Beauvais enjoyed considerable prosperity from the eleventh century onwards, and a textile industry developed there; draperies made in Beauvais were exported as far as Byzantium. It was in 1225 that the count-bishop Milon de Nanteuil began building the Saint-Pierre Cathedral (three Michelin stars, *worth the journey*), and, though incomplete, it nonetheless boasts one of the highest Gothic vaults in Europe. The decline of Beauvais, accompanying that of the textile industry, was to start at the end of the eighteenth century; it hadn't really stopped since, and Jed had no difficulty finding a room in the Kyriad Hotel. He even thought he was the only guest, until dinner. As he tucked into his *blanquette de veau* – the dish of the day – he saw come in a solitary Japanese man, aged about thirty, who shot terrified looks around the room, then sat down at the next table.

The suggestion of a *blanquette de veau* plunged the Japanese man into anxiety; he opted for an entrecôte which arrived a few minutes later and which he prodded sadly, and irresolutely, with the end of his fork. Jed feared he was going to strike up a conversation, which he did, in English, after sucking on a few chips. The poor man was employed by Komatsu, a machine-tool business that had managed to place one of its new-generation textile robots with the last cloth-manufacturing company still going in the area. The programming of the machine had broken down, and he had come to try and repair it. For a journey of this order, he lamented, his firm used to send three or four technicians, or two at the very least; but budgetary restrictions were terrible, and he found himself alone, in Beauvais, faced with a furious client and a machine with defective programming.

He was, indeed, in a nasty situation, agreed Jed. But wasn't there some sort of helpline he could call? 'Time difference,' the Japanese man said sadly. Maybe, around one in the morning, he would get through to someone in Japan, when the offices opened; but until then he was on his own, and he didn't even have Japanese cable channels in his room. For a moment he looked at his steak knife, as if he was contemplating seppuku, then decided to start eating his entrecôte.

In his bedroom, while watching *Thalassa* with the sound off, Jed switched on his mobile. Franz had left three messages. He answered after the first ring.

'So? How did it go?'

'Well. Almost well. Except that I think he'll be a bit late with the text.'

'Oh no, that's not possible. I need it by the end of March, otherwise I can't print the catalogue.'

'I told him . . .' Jed hesitated, then came to the point. 'I told him that it wasn't a problem; that he could take all the time he needed.'

Franz uttered a sort of incredulous grumbling, then went silent before speaking in a voice that was tense and on the verge of exploding.

'Listen, we've got to meet up and talk about this. Can you come by the gallery now?'

'No, I'm in Beauvais.'

'*Beauvais*? What the fuck are you doing in *Beauvais*?'

'I'm taking some time out. It's good, taking time out in Beauvais.'

There was a train at 8:47 a.m., and the journey to Gare du Nord took a little over an hour. At eleven Jed was at the gallery, facing a downcast Franz. 'You're not my only artist,' he said reproachfully. 'If the exhibition can't take place in May, I'm obliged to put it back to December.'

The arrival of Marylin, ten minutes later, improved the mood a little. 'Oh, December's perfectly fine by me,' she announced immediately, then continued with ferocious joviality. 'That'll give me more time to work the English magazines; you have to go right to the top with the English magazines.'

'Good, then December it is,' Franz conceded, morose and beaten.

'I am . . .' began Jed lifting his hands slightly, then he stopped. He was going to say 'I am the artist', or words to that effect, but he came to his senses and simply added: 'I also need the time to make the portrait of Houellebecq. I want it to be a good painting. I want it to be my best painting.'

17

In *Michel Houellebecq, Writer*, as most art historians stress, Jed Martin breaks with that practice of realistic backgrounds which had characterised his work all through the period of the 'Professions'. He has trouble breaking with it, and you can sense that this break comes with much effort, that he strives through various artifices to maintain the illusion of a possible realistic background as much as possible. In the painting, Houellebecq is standing in front of a desk covered with written or half-written pages. Behind him, at a distance of some five metres, the white wall is entirely papered with handwritten pages stuck to one another, without any interstices whatsoever. Ironically, those art historians stress, Jed Martin seems in this work to accord an enormous importance to the text, and focuses on it detached from any real referent. Now, as all the historians of literature confirm, if Houellebecq liked in the course of his work to pin various documents to the wall, most often photos, representing the places where he situated the scenes of his novels, and rarely written or half-written scenes. Jed Martin probably chose to portray him in the middle of a universe of paper neither to make a statement about realism in literature nor to bring Houellebecq closer to a formalist position that he had explicitly rejected. Without doubt, more simply, he was taken by a purely plastic fascination with the image of these branching blocks of text, engendering one another like some gigantic octopus.

Few people, when the painting was first put on display, would pay much attention to the background, which was eclipsed by the incredible expressiveness of the main figure. Captured at the moment of noticing a mistake on one of the pages on the desk in front of him, the author appears to be in a trance, possessed by a fury that some have not hesitated to describe as demonic; his hand holding the pen, treated with a certain blurring movement, throws itself on the page 'with the speed of a cobra stretching to strike its prey', as Wong Fu Xin writes in a visual way, probably giving an ironic twist to the clichés of metaphorical exuberance tradition- ally associated with the authors of the Far East (Wong Fu Xin wanted, above all, to be a poet; but his poems are almost never read now, and aren't even easily available, while his essays on the work of Jed Martin remain a central reference point in art-history circles). The lighting, which is far more contrasting than in Martin's previous paintings, leaves in shadow a large part of the writer's body, concentrating uniquely on the upper half of the face and on the hands with their hooked, long, and scrawny fingers, like the talons of a raptor. The expression in the eyes appeared at the time so strange that it could not, in the critics view, be compared to any existing pictorial tradition, but had rather to be compared to certain archival ethnological images taken during voodoo ceremonies.

Jed phoned Franz on 25 October to announce that his painting was finished. For a few months they hadn't seen much of each other; contrary to his usual practice he hadn't called to show him prepara- tory work or sketches. Franz for his part had concentrated on other exhibitions, which had gone rather well. His gallery had been quite prominent for a few years now, its reputation gradually increasing – though that hadn't yet translated into substantial sales.

Franz arrived at about 6 p.m. The canvas was in the centre of the studio, hung on a standard chassis of 116 centimetres by 89, well lit by halogen lamps. Franz sat on a folding canvas chair, just opposite, and looked at it wordlessly for about ten minutes.

'OK . . .' he finally said. 'You can be fucking annoying at times, but you're a good artist. I must admit it was worth the wait. It's a good painting; a very good painting. You sure you want to give it to him?'

'I promised.'

'And the text, is it arriving soon?'

'By the end of the month.'

'But are you in contact or not?'

'Not really. He just sent me an email in August to tell me he was coming back to settle in France, that he had managed to buy his childhood home in the Loiret. But he added that this didn't change anything, and that I'd have the text by the end of October. I trust him.'

18

In fact, on the morning of 31 October, Jed received an email accompanied by an untitled text of about fifty pages, which he immediately forwarded to Marylin and Franz, although he was a bit concerned: wasn't it too long? Marylin reassured him immediately: on the contrary, she said, it was always preferable 'to go big'.

Even if today it is considered a historical curiosity, Houellebecq's text – the first of this size devoted to Martin's work – nonetheless contains some interesting intuitions. Beyond the variation of themes and techniques, he asserts for the first time the unity of the artist's work, and discovers a deep logic in the fact that having devoted his formative years to hunting for the essence of the world's manufactured products, he is interested, during the second half of his life, in their producers.

Jed Martin's view of the society of his time, Houellebecq stresses, is that of an ethnologist much more than that of a political commentator. Martin, he insists, is in no way a committed artist, and even if *The Stock Exchange Flotation of Shares in Beate Uhse*, one of the rare crowd scenes, is reminiscent of the expressionist period, we are very far from the scathing, caustic treatment of a George Grosz or an Otto Dix. His traders in trainers and hooded sweatshirts, who acclaim with blasé world-weariness the great German porn businesswoman, are the direct descendants of the suited bourgeois who meet endlessly in the receptions directed by Fritz Lang in the *Mabuse* films; they are treated with the same detachment, the same objective coldness. In his titles as in his painting itself, Martin is always simple and direct: he describes the world, rarely allowing himself a poetic notation or a subtitle serving as commentary. He does this, however, in one of his most successful works, *Bill Gates and Steve Jobs Discussing the Future of Information*

Technology, which he chose to subtitle *The Conversation at Palo Alto*.

Sunk in a wicker chair, Bill Gates was spreading his arms out wide while smiling at his interlocutor. He was dressed in canvas trousers and a khaki short-sleeved shirt; his bare feet were in flip-flops. It was no longer the Bill Gates in a sea-blue suit at the time when Microsoft was consolidating its global domination, and when he himself, dethroning the Sultan of Brunei, became the world's richest man. Nor was it yet the concerned, sorrowful Bill Gates, visiting Sri Lankan orphanages or calling on the international community to be vigilant about the outbreak of smallpox in West Africa. It was an intermediary Bill Gates, relaxed, manifestly happy about retiring from his post as chairman of the planet's biggest software business; in short, a Bill Gates on holiday. Only his metal-framed glasses, with their strongly magnifying lenses, recalled his past as a nerd.

In front of him, Steve Jobs, although sitting cross-legged on the white leather sofa, seemed paradoxically an embodiment of austerity, of the *Sorge* traditionally associated with Protestant capitalism. There was nothing Californian in the way his hand clutched his jaw as if to help him in some difficult reflection, nothing in the look full of uncertainty which he sent his interlocutor; and even the Hawaiian shirt that Martin had decked him out in did nothing to dispel the impression of a general sadness produced by his slightly slumped position, and by the expression of disarray that could be read in his features.

The encounter, quite obviously, took place in Steve Jobs' home. A mixture of coolly designed white furniture and brightly coloured ethnic draperies, everything in the room recalled the aesthetic universe of the founder of Apple, the polar opposite of the profusion of high-tech gadgets, at the limit of science fiction, which, legend would have it, characterised the home the founder of Microsoft had built in the Seattle suburbs. Between the two men, a chessboard with hand-crafted wooden pieces sat on a coffee table;

they had just interrupted the game in a stage unfavourable to the blacks – namely to Jobs.

In certain pages of his autobiography, *The Road Ahead*, Bill Gates occasionally lets slip what could be considered total cynicism – particularly in the passage where he confesses quite plainly that it is not necessarily advantageous for a business to offer the most innovative products. More often it is preferable to observe what the competitors are doing (and there he clearly refers, without using the name, to Apple), to let them bring out their products, confront the difficulties inherent in any innovation, and, in a way, surmount the initial problems; then, in a second phase, flood the market by offering low-price copies of the competing products. This apparent cynicism is not, however, Houellebecq stresses, the true nature of Gates; this is expressed instead in the surprising, almost touching passages in which he reasserts his faith in capitalism, in the mysterious 'invisible hand'; his absolute, unshakeable conviction that whatever the vicissitudes and apparent counter-examples, the market, at the end of the day, is always right, and that the good of the market is always identical to the general good. It is then that the fundamental truth about Bill Gates appears, as a creature of faith, and it is this faith, this candour of the sincere capitalist, that Jed Martin was able to render by portraying him, arms open wide, warm and friendly, his glasses gleaming in the last rays of the sun setting on the Pacific Ocean. Jobs however, made thin by illness, his face careworn and dotted with stubble, sorrowfully leaning on his right hand, is reminiscent of one of those travelling evangelists who, on finding himself preaching for perhaps the tenth time to a small and indifferent audience, is suddenly filled with doubt.

And yet it was Jobs, motionless, weakened, in a losing position, who gave the impression of being the master of the game; such was, according to Houellebecq's text, the profound paradox of this canvas. In his eyes still burned that flame common not only to preachers and prophets but also to the inventors so often described by Jules Verne. By looking more closely at the position of Jobs's chess pieces as portrayed by Martin, you realised that it was not necessarily a losing one; and that Jobs could, by sacrificing his queen, conclude in three moves with an audacious bishop–knight checkmate. Similarly, you had the sense that he could, through the brilliant intuition of a new product, suddenly impose new norms on the market. Through the bay window behind them one could be made out a landscape of meadows, of an almost surreal emerald green, gently descending to a line of cliffs, where they joined a forest of conifers. Further away, the Pacific Ocean unfurled its endless, golden-brown waves. On the lawn, some young girls, had started a game of Frisbee. Evening was falling, magnificently, in the explosion of a setting sun that Martin had wanted to be almost improbable in its orangey magnificence, on north California, and the evening was falling on the most advanced part of the world; it was that too, that indefinite sadness of farewells, which could be read in Jobs' eyes.

Two convinced supporters of the market economy; two resolute supporters also of the Democratic Party, and yet two opposing facets of capitalism, as different as a banker in Balzac could be from Verne's engineer. *The Conversation at Palo Alto*, Houellebecq stressed in his conclusion, was far too modest a subtitle; instead, Jed Martin could have entitled his painting *A Brief History of Capitalism*; for that, indeed, is what it was.

19

After much equivocation, the *vernissage* was fixed for 11 December, a Wednesday – the ideal day, according to Marylin. Urgently produced by an Italian printer, the catalogues arrived just in time. They were elegant, luxurious objects – you don't skimp on that, had decided Marylin, to whom Franz was more and more beholden. It was becoming curious; he followed her around everywhere, like a bichon, while she made her phone calls.

After stacking a pile of catalogues by the entrance, and checking that all the canvases were hung correctly, they had nothing to do until the opening, scheduled for seven, and the gallerist began to show palpable signs of nervousness; he was wearing a curious embroidered Slovakian peasant shirt over his black Diesel jeans. Marylin, still composed, was checking a few details on her mobile and wandering from one painting to another, with Franz at her heels. *It's a game, it's a million-dollar game.*

By six-thirty, Jed began to tire of his two sidekicks's antics, and announced he was going out for a walk. 'Just a walk around the neighbourhood, I'm taking a little walk. Don't worry, walking does you good.'

The remark showed exaggerated optimism, as he realised once he set foot on the boulevard Vincent-Auriol. Some cars raced by, splashing him; it was cold and rainy, that's all you could say, that evening, for the boulevard Vincent-Auriol. A Casino hypermarket and a Shell service station were the only perceptible centres of energy, the only social propositions likely to provoke desire, happiness or joy. Jed already knew these lively places: he had been a regular customer of the Casino hypermarket for years, before switching to the Franprix in the boulevard de l'Hôpital. As for the Shell station, he also knew it well: on many a Sunday, he had appreciated being able to go there for Pringles and bottles of

Hepar. But there was no point this evening. A cocktail party had obviously been scheduled, and they'd called on the services of a caterer.

However, along with dozens of other customers, he went into the hypermarket and immediately noticed various improvements. Near the book section, a shelf of newspapers now offered a large choice of dailies and magazines. The range of fresh Italian pasta had expanded yet again (undoubtedly, nothing seemed able to stop the advance of fresh Italian pasta), and above all the food-court had been enriched with a magnificent, brand-new self-service Salad Bar, which lined up about fifty varieties, some of which looked delicious. That's what gave him the desire to come back, what gave him the *stupefyingly strong* desire to come back, as Houellebecq would have said. Jed suddenly missed him a lot, standing in front of the Salad Bar where a few middle-aged women calculated, sceptically, the calorie content of the ingredients on offer. He knew the writer shared his taste for big food retailers – *real* retail, as he would say – and like him he wished, in a more or less utopian and distant future, for the fusion of the various chain stores in one total hypermarket, which would cover all the needs of mankind. How nice it would have been to visit this refurbished Casino hypermarket together, to nudge each other and point out the sections of completely new products, or particularly clear and exhaustive nutritional labelling!

Was he experiencing a *feeling of friendship* for Houellebecq? That would be an exaggeration. Jed didn't think he was capable of such a feeling: he had gone through childhood and the start of adolescence without falling prey to strong friendships, while these periods of life are considered particularly propitious for their birth. It was scarcely probable that friendship would come to him now, *late in life*. But, still, he had appreciated their encounter, and above all he liked his text. He found in it a surprising quality of intuition, given the author's obvious lack of artistic education. Of course, he had invited him to the *vernissage*; Houellebecq had replied that he would 'try to pop in', which meant that the chances of seeing him were almost nil. When they'd spoken on the phone, he was very excited

by the renovation of his new home. When he'd returned, two
months ago, in a sort of sentimental pilgrimage, to the village
where he had spent his childhood, his family home was up for sale.
He had considered this 'absolutely miraculous'. It was fate, and he
had bought it immediately, without even discussing the price, and
moved in his things – most of which, it's true, had never left their
boxes – and now was busy furnishing it. That's all he'd talked about,
and Jed's painting seemed the least of his concerns; Jed had,
however, promised to bring it to him after the *vernissage* and the
first days of the exhibition, when occasionally a few latecomer
journalists would show up.

At about seven-twenty, when Jed returned to the gallery, through
the bay windows he noticed people circulating in the rows between
the paintings. They had come on time, which was probably a good
sign. Marylin saw him from afar, and shook her fist at him in a
victory sign.

'There are heavyweights here,' she said when he rejoined her.
'Some real heavyweights.'

In fact, a few metres away, he saw Franz in conversation with
François Pinault, flanked by a ravishing young woman, probably
of Iranian origin, who was assisting him as director of his artistic
foundation. His gallerist seemed to be struggling, waving his arms
around distractedly, and for an instant Jed wanted to come to his
aid, before remembering what he'd always known, and what
Marylin had categorically told him a few days before: he was never
better than when silent.

'It's not over yet,' the press officer went on. 'You see that guy
in grey, over there?' She pointed to a young man aged about thirty,
with an intelligent face and extremely well dressed, his suit, tie,
and shirt forming a delicate colour-chart of grey. He had stopped
in front of *The Journalist Jean-Pierre Pernaut Chairing an Editorial
Meeting*, a relatively old painting, the first in which Jed had portrayed
his subject in the company of work colleagues. That had been, he
remembered, a particularly difficult one to paint: the expressions
of Jean-Pierre Pernaut's staff, listening to the directives of their

charismatic leader with a curious mixture of veneration and disgust, had not been easy to render; he'd spent almost six months on it. But this painting had liberated him, and he immediately launched into *The Architect Jean-Pierre Martin Leaving the Management of his Business*, and in fact all his big compositions that took the world of work as their setting.

'That guy's Roman Abramovich's buyer for Europe,' Marylin told him. 'I've already seen him in London and Berlin, but never in Paris; never in a contemporary art gallery, in any case.

'It's good if you've got a competitive situation right from the evening of the *vernissage*,' she went on. 'It's a small world and they all know each other, so they're going to start calculating, imagining the prices. Obviously, you need at least two bidders. And there . . .' She made a charming, cheeky smile, which made her look like a little girl, and which surprised Jed. 'Look, there's three of them . . . You see the guy over there, in front of the Bugatti painting?' She pointed at an old man with an exhausted and slightly puffy face and a small grey moustache, dressed in a badly cut black suit. 'That's Carlos Slim Helu. A Mexican of Lebanese origin. He doesn't look much, I know, but he made an enormous amount of money in telecommunications; according to estimates, he's the third or fourth richest man in the world. And he's a collector . . .'

What Marylin meant by *the Bugatti painting* was in fact *The Engineer Ferdinand Piëch Visiting the Production Workshops at Molsheim*, where the Bugatti Veyron 16.4 – the fastest, and most expensive, car in the world – was produced. Fitted with a 16-cylinder W engine with 1,001 horsepower, complete with four turbochargers, it could go from 0 to 110 km per hour in 2.5 seconds and had a top speed of 407 km per hour. No tyres available on the market could withstand such accelerations, and for this car Michelin had developed a special rubber.

Carlos Slim Helu stayed in front of the painting for at least five minutes, moving very little, stepping back and then forward a few centimetres. He had chosen, Jed noted, the ideal distance from which to view a canvas of this size; obviously, he was a real collector.

Then the Mexican billionaire turned around and made for the exit; he'd neither greeted nor spoke to anyone. As he passed, François Pinault gave him a cutting look; in the face of such a competitor, the Breton businessman wouldn't have counted for much. Without making eye contact, Slim Helu got into the back of a black Mercedes limousine parked in front of the gallery.

Roman Abramovich's envoy took his turn to go up to *the Bugatti painting*. It was, indeed, a curious work. A few weeks before starting it, at the flea market of Montreuil, Jed had bought for a tiny price – no more than the price of the paper – some old issues of *Peking-Information* and *China in Construction*, and the treatment had something ample and airy about it that resembled Chinese socialist realism. The wide V-shaped formation of the small group of engineers and mechanics following Ferdinand Piëch on his visit to the workshops recalled very precisely, as a particularly pugnacious and well-informed art historian noted later, that of the group of agronomists and middle-poor peasants accompanying President Mao Zedong in a watercolour reproduced in issue 122 of *China in Construction*, entitled: *Forwards to Irrigated Rice-growing in the Province of Hu Nan!* Besides, it was the only time, as other art historians have long pointed out, that Jed had tried watercolour. The engineer Ferdinand Piëch, two metres in front of the group, seemed to float rather than walk, as if levitating a few centimetres above the light epoxy floor. Three aluminium work-stations accommodated the Bugatti Veyron chassis at various stages in its manufacture; in the background, the walls, made entirely of glass, opened out onto a panorama of the Vosges. By a curious coincidence, as Houellebecq observed in his text for the catalogue, this village of Molsheim, and the Vosges landscapes surrounding it, were already at the centre of the Michelin map and satellite photographs with which Jed had chosen, ten years before, to open his first solo exhibition.

This simple remark, in which Houellebecq, a man of rational if narrow mind, certainly didn't see anything more than an interesting but anecdotal fact, would inspire Patrick Kéchichian to write a passionate article, more mystical than ever: having shown us a God co-participating, with man, in the creation of the world, he wrote, the artist, completing his move towards incarnation, now showed us God descended among men. Far from the harmony of celestial spheres, God had now come 'to plunge his hands in the dirty grease' so as to pay homage, with his full presence, to the sacerdotal dignity of human labour. Being himself both a true man and a true God, he had come to offer working mankind the sacrificial gift of his burning love. In the posture of the mechanic on the left leaving his workstation to follow the engineer Ferdinand Piëch, how could you not recognise, he stressed, that of Peter as he put down his nets at the invitation of Christ? 'Come, I will make you a fisher of men'. And in the absence of the Bugatti Veyron 16.4 at the final stage of manufacture, he spotted a reference to the new Jerusalem.

The article was rejected by *Le Monde*, whose art editor Pépita Bourguignon, threatened to resign if they published this 'Jesus-freak shit'; but it would appear in *Art Press* the following month.

'Anyway, at this stage, we don't give a toss about the reviews. It's no longer there that the real decisions are made,' Marylin summed up at the end of the soirée, while Jed worried about the continual absence of Pépita Bourguignon.

At around ten, after the last guests had left, and while the catering staff was folding up the tablecloths, Franz collapsed in a soft plastic chair near the gallery entrance. 'Fuck, I'm exhausted,' he said. 'Absolutely exhausted.' He'd given his all, tirelessly retracing, for anyone interested, Jed's artistic career or the history of his gallery, speaking non-stop all evening. Jed, for his part, had just nodded his head from time to time.

'Can you go get me a beer, please? From the fridge in the stockroom.'

Jed came back with a six-pack of Stella Artois, Franz gulped one down before speaking again.

'OK, now all we have to do is wait for the offers,' he said. 'We'll assess the situation in a week's time.'

20

When Jed came out onto the square of Notre-Dame de la Gare, a light and icy rain suddenly began to fall, like a warning, then stopped just as suddenly after a few seconds. He climbed the few steps leading to the entrance. The double doors of the church were wide open; it looked deserted inside. He hesitated, then turned around. The rue Jeanne-d'Arc descended as far as the boulevard Vincent-Auriol, which the Métro passed over; in the distance you could see the dome of the Panthéon. The sky was a dark and dull grey. Basically, he didn't have much to tell God; not at that moment.

The place Nationale was deserted, and trees stripped of their leaves revealed the rectangular and perfectly fitting structures of the campus at Tolbiac. Jed turned into the rue du Château-des-Rentiers. He was early, but Franz was already there, sitting in front of a glass of cheap red wine, and it was visibly not his first. Bloodshot-eyed and hirsute, he looked like he hadn't slept for weeks.

'OK,' he summed up as soon as Jed had sat down. 'I've had offers for almost all the paintings now. I've pushed up the bidding, maybe I can push it up a bit more; let's say that for the moment the average price has stabilised at around five hundred thousand euros.'

'Pardon?'

'You heard right: five hundred thousand euros.'

Franz was nervously twisting locks of his untidy white hair; it was the first time that Jed had noticed this tic. He emptied his glass and immediately ordered another one.

'If I sell now,' he continued, 'we'll make thirty million euros; approximately.'

Silence fell again in the cafe. Next to them, a very thin old man in a grey overcoat was dozing in front of his Picon beer. At his feet, an obese little white-and-ginger ratter was half asleep, like its master. The light rain began to fall again.

'So?' Franz asked a minute later. 'What do I do? Do I sell now?'

'As you wish.'

'What the fuck do you mean, as I wish? Do you realise how much money that represents?' He'd almost shouted, and the old man next to them woke up with a start; the dog got up with difficulty and growled in their direction.

'Fifteen million euros . . . Fifteen million euros each,' Franz went on more softly, but in a choked voice. 'And I get the impression that doesn't mean anything to you.'

'No, no, sorry,' Jed quickly replied. 'Let's just say I'm in shock,' he added a little later.

Franz looked at him with a mixture of suspicion and dismay. 'Well, OK,' he said finally, 'I'm not Larry Gagosian. I don't have the nerves for this kind of thing. I'm going to sell now.'

'You're surely right,' Jed said a good minute later. Silence had fallen again, troubled only by the snores of the ratter, who had lain down again, reassured, at the feet of its master.

'In your view,' Franz went on. 'In your view, which painting should've got the best offer?'

Jed reflected for a moment. 'Maybe *Bill Gates and Steve Jobs*,' he finally suggested.

'Exactly. It's gone up to one and a half million euros. From an American broker, who apparently works for Jobs himself.

'For a long time,' he continued his voice tense, on the brink of exasperation. 'For a long time, the art market has been dominated by the richest businessmen on the planet. And now, for the first time, as well as buying what is most avant-garde in the aesthetic domain, they have the opportunity to buy a painting that portrays themselves. I can't tell you the number of proposals I've received, from businessmen or industrialists, who would like you to paint their portrait. We've returned to the time of Ancien Régime court painting . . . Well, what I mean is that there's pressure, a big pressure, on you at this time. Do you still intend to give Houellebecq his painting?'

'Obviously. I promised.'

'As you wish. It's a beautiful gift. A gift worth seven hundred and fifty thousand euros . . . Look, he deserves it. His text's played an important role. By insisting on the systematic, theoretical side of your approach, he's enabled you to avoid being likened to the new figurative painters, all those losers . . . Obviously, I haven't left the paintings in my warehouse in Eure-et-Loir, I've rented the vaults of a bank. I'm going to sign a paper, so you can pass by and take the Houellebecq portrait whenever you want.'

'I had a visitor, as well,' he went on after a brief pause. 'A young Russian woman, I guess you know who she is.' He took out a business card and handed it to Jed. 'A very pretty young woman . . .'

Light was beginning to fade. Jed put the business card in the inside pocket of his jacket, then started pulling it on.

'Wait,' Franz interrupted. 'Before you leave, I'd just like to make sure that you completely understand the situation. I've received about fifty calls from men who are among the richest in the world. Sometimes they've had an assistant call, but they've mainly phoned themselves. They'd all like you to do their portraits. They're all offering you a million euros – minimum.'

Jed finished putting on his jacket and took out his wallet to pay.

'I'm inviting you,' said Franz with a mocking grimace. 'Don't reply, there's no point, I know exactly what you're going to say. You'll ask to have time to think; and in a few days you'll phone to tell me you're saying no. And then you're going to stop. I'm starting to know you, you've always been like that, even at the time of the Michelin maps: you work, you work away in your little corner for years; and then, once your work is exhibited, as soon as you get recognition, you drop it all.'

'There are small differences. I was at a dead end when I gave up *Damien Hirst and Jeff Koons Dividing Up the Art Market.*'

'Yes, I know; that's what made me organise the exhibition. Besides, I'm happy you didn't finish that painting. However, I liked the idea, the project had a historical relevance, it was quite an accurate reflection of the art world at a given time. There was, indeed, a sort of dividing up; on the one hand, fun, sex, kitsch, and innocence; on the other, trash, death, and cynicism. But, in your situation, that would inevitably have been interpreted as the work of a minor artist, jealous of the success of his richer counterparts; anyway, we're at a point where success in market terms justifies and validates anything, replacing all the theories. No one is capable of seeing further, absolutely no one. Now you could indulge in this painting, because you've become the best-paid French artist of the moment; but I know you won't paint it, you'll move on to something else. Maybe you'll simply stop doing the portraits; or stop figurative art in general; or stop painting completely, and perhaps return to photography, I don't know.'

Jed kept his silence. At the neighbouring table the old man roused himself from his slumber, got up, and went over to the door; his dog followed him with difficulty, its fat body bobbing on its short legs.

'In any case,' Franz said, 'I want you to know that I remain your gallerist. Whatever happens.'

Jed nodded. The cafe owner came out of the cellar, lit the ramp of neon lights above the counter, and nodded to Jed, who nodded back. They were regular customers, but no real familiarity had been established between them. The owner of the establishment had even forgotten that, ten years previously, he'd allowed Jed to take pictures of him and his cafe. Those pictures inspired Jed to make *Claude Vorilhon, Bar-Tabac Manager*, the second painting in the 'Series of Simple Professions' – for which an American stockbroker had just offered three hundred and fifty thousand euros. He had always considered them untypical customers, not of the same age or background as the rest of his regulars; in short, they weren't part of his *core market*.

Jed stood up. He wondered when he would see Franz again; at

the same time he became aware that all of a sudden he was a *rich man*. Just before he went to the door, Franz asked him: 'What are you doing for Christmas?'

'Nothing. I'm seeing my father, as usual.'

21

Not quite as usual, thought Jed as he walked back up towards the rue Jeanne-d'Arc. On the phone his father had sounded completely broken, and he'd initially proposed cancelling their annual dinner. 'I don't want to be a burden to anyone . . .' His rectal cancer had suddenly worsened, he had *losses of matter* now, he announced with masochistic delight. They were going to have to fit him with an artificial anus. After Jed insisted, he agreed to meet, on the condition that his son received him at home. 'I can no longer bear to see human beings . . .'

Arriving on the square of Notre-Dame de la Gare he hesitated, then went in. At first the church seemed empty, but on advancing towards the altar he saw a young black girl, eighteen at most, in front of a statue of the Virgin; she was speaking very softly. Concentrated in prayer, she paid no attention to him. Her arse, arched by kneeling, was hugged very precisely by her thin white trousers, Jed noted against his will. Did she have sins to be forgiven? Sick parents? Both, probably. Her faith seemed deep. It must have been very practical, that belief in God; when you could no longer do anything for others – and that was often the case in life, it was basically almost always the case, and particularly concerning his father's cancer – there remained the resource of *praying for them.*

He went out, ill at ease. Night was falling on the rue Jeanne d'Arc, the red lights of the cars edging slowly towards the boulevard Vincent-Auriol. In the distance, the dome of the Panthéon was bathed in an inexplicable greenish light, a bit like some spherical aliens were planning a massive attack on the Paris region. Some people were doubtless dying, at that very minute, here and there, in the city.

★   ★   ★

However, at the same time the following day, he found himself lighting candles and putting out *coquilles de saumon* on his trestle table while darkness spread over the place des Alpes. His father had promised to be there at six.

He rang down below at one minute past six. Jed buzzed him in and breathed slowly and deeply, several times, as the lift came up.

He lightly kissed his father's rough cheeks as he stood still in the centre of the room. 'Sit down, sit down,' he said. Obeying immediately, his father took a seat on the edge of a chair and looked timidly around him. He's never come here, Jed suddenly realised, he's never been to my flat. He then had to tell him to take off his coat as well. His father was trying to smile, a bit like a man trying to show how valiantly he's bearing an amputation. Jed wanted to open the champagne, but his hands were trembling and he almost dropped the bottle he'd just taken out of the refrigerator, and he was sweating. His father was still smiling, with a rather fixed smile. Here was a man who, with dynamism and sometimes harshness, has led a firm of about fifty people, who'd had to hire and fire, who'd negotiated contracts involving tens, sometimes hundreds of millions of francs. But the approach of death makes you humble, and he seemed, this evening, to want everything to go as smoothly as possible, he seemed above all to want to avoid trouble; that was apparently his only ambition now on this earth. Jed managed to open the champagne, and relaxed a little.

'I've heard about your success,' his father said, lifting his glass. 'We drink to your success.'

That was a way forward, Jed immediately thought, an opening for a possible conversation, and he began talking about his paintings, this work he had started ten years ago, his will to describe, through painting, the different parts that contributed to the funcioning of society. He spoke with ease, for almost an hour, regularly serving champagne and then wine, while they ate dishes bought from the caterer the day before, and what he was saying then, he realised to his astonishment the following day, he'd never said to anyone. His father listened attentively, asking a question from time to time, with the surprised and curious expression of a little child. In short, everything went marvellously well until the cheese course, when Jed's inspiration began to dry up and his father, as if under the effect of gravity, fell back into a sorrowful despondency. He was, however, cheered up by the dinner, and it was without any real sadness, rather shaking his head incredulously, that he said in a low voice, 'Fucking hell . . . an artificial anus.

'You know,' he added, now in a voice which betrayed a slight drunkenness, 'in a sense I'm happy that your mother's no longer here. She who was so refined, so elegant . . . she would've found physical decline unbearable.'

Jed went rigid. That's it, he thought. That's it, *we're there*; after all these years, he's going to speak. But his father had noticed his change in expression.

'I'm not going to reveal why your mother committed suicide!' he declaimed in a loud, almost angry voice. 'I'm not going to reveal it to you because I don't know!' He calmed down almost immediately, and shrank into his chair. Jed was sweating again. Maybe it was too hot. The heating was almost impossible to set, and he was always worried it would break down. He was going to move now that he had money, surely that's what people do when they have money, they try to improve their living situation, but move where? He had no particular desire for property. No, he was going to stay, maybe do some improvements, in any case replace the boiler. He stood up again and tried to manipulate the thermostat. His father was nodding gently, muttering softly. Jed returned to his side. All he needed to do was put his hand out, touch his shoulder or something, but how could he do that? He'd never done that. 'An artificial anus . . .' his father murmured again dreamily.

'I know she wasn't satisfied with our life,' he continued, 'but is that sufficient reason for dying? I wasn't satisfied with my life either. I confess I was hoping for something more from my career as an architect than building stupid fucking seaside resorts for dumb tourists, under the control of fundamentally dishonest and almost infinitely vulgar property developers. But, OK, it was work, a routine . . . Probably she just didn't like life. What shocked me the most is what the neighbour, whom I'd only just met, told me. She was coming back from her shopping, she had probably just procured the poison – we've never known how, by the way. What this woman told me was that she seemed happy, incredibly enthusiastic and happy. She had exactly, she said, the expression of someone who is preparing to go on holiday. It was cyanide, and she must have died almost instantly; I'm absolutely certain she didn't suffer.'

Then he stopped speaking, and the silence continued for a long time. Jed ended up slightly losing consciousness. He had the vision of immense meadows whose grass was waving in the wind, and the light was that of an eternal spring. When he woke suddenly, his father was still nodding his head and muttering, pursuing a painful internal debate. Jed hesitated; he'd planned a dessert – there were chocolate profiteroles in the fridge. Did he have to take them out? Or did he have to learn more about his mother's suicide? He had basically almost no memory of her. It was more important for his father, probably. He decided to let the profiteroles wait a little.

'I've known no other woman,' his father said in a lifeless voice. 'No other, absolutely. I didn't even feel the desire.' Then he started again to mutter and nod his head gently. Jed decided, finally, to take out the profiteroles. His father stared at them in astonishment, like a completely new object, for which nothing, in his previous life, had prepared him. He took one, turned it between his fingers, looking at it with as much interest as he would a dog turd; but he finally put it in his mouth.

There then followed two to three minutes of mute frenzy, as they took the profiteroles one by one, from the decorated box provided by the *pâtissier*, and promptly ate them. Then things calmed down, and Jed proposed coffee. His father accepted immediately.

'I feel like smoking a cigarette,' he said. 'Do you have any?'

'I don't smoke,' Jed said, then leapt up. 'But I can go out for them. I know a tobacconist on the place d'Italie that's open late in the evening. And then . . .' He consulted his watch in disbelief. 'It's only eight.'

'Even on Christmas Eve, you think they're open?'

'I can try.'

He put on his coat. Outside, he was struck by a violent blast of wind; snowflakes were swirling around in the freezing air. It must have been several degrees below zero. On the place d'Italie, the *bar-tabac* was closing. The owner returned to his counter, grumbling.

'What will it be?'

'Cigarettes.'

'What brand?'

'I don't know. Some good cigarettes.'

The man looked at him furiously. 'Dunhill! Some Dunhill and some Gitanes! And a lighter!'

His father hadn't moved, still shrunk in his chair, and didn't even react on hearing the door open. Nevertheless, he took a Gitane from the pack, and looked at it with curiosity before lighting up. 'It's twenty years since I last smoked,' he remarked. 'But what's the importance of all that now?' He drew a puff, then another. 'It's strong,' he said. 'It's good. When I was young, everybody smoked. In meetings, discussions in the cafes, we smoked all the time. It's funny how things change . . .'

He sipped the cognac his son had placed in front of him, then again fell silent. In the silence, Jed could make out the increasingly violent whistling of the wind. He looked through the window: the snowflakes were swirling, very dense, it was turning into a real storm.

'I always wanted to be an architect, I think,' his father continued. 'When I was small I was interested in animals, like all children probably; when asked I would say I wanted to become a vet later in life, but deep down I think I was already attracted by architecture. At the age of ten, I remember I tried to build a nest for the swallows who spent the summer in the shed. In an encyclopedia I'd found some indications on how swallows built their nests, with earth and saliva. I spent weeks on it . . .' His voice quavered slightly and he stopped again. Jed looked at him worriedly, but then he took a big sip of cognac before continuing.

'But they never wanted to use my nest. Never. They even stopped nesting in the shed . . .' The old man suddenly began to cry. Tears were pouring down his face and it was awful.

'Dad,' Jed said, completely distraught. 'Dad.' It seemed he could no longer stop crying.

'Swallows never use nests built by human hand,' said Jed very quickly, 'it's impossible. If a man so much as touches their nest, they leave it to build a new one.'

'How do you know that?'

'I read it a few years ago in a book on animal behaviour – I'd done some research for a painting.'

This was untrue, he'd read nothing of the sort, but his father seemed instantly relieved and calmed down immediately. And to think, Jed thought, that he had been carrying this weight on his heart for more than sixty years . . . That it had probably plagued him throughout his career as an architect . . .

'After the baccalaureate, I matriculated at the Beaux-Arts de Paris. That worried my mother a little, she would've preferred that I'd gone to an engineering school; but I received a lot of support from my grandfather. I think he had an artistic ambition, as a photographer, but he never had the chance to photograph anything other than marriages and communions.'

Jed had never seen his father busy with anything other than technical problems, and at the end more and more with financial problems; the idea that his father had also gone to Beaux-Arts, that architecture belonged to the artistic disciplines, was surprising, and it made Jed uncomfortable.

'Yes, I too wanted to be an *artist*,' his father said acrimoniously, almost nastily. 'But I didn't succeed. The dominant current when I was young was functionalism, and in truth it had already been dominating everything for several decades. Nothing had happened in architecture since Le Corbusier and Mies van der Rohe. All the new towns, all the housing estates that were built in the suburbs in the 1950s and 60s were marked by their influence. With a few others, at the Beaux-Arts, we had the ambition to do something different. We didn't really reject the primacy of function, nor the notion of a "machine for living"; but what we were challenging was what was meant by the fact of living somewhere. Like the Marxists, like the liberals, Le Corbusier was a productivist. What he imagined for man were square, utilitarian blocks of offices, with no decoration whatsoever, and residential buildings that were almost identical, with a few supplementary functions – crèche, gymnasium, swimming pool. Between the two were fast lanes. In his cell for living, man was to benefit from pure air and light, this was very important in his view. And between the structures of work and inhabitation, free space was reserved for wild nature: forests, rivers. I imagine that, in his mind, human families would be able to walk there on Sundays, but he nonetheless wanted to conserve this space, he was a sort of *proto-ecologist*. For him mankind had to confine itself to circumscribed modules of inhabitation, which were in the midst of nature, but which in no case should modify it. It's terrifyingly primitive when you think about it, a terrifying regression from any true rural landscape, which is a subtle, complex and evolving mixture of meadows, fields, forests and villages. It's the vision of a brutal, totalitarian mind. Le Corbusier seemed to us both totalitarian and brutal, motivated by an intense taste for ugliness; but it's his vision that prevailed throughout the twentieth century. As for us, on the other hand, we were influenced by Charles Fourier . . .' He smiled on seeing the surprise on his son's face. 'We've mainly remembered the sexual theories of Fourier, and it's true that they're quite burlesque. It's difficult to read Fourier with a straight face, with his stories of whirlwinds, fakiresses and fairies of the Rhine Army. It's hard to believe he had any disciples, people who took him seriously, who really thought of constructing a new model of society on the basis of his books. It's incomprehensible if you try to see him as a *thinker*, because his thought is completely incomprehensible, but fundamentally Fourier isn't a thinker, he's a *guru*, the first of his kind, and, as with all gurus, his success came not from intellectual adherence to a theory but, on the contrary, from general incomprehension, linked with an inexhaustible optimism, especially on the sexual level: people need sexual optimism to an incredible degree. Yet Fourier's real subject, the one which interests him above all else, isn't sex, but the organisation of production. The big question he asks is: Why does man work? What makes him occupy a determined place in the social organisation and agree to stay there and carry out his task? To this question, the liberals replied that it was the lure of profit, pure and simple; we thought this was an inadequate reply. As for the Marxists, they didn't reply at all, they weren't even interested, and, besides, that's what made communism fail: as soon as you got rid of the financial incentive, people stopped working, they sabotaged their task, absenteeism grew in enormous proportions. Communism never was able to ensure the production and distribution of the most elementary goods. Fourier had lived under the Ancien Régime, and he was conscious that, well before the appearance of capitalism, scientific research and technical progress had taken place, and that people worked hard, sometimes very hard, without being pushed by the lure of profit but by something, in the eyes of a modern man, much vaguer; the love of God, in the case of monks, or more simply the honour of the function.'

Jed's father stopped speaking and noticed that his son was now listening to him with rapt attention. 'Yes,' he commented, 'there's doubtless a rapport with what you've tried to do in your paintings. There's a lot of rubbish in Fourier's work, and overall it's almost unreadable; there is, however, still something to be drawn from it. Well, at least that's what we thought at the time . . .'

He fell silent, and seemed to plunge back into his memories. The gusts of wind had calmed down, making way for a starry, silent sky; a thick layer of snow covered the rooftops.

*   *   *

'I was young,' he finally said with a sort of serene incredulity. 'Maybe you can't completely understand this, because you were born into a family that was already rich. But I was young, I was preparing to become an architect, and I was in Paris – everything seemed possible. And I wasn't the only one. Paris was gay at the time, and you had the impression you could remake the world. It's there that I met your mother – she was studying at the Conservatoire, she played violin. We were like a band of artists, really. Well, that was limited to writing four or five articles in an architecture review, which several of us signed. They were political texts, mainly. We defended the idea that a complex, ramified society, with multiple levels of organisation, like that proposed by Fourier, went hand in hand with a complex, ramified, multiple architecture that left space for individual creativity. We violently attacked Mies van der Rohe – who made empty, multi-purpose structures, the same ones that were going to be a model for the open spaces in businesses – and above all Le Corbusier, who tirelessly built concentration-camp-like spaces, divided into identical cells that were suited, we wrote, only for model prisons. These articles had a certain impact – I think Deleuze spoke about them – but we all had to work, and we entered the big architectural practices, and life immediately became much less fun. Quite quickly my financial situation improved, as there was a lot of work at the time with France rebuilding herself at high speed. I bought the house in Raincy; I thought it was a good idea, and back then it was a pleasant town. I also got it for a very good price – it was a client who put me on to it, a property developer. The owner was an old guy, visibly an intellectual, still in a grey three-piece suit, with a flower in the buttonhole – every day I saw him it was a different flower. He looked like he'd stepped out of the belle époque, or the 1930s at the latest. I couldn't fit him with his environment. You could've imagined coming across him, I don't know, on the Quai Voltaire . . . well, certainly not in Raincy. He was a former university professor, specialising in esoterism and the history of religions – I remember he was very clued up on the Kabbala and gnosis, but he was interested in this in a very particular way. For example, he had nothing but contempt for Rene Guénon. "That imbecile Guénon", that's how he spoke about him. I think he'd written several virulent critiques of his books. He'd never been married, he'd *lived for his work*, as we say. I read a long article he'd written in a social-science journal, in which he developed some quite curious considerations on Fate, on the possibility of developing a new religion based on the principle of synchronicity. His library alone would have been worth the price of the house, I think – there were more than five thousand volumes, in French, English and German. It's there that I discovered the works of William Morris.'

He stopped on seeing a change in Jed's expression.

'You know William Morris?'

'No, Dad. But I also lived in that house, and I remember the library . . .' He hesitated and sighed. 'I don't understand why you've waited so many years to tell me about all this.'

'It's because I'm going to die soon, I think,' his father said simply. 'Well, not straight away, not the day after tomorrow, but it's obvious I don't have very long left.' He looked around him and smiled almost cheerily. 'Can I have some more cognac?' Jed served him immediately. He lit a Gitane, inhaling the smoke with delight.

'And then your mother became pregnant with you. The end of her pregnancy went badly, she had to have a Caesarean. The doctor informed her that she would no longer be able to have children; what's more, she had some quite terrible scars. That was hard for her; she was a beautiful woman, you know . . . We weren't unhappy together, and never had any serious arguments, but it's true I didn't speak to her enough. There's the violin as well. I think she should never have stopped playing. I remember one evening at the Porte de Bagnolet, I was coming back from work in my Mercedes, it was already nine o'clock but there were still traffic jams. I don't know what triggered it, maybe the Mercuriale Towers because I was working on a very similar project, which I found ugly and uninteresting, but I saw myself in my car in the middle of these fast-entry slip roads, in front of those appalling buildings, and all of a sudden I told myself I couldn't go on. I was nearly forty, my professional life was a success, but I couldn't go on. In a few minutes I decided to start my own business, to try and practise architecture as I understood it. I knew it would be difficult, but I didn't want to die without at least trying. I called on the ex-students I knew at the Beaux-Arts, but all of them had settled down – they'd succeeded too, and no longer wanted to take risks. So, I launched into it on my own. I made contact again with Bernard Lamarche-Vadel, we'd met a few years before and got on rather well, and he introduced me to people interested in free figuration: Combas, Di Rosa . . . I don't know if I've already spoken to you about William Morris?'

'Yes, you just mentioned him five minutes ago.'

'Ah?' He stopped, and a lost expression crossed his face. 'I'm going to try a Dunhill . . .' He took a few puffs. 'It's good as well; different from the Gitanes, but it's good. I don't understand why everyone has given up smoking all of a sudden.'

He savoured the rest of his cigarette without speaking. Jed was waiting. Very far away outside, a solitary klaxon was trying to play 'Born is Jesus, the Infant King' but got the notes wrong and started again; then silence returned – there was no concert of klaxons. On the roofs across Paris, the snow was now thick, stabilised; there was something definitive in this stillness, Jed thought.

'William Morris was close to the Pre-Raphaelites,' his father went on, 'to Gabriel Dante Rossetti at the beginning, and to Burne-Jones right until the end. The fundamental idea of the Pre-Raphaelites was that art had begun to degenerate just after the Middle Ages, that from the start of the Renaissance it had cut itself off from any spirituality, any authenticity, to become a purely industrial and commercial activity, and that the so-called *great masters* of the Renaissance – be they Botticelli, Rembrandt or Leonardo da Vinci – behaved in fact exclusively as the heads of commercial enterprises. Exactly like Jeff Koons or Damien Hirst today, with an iron hand the so-called *great masters* of the

Renaissance ruled workshops of fifty, even a hundred assistants, who chain-produced paintings, sculptures, and frescos. They just gave general guidelines, signed the finished work, and above all devoted themselves to public relations with the patrons of the moment – princes or popes. For the Pre-Raphaelites, as for William Morris, the distinction between art and the worker, between design and execution, had to be abolished. Any man, at his own level, could be a producer of beauty – be it in the making of a painting, a piece of clothing or furniture – and he also had the right, in his daily life, to be surrounded by beautiful objects. He allied this conviction with a socialist activism that led him to become more and more involved in movements for the emancipation of the proletariat; he wanted simply to put an end to the system of industrial production.

'What's curious is that Gropius, when he founded Bauhaus, was on exactly the same wavelength – maybe less political, with more spiritual preoccupations, although he too was a socialist. In the *Bauhaus Proclamation* of 1919, he declares that he wants to go beyond the opposition between art and industry, and proclaims the right to beauty for all: exactly the aim of William Morris. But gradually, the more Bauhaus moved closer to industry, the more it become functionalist and productivist; Kandinsky and Klee were marginalised within the teaching establishment, and when the institute was closed by Göring it had anyway been passed over entirely to the service of capitalist production.

'We ourselves weren't really political; but the thought of William Morris helped us to free ourselves from the taboo that Le Corbusier had placed on any form of ornamentation. I remember that Combas had a few reservations at the start – the Pre-Raphaelite painters weren't really his universe – but he came to agree that the wallpaper motifs designed by William Morris were very beautiful, and when he really understood what it was all about he became completely enthusiastic. Nothing could've given him more pleasure than to design motifs for furniture covers, wallpaper or external friezes, used in a whole group of buildings. They were, however, quite isolated at the time, the people in free figuration; the minimalist current remained dominant, and the *graff* didn't yet exist – or at least it wasn't spoken about. So we put together some dossiers for all the more or less interesting projects that were up for competition, and we waited . . .'

His father stopped again, as if suspended in his memories, then seemed to shrink, diminish, and Jed then became aware of the elan, the enthusiasm with which he'd spoken for the last several minutes. He'd never heard him speak like this, even as a child – and never again, he immediately thought, would he ever hear him speak like this. His father had just relived, for the last time, the hopes and failures which formed the story of his life. It doesn't amount to much, generally speaking, a human life; it can be summed up in a small number of events, and this time Jed had well and truly understood the bitterness and the wasted years, the cancer and the stress, as well as the suicide of his mother.

'The functionalists dominated all the juries,' his father concluded in a soft voice. 'I banged my head against a window; we all banged our heads against a window. Combas and Di Rosa didn't drop us immediately, in fact they phoned me for years to find out if things were freeing up . . . Then, seeing that nothing was coming, they concentrated on their work as painters. As for me, I ended up having to accept normal commissions. The first was Port-Ambarès – and then it built up, especially the construction of seaside resorts. I packed away my projects, they're still in a cupboard in my office, in Raincy, you can go and have a look . . .' He kept himself from adding: 'when I'm dead', but Jed understood completely.

'It's late,' he said, getting up from his chair. Jed glanced at his watch: four in the morning. His father went to the toilet, then came back to put on his coat. For the two to three minutes this took, Jed had the fleeting, contradictory impression that they'd either just started a new stage in their relationship, or would never see each other again. As his father finally stood in front of him with an expectant look, he said: 'I'm going to call you a taxi.'

22

When he woke up on the morning of 25 December, Paris was covered with snow; on the boulevard Vincent-Auriol, he passed a beggar with a thick hairy beard and skin almost brown with filth. He put two euros in his bowl, then, turning back, added a ten-euro note. The beggar groaned in surprise. Jed was now a rich man, and the metal arches of the overground Métro stood above a softened but lethal landscape. During the day, the snow was going to melt and it would all turn into mud and dirty water; then life would start again, at quite a slow pace. Between these two high points of high relational and commercial intensity that are Christmas and New Year's Eve, an interminable week passes, which is basically downtime, until activity restarts, violently and explosively early in the evening on the 31st.

Back home, he looked at Olga's business card: *Director of Programmes, Michelin TV, avenue Pierre Ier de Serbie*. She too had made it on the professional level, without particularly striving for it; but she hadn't married, and that thought made him uncomfortable. Without thinking much about it, all those years, he'd always imagined that she'd found love, or at least a *family life*, somewhere in Russia.

He called late the following morning, expecting everyone to be on holiday, though that wasn't the case: after five minutes, a stressed secretary told him that Olga was in a meeting, but that she would tell her he had phoned.

Over the next few minutes, waiting for her call, his nervousness increased. The painting of Houellebecq was facing him, standing on its easel; he'd withdrawn it from the bank that very morning. The look in the author's eyes, much too intense, added to his unease. He got up and turned the canvas around. Seven hundred and fifty thousand euros . . . he thought: that made no sense. Picasso made no sense either; even less, probably, if you could establish a grading in senselessness.

As he went to the kitchen, the phone rang. He ran to pick it up. Olga's voice hadn't changed. People's voice's never change, no more than the expressions in their eyes. Amid the generalised physical collapse that is old age, the voice and the eyes bear painfully indisputable witness to the persistence of character, aspirations, and desires, everything that constitutes a human personality.

'Did you pass by the gallery?' he asked, in an attempt to start the conversation on *neutral ground*. He was astonished that in his own view his pictorial work had become *neutral ground*.

'Yes, and I liked it a lot. It's . . . original. It looks like nothing I've seen before. But I always knew you had talent.'

A heavy silence followed.

'Little Frenchman,' said Olga, her ironic tone failing to disguise her true emotion, and again Jed felt uncomfortable, on the verge of tears. '*Successful* little Frenchman . . .'

'We could meet,' Jed replied quickly. Someone had to say it first; there, it was him.

'I've an enormous amount of work this week.'

'Oh, really? How come?'

'We start our broadcasts on 2 January. There are still lots of things to sort out.' She thought for a few moments. 'There's a party the channel is throwing on the 31st. I can invite you.' She stopped again for a few seconds. 'It would give me great pleasure if you came.'

That evening, he received an email containing all the details. The party was taking place in the private home of Jean-Pierre Pernaut, who he lived in Neuilly, on the boulevard des Sablons. His theme was, unsurprisingly, 'the Provinces of France'.

Jed thought he knew everything about Jean-Pierre Pernaut, but the Wikipedia entry contained a few surprises. Thus he learned the popular presenter was also the author of many books. Alongside

A Taste of France, Festive France and *At the Heart of Our Regions*, he found *The Magnificent Crafts of the Artisans*, in two volumes, all published by Éditions Michel Lafon.

He was also surprised by the laudatory, almost ecstatic tone of the entry. He remembered that Jean-Pierre Pernaut had sometimes been the target of criticism, but all that seemed forgotten now. Jean-Pierre Pernaut's stroke of genius, the author stressed from the outset, had been to understand that after the 'flash your cash' 1980s, the public hungered for ecology, authenticity and true values. Even if Martin Bouygues could be credited with putting his trust in him, the one o'clock news on TF1 completely bore the imprint of his visionary personality. Taking as his point of departure the current news – violent, rapid, frenetic, and senseless – Jean-Pierre Pernaut carried out a messianic task that consisted of guiding the terrorised and stressed viewer towards the idyllic regions of a protected countryside, where man lived in harmony with nature, with the rhythm of the seasons. More than a mere news programme, the one o'clock news on TF1 took on the dimension of a march to the star, ending in a psalm. The author of this entry – though he admitted that he himself was a Catholic – did not, however, hide the fact that if the *Weltanschauung* of Jean-Pierre Pernaut perfectly suited a France both rural and 'the eldest daughter of the Church', it would have gone just as well with a pantheistic, or even epicurean wisdom.

The following day, at the France Leisure bookshop in the Italie 2 mall, Jed bought the first volume of *The Magnificent Crafts of the Artisans*. The subdivision of the book was simple, based on the materials used: earth, stone, metal, wood . . . Reading it (which was quite easy, as it was made up almost uniquely of photos) did not suggest a particular attachment to the past. By systematically dating the appearance of the different crafts he described, and the major developments made in their practice, Jean-Pierre Pernaut seemed to make himself less an apologist for immobility than one for *gradual progress*. There perhaps were, Jed thought, some points of convergence between Jean-Pierre Pernaut's thinking and that of William Morris – socialist commitment apart, of course. If most viewers placed him *rather on the right*, Jean-Pierre Pernaut had always demonstrated, in the daily content of his programme, extreme deontological care. He had even avoided appearing to support Hunting, Fishing, Nature, and Traditions, a movement founded in 1989 – exactly one year after he'd taken control of the one o'clock news on TF1. There had certainly been a shift at the very end of the 1980s, Jed thought, a major historical shift, that at the time went unnoticed, as was almost always the case. He also remembered 'Calm Strength', the slogan invented by Jacques Séguéla that had made possible, against all expectations, the re-election of François Mitterrand in 1988. He could still picture the posters depicting the old Pétainist mummy against a background of church towers and villages. He was thirteen years old, and it was the first time in his life that he paid any attention to a political slogan or a presidential election.

If he constituted the most significant and durable element of this serious ideological shift, Jean-Pierre Pernaut had always refused to reinvest his immense fame in any attempt at a political commitment or career; right to the end, he had wanted to remain in the camp of the *entertainers*. Unlike Noël Mamère, he hadn't even grown a moustache. And while he probably shared the values of Jean Saint-Josse, the first president of Hunting, Fishing, Nature, and Traditions, he'd always refused to support him publicly. Nor had he done so for Frédéric Nihous, his successor.

Born in 1967 in Valenciennes, Frédéric Nihous had received his first rifle at the age of fourteen, a present from his father, after gaining the high-school diploma. With a degree in international and European Community law, as well as a degree in national defence and European security, he had taught administrative law at the University of Cambrai; he was also president of the Association of Pigeon and Migrant Bird Hunters in the Nord department. In 1988, he had finished first in a fishing tournament in the Hérault by catching a nakin carp weighing 7,256 kilograms. Twenty years later, he would provoke the collapse of the movement he now led by making the mistake of concluding an alliance with

Catholic right-winger Philippe de Villiers – for which the hunters of the South-West, traditionally anticlerical and rather radical or socialist, would never forgive him.

On 30 December, in the middle of the afternoon, Jed telephoned Houellebecq. The writer was on top form. He'd just spent an hour chopping wood, he announced. Chopping wood? Yes, his house in the Loiret now had a fireplace. He also had a dog – a two-year-old mongrel that he'd taken in on Christmas Day from the pet refuge in Montargis.

'Are you doing anything on New Year's Eve?' Jed enquired.

'No, nothing in particular; I'm rereading Tocqueville at the moment. You know, in the countryside we go to bed early, especially in winter.'

For an instant Jed had the idea of inviting him, but realised just in time that he could hardly invite someone to a party he wasn't giving himself; anyway, the author would certainly have refused.

'I'm going to bring your portrait, as promised. In the first days of January.'

'My portrait, yes . . . Please do, please do.' He didn't seem to care at all. They chatted pleasantly for a few more minutes. There was in the voice of the author of *Atomised* something that Jed had never noticed before, that he'd never expected to find, and that he took some time to identify, because basically he hadn't found it in anyone, for many years: he seemed happy.

Some Vendée peasants armed with pitchforks mounted the guard at each side of the porch leading to Jean-Pierre Pernaut's townhouse. Jed handed one of them the email invitation he'd printed out and proceeded into the large cobbled courtyard, which was entirely lit by torches. A dozen guests were walking towards the big, open doors that led into the reception rooms. With his velvet trousers and his C&A Sympatex blouson, he felt awfully *underdressed*: the women were in long dresses, and most of the men in dinner jackets. Two metres in front of him he recognised Julien Lepers, accompanied by a magnificent black girl who was easily a foot taller; she was wearing a sparkling long white dress, with gold facing and open at the back right down to her arse; the torchlight reflecting on her bare skin. The presenter himself – wearing an ordinary dinner jacket, the one he used for '*grandes écoles* special editions', his working dinner jacket in a way – seemed buried in some difficult discussion with a small, hot-headed man who looked nasty and gave the impression of having corporate responsibilities. Jed moved past them, and, entering the first reception room, was greeted by the insistent complaint of a dozen Breton bagpipers, who had just started a tortured and inter- minable Celtic tune that was almost painful to listen to. Keeping a good distance, he entered the second room and accepted an Emmental-flavoured canapé and a glass of '*vendange tardive*' Gewürztraminer, offered by two Alsatian waitresses wearing head- dresses and white-and-red aprons, who circulated among the guests with their trays; they were so alike that they could've been twins.

The reception area was made up of four conjoining rooms with ceilings at least eight-metres-high. Jed had never seen such a huge apartment; he'd no idea that such an apartment could exist. However, it probably wasn't much, he thought in a flash of lucidity, compared to the residences of those who bought his paintings.

There must have been two or three hundred guests, and the din of the conversations gradually drowned the wailing of the pipes. Feeling he was going to pass out, he leaned against a stand of Auvergnat products, and accepted a Jésus-Laguiole brochette and a glass of Saint-Pourçain. The powerful, earthy smell of the cheeses restored his balance a little; he emptied his glass of Saint-Pourçain, asked for another and resumed his advance through the crowd. He was beginning to feel a bit too hot, and realised he should have left his coat at the cloakroom. His coat was truly at odds with the *dress code*, he scolded himself again. All the men were in evening dress, absolutely all of them, he repeated desperately to himself, and at just that instant he found himself in front of Pierre Bellemare, dressed in Tergal petrol-blue trousers and a white shirt with a jabot covered in grease stains, his trousers were held up by wide braces in the colours of the American flag. Jed warmly held his hand out to the French king of teleshopping, who, taken aback, shook it and started off again, slightly reassured.

It took him more than twenty minutes to find Olga. Standing in a doorway, half hidden by a curtain, she was deep in a clearly professional conversation with Jean-Pierre Pernaut. He was the main one speaking, declaiming sentences punctuated by determined movements of his right hand; she nodded from time to time, absorbed and attentive, and formulated very few objections or remarks. Jed stood there frozen, just a few metres from her. Two bands of cream-coloured cloth – tied behind her neck and encrusted with small crystals – covered her breasts and joined at her navel, pinned together by a silver brooch representing the sun, before attaching to a short figure-hugging skirt, also studded with crystals, that revealed her white garters; her tights, also white, were extremely fine. Ageing, and especially apparent ageing, is in no respect a continuous process. Life could rather be characterised as a succession of levels, separated by sudden falls. When we meet someone we have lost sight of for some years, we sometimes have the impression that he has *aged*; sometimes, on the other hand, that he hasn't changed at all. This is a complete fallacy, since decay is still secretly making its way inside the organism before bursting out into the broad daylight. For ten years, Olga had kept herself at a radiant level of beauty – without this being enough to make her happy. Nor had he, Jed believed, changed all that much over the last ten years; he had *produced a body of work*, as they say, without ever encountering, or even contemplating happiness.

Jean-Pierre Pernaut stopped talking and drank some Beaumes-de-Venise; Olga looked a few degrees away and suddenly saw Jed, standing there in the crowd. A few seconds can be enough to decide a life, or at least to reveal its main direction. She put her hand lightly on the presenter's forearm, giving him a word of apology, and in a few bounds she was in front of Jed and kissing him on the mouth. Then she stepped back, taking him by the hands. For a few seconds they remained silent.

Avuncular in his Arthur van Aschendock tails, Jean-Pierre Pernaut saw them turn towards him. His unguarded expression in that moment suggested that he understood life and even felt at ease with it. Olga made the introductions.

'I know you!' the presenter exclaimed, his smile widening even more. 'Come with me!'

Quickly crossing the last room, accidenetally brushing the arm of Patrick Le Lay (who had tried, unsuccessfully, to buy shares in the channel), he led them down a wide corridor with high, and vaulted walls made of thick limestone. More than a townhouse, Jean-Pierre Pernaut's residence reminded you of a Romanesque abbey, with its corridors and crypts. They stopped in front of a thick door padded with brown leather. 'My office,' said the presenter.

He stopped at the doorway, letting them enter the room. A line of acajou bookcases mainly contained tourist guides, of all kinds – the *Guide du Routard* next to the *Guide Bleu*, the *Petit Futé* the *Lonely Planet*. The books by Jean-Pierre Pernaut himself, from *The Magnificent Crafts of the Artisans* to *A Taste of France*, were exhibited on display shelves. A windowsill contained the five Sept d'Or he had won in the course of his career, as well as sports trophies of uncertain origin. Deep leather armchairs spread themselves around a mahogany executive desk. Behind the desk, which was discreetly lit by halogen lamps, Jed immediately recognised one of the photos from his Michelin period. Curiously, the presenter had not chosen a spectacular, immediately picturesque image, like those he had made of the Var corniche or of the gorges of Verdon. The photo, centred on Gournay-en-Bray, was treated with solid colours, without any lighting or perspective. Jed remembered that he had taken it directly from above. The white, green and brown spots were distributed equally, traversed by the symmetrical network of the departmental roads. No agglomeration stood out clearly, each seeming to have the same importance, which gave the overall impression of calm, balance and almost abstraction. This landscape, he realised, was probably the one he had flown over at low altitude, immediately after departing from Beauvais, when he went to visit Houellebecq in Ireland. In the presence of the concrete reality, of that discreet juxtaposition of meadows, fields and villages, he had felt the same thing: balance, a peaceful harmony.

'I know that you've now turned to painting,' Jean-Pierre Pernaut went on, 'and that you've made a painting of me. To tell you the truth, I tried to buy it; but François Pinault bid higher, and I couldn't follow.'

'François Pinault?' Jed was surprised. *The Journalist Jean-Pierre Pernaut Chairing an Editorial Meeting* was a quiet painting, classical in technique, which didn't correspond at all to the Breton businessman's usual, much *wilder* choices. No doubt he'd decided to diversify.

'Perhaps I should have . . .' He paused. 'I'm sorry . . . Perhaps I should have introduced a sort of preference clause for the subjects portrayed.'

'It's the market,' Pernaut said with a wide, beaming, rancourless smile, going so far as to pat him on the shoulder.

The presenter led them back down the vaulted corridor, the basques of his tails slowly floating behind him. Jed glanced at his watch: it was almost midnight. They again passed through the double doors leading to the reception rooms: the din was now at its peak; new guests had arrived, swelling the gathering to four or five hundred people. In the middle of a small group, a very inebriated Patrick Le Lay was perorating noisily; he had swiped a bottle of Châteauneuf-du-Pape and was guzzling long swigs of it. The presenter Claire Chazal, visibly tense, put her hand on his arm, trying to interrupt him; but the president of the channel had manifestly crossed certain red lines. 'TF1 are the biggest!' he was shouting. 'I don't give Jean-Pierre's channel six months! M6 are the same, they thought they could screw us with *Loft Story*, but we doubled the price with Koh Lanta and we fucked them up the arses! Up the arse!' he repeated, and threw the bottle over his shoulder. It grazed the skull of Julien Lepers and smashed at the feet of three middle-aged men, in grey three-piece suits, who stared at him sternly.

Without hesitation, Jean-Pierre Pernaut walked over to his former president, and stood straight in front of him. 'You've drunk too much, Patrick,' he said calmly; his muscles were tense under the fabric of the tails, his face hardened as if he was preparing for a fight. 'OK, OK . . .' said Le Lay, obsequiously indicating that he'd calmed down. 'OK OK . . .' At that moment, a resonant tenor voice, of incredible power, rose up from the second room. Other baritone and then bass voices took up the same theme, without words, in a round. Many guests turned in this direction, recognising a famous Corsican polyphony group. Twelve men of all ages, wearing black trousers, smocks and berets, gave a vocal performance that lasted a little more than two minutes: it was at the limit of what one could call music, more a war cry, of surprising savagery. Then they suddenly stopped. Spreading his arms slightly, Jean-Pierre Pernaut went to meet the crowd, waited for silence to fall, then said in a loud voice: 'Happy New Year to you all!' A volley of champagne corks popped. The presenter then went over to the three men in grey suits and shook hands with each of them. 'They belong to the Michelin board of directors . . .' Olga whispered to Jed before approaching the group. 'Financially, TF1, next to Michelin, counts for nothing. And it seems that Bouygues is sick of mopping up their losses,' she had the time to add before Jean-Pierre Pernaut introduced her to the three men. 'I was slightly expecting Patrick to make a scene,' he was saying to the directors, 'he took my departure very badly.'

'At least that proves our project doesn't leave him cold,' the oldest one said. At that very moment, Jed saw a man of about forty approach, wearing tracksuit bottoms and a hooded sweater, with a rapper's cap stuck backwards on his head, whom he recognised incredulously as Patrick Forestier, the communications director of Michelin France. 'Yo!' he shouted to the three directors before slapping their hands. 'Yo,' they each replied in turn, and it was at that moment that things started spiralling out of control. The conversation din intensified all of a sudden, while the Basque and Savoyard orchestras began to play at the same time. Jed was sweating; for a few minutes he tried to follow Olga, who was going from one guest to another to wish each a Happy New Year, all smiling and warm. From the friendly but serious expressions worn by the people she approached he understood that she was making a tour of her staff.

Feeling the nausea rising, he ran out into the courtyard and vomited on a dwarf palm tree. The night was curiously mild. A few guests were already departing, including the three directors. (Where did they come from? Had they checked into the same hotel?) They were advancing smoothly, in triangular formation, and silently passed the Vendée peasants, conscious of representing power and the real world. They would have made a good subject for a painting, thought Jed, discreetly leaving the reception while behind them the stars of French television laughed and yelled. A dirty song competition was being orchestrated by Julien Lepers. Enigmatic in his midnight-blue costume, Jean-Pierre Pernaut surveyed everything impassively, while Patrick Le Lay, inebriated and browbeaten, stumbled on the cobblestones, hailing the departing Michelin directors, who didn't turn round to look at him. *A Mutation in the History of West European Television*: that could have been the title of this painting Jed would never make. He vomited again, still having a little bile left in his stomach; it had probably been a mistake to mix Creole punch and absinthe.

Patrick Le Lay, his forehead bloody, crawled across the ground, having now lost all hope of rejoining the directors who were turning the corner of the avenue Charles-de-Gaulle. The music had calmed down. From the reception rooms came the slow beat of a Savoyard groove. Jed looked to the heavens, to the indifferent constellations. Spiritual configurations of a new type were appearing, something in any case was shifting durably in the structure of the French television scene. That's what Jed could deduce from the conversations of the guests who, having recovered their coats, were slowly moving towards the carriage entrances. He caught in passing the words 'new blood' and 'test run', and realised that many of the conversations had to do with Olga, who was a novelty in the French television scene. She 'came from the corporation': this was one of the most frequent comments, along with those concerning her beauty. The outside temperature was difficult to gauge, as it alternated between cold and warm. He was seized again by a spasm, and belched with difficulty on the palm tree. On getting up again, he saw Olga, dressed in a white leopard-skin coat, who gave him a worried look.

'We're going home.'

'Home . . . To your place?'

Without replying she took him by the arm, and led him to her car. 'Fragile little Frenchman . . .' she said with a smile before starting the engine.

24

The first light of day filtered through the gaps between the thick, fleece-lined double curtains with scarlet and yellow motifs. Olga was breathing regularly at his side, her short nightshirt drawn up to the waist. Jed softly caressed her round white buttocks without waking her. Her body had hardly changed in ten years, but her breasts had got a bit heavier. This magnificent flower of flesh had begun to wither; and the degradation, now, would only accelerate. She was two years older than he was, and Jed realised that he would turn forty the following month. They were almost at the midpoint of their lives; things had passed quickly. He got up and gathered the clothes strewn on the floor. He couldn't remember undressing the previous evening, and it was no doubt Olga who had done it; he seemed to recall having fallen asleep once his head touched the pillow. Had they made love? Probably not, and this simple fact was already serious, because after so many years of separation they should have, or should have at least tried. His predictable absence of an immediate erection would have been too easily explained by the excessive consumption of alcohol, but she could have tried to suck him off. He didn't remember her doing it. Maybe he should have asked? This hesitation, too, about his sexual rights, about what seemed natural and normal in the framework of their relationship, was worrying, and probably announced the end. Sexuality is a fragile thing: it is difficult to enter, and easy to leave.

He closed the padded white leather bedroom door behind him, and entered a long hallway which on the right side led to other bedrooms and an office, and, on the left, reception rooms – little salons with Louis XVI mouldings and hardwood floors. In the darkness intermittently lit by big shaded lamps, the apartment seemed immense. He crossed one of the salons and opened a curtain: the avenue Foch extended infinitely, abnormally wide, covered with a thin layer of frost. The only sign of life was the exhaust of a black Jaguar XJ whose engine purred by the pavement. Then a woman in evening dress staggered out of a building, and got in next to the driver; the car went off towards the Arc de Triomphe. A total silence fell again on the urban landscape. Everything appeared to him with an unusual clarity as a faint winter sun rose between the towers of La Défense, making the immaculate surface of the avenue sparkle. At the end of the hallway, he found himself in a vast kitchen furnished with brushed aluminium cupboards surrounding a basalt central worktop. The fridge was bare, except for a box of Debauve & Gallais chocolates and an opened carton of Leader Price orange juice. Looking around him he noticed a coffee machine and he made himself a Nespresso. Olga was nice, she was nice and loving, Olga loved him, he repeated to himself with a growing sadness as he also realised that nothing would ever happen between them again; life sometimes offers you a chance, he thought, but when you are too cowardly or too indecisive to seize it life takes the cards away; there is a moment for doing things and entering a possible happiness, and this moment lasts a few days, sometimes a few weeks or even a few months, but it only happens once and one time only, and if you want to return to it later it's quite simply impossible. There's no more place for enthusiasm, belief and faith, and there remains just gentle resignation, a sad and reciprocal pity, the useless but correct sensation that something could have happened, that you just simply showed yourself unworthy of this gift you had been offered. He made another coffee, which definitively dispelled the mists of sleep, then thought of leaving Olga a note. 'We must think,' he wrote, before crossing that out and scribbling: 'You deserve better than me.' He crossed out that sentence again, and wrote: 'My father is dying', then realised that he'd never mentioned his father to Olga, and scrunched up the paper before throwing it in the bin. He would soon be the same age his father was when he was born; for his father, having a child had meant the end of all artistic ambition and, more generally, the acceptance of death, as for most people, no doubt, but in his father's case more particularly so. He went back down the hallway to the bedroom, where Olga was still sleeping peacefully, huddled up. He stayed for almost a minute, attentive to her regular breathing, incapable of achieving any kind of synthesis, and suddenly he thought again of Houellebecq. A writer must have some knowledge about life, or at least make you believe that he does. One way or another, Houellebecq had to be part of the synthesis.

It was broad daylight now, but the avenue Foch was still just as deserted. Never had he spoken of his father to Olga, nor of Olga to his father, no more than he had spoken of them to Houellebecq and Franz. He had certainly maintained the residue of social life but this hardly constituted a network or an organic tissue or anything truly alive. You were dealing simply with an elementary and minimal graph lacking interconnections, made up of independent and dry branches. Back home, he put the writer's portrait in a titanium case, which he secured to the roof rack of his Audi Sport Wagon. At the Porte d'Italie, he took the direction of the A10 motorway.

As soon as he was past the outer suburbs and the last storage depots, he noticed that the snow had settled. The outside temperature was below freezing but the heater worked perfectly and a uniform mildness filled the interior. Audis characterise themselves by a particularly high level of finishing which can only be rivalled, according to *Auto-Journal*, by certain Lexus models. This car was the first one he'd bought since reaching a new wealthy status; from his first visit to the dealer, he'd been seduced by the rigour and precision of the metal assemblages, the gentle click of the doors when he closed them, all that was machine-tooled like a safe. Turning the speed-regulator control, he opted for a cruising speed of 105 km per hour. Some small notches, marking every 5 kph, made driving all the smoother; this car was indeed perfect. A layer of untouched snow covered the horizontal plain; the sun was shining valiantly, almost gaily, on the sleepy Beauce. Just before Orléans, he took the E60 in the direction of Courtenay. A few centimetres below the surface of the soil, some seeds awaited germination, awakening. The journey was going to be too short, he realised. It would have taken hours, even entire days on the motorway at constant speed to begin to sketch a clear thought. However, he forced himself to stop at a service station, and on starting off again thought that he had to phone Houellebecq to warn him of his arrival.

He left at Montargis-Ouest, parked about fifty metres before the motorway tollbooths, dialled the writer's number, and let it ring a dozen times before hanging up. The sun had disappeared, and the sky was now a milky white above the snowy landscape. The dirty-white tollbooths completed this symphony of light tones. He got out and was struck by the cold, which was much sharper than in urban areas, and walked for a few minutes on the tarmac of the hard shoulder. Noticing the titanium case tied to the roof of his car, he suddenly remembered the motive of his journey and imagined he would finally be able to read Houellebecq after it was all over. After *what* was over? At the same time as he asked the question he answered it, and he understood that Franz had got it right: *Michel Houellebecq, Writer* would be his last painting. No doubt he would have other ideas for paintings, daydreams about paintings, but never again would he feel the energy or motivation necessary to give them form. You can always take notes, Houellebecq had told him when talking about his career as a novelist, and try to string together sentences; but to launch yourself into the writing of a novel you have to wait for all of that to become compact and irrefutable. You have to wait for the appearance of an authentic core of necessity. You never *decide* to write a novel, he had added; a book, according to him, was like a block of concrete that had decided to set, and the author's freedom to act was limited to the fact of being there, and of waiting, in frightening inaction, for the process to start by itself. At that moment Jed understood that inaction, more than ever, would cause him anguish, and the image of

Olga floated back into his memory like the ghost of a thwarted happiness; if he'd been able to, he would've prayed for her. He got back in his car, started off slowly towards the tollbooths, and took out his credit card to pay.

It was almost midday when he reached Houellebecq's village, but there was no one in the streets. Was there ever anyone in the streets of this village? It was an alternation of limestone houses, with ancient tiled roofs, which must have been typical of the region, and others with whitewashed half-timbering, which you would have expected to find instead in the Normandy countryside. The church, with its ivy-clad flying buttresses, bore the traces of a thorough renovation; here, manifestly, they didn't take heritage lightly. Everywhere there were ornamental bushes and lush lawns; brown wood noticeboards invited the visitor to take an adventure holiday on the edge of the Puisaye. The multi-purpose cultural centre offered a permanent exhibition on local crafts. For a long time there had probably only been second homes here.

The writer's house was situated a little outside the village; his directions had been exceptionally clear once Jed had managed to get him on the phone. He'd just taken a long walk with his dog, he had said, a long walk in the frozen countryside, and he was delighted to invite him for lunch.

Jed parked at the gate in front of a vast L-shaped farm building, with limewashed walls. He detached the case containing his painting, then rang the doorbell. There was sudden barking in the house. A few minutes later, the door opened and a big, hairy black dog rushed out to the gate, still barking. The author of *Atomised* appeared in turn, wearing a sheepskin jacket and velvet trousers. He had changed, Jed realised. More robust, probably more muscular, he walked energetically, a welcoming smile on his lips. At the same time he had become thinner, his face was finely wrinkled, and his hair, cut very short, had gone white. He was, thought Jed, like an animal that has put on its winter coat.

★   ★   ★

A fire was roaring in the living room hearth, and they sat down on bottle-green sofas. 'Some original furniture was left,' said Houellebecq, 'I bought the other things from an antique dealer.' On a coffee table he had put out some sliced sausage and some olives, and he now opened a bottle of Chablis. Jed took the portrait out of its case and rested it against the back of the sofa. Houellebecq looked distractedly at it, then glanced around the room. 'Above the fireplace would be good, don't you think?' he asked finally. It was the only thing that seemed to interest him. It's maybe good this way, Jed thought. What is a painting, basically, but a particularly expensive piece of furniture? He was sipping his wine.

'Do you want to look around?' Houellebecq asked. Of course, Jed agreed. He liked the house, which reminded him a little of his grandparents'; but of course all these traditional country houses are more or less alike. Outside the living room there was a big kitchen, extended by a storeroom that also served as a woodshed and a cellar. The doors of two bedrooms opened on the right. The first one, unoccupied but furnished with a narrow and high double bed, was freezing. In the second one there was a single bed, a cot, set in a cosy corner, and a writing desk with a flap. Jed made out the titles of the books in the shelf of the cosy, near the head of the bed: Chateaubriand, Vigny, Balzac.

'Yes, that's where I sleep,' confirmed Houellebecq as they returned to the living room, and sat down again in front of the fire. 'In my old cot . . . You end where you began,' he added with an expression that was difficult to interpret (satisfaction? resignation? bitterness?). Jed could think of no appropriate comment to make.

After the third glass of Chablis, he felt overcome by a light torpor. 'Lunch is ready,' said the writer. 'I made a *pot-au-feu* yesterday, it will be better today. It heats up very well, *pot-au-feu*.'

The dog followed them into the kitchen and curled up in a big cloth basket, sighing with pleasure. The *pot-au-feu* was indeed good. The grandfather clock ticked softly. Through the window could be made out meadows covered with snow and, on the horizon, a copse of black trees.

'You've chosen a peaceful life,' said Jed.

'We're approaching the end; we're ageing peacefully.'

'Do you no longer write?'

'At the start of December, I tried to write a poem about birds – almost at the moment when you invited me to your exhibition. I'd bought a bird feeder and left out bits of fat for them; it was already cold, winter had come early. They showed up in great numbers: chaffinches, bullfinches, robins. They greatly appreciated the bits of fat, but from there to writing a poem . . . Finally, I wrote about my dog. It was the year of Ps, so I called my dog Plato, and I wrote a good poem; it's one of the best poems ever written about Plato's philosophy – and probably also about dogs. It will be one of my last works. Perhaps the very last.'

At that same instant, Plato stirred in his basket, his paws beat the air, and he made a long groan in his dream, before settling down again.

'Birds are nothing,' Houellebecq went on, 'just small living spots of colour who sit on their eggs and devour thousands of insects while fluttering pathetically here and there. A busy and stupid life, entirely devoted to the devouring of insects – and with, occasionally, a modest feast of larvae – and the reproduction of the same. A dog already carries within it an individual destiny and a representation of the world, but his drama has something undifferentiated about it, that's neither historical nor even genuinely narrative. I think I've more or less finished with *the world as narration* – the world of novels and films, the world of music as well. I'm now only interested in *the world as juxtaposition* – that of poetry and painting. Do you want a little more *pot-au-feu?*'

Jed declined the offer. Houellebecq took out of the fridge a Saint-Nectaire and an Epoisses, cut some slices of bread and opened another bottle of Chablis.

'It's nice of you to bring me this painting,' he added after a few seconds. 'I'll look at it sometimes. It'll remind me I had an intense life – sometimes.'

* * *

They went back into the living room to have some coffee. Houellebecq added two logs to the fire, then went away to busy himself in the kitchen. Jed went back to examining the bookcase, and was surprised by the small number of novels – classics, essentially. However, there was an astonishing number of books by social reformers of the nineteenth century: the best known, like Marx, Proudhon and Comte; but also Fourier, Cabet, Saint-Simon, Pierre Leroux, Owen, Carlyle, as well as others whose names meant almost nothing to him. The author came back, carrying on a tray a cafetière, some macaroons, and a bottle of plum eau-de-vie. 'You know what Comte asserts,' he said, 'that mankind's dead outnumber the living. Well, I agree with him now. Above all I'm in contact with the dead.' Jed couldn't find anything to say in reply to that. An old edition of Tocqueville's *Memoirs* was lying on the coffee table.

'He was an astonishing case, Tocqueville,' the writer continued. '*Democracy in America* is a masterpiece, a book of unheard-of visionary power, which innovates absolutely, in every domain; it's undoubtedly the most intelligent political book ever written. And after producing this astounding work, instead of continuing, he devotes all his energy to being elected deputy for a modest arrondissement of the Manche, then taking responsibilities in the governments of his day, just like an ordinary politician. And yet he had lost nothing of his acuity, his powers of observation.' He leafed through the *Memoirs* while stroking the back of Plato, who had stretched out at his feet. 'Listen to this, when he talks about Lamartine! Ah, he really goes after Lamartine!. . .' He read, in a pleasant and well-accentuated voice:

'I do not know if I have ever met, in this world of selfish ambitions in which I have lived, a mind as empty of thought for the public good as his. I have seen a crowd of men trouble the country for self-aggrandisement; but he is the only one, I believe, who seemed to me always ready to change the world for personal entertainment.'

'Tocqueville can't get over being in the presence of such a specimen. He himself is fundamentally an honest guy, who tries to do what he thinks is best for his country. Ambition, greed, he can understand all that; but such a thespian temperament, such a mixture of irresponsibility and dilettantism, that leaves him flabbergasted. Listen to this next part:

'Nor have I ever known a less sincere mind, who had nothing but the utmost contempt for the truth. When I say that he had contempt for it, I am wrong; he did not honour it enough to be bothered about it in the slightest. When speaking and writing, he leaves the truth and returns to it without paying attention; uniquely concerned with a certain effect that he wants to have at that moment . . .'

Forgetting his guest, Houellebecq continued to read to himself, turning the pages with increasing jubilation.

Jed waited, hesitated, then emptied his glass of plum brandy and cleared his throat. Houellebecq looked up at him. 'I've come . . .' said Jed, 'to give you this painting, of course, but also because I'm waiting for a message from you.'

'A message?' The writer's smile gradually disappeared, and his face was overcome with an earthy, mineral sadness. 'The impression you have,' he finally said slowly, 'is that my life is ending, and that I'm disappointed, is that it?'

'Um . . . yes, more or less.'

'Oh well, then you're right: my life is coming to an end, and I am disappointed. Nothing I'd hoped for in my youth has happened. There were interesting moments, but they were always difficult to reach, always won at the limit of my strength. Nothing was ever offered to me on a plate, and now I've just had enough. I would just like everything to end without excessive suffering, without debilitating illness, without infirmity.'

'You sound like my father,' Jed said softly. Houellebecq started at the word *father*, as if he'd pronounced an obscenity, then his face filled with a blasé smile that was courteous without being warm. Jed swallowed three macaroons in succession, then a big glass of plum brandy, before continuing.

'My father,' he finally repeated, 'spoke to me of William Morris. I wanted to know if you know him, what you think of him.'

'William Morris . . .' His tone was again disengaged, objective. 'It's funny that your father talked to you about him; almost no one knows William Morris.'

'Apparently they do in his circle of architects and artists.'

Houellebecq got up and rummaged in his bookcase for at least five minutes before taking out a thin volume with a faded yellowish cover, adorned with a tracery of art-nouveau motifs. He sat down again and carefully turned the blemished and stiffened pages; the book obviously hadn't been opened in years.

'Look,' he finally said, 'this situates his point of view a little. It's taken from a lecture he gave in Edinburgh in 1889: "There, in short, is our position as artists: we are the last representatives of the artisans to whom commodity production has dealt a fatal blow."

'In the end he rallied to Marxism, but at the beginning it was different, truly original. He starts from the point of view of the artist when he produces a work, and then he tries to generalise it to the whole of the world of production – industrial and agricultural. Today we have difficulty imagining the richness of political thought at that time. Chesterton paid homage to William Morris in *The Return of Don Quixote*. It's a curious novel, in which he imagines a revolution based on the return to artisan industry and medieval Christianity spreading gradually over the British Isles, supplanting the other socialist and Marxist workers' movements, and leading to the abandonment of the industrial system of production for both artisan and agrarian communities. Something completely implausible, treated in a fairy-tale atmosphere, not very far from *Father Brown*. Chesterton put a lot of his personal convictions into it, I believe. But it must be said that

William Morris, according to all we know about him, was someone quite extraordinary.'

A log collapsed in the fireplace, projecting a cascade of sparks. 'I should've bought a fireguard,' Houellebecq grumbled before his glass of brandy. Jed was still staring at him, motionless and attentive, filled with an extraordinary and incomprehensible nervous tension. Houellebecq looked back at him with surprise, and Jed realised with embarrassment that his left hand was trembling convulsively. 'I'm sorry,' he finally said, relaxing all of a sudden. 'I'm going through . . . a peculiar period.'

'William Morris didn't lead a very happy life, according to the usual criteria,' Houellebecq continued. 'However, all the accounts show him to be joyful, optimistic, and active. At the age of twenty-three he met Jane Burden, who was eighteen and worked as a painter's model. He married her two years later, and considered going into painting himself before giving up this idea, not feeling gifted enough – he respected painting above all else. He built a house according to his own plans, in Upton, on the banks of the Thames, and decorated it to live there with his wife and their two young daughters. His wife was, according to all those who met her, a great beauty; but she wasn't faithful. In particular she had a liaison with Dante Gabriel Rossetti, the head of the Pre-Raphaelite movement. William Morris had a lot of admiration for him as a painter. At the end he came to live with them, and basically supplanted Morris in the conjugal bed. Morris then made the journey to Iceland, learned the language, and started translating the sagas. After a few years he came back, and decided to have it out with them. Rossetti agreed to leave, but something had broken, and never again was there any real carnal intimacy between the couple. He was already involved in several social movements, but he left the Social Democratic Federation, which appeared to him too moderate, to create the Socialist League, which openly defended communist positions, and right until his death he gave all his energy to the communist cause, with countless articles, lectures, and meetings.'

Houellebecq stopped, shook his head in resignation, and passed his hand gently over Plato's spine, provoking a satisfied moan.

'Also right until the end,' he said slowly, 'he fought Victorian prudishness and, he campaigned for free love.'

'You know,' he added, 'I've always hated that disgusting yet so credible idea that militant, generous, and apparently disinterested action is merely compensation for problems in your private life.'

Jed said nothing, and waited for at least a minute. 'Do you think he was a utopian?' he finally asked. 'Completely unrealistic?'

'In a sense, yes, undoubtedly. He wanted to abolish school, thinking that children would learn better in an atmosphere of total freedom; he wanted to abolish prisons, thinking that remorse would be sufficient punishment for the criminal. It's difficult to read all those absurdities without a mixture of compassion and dismay. And yet, and yet . . .' Houellebecq hesitated, searching for his words. 'Paradoxically, he had a certain success on the practical level. To put into practice his ideas on the return to artisanal production, very early on he created a firm for decoration and furniture; his employees worked much less than those in the factories of the time, which were nothing other than labour camps, but above all they worked freely and each was responsible for his task from start to finish. The essential principle of William Morris was that design and execution should never be separated, no more than they were in the Middle Ages. According to all the reports, the working conditions were idyllic: well-lit, well-aired workshops on the bank of a river. All the profits were redistributed to the workers, except a small percentage, which served to finance socialist propaganda. Well, against all expectations, success was immediate, including on the commercial level. After carpentry they became interested in jewellery, leatherwork, then stained-glass windows, cloth and tapestries, always with the same success: the firm Morris & Co. was constantly in profit, throughout its existence. This was achieved by none of the workers' cooperatives that proliferated in the nineteenth century, be they the Fourierist phalansteries or Cabet's Icarian community: not one of them managed to organise the efficient production of goods and foodstuffs. With the exception of the firm founded by William Morris you can only cite a succession of failures. Not to mention the communist societies that came later . . .'

He stopped speaking again. In the room, the light was beginning to fade. He got up, lit a lamp, and added a log to the fire before sitting down again. Jed was still staring at him intently, his hands on his knees, totally silent.

'I don't know,' said Houellebecq, 'I'm too old, I no longer have the desire or the habit to come to conclusions, even to do very simple things. There are portraits of him, you know, drawn by Burne-Jones: trying a new mixture of vegetable dyes, or reading to his daughters. A stocky, hirsute guy, with a ruddy and lively face, small glasses and a bushy beard, in all the drawings he gives an impression of permanent hyperactivity, of inexhaustible goodwill and candour. What can undoubtedly be said is that the model of society proposed by William Morris certainly would not be utopian in a world where all men were like William Morris.'

Jed waited again, for a long time, while night fell on the surrounding fields. 'Thank you,' he finally said as he got up. 'I'm sorry to have disturbed you in your retreat, but your opinion means a lot to me. You've helped me a lot.'

In the doorway, they were struck by the cold. The snow gleamed faintly. The black branches of the denuded trees stood out against the dark grey sky. 'There'll be some black ice,' said Houellebecq, 'drive carefully.' When he turned the car to leave, Jed saw him waving his hand very slowly at shoulder height, in farewell. His dog, squatting at his side, seemed to nod as if in approval of his departure. Jed intended to see the writer again, but he had a feeling this wouldn't happen, that there would be all sorts of unforeseen difficulties, and various setbacks. His social life was undoubtedly going to be simplified now.

★   ★   ★

Via winding and deserted departmental roads he slowly reached, without going faster than 30 km per hour, the A10 motorway. When he entered the access slip road he noticed, down below, an immense luminous ribbon of headlights and realised that he was about to be caught up in an endless traffic jam. The outside temperature had fallen to –12°C but the inside temperature was still 19°C. The heater was working perfectly, so he felt no impatience.

Putting on France-Inter, he came across a programme that analysed the cultural news of the week; the commentators guffawed loudly and their scripted yelps of laughter were unbearably vulgar. France-Musique was broadcasting an Italian opera whose grandiose and fake brio quickly annoyed him and he switched the radio off. He'd never liked music, and now apparently liked it even less. He fleetingly wondered what had led him to embark on an artistic representation of the world, or even to think that any such thing was possible. The world was anything but a subject for artistic emotion. The world presented itself absolutely as a rational system, devoid of magic or any particular interest. He switched on Motorway FM, which confined itself to giving concrete information: there had been accidents near Fontainebleau and Nemours, and the delays would probably continue as far as Paris.

It was Sunday 1 January, thought Jed; it was the end not only of a weekend but of a holiday period, and the start of a new year for all these people who were going home, slowly, probably cursing the slowness of the traffic, who would now reach the outermost Paris suburbs in a few hours, and who, after a short night's sleep, would retake their places – subordinate or high-ranking – in the Western system of production. Near Melun-Sud the atmosphere filled with a whitish mist, and the cars slowed even further, crawling for more than five kilometres before the road gradually became unblocked near Melun-Centre. The outside temperature was –17°C. He himself had been singled out, less than a month before, by *the law of supply and demand*. The wealth that had suddenly enveloped him like a rain of sparks had delivered him from any financial yoke, and he realised that he was now going to leave a world he'd never genuinely been a part of. His human relations, already few, would one by one dry up and disappear, and he would be in life like he was at present in the perfectly finished interior of his Audi Allroad A6: peaceful and joyless, completely neutral.

Part Three

25

As soon as he opened the door of the Safrane, Jasselin knew that he was going to experience one of the worst moments of his career. Sitting on the grass a few steps from the cordon, his head in his hands, Lieutenant Ferber was utterly still. It was the first time Jasselin had seen a colleague in such a state – in the detective branch, either they developed a hard surface that enabled them to control their emotions or they resigned, and Ferber had been in the profession for over a decade. A few metres further away, the three men from the Montargis gendarmerie were in a state of shock: two of them were kneeling in the grass, staring vacantly, and the third – probably their commanding officer; Jasselin thought he recognised the insignia of a brigadier – was swaying slightly, on the brink of passing out. Waves of stench emanated from the farm building, carried by a breeze which gently bent the butter-cups on a bright green meadow. None of the four men had reacted when the car pulled up.

He went towards Ferber, who remained still. With his pale complexion, his very pale blue eyes and his black medium-length hair, Christian Ferber had at thirty the romantic physique of a sensitive, darkly handsome kid, which was quite unusual in the police; he was, however, a competent and stubborn policeman, one of those you preferred to work with. 'Christian,' said Jasselin softly, then more loudly. Slowly, like a scolded child, Ferber looked up, with an expression of plaintive rancour.

'It's as bad as that?' Jasselin gently asked.

'It's worse. Worse than you can even imagine. Whoever did that . . . should not exist. He should be wiped off the face of the earth.'

'We'll catch him, Christian. We always catch them.'

Ferber nodded and began to cry. All this was becoming very unusual.

After what seemed a very long time, Ferber stood up, still unsure on his feet, and led Jasselin over to a group of gendarmes. 'My superior, Inspector Jasselin,' he said in a low voice. At these words, one of the younger gendarmes began to vomit at length, got his breath back and then vomited on the ground again, without paying attention to anyone. This wasn't very usual, either, for a gendarme. 'Brigadier Bégaudeau,' his superior said mechanically, still swaying meaninglessly. In short, nothing could be expected from the Montargis gendarmerie.

'They're going to be taken off the case,' said Ferber. 'We're the ones who started the investigation: the victim had a meeting in Paris he didn't go to, so we were called. As he lived here, I asked them to check; and they found him.'

'If they found the body, they can ask to be given the case.'

'I don't think they will.'

'What makes you say that?'

'I think you'll agree with me on seeing . . . the state of the victim.' He stopped, shuddered, and again felt sick, but he had nothing to vomit, just a little bile.

Jasselin looked at the door to the house, which stood wide open. A cloud of flies had accumulated nearby; they hovered buzzing, as if awaiting their turn. From a fly's point of view a human corpse is meat, pure and simple meat. More stinking air wafted over to them, and the stench was truly atrocious. If he was going to assess the crime scene without going to pieces, he should, he was clearly aware, adopt the fly's point of view for a few minutes. The remarkable objectivity of the housefly, *Musca domestica*. Each female of *Musca domestica* can lay up to five hundred eggs, and occasionally a thousand. These eggs are white and measure around 1.2 mm long. After only a day, the larvae (maggots) leave them; they live and feed on organic matter (generally dead and in an advanced state of decomposition, such as a corpse, detritus or excrement).

The maggots are pale white, about 3 to 9 mm long. They are slender in the mouth region and do not have legs. At the end of their third metamorphosis, the maggots crawl towards a cool, dry place and transform into pupae of a reddish colour.

The adult flies live from two weeks to a month in nature, longer in laboratory conditions. After emerging from the pupa, the fly stops growing. Small flies aren't young flies, but flies that didn't get enough food in the larval stage.

Around thirty-six hours after its emergence from the pupa, the female is receptive to coupling. The male mounts on its back to inject sperm. Normally the female couples only once, storing the sperm in order to use it for several clutches of eggs. The males are territorial: they defend a certain territory against the intrusion of other males, and try to mount any female entering this territory.

'What's more,' added Ferber, 'the victim was famous.'

'Who was it?'

'Michel Houellebecq.'

At his superior's lack of reaction, he explained: 'He's a writer. Well, he *was* a writer. He was very well known.'

Ah well, *the famous writer* was now a nutritional support for numerous maggots, thought Jasselin in a brave attempt at *mind control*.

'You think I should go in there?' he finally asked his subordinate. 'Go inside and see?'

Ferber hesitated at length before replying. The one responsible for an investigation should always examine the crime scene in person; Jasselin always insisted on that in the lectures he gave to the training institute for inspectors at Saint-Cyr-au-Mont-d'Or. A crime, and especially one that is villainous and brutal, is a very intimate thing, where the murderer necessarily expresses something of his personality and of his relationship with the victim. Hence in the crime scene something individual and unique, practically a signature of the criminal; and this is particularly true, he would add, of atrocious or ritual crimes, of those for which you are naturally disposed to steer the investigation towards a psychopath.

'If I were you,' Ferber finally replied, 'I'd wait for the crime scene investigators. They'll have sterilised masks that will allow you, at least, to escape the smell.'

Jasselin reflected, then decided it was a good compromise.

'When do they arrive?'

'In two hours' time.'

Brigadier Bégaudeau was still swaying to and fro, but he had reached a cruising speed in his swaying and no longer seemed in danger – he just had to go and lie down, that's all, in a hospital bed or even at home, but after taking some strong tranquillisers. His two subordinates, still kneeling at his side, began to nod their heads and sway slowly in imitation of their chief. They're rural gendarmes, Jasselin thought benevolently, authorised to issue speeding tickets or investigate minor credit-card fraud.

'If you don't mind,' he told Ferber, 'I'm going to take a walk around the village in the meantime. Just to soak in the atmosphere.'

'Go on, go on . . . You're the one in charge,' Ferber smiled wearily. 'I'll look after everything, I'll *receive the guests* in your absence.'

He sat back down on the grass, sniffed several times and took a paperback from his jacket – it was *Aurelia* by Gérard de Nerval, Jasselin noticed. Then he turned around and started for the village – a tiny little village, no more than a group of sleepy homes in the heart of the forest.

26

Police detectives constitute the leadership and coordination corps of the national police force, which is a superior technical corps with an interministerial vocation answerable to the Ministry of the Interior. They are responsible for elaborating and putting into effect policing doctrines and managing the various services, for which they assume operational and organic responsibility. They have authority over the personnel appointed to these services. They participate in the design, execution and evaluation of the programmes and projects relative to the prevention of insecurity and the struggle against crime. They have the magistrate's powers conferred on them by law. They are given uniforms.

The remuneration at the start of their career is in the order of 2,898 euros a month.

Jasselin was walking slowly along a road that led to a copse that was of an abnormally intense green colour, and where snakes and flies probably proliferated – even, in the worst case, scorpions and horseflies. Scorpions were not rare in the Yonne, and some ventured as far as the limits of the Loiret. He had read that in Gendarmeries Info before he left, an excellent site, that put only carefully checked information online. In short, Jasselin thought sadly, in the countryside, contrary to appearances, you could expect to find anything and frequently the worst. The village itself had given him a very bad impression: the white houses with black shingle roofs, impeccably clean; the church pitilessly restored; the supposedly playful information noticeboards – it all gave the impression of a decor, a fake village recreated for a television series. What's more, he hadn't met a single inhabitant. In such an environment, he could be sure that no one would have seen or heard anything. The gathering of statements immediately seemed an almost impossible task.

But he turned back, rather through idleness. If I meet a human being, just one, he told himself with childlike enthusiasm, I'll solve this murder. For an instant, he thought he was lucky to catch sight of a cafe, Chez Lucie: the door onto the main street was open. He hurried over in this direction but, when he was about to go in, an arm (a woman's, perhaps Lucie herself?) emerged to shut the door violently. He heard the lock click closed twice. He could've forced his way into the establishment and demand she give a statement, he had the necessary police powers, but the approach seemed to him premature. Anyway, it would be someone from Ferber's team who would look after it. Ferber himself excelled at gathering statements: no one, on meeting him, felt they were dealing with a cop, and even after he had shown his card people forgot it instantly (he rather gave the impression of being a psychologist, or an ethnology research assistant) and confided in him with disconcerting ease.

Just next to Chez Lucie, the rue Martin-Heidegger descended towards a part of the village he had not yet explored. He went down it, meditating on the almost absolute power that mayors had been given to name the streets of their towns. At the corner of the impasse Leibniz he stopped in front of a grotesque painting, with strident acrylic colours on a tin sheet, which portrayed a man with a duck's head and an excessively large penis; his torso and his legs were covered with a thick brown fur. An information board told him that he was standing in front of the 'Muze'eretical', dedicated to *art brut* and pictorial productions by the residents of the Montargis mental home. His admiration for the inventiveness of the municipality grew more when, on arriving at the place Parmenides, he discovered a brand-new car park: the lines of white paint delimiting the parking spaces could not have been more than a week old, and it was equipped with an electronic payment system that accepted European and Japanese credit cards. A sole car was parked there for the moment, a sea-green Maserati GranTurismo, and Jasselin noted at random its licence plate. In the course of an investigation, as he always said to his students at Saint-Cyr-au-Mont-d'Or, it is fundamental to take notes – at this stage of his exposé he would take out his own notebook, a standard 105 × 148 mm Rhodia pad. You should never let a day of an investigation pass by without taking at least one note, he insisted, even if the fact noted seemed to be totally lacking in importance. The rest of the investigation would, almost always, confirm this lack of importance, but this wasn't the essential point: the essential point was to remain active, to maintain a minimum intellectual activity, for a completely inactive policeman becomes discouraged, and therefore becomes incapable of reacting when important facts do start to manifest themselves.

Curiously, Jasselin was thus unknowingly formulating recommendations almost identical to those that Houellebecq had given on the subject of his work as a writer, the one time he agreed to teach a creative writing workshop, at the University of Louvain-la-Neuve, in April 2011.

In the southerly direction the village ended at the Immanuel Kant roundabout, a purely urbanistic creation of great aesthetic sobriety – a simple circle of totally grey tarmac which led to nothing, enabled access to no road, and around which no house had been built. A bit further on, a river flowed slowly. The sun shot its rays, more and more intensely, on the meadows. Bordered with aspen, the river offered a relatively shaded space. Jasselin followed its course for a little more than two hundred metres before running into an obstacle: a wide and inclined concrete wall, whose upper part was at the level of the riverbed, fed a diversion channel which, he realised after a few metres, was more of an extended pond.

He sat down in the thick grass on the edge of the pond. Of course he didn't know it, but this part of the world where he sat, tired, suffering from lumbar back pains and a digestion that was becoming more difficult with the passing years, was the exact place which had served as a theatre for Houellebecq's games as a child. Most often they were solitary games. In his mind Houellebecq was simply a *case*, one that he could already feel was difficult. When *personalities* are murdered, the public's expectation of a solution is high, and its propensity to denigrate the police and attack their inefficiency becomes manifest after a few days; the only thing worse that could happen to you was to have on your hands the murder of a child, and worst still the murder of a *baby*. In the case of babies it was awful; a baby murderer would have to be apprehended immediately, before even turning the street corner. A delay of forty-eight hours was already considered unacceptable by the public. He looked at his watch: he had been away for more than an hour, and he chided himself for having left Ferber on his own. The surface of the pond was covered in duckweed, its colour was opaque, unhealthy.

27

When he returned to the scene of the crime, the temperature had fallen slightly. He also had the impression that the flies were less numerous. Stretched out on the grass, his rolled-up jacket serving as a pillow, Ferber was still engrossed in *Aurelia*. He now looked like he had been invited on a day out in the countryside. 'He's made of strong stuff, that boy,' Jasselin said to himself, doubtless for the twentieth time since he'd known him.

'Have the gendarmes left?' he asked, surprised.

'Someone came to look after them. People from the psychological assistance unit – they came from the hospital in Montargis.'

'Already?'

'Yes, that astonished me too. The work of a gendarme has become harder these last years, they now have almost as many suicides as we do; but you have to accept that psychological support has made a lot of progress.'

'How do you know that? The statistics on suicides?'

'Don't you ever read the *Internal Bulletin of the Forces of Law and Order*?'

'No.' He sat down heavily on the grass next to his colleague. 'I don't read enough, in general.' Shadows were beginning to lengthen between the lime trees. Jasselin regained hope; he had almost forgotten the materiality of the corpse, a few metres from there, when the Peugeot Partner of the crime scene investigators drew up noisily in front of the barrier. The two men got out immediately, perfectly synchronised, wearing those ridiculous suits which made you think of a nuclear decontamination team.

Jasselin hated the investigators from the criminal records office, their way of always functioning in pairs, in their specially equipped little cars stuffed with expensive and incomprehensible machines, their open contempt for the hierarchy of the crime squad. But in

truth the people from the criminal records office in no way sought
to be loved; on the contrary, they did their utmost to differentiate
themselves as much as possible from ordinary policemen, showing
in all circumstances the insulting arrogance of the technician
towards the layman – this no doubt in order to justify the growing
inflation of their annual budget. It's true that their methods had
made spectacular progress, and that they now succeeded in taking
fingerprints or DNA samples in conditions inconceivable only a
few years before, but to what extent could they deserve the credit
for this progress? They would have been completely incapable of
inventing or even improving the equipment that enabled them to
obtain those results; they just used them, which demanded no
particular intelligence or talent, just an appropriate technical
training that it would have been more effective to give directly to
the policemen on the ground. At least that was the thesis that
Jasselin defended, regularly and up to now unsuccessfully, in the
annual reports he submitted to his superiors. While, he had no
hope of being heard – the division between the services was ancient
and established – he did it mainly to calm his nerves.

Ferber had got up, elegant and affable, to explain the situation
to the two men. Their brief nods were calculated to show their
impatience and professionalism. At a given moment, Ferber pointed
to Jasselin, no doubt to identify him as the leader of the investigation. They made no reply and didn't even make a step in his direction, just put on their masks. Jasselin had never been especially
strict on questions of hierarchical precedence. Never had he
demanded strict observance of the formal deference to which he
was entitled as an inspector. No one could say he had, but these
two clowns were beginning to exasperate him. Accentuating the
natural heaviness of his gait, like the oldest monkey of the tribe,
he went towards them breathing heavily, waited for a salute which
did not come, and announced 'I'm coming with you' in a tone that
needed no reply. One of them gave a start: obviously they were
used to doing their business in peace, going into the crime scene
without letting anyone else approach the perimeter, taking their

absurd little notes on their hand-held terminals. But what could they do? Object? They could do absolutely nothing, and one of them handed him a mask. As he put it on, he became aware again of the reality of the crime, and even more so on approaching the building. He let them go ahead, walking a few steps ahead of him, and noted with a vague satisfaction that the two zombies stopped dead, afraid, at the entrance to the house. He joined and then over-took them, strolling into the living room, albeit uncertainly. 'I am the living body of the law,' he said to himself. The luminosity began to fade. These surgical masks were amazingly effective, and the smells were almost completely blocked. Behind him he no longer felt or heard the two crime scene investigators who, emboldened, had penetrated the living room, but stopped almost immediately in the doorway. 'I am the body of the law, the imperfect body of the moral law,' he repeated to himself, a little like a mantra, before accepting, before looking fully at what his eyes had already seen.

A policeman reasons on the basis of the *body*. His training demands that: he is trained to note and describe the position of the body, the wounds inflicted on the body, the state of conserva-tion of the body; but here, strictly speaking, there wasn't a body. He turned around and saw behind him the two investigators from the criminal records office who began to nod and sway to and fro, exactly like the gendarmes of Montargis. The head of the victim was intact, cut off cleanly and placed on one of the armchairs in front of the fireplace. A small pool of blood had formed on the dark green velvet. Facing him on the sofa, the head of a big black dog had also been cleanly cut off. The rest was a massacre, a senseless carnage of strips of flesh scattered across the floor. However, neither the head of the man nor that of the dog were frozen in an expression of horror, but rather one of incredulity and anger. In the midst of the strips of mixed human and canine meat, a clear passage, fifty centimetres wide, led to the fireplace filled with bones to which some remains of flesh were still attached. Jasselin went in carefully, thinking that it was probably the murderer who had made this passage, and turned around; with his back to the fireplace, he looked around the living room, which could have been about sixty square metres. The whole surface of the carpet was spattered with trails of blood, which in places formed complex arabesques. The strips of flesh in themselves, of a red colour which sometimes became blackish, did not seem arranged at random but followed motifs that were difficult to decrypt; he felt it was like being in the presence of a puzzle. No traces of footprints were visible: the murderer had acted methodically, first cutting the strips of skin that he wanted to place in the corners of the room, then returning gradually towards the centre while leaving a path to the exit. They would need photos to help try and recreate the design of the whole. Jasselin glanced at the two investigators from the criminal records office: one of them continued to sway to and fro like a madman; the other, in an effort to get a grip of himself, had taken a digital camera out of his bag and was holding it at arm's length, but didn't seem able to switch it on. Jasselin took out his mobile.

'Christian? It's Jean-Pierre. I've a favour to ask you.'

'I'm listening.'

'You have to come and get these criminal records guys, they're already out of action, and what's more there's a special thing to be done with photos in this case. They mustn't do just close-ups as usual, I need views of every part of the room, and if possible of the room as a whole. But I can't brief them immediately, we'll have to wait until they come back to their senses a little.'

'I'll look after it. In fact, the team's arriving soon. They just called me from outside Montargis. They'll be here in ten minutes.'

Jasselin hung up pensively: that boy continued to astonish him. Ferber's entire team was arriving, a few hours after the fact, and probably in personal vehicles. His ethereal, evanescent appearance was indeed deceptive: he had complete authority over his team, and was undoubtedly the best team leader Jasselin had ever had under his orders. Two minutes later, he saw him discreetly enter the back of the room, patting the shoulders of the two investigators to usher them gently out of the house. Jasselin was nearing the end of his career, having scarcely a year left, which he could perhaps prolong to two or three, four at most. He implicitly knew, and at their bimonthly interviews his division commander sometimes made this explicit, that what was expected from him now was no longer *solving* crimes, but rather designating his successors, co-opting those who, after him, should, solve them.

After Ferber and the two investigators left, he found himself alone in the room. The luminosity was fading again but he had no desire to turn on the light. He felt, without being able to explain it to himself, that the murder had been committed in broad daylight. The silence was almost unreal. He had the sensation that there was, in this case, something that concerned him particularly, personally, but why? He observed again the complex motif composed by the strips of flesh spread across the floor of the room. What he felt was less disgust than a sort of general pity for the entire earth, for mankind which can, in its heart, give birth to such horrors. In truth, he was a bit astonished he could bear this spectacle which had even revolted crime scene investigators inured to the worst. A year before, feeling that he was beginning to have difficulty bearing crime scenes, he had gone to the Buddhist centre of Vincennes to ask them if it would be possible for him to practise *asubha*, the meditation on the corpse. The lama had first tried to dissuade him: this meditation, he had opined, was difficult, and not adapted to the Western mentality. But when he learned of Jasselin's profession, he had changed his mind, and asked for time to reflect. A few days later he phoned to say that yes, in his particular case, *asubha* could undoubtedly be appropriate. It wasn't practised in Europe, where it was incompatible with health and safety regulations, but he could give Jasselin the address of a Sri Lankan monastery which occasionally received Westerners. He had spent two weeks' holiday there, after having found an airline that agreed to transport his dog (that had been the most difficult part). Every evening, while Hélène went to the beach, he went to a mass grave where they deposited the recently deceased, without precaution against predators or insects. After concentrating all of his mental faculties by trying to follow the precepts laid down by Buddha in the sermon on the direction of attention, he had thus been able to intently observe the wan corpse, the suppurating corpse, the dismembered corpse, the corpse eaten by worms. At each stage, he had to repeat to himself, forty-eight times: 'This is my fate, the fate of all mankind, I cannot escape it.'

Asubha, he now realised, had been a total success, so much so that he would have recommended it without hesitation to any policeman. He had not, however, become a Buddhist, and even if his feelings of repulsion at the sight of a corpse had been reduced by notable proportions, he still felt *hatred* for the murderer, hatred and fear. He wanted to see the murderer annihilated, eradicated from the surface of the globe. On passing through the writer's door, enveloped by the rays of the setting sun which illuminated the meadow, he rejoiced at the persistence, in him, of that hatred, which was necessary, he thought, for effective police work. The rational motivation, that of the quest for truth, was not generally sufficient; it was, however, sometimes unusually strong. He felt confronted by a complex, monstrous but rational mind, probably that of a schizo-phrenic. On their return to Paris, they would have to consult the files of serial killers, and probably ask for the delivery of foreign files, as he had no memory of such a crime ever being committed in France.

When he left the house he saw Ferber, among his team, giving them instructions: lost in his thoughts, he hadn't heard the cars arrive. There was also a big guy, in suit and tie, whom he didn't know – probably the deputy public prosecutor from Montargis. He waited for Ferber to finish distributing the tasks to explain again what he wanted: general shots of the crime scene, wide shots.

'I'm returning to Paris,' he then announced. 'You coming with me, Christian?'

'Yes, I think everything's in place. Will we have a meeting tomorrow morning?'

'Not too early. Around midday will be fine.' He knew they would have to work late, no doubt until dawn.

28

Night was falling when they got onto the A10 motorway. Ferber turned the cruise-control to 130 kph and asked if Jasselin minded him putting on some music. He replied no.

There is perhaps no music that better expresses than Franz Lizst's last pieces of chamber music that funereal and gentle feeling of the old man whose friends are all dead, who in some way already belongs to the past and who in turn feels death approaching, who sees it as a sister, a friend, the promise of a return to the childhood home. In the middle of 'Prayer to the Guardian Angels', Jasselin began to think about his youth, his student days.

Quite ironically, he had interrupted his medical studies between the first and second year because he could no longer bear the dissections, nor even the sight of corpses. Law had immediately interested him a lot, and like almost all his classmates he considered a career as a lawyer, but his parents' divorce was to make him change his mind. It was a divorce between old people; he was already twenty-three and their only child. In young people's divorces, the presence of children, whose care they have to share, and who are loved more or less despite everything, often lessens the violence of the confrontation; but in old people's divorces, where there remain only financial and heritage interests, the savagery of the fight no longer knows any limits. He had then realised exactly what a lawyer is, he had got a full sense of that mixture of deceit and laziness which sums up the professional behaviour of a lawyer, and most particularly of a lawyer specialising in divorce. The procedure had lasted more than two years, two years of endless struggle at the end of which his parents felt for each other a hatred so violent that they were never to see or even phone each other for the rest of their lives, and all that just to reach a divorce agreement of depressing banality, that any cretin could have written in a quarter of an hour after reading *Divorce for Dummies*. It was surprising, he'd thought several times, that spouses engaged in divorce proceedings do not more frequently murder their former partners – either directly or via a professional. The fear of the gendarme, he realised, was undoubtedly the true basis of human society, and it was in some way natural that he sat the police entrance exam. He had entered at a good rank, and, being from Paris, did a year's training at the police station in the 13th arrondissement. It was demanding. Nothing, in all the cases he would be confronted with later, was to surpass in complexity and impenetrability the settling of accounts in the Chinese mafia which he'd been confronted with at the start of his career.

Among the students at the police academy of Saint-Cyr-au-Mont-d'Or, many dreamed of a career at the Quai des Orfèvres, sometimes since childhood. Some had joined the police solely for this reason, so he was a bit surprised that his application for a transfer to the crime squad was accepted, after five years' service in local police stations. He had then just *set up home* with a woman he'd met while she was studying economics, who then went into teaching and was subsequently appointed a lecturer at the University of Paris-Dauphiné; but he never considered marrying her, or even having a civil partnership: the mark left by his parents' divorce was to remain indelible.

'Should I drop you off at your place?' Ferber asked him gently. They had arrived at the Porte d'Orléans. He noticed that they hadn't exchanged a word during the entire journey; lost in his thoughts, he hadn't even noticed the stops at the tollbooths. Anyway, it was too early to say anything about the case; a night would allow them to settle, to absorb the shock. But he had no illusions: given the horror of the crime, and the fact that, what's more, the victim was a *personality*, things would move very quickly; the pressure was going to be enormous. The press had not yet been informed, but this respite would only last one night; that very evening, he was going to have to phone the detective chief inspector on his mobile. And the latter, probably, would immediately call the prefect of police.

He lived in the rue Geoffroy-Saint-Hilaire, almost at the corner of the rue Poliveau, two steps from the Jardin des Plantes. At night, during their nocturnal strolls, they sometimes heard the trumpeting of the elephants and the impressive roaring of the wild cats – lions? panthers? cougars? – they were unable to tell them apart by the noise. They could also hear, especially when there was a full moon, the conjugated howling of the wolves, which plunged Michou, their Bolognese bichon, into fits of atavistic and insurmountable terror. They were childless. A few years after they had begun living together, and while their sex life was – according to the classic expression – 'completely satisfying', and Hélène took 'no particular precaution', they decided to consult a doctor. Some slightly humiliating but quick examinations showed he was *oligospermic*. The name of the affliction appeared, in this case, quite euphemistic; his ejaculations, besides being of moderate quantity, didn't contain *an insufficient quantity of spermatozoa,* they didn't contain *any spermatozoa at all.* Oligospermia can have very different origins: testicular varicocela, testicular atrophy, hormonal deficit, chronic infection of the prostate, flu, or other causes. Most of the time it has nothing to do with virile strength. Some men who produce very few or no spermatozoa can have hard-ons *like stags,* while men who are almost impotent have ejaculations so abundant and fertile that they could repopulate Western Europe; the conjunction of these two qualities is enough to characterise the male ideal promoted in pornographic productions. Jasselin didn't fit into this perfect configuration: if he could still, aged over fifty, gratify his partner with firm and durable erections, he would certainly not have been able to offer her a *sperm shower,* should she have so desired; his ejaculations, when they took place, were no more than a teaspoon-full.

Oligospermia, the main cause of male sterility, is always difficult and often impossible to treat. There remained only two solutions:

the spermatozoa of a male donor, or adoption. After discussing it several times, they decided to give up. Hélène, in truth, didn't have that strong a desire to have a child, and a few years later it was she who proposed that they buy a dog. In a passage where he laments French decadence and the fall in the birth rate (already in the news in the 1930s), the fascist author Drieu la Rochelle imitates, in order to attack it, the conversation between a decadent French couple of his times, which goes more or less like this: 'And then Kiki, the dog, that's easily enough to amuse us.' She was basically in total agreement with this view, she ended up confessing to Jasselin. A dog was as amusing as, and even much more amusing than, a child, and if she had at one moment considered having a child it was above all out of conformism, a little also to please her mother. But in fact she didn't really like children, she had never really liked them, and nor did he like children when he thought about it. He didn't like their natural and systematic selfishness, their innate ignorance of the law, their utter immorality that required an exhausting and almost always fruitless education. No, he really didn't like children, or in any case human children.

He heard a screeching on his right and noticed suddenly that they had stopped outside his home, possibly for a long time. The rue Poliveau was deserted under the line of street lights.

'Sorry, Christian,' he said, embarrassed. 'I was . . . distracted.'

'No problem.'

It was only nine, he thought as he climbed the stairs, and Hélène had probably waited to have dinner with him. She liked to cook. Sometimes he accompanied her on Sunday mornings when she did her shopping at the market in the rue Mouffetard; every time he was always charmed by that corner of Paris, the Saint-Médard church by its little square, with a weathercock on top of the steeple, just like a village church.

Indeed, on arriving on the third floor landing, he was greeted by the characteristic smell of rabbit in mustard sauce and the joyful yapping of Michou, who had recognised his footsteps. He turned his key in the lock. They were an old couple, he thought, a traditional couple, of a model quite rare in the 2010s among people their age, but which again, it seems, constituted for young people an ideal to be hoped for, although it was generally inaccessible. He was aware of living on an improbable islet of happiness and peace; he was aware that they had created for themselves a sort of peaceful niche, far from the noises of the world, of an almost childlike mildness, in absolute opposition to the barbarism and violence that confronted him every day in his work. They had been happy together; they were still happy together, and probably would be *until death do they part.*

He took Michou, who was leaping and yapping happily, in his hands and lifted him to his face, the little body frozen in an ecstatic joy. If the origin of bichons goes back to antiquity (statues of bichons were found in the tomb of the pharaoh Ramses II), the introduction of the Bolognese bichon to the court of François I came as a present from the Duke of Ferrara; the delivery, accompanied by two miniatures from Correggio, was enormously appreciated by the French sovereign, who judged the animal 'more lovable than a hundred maidens', and sent the Duke military aid that was decisive in his conquest of the principality of Mantua. The bichon then became the favourite breed of several French kings, including Henri II, before being dethroned by the pug and the poodle. Unlike such dogs as the Shetland or the Tibetan terrier, who have only lately attained the status of *pet dog* after a difficult past as *working dogs*, the bichon seems from the start to have had no reason to exist other than to bring joy and happiness to human beings. It has acquitted itself of this task with great constancy, being patient with children and gentle with old people, for innumerable generations. It suffers enormously from being alone, and this must be taken into account when buying a bichon: any absence of its masters will be considered by it an abandonment, and its entire world, the structure and essence of its world, will collapse in an instant. It will be subject to severe bouts of depression and will frequently refuse to eat; in fact, you are strongly advised never to leave a bichon alone, even for a few hours. The French university system had ended up accepting that, and Hélène could take Michou to her classes, or at least the habit had taken hold, without any formal authorisation. He stayed calmly in his carrier, moving a little, sometimes asking to come out. Hélène would then put him on the desk, to the joy of the students. He walked across the desk for a few minutes, looking up from time to time at his mistress, occasionally reacting with a yawn or a brief bark to such-and-such a quotation from Schumpeter or Keynes; then he returned to his flexible bag. On the other hand, the airline companies, intrinsically fascist organisations, refused to display the same tolerance, and they had been obliged, with regret, to abandon any plans for long-distance travel. They left by car every summer in August, confining themselves to the discovery of France and neighbouring countries. With its status classically categorised by jurisprudence as belonging to the individual home, the car remained, for pet-owners as well as for smokers, one of the last spaces of freedom, one of the last *temporary autonomous zones* available to humans at the start of the third millennium.

It wasn't their first bichon: they had bought his predecessor and father, Michel, shortly after the doctors had informed Jasselin of the probably incurable nature of his sterility. They had been very happy together, so much so that they genuinely were shocked when Michel was struck down with dirofilariasis, at the age of eight. Dirofilariasis is a parasitic illness; the parasite is a nematode that lodges in the right ventricle of the heart and in the pulmonary artery. The symptoms are increased tiredness, then coughing, and heart trouble that can provoke fainting. The treatment is not without risks: several dozen worms, some of which can reach thirty centimetres in length, sometimes coexist in the dog's heart. For several days, they feared for its life. The dog is a sort of definitive child, more docile and gentle, a child who could be said to have stopped growing at the age of reason, but it is also a child which will be outlived: to accept to love a dog is to accept to love a being which will, inevitably, be torn from you, and, curiously, they had not become aware of that before Michel's illness. On the day after he was cured, they decided to give him descendants. The breeders they consulted displayed certain misgivings: they had waited too long, the dog was already a bit old, the quality of his spermatozoa risked being degraded. Finally, one of them, based near Fontainebleau, agreed, and from the union of Michel and a young bitch called Lizzy Lady de Heurtebise were born two pups, a male and a female. As owners of the stud (according to the classic expression), custom gave them the choice of the first puppy. They chose the male, which they called Michou. It had no apparent imperfection, and, contrary to their fears, was accepted very well by its father, who did not display any particular jealousy.

After a few weeks, however, they noticed that Michou's testicles had not yet dropped, which began to become abnormal. They consulted one vet, then another: both agreed that the sire had been too old. The second hazarded the hypothesis of a surgical inter-vention before changing his mind, declaring it dangerous and almost impossible. It was a terrible blow for them, much more than Jasselin's own sterility had been. This poor dog would not only have no descendants but also would experience no sexual drive or satisfaction. It would be a diminished dog, incapable of transmit-ting life, cut off from the elementary appeal of the race and limited in time – definitively.

Gradually they got used to the idea, just as they realised that their little dog wouldn't miss the sexual life of which it had been deprived. Anyway, dogs are scarcely hedonistic or libertine, and any kind of erotic refinement is unknown to them. The satisfac-tion it feels at the moment of coitus doesn't go beyond the brief and mechanical relief of the life instincts of the species. The bichon's willpower is in all cases very weak; but Michou, delivered from the ultimate attachments of the propagation of the genome, seemed even more submissive, gentle, joyful and pure than his father had been. He was an absolute mascot, innocent and flaw-less, whose life was entirely devoted to his adored masters, a continual and unfailing source of joy. Jasselin was by this point approaching fifty. While watching that small being play with its soft toys on the living-room carpet, he was occasionally, despite himself, filled with dark thoughts. Marked no doubt by the ideas fashionable in his generation, he had up until then considered sexuality to be a positive power, a source of union that increased the concord between humans through the innocence of shared pleasure. On the contrary, he now saw in it more and more often the struggle, the brutal fight for domination, the elimination of the rival and the hazardous multiplication of coitus without any reason other than ensuring the maximum propagation of genes. He saw in it the source of all conflict, of all massacres and suffering. Sexuality increasingly appeared to him as the most direct and obvious manifestation of evil. And his career in the police was not going to change his mind: the crimes which were not motivated by money were motivated by sex. It was one or the other. Mankind seemed incapable of imagining anything beyond it, at least concerning crime. The new case on their hands seemed original at first sight, but it was his first murder in at least three years, and the uniformity of criminal motives was, on the whole, tedious. Like most of his colleagues, Jasselin rarely read detective novels; he had, however, the previous year, come across a book which wasn't strictly speaking, a novel, but the memoirs of a former private detective who had worked in Bangkok, and who had chosen to retrace his career in the form of about thirty short stories. In almost all the cases, his clients were Westerners who'd fallen in love with a young Thai girl, and who wanted to know if, as she assured them, she was faithful in their absence. And in almost every case the girl had one or several lovers – with whom she blithely spent their money – and often a child from a previous union. In a sense it was certainly a bad book, or at least a bad detective novel: the author made no imaginative effort and never tried to vary the motives or the plots; but it was precisely this crushing monotony that gave it a unique flavour of authenticity, of realism.

'Jean-Pierre!' Hélène's voice came to him as if muffled, but then he came back to full consciousness and realised that she was standing a metre in front of him, her hair undone, wearing a housecoat. He was still clutching Michou, his arms raised to chest height, and had been for a time that was difficult to calculate; the little dog looked at him with surprise, but without fear.

'Are you OK? You look bizarre.'

'A strange case has come my way.'

Hélène went silent and waited for what would follow. During the twenty-five years they had been together, Jean-Pierre had practically never spoken to her about his work. Confronted daily with horrors that surpass the dimensions of normal understanding, virtually all policemen choose, once back at home, to keep quiet. The best prophylaxis for them consists of creating a vacuum, or trying to create a vacuum, during the few hours of respite they are given. Some indulge in drink, and end their dinners in an advanced state of alcoholic mindlessness that leaves them nothing else to do but drag themselves off to bed. Others, among the younger ones, indulge in pleasure and the vision of mutilated and tortured corpses ends up disappearing in a loving embrace. Almost none of them choose to speak, and again that evening, Jasselin, after putting Michou back down, went over to the table, sat down at his usual place, and waited for Hélène to bring the celeriac remoulade – he had always greatly liked celeriac remoulade.

29

The following day, he walked to work, turned at the top of the rue des Fossés-Saint-Bernard, then strolled along the quais. He stopped for a long time on the pont de l'Archevêché: it was from there that you had, in his opinion, the most beautiful view of Notre-Dame. It was a fine October morning with fresh and limpid air. He stopped again for a few moments in the square Jean-XXIII, observing the tourists and the homosexuals who were out for a stroll, mostly in couples, kissing or hand in hand.

Ferber arrived at the office at almost the same time and joined him on the stairs near the third-floor control centre. They would never install a lift in the Quai des Orfèvres, he thought resignedly; he noticed that Ferber was limiting his strides, abstaining from going ahead of him in the last part of the climb.

Lartigue was the first to join them in the team's office. Usually a rather jovial guy, he didn't look at all well; his dark and smooth southern face was tense, worried. Ferber had asked him to gather witness statements on the spot.

'We drew a blank,' he announced at the outset. 'I've nothing at all. No one saw or heard anything. No one has even noticed a car from outside the village in weeks.'

Messier arrived a few minutes later, greeted them, and put on the desk the backpack he carried on his right shoulder. He was only twenty-three. Having joined the crime squad six months before, he was the junior member of the team. Ferber liked him, and disregarded his casual clothes, generally tracksuit bottoms, sweatshirt or canvas jacket, that went quite badly with his angular, austere face which was almost never crossed by a smile; and if he occasionally advised him to change the general design of his clothing, he did so in a friendly way. Messier went to get himself a Diet Coke from the machine before giving them the results of his investigations. His features were more drawn than usual; he looked like he hadn't slept all night.

'As for the mobile, there was no problem,' he announced, 'it didn't even have a code. But that wasn't very interesting either. Some conversations with his publisher, with the guy who was to deliver him fuel, another who was to install some double glazing . . . only practical and professional conversations. This guy seemed to have no private life.'

Messier's astonishment was, in a sense, incongruous: a statement of his own phone conversations would have given almost identical results. But he didn't, it's true, intend to get murdered; and it's always supposed that the victim of a murder has something in his life that justifies and explains it; that something interesting is happening or has happened, at least in some obscure corner of his life.

'As for the computer, that was something else,' he went on. 'Already there were two consecutive passwords, passwords without capitals, and rare punctuation marks . . . Then, all the files were encrypted – a serious code, SSL Double Layer, 128 bits. In short, I couldn't do anything, I've sent it to the Investigation Brigade for IT Fraud. What was this guy – paranoid?'

'He was a writer,' said Ferber. 'He maybe wanted to protect his work, to keep it from being pirated.'

'Yeah,' said Messier, who didn't look convinced. 'That level of protection rather makes me think of a guy who exchanges paedophile videos.'

'It's not incompatible,' Jasselin observed with common sense. This innocuous remark ended up dampening the atmosphere of the meeting by emphasising the deplorable uncertainty that surrounded this murder. They possessed, they had to admit, absolutely nothing: no obvious motive, no witness, not a single lead. It threatened to be one of those difficult cases, characterised by an empty file, which sometimes takes years to be solved – if at all – and owes its solution only to pure chance, a repeat murderer arrested for another crime and who, in the course of his statement, confesses to an extra murder.

Things got a little better with the arrival of Aurélie. She was a pretty girl, with curly hair and a face spotted with freckles. Jasselin found her a bit scatterbrained, lacking in rigour. You couldn't count on her 100 per cent for tasks demanding precision; but she was dynamic, and of inexhaustible good humour, which is precious in a team. She had just received the first conclusions of the criminal records office. She began by handing Jasselin a thick file. 'The photos you asked for . . .' There were about fifty A4 prints on glossy paper. Each represented a rectangle of the living room floor where the murder had taken place, of basically a square metre. The photographs were clear and well exposed, devoid of shadow, taken from practically directly above. They overlapped only very slightly, and put together they faithfully recreated the floor of the room. She had also received some preliminary conclusions on the weapon used for the beheading of the man and the dog, which had been exceptionally clean and precise: there had been almost no projections of blood, though the sofa and the entire zone should have been spattered. The murderer had proceeded with a very particular tool, a laser cutter, a sort of cheese wire where the role of the wire was played by an argon laser that severed limbs while cauterising the wound as it went on. This equipment, which cost tens of thousands of euros, could be found only in the surgery departments of hospitals, where it was used for radical amputations. In fact, all the cutting up of the body had prob-ably, given the precision and the cleanness of the incisions, been carried out with professional surgical tools.

Some appreciative murmurs went around the office. 'That puts us on the trail of a murderer belonging to the medical world?' suggested Lartigue.

'Maybe,' said Ferber. 'Anyway, we'll have to check with the hospi-tals to see if any equipment of this kind is missing; although, of course, the murderer could just have borrowed it for a few days.'

'What hospitals?' asked Aurélie.

'All French hospitals, to begin with. And, of course, the clinics as well. We'll also have to check with the manufacturer to see if they've made an unusual sale in the last few years. I guess there aren't that many manufacturers of this kind of equipment?'

'Just one. One for the whole world. It's a Danish company.'

Michel Khoury, who had just arrived, was briefed. Of Lebanese origin he was the same age as Ferber. Chubby and well turned-out, he physically was as different from Ferber as could be; but he shared with him that quality, so rare among policemen, of *inspiring trust* and, with that, of effortlessly drawing out the most intimate secrets. That very morning, he had dealt with informing and questioning those close to the victim.

'Well, if you can say they were close.' he added. 'You could say that he was very much alone. Divorced twice, with a child he never saw. For more than ten years, he had had no contact with anyone in his family. No love affairs either. Perhaps we'll learn some things by going through his phone conversations, but for the moment I've found only two names: Teresa Cremisi, his publisher, and Frédéric Beigbeder, another writer. And what's more: I had Beigbeder on the phone this morning, he seemed devastated, sincerely I think, but he nevertheless told me that they hadn't seen each other for two years. Curiously, he and his publisher repeated the same thing: he had lots of enemies. I'm meeting them this afternoon, and maybe I'll learn more about that.'

'Lots of enemies . . .' Jasselin interjected pensively. 'That's interesting: generally victims have no enemies, and you get the impression they were loved by everyone . . . We'll have to go to his funeral. I know that's not done very often, but sometimes you can learn things there. Friends come to the funeral, but sometimes enemies too. They seem to take a sort of pleasure in it.'

'By the way,' remarked Ferber, 'do we not know what he died of? What killed him exactly?'

'No,' replied Aurélie. 'We'll have to wait . . . for them to perform an autopsy on the pieces.'

'The beheading couldn't have taken place when he was alive?'

'Surely not. It's a slow operation, which can take an hour.' She shuddered a little, and shook herself.

They broke up immediately afterwards to get on with their tasks, and Ferber and Jasselin found themselves alone in the office. The meeting was ending better than it had begun; they each had things to do; without really having a lead yet, they at least had some directions for the investigation.

'Nothing has come out in the press,' Ferber remarked. 'No one knows the situation.'

'No,' replied Jasselin, looking at a barge going down the Seine. 'It's funny, I thought that would happen right away.'

30

That did happen the following day. AUTHOR MICHEL HOUELLEBECQ SAVAGELY MURDERED, was the headline in *Le Parisien*, which devoted half a column to the news, though quite uninformed. The other papers gave it almost the same amount of space, without giving more details, mainly just repeating the communiqué from the prosecutor in Montargis. None of them, it seemed, had sent a reporter to the spot. A little later the declarations of different personalities, including the Minister of Culture, were printed: all declared themselves 'shattered', or at least 'deeply saddened', and saluted the memory of 'an immense creator, who would forever remain present in our memories'. In short it was a classic celebrity death, with its consensual chatter and its appropriate inanities, none of which were of much help.

Michel Khoury came back disappointed from his rendezvous with Teresa Cremisi and Frédéric Beigbeder. The sincerity of their sadness, according to him, was in no doubt. Jasselin had always been astounded by the calm assurance with which Khoury asserted things, which in his view belonged to the eminently complex and uncertain domain of human psychology. 'She really liked him,' he said, or 'the sincerity of their sadness is in no doubt', and he said that completely as if he was relating experimental, observable facts; the strangest thing was that the rest of the investigation generally proved him right. 'I know human beings,' he had told Jasselin once, in the same tone in which one would say 'I know cats' or 'I know computers'.

That said, neither of these witnesses had anything useful to tell him. Houellebecq had lots of enemies, they had repeated, people had shown themselves to be unjustly aggressive and cruel towards him; when asked for a more precise list of them, Teresa Cremisi, impatiently shrugging her shoulders, offered to send him a press file. But, when asked if one of these enemies could have murdered him, they both replied in the negative. Expressing herself with exaggerated clarity, a little like the way you address a madman, Teresa Cremisi had explained to him that you were dealing with *literary* enemies, who expressed their hatred on Internet sites, in newspaper or magazine articles and, in the worst case, books, but that none of them would have been capable of committing physical murder. Less for moral reasons, she went on with notable bitterness, than because they would simply not have had the guts. No, she concluded, it was not (and he had the impression that she had almost said 'unfortunately not') in the literary milieu that you had to look for the culprit.

As for Beigbeder, he had said almost the same thing. 'I have complete trust in my country's police . . .' he began by saying, before laughing out loud, as if he had just made an excellent joke. But Khoury hadn't held this against him; the author was visibly tense, lost, completely destabilised by the sudden death. He then added that Houellebecq had as enemies 'almost all the arseholes on the Parisian scene'. When pushed by Khoury, he had cited journalists on the site nouvelobs.com, while pointing out that, if they currently rejoiced at his death, none of them seemed to him capable of taking the slightest personal risk. 'Can you imagine Didier Jacob driving through a red light? Even on a bike, he wouldn't dare,' the author of *A French Novel* had concluded, visibly upset.

In short, Jasselin concluded as he put the two statements into a yellow folder, you were dealing with an ordinary professional milieu, with its ordinary jealousies and rivalries. He put the folder at the back of the 'Statements' file, aware that he was at the same time closing the *literary milieu* part of the investigation, and that he would doubtless never again be in contact with the *literary milieu*. He was painfully aware, too, that the investigation wasn't going very far. The conclusions of the criminal records office had just arrived: both man and dog had been killed with a Sigsauer M-45, in both cases with a single bullet, shot in the heart, from close range; the gun was fitted with a silencer. They had first been knocked unconscious with a long, blunt object – something like a baseball bat. A precise crime, committed without needless violence. The cutting up and laceration of their bodies had happened afterwards. All this took, and the investigators had performed a rapid simulation to arrive at this figure, a little over seven hours. The death had occurred three days before the body was discovered. Therefore the murder had taken place on a Saturday, probably in the middle of the day.

Examination of the victim's phone communications, which, in accordance with the law, the operator had kept for a full year, had brought nothing. Houellebecq had, indeed, phoned very little during that period: ninety-three calls in total, not one of which was of an even slightly personal nature.

31

The funeral had been arranged for the following Monday. On this subject the writer had left extremely precise instructions, which he had put in his will, accompanied by the necessary sum. He did not wish to be cremated, but very classically buried. 'I want the worms to free my skeleton,' he added, allowing himself a personal note in an otherwise very official text. 'I have always had excellent relations with my skeleton, and I am delighted that it can free itself from its straitjacket of flesh.' He wanted to be buried in the cemetery of Montparnasse, and had even bought the plot in advance, which by chance was a few metres away from that of Emmanuel Bove.

Jasselin and Ferber were both *quite good* at funerals. Often dressed in sombre colours, slightly emaciated, and with a naturally pale complexion, Ferber had no difficulty in putting on the sadness and gravitas required in these circumstances; as for Jasselin, his exhausted, resigned attitude of a man who knows life, and no longer has any illusions about it, was also completely appropriate. They had, in fact, already attended together quite a few funerals, sometimes of victims, more often of colleagues: some who had committed suicide, others who had died in the course of duty – and the latter was the most impressive kind: there was, generally, the award of a medal which was solemnly pinned to the coffin, and the presence of a high-ranking official or even the minister; in short, with all the honours of the Republic.

They met at ten in the police station of the 6th arrondissement; through the windows of the reception rooms of the town hall, which had been opened to them for the occasion, there was a very good view onto the place Saint-Sulpice. It had been discovered, to everyone's surprise, that the author of *Atomised*, who throughout his life had displayed an intransigent atheism, had very discreetly been baptised, in a church in Courtenay, six months before. This news drew the ecclesiastical authorities out of a painful uncertainty: for obvious media reasons, they did not want to be kept away from the funerals of personalities; but the regular progress of atheism, the steady fall in the rate of baptism and even baptisms of pure convenience, and the rigid perpetuation of their rules led them more and more often to this disheartening solution.

Alerted by email, the cardinal archbishop of Paris enthusiastically gave his agreement to a Mass, which would take place at eleven. He himself wrote the homily, which emphasised the universal human value of the novelist's work and recalled only very discreetly, as a coda, his secret baptism in the church in Courtenay. The whole ceremony, with the communion and the other fundamentals, was to last about an hour; it was therefore at about midday that Houellebecq would be *led to his last resting place.*

There too, Ferber informed him, he had left very precise instruct-ions, going as far as designing his gravestone: a simple black basalt tombstone, at ground level; he insisted on the fact that it was not to be raised at all, even by a few centimetres. The tombstone carried his name, without dates or any other facts, and the design of a Möbius strip. He'd had it made before his death, by a Parisian marble mason, and had personally overseen the work.

'So,' Jasselin remarked, 'he didn't think he was a piece of shit.'

'He was right,' Ferber replied softly. 'He wasn't a bad writer, you know . . .'

Jasselin immediately felt ashamed of his remark, formulated without any real reason. What Houellebecq had done for himself was no more, and even rather less, than what would have been done by any notable of the nineteenth century, or any minor nobleman of previous centuries. Indeed, when he thought about it, he realised that he totally disapproved of the modest, modern trend, consisting of having yourself cremated and your ashes scattered somewhere in the heart of the countryside, as if to show more clearly that you were returning to its bosom and mixing again with the elements. And even in the case of his dog, who died five years before, he'd made a point of burying it – placing next to its little corpse, at the moment of burial, a toy he'd particularly liked – and erecting a modest monument to it, in the garden of his parents' house, in Brittany, where his father himself had died the previous year, and that he had chosen not to sell, with the idea perhaps that they, he and Hélène, would go and spend their retirement there. Man *was not a part of* nature, he had raised himself above nature, and the dog, since its domestication, had also raised itself above it, that's what he thought in his heart of hearts. And the more he thought about it the more it seemed to him *impious*, even though he didn't believe in God, the more it seemed to him in some way *anthropologically impious* to scatter the ashes of a human being on the fields, the rivers or the sea, or even, as he remembered had been done by the clown Alain Gillot-Pétré, who had been considered in his time as having *given a flush of youth* to weather presenting on television, in the eye of a cyclone. A human being had a conscience, a unique, individual and irreplaceable conscience, and thus deserved a monument, a stele, or at least an inscription – well, something which asserts and bears witness to his existence for future centuries, that's what Jasselin truly believed.

'They're coming,' Ferber said softly, drawing him out of his meditation. Indeed, although it was only half past ten, about thirty people had already gathered in front of the entrance to the church. Who could they be? Some anonymous people, readers of Houellebecq probably. It could happen, mainly in the case of murders committed for revenge, that the criminal would come and attend his victim's funeral. He didn't believe it was the case here, but he had nonetheless arranged for two photographers, two men from the criminal records office who had taken up position in a flat in the rue Froidaux, equipped with cameras and telescopic lenses.

Ten minutes later, he saw Teresa Cremisi and Frédéric Beigbeder arrive on foot. They caught sight of each other and embraced.

With her Oriental physique, the publisher could have been one of those hired mourners who were until very recently employed at certain Mediterranean funerals; and Beigbeder seemed deep in particularly dark thoughts. In fact, although the author of *A French Novel* was only fifty-one at the time, and it was undoubtedly one of the first funerals he'd had the occasion to attend for someone of his generation, he had to think that it was far from being the last; that, increasingly, phone conversations with his friends would no longer start with the expression: 'What are you doing tonight?' but rather with: 'Guess who died.'

Discreetly, Jasselin and Ferber left the town hall and came to mingle with the group. About fifty people had now gathered. At five to eleven, the hearse drew up in front of the church – a simple black van from the municipal funeral directors. When the two employees took out the coffin, a murmur of consternation and horror went through the crowd. The investigators from the criminal records office had had a trying task gathering together the rags of skin scattered at the crime scene, grouping them together in hermetically sealed plastic bags which they had sent, with the intact head, to Paris. Once the examinations were finished, all of it formed only a small compact pile, of a volume far inferior to that of an ordinary human corpse, and the employees of the municipal funeral service had judged it right to use a child's coffin, one metre twenty long. This will to rationality was perhaps praiseworthy in principle, but the effect it had, when the two employees took the coffin out onto the church steps, was absolutely awful. Jasselin heard Ferber stifle a gulp of sorrow, and he himself, as hardened as he was, had a heavy heart; several people present had broken down in tears.

As usual, the Mass itself was for Jasselin a moment of total boredom. He had lost all contact with the Catholic faith at the age of ten and, despite the great number of funerals he had attended, he had never succeeded in returning to it. Basically he understood nothing about it, he did not even see exactly what the priest wanted to talk about; there were mentions of Jerusalem which seemed to him irrelevant, but which must have had a symbolic meaning, he thought. However he did feel that the rite seemed *appropriate*, that the promises concerning a future life were in this case obviously welcome. The intervention of the Church was basically much more legitimate in the case of a funeral than in that of a birth, or a marriage. There it was perfectly in its element; it had *something to say* about death, whereas – about love this was more doubtful.

At a funeral, the close members of the family usually stand by the coffin to receive condolences; but here there was no family. Once Mass had been said, the two employees again took the little coffin – once more, a shiver of sadness ran through Jasselin – and put it back in the van. To his great surprise, about fifty people were waiting on the steps, for them to leave the church – probably those readers of Houellebecq who were allergic to any religious ceremony.

Nothing special had been put in place, no blocking of the streets, no traffic control, so the hearse left directly for Montparnasse cemetery, and it was on the pavements that about a hundred people made the same journey, along the Jardin du Luxembourg, through the rue Guynemer, then taking the rue Vavin, the rue Bréa, for a moment going up the boulevard Raspail before cutting through the rue Huyghens. Jasselin and Ferber had joined them. There were people of all ages and all backgrounds, most often alone, sometimes in couples; basically people that nothing in particular seemed to unite, in whom no common trait could be discerned, and Jasselin suddenly had the certainty that they were wasting their time. They were readers of Houellebecq and that was all. It was implausible that anyone involved in the murder would be among them. Too bad, he thought; it was at least a pleasant walk; weather was keeping fine in the Paris region, the sky was a deep, almost winter blue.

Probably briefed by the priest, the gravediggers had waited for them to start shovelling. In front of the grave, Jasselin's enthusiasm for funerals grew again, to the point where he took the firm and definitive decision to be buried himself, and to phone his solicitor the following day and have this made explicit in his will. The first spadefuls of earth fell on the coffin. A lone woman, aged about thirty, threw a white rose – they're good all the same, women, he said to himself. They think of things that men don't have a clue about. In a cremation there are always noises of machinery, the gas burners which make a terrifying din, while here the silence was almost total, troubled only by the reassuring sound of the spadefuls of earth landing on the wood, spreading out gently on the surface of the coffin. At the centre of the cemetery, the noise of the traffic was almost imperceptible. As the earth generally filled the grave, the noise became more muffled and dull; then the tombstone was laid.

32

He received the photos the following day, mid-morning. The investigators from the criminal records office might well have annoyed Jasselin with their arrogance, but he had to acknowledge that they generally provided excellent work. The pictures were clear, well lit, in excellent definition despite the distance, and you could recognise perfectly the features of each of the people who had bothered to go to the writer's funeral. The prints were accompanied by a memory stick containing the photos in digital form. He immediately sent this to the Investigation Brigade by internal mail, with a note asking them to check them against databases with photos of criminals; they were now equipped with face-recognition software which allowed them to carry out the operation in a few minutes. He didn't hold out much hope, but you had to at least try.

He got the results early that evening, when he was preparing to return home; they were, as he expected, negative. At the same time, the Investigation Brigade had added a summary of about thirty pages concerning the contents of Houellebecq's computer – whose codes they had finally succeeded in breaking. He took it with him to study in peace at home.

He was greeted by the yappings of Michou, who leapt around for about a quarter of an hour, and by the aroma of cod *à la galicienne* – Hélène tried to vary the flavours, passing from Burgundy to Alsatian, from Provençal to South-Western; she was also good at Italian, Turkish and Moroccan, and had just joined a workshop initiating her to Far Eastern dishes that was organised by the municipality of the 5th arrondissement. He came over to kiss her; she had put on a pretty silk dress. 'It's ready in ten minutes, if you like,' she said. She looked relaxed, happy, as she always did when she didn't have to go into the university – the All Saints' Day holidays had just begun. Hélène's interest in economics had waned considerably over the years. More and more, the theories which tried to explain economic phenomena, to predict their developments, appeared almost equally inconsistent and random. She was more and more tempted to liken them to pure and simple charlatanism; it was even surprising, she occasionally thought, that they gave a Nobel Prize for economics, as if this discipline could boast of the same methodological seriousness, the same intellectual rigour as chemistry, or physics. And her interest in teaching had also waned considerably. On the whole, young people no longer interested her much. Her students were at such a terrifyingly low intellectual level that, sometimes, you had to wonder what had pushed them into studying in the first place. The only reply, she knew in her heart of hearts, was that they wanted to make money, as much money as possible; aside from a few short-term humanitarian fads, that was the only thing that really got them going. Her professional life could thus be summarised as teaching contradictory absurdities to social-climbing cretins, even if she avoided formulating it to herself in such stark terms. She had planned to take early retirement as soon as Jean-Pierre left the crime squad – he was not in the same state of mind and he still liked his job just as much. Evil and crime appeared to him to be subjects just as urgent and essential as when he had started, twenty-eight years before.

He put on the television: it was time for the news. Michou jumped up at his side on the sofa. After the description of a particularly deadly bomb attack by Palestinian that bombers in Hebron, the presenter moved on to the crisis that had been shaking the financial markets for several days, and which threatened, according to some experts, to be even worse than that of 2008; on the whole, a very typical broadcast. He was about to switch channels when Hélène, leaving her kitchen, came to sit on the arm of the sofa. He put down the remote; this was her domain after all, he thought, so she was perhaps slightly interested.

After a tour of the main financial markets, the programme

returned to an expert on the panel. Hélène listened to him closely, an undefinable smile on her lips. Jasselin looked at her breasts through the neckline of the dress: certainly they were siliconed breasts, the implants had been done ten years before, but it was a success, the surgeon had done a good job. Jasselin was completely in favour of siliconed breasts, which show in the woman a certain *erotic goodwill*, which is, if truth be told, the most important thing in the world on the erotic level, and delays by ten or even twenty years the disappearance of the couple's sex life. And then there were marvels, small miracles: at the swimming pool, during their only stay in a HotelClub, which they had spent in the Dominican Republic (Michel, their first bichon, almost didn't forgive them, and they vowed they would never repeat the experience, unless they found a HotelClub that admitted dogs – but, alas, he never found one), in short, during this sojourn, he had marvelled at Hélène's breasts, as she lay on her back by the swimming pool, pointing skywards in an audacious negation of gravity.

Siliconed breasts are ridiculous when the woman's face is atrociously wrinkled and when the rest of her body degraded, flabby, and fat. But this was not the case with Hélène – far from it. Her body had remained slim, her buttocks firm, scarcely drooping, and her thick and curly auburn hair still gracefully cascaded upon her rounded shoulders. She was a very beautiful woman, and he had been very lucky indeed.

In the long term, of course, any siliconed breast becomes ridiculous. But in the long term you no longer think about these things. You think of cervical cancer, of a haemorrhage of the aorta, and other similar subjects. You also think of the transmission of inheritance, of sharing out property among presumptive heirs. You have concerns more serious than siliconed breasts; but they hadn't yet got there, he thought, not completely. They would perhaps make love that evening (or rather tomorrow morning, he preferred the morning, that put him in a good mood for the rest of the day). You could say that they *still had some beautiful years* ahead of them.

* * *

The economics item had just ended, and they now passed on to the presentation of a romantic comedy which was being released in France the following day. 'Did you hear what that expert said?' asked Hélène. 'Did you see his forecasts?' No, in fact he had listened to nothing at all; he'd just looked at her breasts, but he chose not to interrupt her.

'In a week's time, we'll see that all his forecasts were wrong. They'll call another expert, even the same one, and he'll make new forecasts, with the same self-assurance . . .' She was shaking her head, upset, even indignant. 'How can a discipline that can't even manage to make verifiable forecasts be considered a science?'

Jasselin hadn't read Popper, he had no valid reply to make to her; he simply put his hand on her thigh. She smiled at him and said: 'It'll be ready in a second,' and returned to her cooking, but touched on the subject again during the meal. Crime, she told him, seemed to her a deeply human act, linked of course to the darkest zones of the human, but human all the same. Art, to take another example, was linked to everything: to dark zones, luminous zones and intermediary zones. The economy was linked to almost nothing, except to what was most machine-like, predictable and mechanical in the human being. Not only was it not a science, but it wasn't an art. It was, after all is said and done, almost nothing at all.

He didn't agree, and he told her so. Having dealt with criminals for a long time, he could tell her that they were certainly the most mechanical and predictable individuals you could imagine. In almost all cases they killed for money, and uniquely for money; besides, it was what usually made them so easy to catch. On the contrary, almost no one, ever, worked *uniquely* for money. There were always other motivations: the interest you had in your work, the esteem that could come with it, relations of sympathy with your colleagues . . . And almost no one had entirely rational buying behaviour either. It was probably this fundamental uncertainty surrounding the motivations of both producers and consumers which made economic theories so hazardous and, at the end of the day, so false, while criminal detection could be approached as a science, or at least as a rational discipline. The existence of irrational economic agents had always been the *dark side*, the secret fault in any economic theory. Even if she had distanced herself a lot from her work, economic theory still represented her contribution to the household budget and her status at the university; symbolic benefits, for the most part. Jean-Pierre was right: nor did she herself behave in any way as a *rational economic agent*. She relaxed on the sofa, and looked at her little dog who was resting on its back, belly in the air, ecstatic, in the near left corner of the living-room carpet.

Later that evening, Jasselin looked again at the Investigation Brigade's summary of the contents of the victim's computer. Their first remark was that Houellebecq, despite what he had repeated in numerous interviews, was still writing; he was even writing a lot. That said, what he was writing was quite strange: it resembled poetry, or political proclamations, and Jasselin understood almost nothing of the extracts reproduced in the report. We'll have to send all that to the publisher, he thought.

The rest of the computer didn't contain much that was useful. Houellebecq used the 'Address Book' function of his Mac. The content of his address book was reproduced in its entirety, and it was pathetic: there were, in total, twenty-three names, of which twelve were of workmen, doctors and other providers of services. He also used the 'Diary' function and that wasn't any better; the notes were typically along the lines of 'bin bags' or 'fuel delivery'. When all was said and done, he had rarely seen someone with such an awful fucking life. Even his Internet Explorer revealed nothing very exciting. He visited no paedophile or even porno-graphic sites; his most daring connections concerned sites for female erotic lingerie, such as Beautiful and Sexy or Liberette.com. So, the poor little old man contented himself with leering at girls in tight miniskirts or transparent T-shirts – Jasselin was almost ashamed to have read that page. The crime, undoubtedly, wasn't going to be easy to solve. It is their vices that lead men to their murders, their vices or their money. Money Houellebecq had, although less than you might have thought, but nothing, apparently, had been stolen – they had even found his chequebook, credit card and a wallet containing several hundred euros in the house. He fell asleep when he tried to reread Houellebecq's political proclamations, as if he hoped to find in them an explanation or a meaning.

33

The following day, they went through the eleven names in the address book that were of a personal nature. Apart from Teresa Cremisi and Frédéric Beigbeder, whom they had already questioned, the nine other people were women.

If SMSs are kept by operators for only a year, there is no limit concerning emails, especially when the user has chosen, as was the case with Houellebecq, to store them not on his personal computer but in a disk space allocated by his provider; in this case, even a change of equipment allows you to keep your messages. On the server me.com, Houellebecq had a personal storage space of forty gigaoctets; at the rate of his current exchanges, he would have needed seven thousand years to exhaust it.

There is a real legal fuzziness concerning the status of emails, as to whether they qualify as private correspondence or not. Without delay, Jasselin put the whole team onto reading Houellebecq's emails, all the more so as they would soon have to go through letters rogatory: an examining magistrate would have to be appointed, and if prosecutors and their deputies generally showed themselves to be easy-going, examining magistrates could be a formidable pain in the arse, even for murder investigations.

Working almost twenty hours per day – if Houellebecq had a very reduced Internet correspondence immediately before his death, it had been, at other times, much more substantial, and at certain periods, especially just after the publication of a book, he had received an average of thirty emails per day – the team succeeded by the following Thursday in locating the nine women. The geographical variety was impressive: a Spanish woman, a Russian, a Chinese, a Czech, two Germans – but three French women all the same. Jasselin then remembered that he was dealing with an author who had been translated throughout the world.

'That looks pretty good,' he told Lartigue, who had just finished drawing up the list. He said it rather to put his mind at rest, much like you'd make a predictable joke; in reality, he couldn't muster a drop of envy for the writer. They were all former mistresses, the nature of their exchanges left no doubt – sometimes mistresses from very long ago, the relationship in certain cases going back more than thirty years.

These women turned out to be easy to contact: with all of them he exchanged anodyne and gentle emails, describing the small or great sadnesses of their lives, occasionally also their joys.

The three French women immediately agreed to come to the Quai des Orfèvres – one of them, however, lived in Perpignan, the second in Bordeaux, and the third in Orléans. As for the foreign women, they didn't say no, but just asked for a bit more time to get themselves organised.

Jasselin and Ferber received them separately in order to compare their impressions; and their impressions were remarkably identical. All of these women still felt a great tenderness for Houellebecq. 'We wrote by email quite often,' they said, though Jasselin abstained from saying that he had already read them. Never was the possibility of another meeting considered, but you felt that, if one were necessary, they would have agreed to it. It was terrifying, he thought, absolutely terrifying: women do not forget their *exes*, that's what appeared evident. Hélène herself had had exes, even though he'd met her young there had still been exes. What would happen if their paths crossed again? It's a disadvantage of police investigations: you find yourself confronted, despite yourself, with difficult personal problems. These women had known Houellebecq, some of them very well; Jasselin felt that they wouldn't say any more about it; he expected it, as women remain very discreet about these matters, even if they are no longer in love the memory of their love remains infinitely precious to them. But in any case, they had not seen him for years, some not in decades. The very idea that they would have thought of murdering him, or known someone likely to think of murdering him, was grotesque.

A jealous husband or lover after so many years' separation? He didn't believe it for a second. When you know that your wife has had exes, and you have the misfortune of being jealous, you also know that there would be no point in killing them – that would only put salt in the wound. Well, all the same, he was going to put someone in the team onto it – without forcing it, just part-time. He didn't believe it, certainly; but he also knew that, sometimes, you get it wrong. That said, when Ferber asked him: 'Do we go any further with the foreign women? Of course that will cost money, we'll have to send people, but we're justified in doing it, after all it's a case of murder,' he replied without hesitation that no, it wasn't worth it. At that moment he was in his office and randomly shuffling, as he must have done dozens of times in the last fortnight, photos of the crime scene floor – branching, interweaving traces of blood – and those of the people present at the writer's funeral – technically impeccable close-ups of human beings with sad faces.

'You look worried, Jean-Pierre . . .' remarked Ferber.

'Yes, I think we're floundering, and I no longer know what to do next. Take a seat, Christian.'

Ferber looked for a moment at his superior who continued to mechanically shuffle the photos, without looking at them in detail, a bit like a pack of cards.

'What are you looking for in these photos, exactly?'

'I don't know. I feel there's something here, but I couldn't tell you what.'

'We might try and consult Lorrain.'

'Isn't he retired?'

'More or less. I don't understand his exact status, but he comes in a few hours every week. In any case, he hasn't been replaced.'

Guillaume Lorrain was just a simple crime squad officer, but he possessed that strange aptitude of having a perfect, photographic visual memory: he just had to see a photograph of someone, even if it was only in a newspaper, to recognise it ten or twenty years later. He was the one they called on before the appearance of the Visio software, which allowed instantaneous cross-referencing with the crime database; but quite obviously his particular gift was not restricted to offenders, but to anyone he might, in certain circumstances, have seen in a photo.

They visited him in his office the following Friday. He was a stocky man with grey hair. Level-headed and staid, he gave the impression of having spent his entire life in an office – which was more or less the case. As soon as his strange aptitude had been spotted, he had immediately been transferred to the crime squad, and relieved of all other tasks.

Jasselin explained what he expected of him. He immediately went to work, examining one by one the photographs taken on the day of the funeral. Occasionally he passed very quickly over a picture; other times he stared at it, meticulously, for almost a minute, before putting it to one side. His concentration was terrifying: how did his brain work? It was strange to watch.

After twenty minutes, he seized a photo and began to sway to and fro. 'I've seen him . . . I've seen this guy somewhere,' he said in an almost inaudible voice. Jasselin started nervously, but refrained from interrupting him. Lorrain continued swaying to and fro for a time that seemed to him very long, endlessly repeating in a low voice: 'I've seen him . . . I've seen him . . .' like some kind of personal mantra, and all of a sudden he stopped rocking, and handed Jasselin the picture of a man aged about forty with delicate features, a very pale complexion, and black mid-length hair.

'Who is it?' asked Jasselin.

'Jed Martin. I'm sure that's his name. Where I saw the photo, I can't guarantee 100 per cent, but it seems it was in *Le Parisien*, announcing the opening of an exhibition. This guy must be linked to the art world, in one way or another.'

34

The death of Houellebecq had surprised Jed, as he was expecting instead some sad news concerning his father any day now. Contrary to all his habits, he'd phoned Jed at the end of September to ask him to come and see him. He was now in a nursing home in Vésinet, set in a big Napoleon III manor, much more chic and expensive than the previous one, a sort of elegant high-tech dying room. The apartments were spacious, with a bedroom and a salon, the residents had a big LCD television with a cable and satellite subscription, a DVD player and a broadband Internet connection. There was a park with a little lake where ducks swam, and well-traced avenues of trees where does gambolled. They could even, if they wished, cultivate a corner of the garden which was reserved for them, grow vegetables and flowers – but few requested this. Jed had had to fight to get him to accept this change. He had insisted numerous times that there was no longer any point in making sordid little savings – to make him understand that, now, he was *rich*. Obviously, the establishment only accepted people who, in their working lives, belonged to the highest levels of the French bourgeoisie; 'stuck-up snobs', Jed's father, who remained obscurely proud of his modest origins, had once said.

Jed did not understand, at first, why his father had asked him to come over. After a short walk in the park – he now had difficulty walking – they sat down in a room that aspired to be like an English club, with its wood panelling and leather armchairs, and where they could order a coffee. It was brought in a silver cafetière, with cream and a plate of sweets. The room was empty, with the exception of a very old man sitting alone in front of a cup of hot chocolate, who was nodding his head and seemed on the verge of dozing off. His white hair was long and curly and he was wearing a light suit, with a silk cravat around his neck; he made you think of an over-the-hill opera singer – an operetta singer for example, who would have had his greatest triumphs at the festival of Lamalou-les-Bains. Well, you would have imagined him in some refuge for destitute artists rather than in a home like this, which did not have its equivalent in France, even on the Côte d'Azur: you had to go to Monaco or Switzerland to find something as good.

Jed's father silently studied the handsome old man, before addressing his son. 'He's lucky,' he said finally. 'He has a very rare orphan disease – a demeleumaiosis, or something like that. He doesn't suffer at all. He's permanently exhausted, always falls asleep, even at mealtimes; when he goes for a walk, after a few dozen metres he sits down on a bench and falls asleep. He sleeps a little more every day, and one day he won't ever wake up. Right till the end, there are some people who have all the luck.'

He turned to his son, and looked him straight in the eyes. 'It seemed better for me to warn you, and I couldn't see myself speaking to you about it on the phone. I've contacted an organisation in Switzerland. I've decided to be euthanised.'

Jed didn't react immediately, leaving his father time to develop his argument, which boiled down to the fact that he was sick of being alive.

'Are you not all right here?' his son finally asked, his voice quavering.

Yes, he was all right here, he couldn't have been better, but what he had to get into his head was that he could no longer be all right *anywhere*, that he couldn't be all right *in life generally* (he was starting to get worked up, his flow of words became loud and almost choleric, but anyway the old singer had sunk into sleep and everything was calm in the room). If he was to keep on going they would have to change his artificial anus, well, he thought he'd had enough of that joke. And what's more he felt pain. He couldn't bear it any longer, he was suffering too much.

'Don't they give you morphine?' asked Jed in astonishment.

Oh yes, they gave him morphine, as much as he wanted obviously – they preferred the residents to be quiet – but was it a life, to be constantly under the influence of morphine?

In truth, Jed thought yes, that it was almost even an enviable life, without worries, responsibilities, desires or fears, close to the life of plants, where you could enjoy the moderate caress of the sun and the breeze. However, he suspected that his father would have difficulty sharing this point of view. He was a former chief executive, an active man. Those people often have problems with drugs, he said to himself.

'And, besides, what's it got to do with you?' his father said aggressively (Jed then realised that he'd stopped listening, for some time already, to the old man's recriminations). He hesitated and dithered before replying that yes, all the same, in some sense, he had the impression that it had something to do with him. 'Already, to be a child of a suicide is not much fun,' he added. His father was visibly shaken, and hunched up before violently replying: 'That's got nothing to do with it!'

To have both his parents commit suicide, Jed went on without acknowledging the interruption, inevitably put you in an unstable and uncomfortable position: that of someone whose attachments to life lack solidity. He spoke at length, with an ease that in hindsight would surprise him, because, after all, he too felt only a hesitant love of life, and generally passed for someone rather reserved and sad. But he had immediately understood that the only way to influence his father was to appeal to his sense of duty; his father had always been a man of duty, and only work and duty had counted for much in his life. 'To destroy the subject of morality in his own person is tantamount to obliterating from the world, as far as he can, the existence of morality itself,' he repeated mechanically to himself without truly understanding the sentence, seduced by its plastic elegance, while making one general argument after another: the regression of civilisation that represented the generalised recourse to euthanasia, the hypocrisy and the fundamentally evil character of its most illustrious supporters, the moral superiority of palliative care, etc.

When he left the residence at about five, the light was already fading, coloured with magnificent golden reflections. Sparrows were hopping around on the lawn that was sparkling with frost. Clouds oscillating between purple and scarlet made strange, torn forms in the direction of the setting sun. It was impossible, that evening, to deny the world had a certain beauty. Was his father sensitive to these things? He had never displayed the slightest interest in nature; but on getting older, perhaps, who knows? As for him, while visiting Houellebecq, he had noticed that he was beginning to appreciate the countryside – which, up until then, he had always been indifferent to. He clumsily pressed his father's shoulder before placing a kiss on his rough cheeks – at that precise moment he felt he'd won the match, but that very evening, and even more in the days that followed, he was filled with doubt. There would have been no point in calling his father, nor of visiting him again; on the contrary, it would have risked getting his back up. He imagined him standing on the crest of a hill, hesitating about which side to fall on. It was the last important decision he had to take in his life, and Jed feared that this time again, as he used to do when encountering a problem on a building site, he would choose to *make a clear-cut decision*.

During the following days, his worries only increased; any moment now, he expected to receive a call from the manageress of the establishment: 'Your father left for Zurich this morning at ten o'clock. He has left you a letter.' Thus, when a woman on the phone announced the death of Houellebecq, he didn't understand straight away, and thought it was a mistake. (Marylin hadn't introduced herself, and he hadn't recognised her voice. She knew nothing more than what was in the papers, but she thought it was right to phone him because she had thought – correctly in fact – that he hadn't read the papers.) And even after hanging up he still thought, for a while, that there had been some kind of mistake, because his relationship with Houellebecq was for him only starting. He had always had in his head the idea that they were destined to see each other again, many times, and perhaps to become *friends*, in so far as that term was appropriate to people like them. It's true that they hadn't seen each other since he brought the painting, at the beginning of January, and it was already the end of November. It's also true that he hadn't been the first to call, or taken the initiative of proposing a meeting, but Houellebecq was a man twenty years older, and for Jed the only privilege of age, the single and sad privilege of age, was to have earned the right to be *left alone*, and it had seemed to him during their previous encounters that Houellebecq wanted above all else to be *left alone*. He nonetheless still hoped that Houellebecq would call him, for even after their last meeting he felt he still had many things to tell him, and hear from him in response. Anyway he'd done almost nothing since the start of that year: he had taken out his camera again, without putting away his brushes and canvases. Let's just say his state of uncertainty was extreme. He hadn't even moved home, a thing which was, all the same, easy to do.

Being slightly tired on the day of the funeral, he hadn't understood much of the Mass. There was talk of sorrow, but also of hope and resurrection; well, the message delivered was confusing. In the tidy paths of Montparnasse cemetery, with their geometrical layout and calibrated gravel, things had, however, appeared absolutely clear: the relationship with Houellebecq had come to an end for reasons of *force majeure*. And the people gathered around him, none of whom he knew, seemed to share the same certainty. On thinking again of this moment he suddenly understood, with total certainty, that his father was inevitably going to persist with his lethal project, that sooner or later he was going to receive that call from the manageress, and that things could end this way, without conclusion or explanation, that the last word might never be said, that there would remain only a sense of regret, a weariness.

★   ★   ★

Something else, however, was left for him to live through, and a few days later a guy called Ferber phoned him. His voice was gentle and pleasant, not at all what he imagined from a policeman. He informed him that it would not be him but his superior, Inspector Jasselin, who would receive him at the Quai des Orfèvres.

35

Inspector Jasselin was 'in a meeting', Jed was told on arrival. He sat in a small waiting room with green plastic chairs, leafing through an old issue of *Police Forces*, before deciding to look out of the window: the view over the Pont-Neuf and the Quai de Conti, and further on to the Pont des Arts, was superb. In the winter light the Seine seemed frozen, its surface a matt grey. The dome of the Institut de France had a true grace about it, he had to agree despite himself. Obviously, giving a rounded form to a building could not be justified in any way; on the rational level, it was simply a waste of space. Modernity was perhaps an error, thought Jed for the first time in his life. A purely rhetorical question, that: modernity had ended in Western Europe some time ago.

Jasselin burst in, tearing Jed from his thoughts. He seemed tense, almost annoyed. In fact, his morning had been marked by a new disappointment: the cross-referencing of the murderer's surgery method with the files of serial killers had turned up absolutely nothing. Nowhere in Europe, or the United States, nor in Japan had anyone cut his victim into strips before spreading them out in the room; it was absolutely unprecedented. 'For once, France is on the cutting edge,' Lartigue had joked, in a pathetic attempt to lighten the mood.

'I'm sorry,' Jasselin said, 'but my office is occupied for the moment. Can I offer you a coffee? It isn't bad, just got a new machine.'

He came back two minutes later with two small plastic cups containing a coffee which was in fact excellent. It's impossible to perform serious police work, he told Jed, without a suitable coffee machine. Then he asked him to talk about his relationship with the victim. Jed recounted its history: the plan for the exhibition, the text for the catalogue, the portrait he had made of the writer . . . As he went on, he felt his interlocutor's mood darkening as he slumped back in his plastic chair.

'I see . . . So you weren't especially close,' concluded the inspector.

Yes, he could say that, agreed Jed; but he didn't really sense that Houellebecq had had what could be called *intimates*, at least in the final part of his life.

'I know, I know.' Jasselin looked completely discouraged. 'I don't know what made me hope for more . . . I think I've bothered you for nothing. Well, we can still go into my office and take down your statement.'

The surface of his work table was almost entirely covered with photos of the crime scene, which he had, for perhaps the fiftieth time, vainly spent most of his morning examining. Jed approached with curiosity, and picked up one of the photos. Jasselin tried to stifle his look of surprise.

'Forgive me,' said Jed, embarrassed. 'I don't suppose I have the right to see that.'

'Indeed, in principle it's covered by the secrecy of the investigation. But go on, feel free – maybe it will remind you of something.'

Jed examined several of the enlargements, which for Jasselin looked virtually all alike: drips, lacerations, a formless puzzle. 'It's funny . . .' he finally said. 'It looks like a Pollock, but a Pollock who would have worked almost in monochrome. In fact, he did do that, but not often.'

'Who's Pollock? Forgive my ignorance.'

'Jackson Pollock was a post-war American painter. An abstract expressionist, even a leader of that movement. He was very influenced by shamanism. He died in 1956.'

Jasselin stared at him intently, suddenly interested.

'And what are these photos?' asked Jed. 'I mean: what do they represent in reality?'

Jed's reaction surprised Jasselin by its intensity. He scarcely had the time to bring up a chair before Jed collapsed into it, trembling, and shaking with spasms. 'Don't move . . . you must drink something,' he said. He hurried into Ferber's office and came back with a bottle of Lagavulin and a glass. It is impossible to perform serious police work without a reserve of high-quality spirits, that was his conviction, but he abstained from mentioning it. Jed downed an entire glass, in long sips, before his trembling calmed down. Jasselin made himself wait, holding back his excitement.

'I know it's horrible,' he finally said. 'It's one of the most horrible crimes we've had to deal with. Do you think,' he went on carefully, 'do you think that the murderer could have been influenced by Jackson Pollock?'

Jed said nothing for a few seconds, shaking his head in disbelief, before replying: 'I don't know . . . It resembles his work, that's true. There were quite a few artists who used their bodies at the end of the twentieth century, and in fact some partisans of body art presented themselves as the heirs to Pollock. But the bodies of other people . . . There are only the Viennese actionists who crossed the limit, in the 1960s, but that didn't last long and has no influence today.'

'I know this may seem absurd,' Jasselin insisted. 'But given where we are . . . You know, I shouldn't tell you this, but the investigation is going absolutely nowhere. It's already two months since the corpse was discovered, and we're still stuck.'

'Where did it take place?'

'At his home, in the Loiret.'

'Ah yes, I should have recognised the carpet.'

'Have you been to his place? In the Loiret?'

This time Jasselin couldn't contain his excitement. He was the first person they had questioned who knew the place where Houellebecq lived. Even his publisher had never been: when they met, it was always in Paris.

'Yes, once,' Jed calmly replied. 'To give him his painting.'

Jasselin went out of his office, and called Ferber. In the corridor, he summarised what he had just learned.

'That's interesting,' said Ferber pensively. 'Truly interesting. More
than all we've had since the start, it seems.'

'How are we going to take this further?' said Jasselin.

They held an impromptu meeting, including Aurélie, Lartigue,
Michel Khoury. Messier was absent, held up by an investigation
which seemed to passionately interest him – a psychotic teenager,
a sort of otaku who had apparently found the operating procedure
for his murders on the Internet. They're beginning to lose interest
in the case, Jasselin thought sadly, they're starting to resign themselves to the eventuality of failure . . .. Proposals flew in all directions, for quite some time. None of them knew anything
whatsoever about the art world, but it was Ferber who had the
decisive idea.

'I think we should return with him to the Loiret. To the crime
scene. He'll perhaps see something that escaped us.'

Jasselin looked at his watch: it was half past two; the lunch hour
had long since passed – but, above all, that made it three hours
that the witness had been waiting, alone in his office.

When he entered the room, Jed glanced at him absent-mindedly.
He didn't seem at all bored. Sitting behind the inspector's desk, he
was closely examining the photos. 'You know,' he said finally, 'it's
just a rather mediocre imitation of Pollock. There are forms, and
drips, but the whole thing is arranged mechanically, there's no force,
no vital elan.'

Jasselin hesitated: he didn't want to get his back up. 'That's my
desk . . .' he ended up saying, unable to find the best wording. 'Oh
sorry!' Jed leapt up, giving him his seat, though he was not particularly concerned. Jasselin then explained his idea. 'No problem,' Jed
quickly replied. They arranged to leave the following day, in
Jasselin's private car. On arranging a meeting place, they noticed
they lived only a few hundred metres from each other.

'Strange guy,' thought Jasselin after he left, and, as so often in
the past, he thought of all the people who coexist in the heart

of a city without any particular reason, without any common interests or preoccupations, following incommensurate and separate trajectories, sometimes joined (more and more rarely) by sex or (more and more often) by crime. But for the first time this thought – and which fascinated him at the start of his career as a policeman, and which made him want to dig further, to know more, to go right to the heart of human relations – now aroused in him just an obscure weariness.

36

Although he knew nothing about his life, Jed was hardly surprised to see Jasselin arrive at the wheel of a Mercedes Class A. The Mercedes Class A is the ideal car for an old couple without children, who live in an urban or periurban area, yet do not hesitate to treat themselves from time to time to an escapade in a *hôtel de charme*; but it can also suit a young couple of conservative temperament – it will, then, often be their first Mercedes. An entry into the range offered by the firm with the Silver Star, it is a discreetly *different* car; the Mercedes four-door saloon Class C and the Mercedes four-door Class E are more paradigmatic. The Mercedes in general is the car preferred by those who aren't really interested in cars, who place security and comfort over driving sensations – also for those, of course, who have sufficient means. For more than fifty years – despite the impressive commercial strike force of Toyota, despite the pugnacity of Audi – the global bourgeoisie had, on the whole, remained loyal to Mercedes.

The traffic was moving freely on the motorway to the South, and both remained silent. You have to *break the ice*, thought Jasselin after half an hour, it's important to put the witness at ease, as he often repeated in his lectures at Saint-Cyr-au-Mont d'Or. Jed was completely absent, lost in his thoughts – unless, more simply, he was falling asleep. This guy intrigued him, and impressed him a little. He had to admit that his career as a policeman had allowed him to meet, in the person of *criminals*, only simplistic and evil beings, incapable of any original thought and generally almost any thought, degenerate animals which it would have been better, in their own interest as well as that of others and of any possibility of a human community, to kill on capture; at least this was – more and more often – his opinion. Well, that wasn't his business, it was up to the *judges*. His own work was to hunt the game, then bring it back to drop it at the feet of the judges, and more generally of the *French people* (they operated in its name, and this was at least the time-honoured expression). In the course of a hunt, the game dropped at the feet of the hunter is most often dead – its life ended during its capture, the explosion of a bullet fired in the appropriate place putting an end to its vital functions; sometimes, the fangs of the dogs finished the job. In the course of a police investigation, the guilty person dropped at the feet of the judges was almost always alive – which enabled France to still receive good marks in the reports on human rights regularly published by Amnesty International. The judge – subordinate to the *French people*, which he represented in general, and to which he was more precisely subordinate in the case of serious crimes involving a *jury*, which was almost always such for the cases Jasselin dealt with – was then to give a ruling on his or her fate. Various international conventions forbade (and even in the case where the *French people* had in their majority pronounced themselves in favour) putting him to death.

Once past the tollbooths of Saint-Arnoult-en-Yvelines, he proposed to Jed that they stop for a coffee. The motorway service station made an ambiguous impression on Jasselin. In some ways, it clearly reminded him of the Paris region: the choice of magazines and national dailies was vast – it would reduce rapidly as they penetrated the depths of the provinces – and the main souvenirs offered to tourists were Tour Eiffels and Sacré Coeurs available in different forms. On the other hand, it was difficult to pretend that you were in the suburbs: passing through the toll barrier, as through the limit of the last travel-card zone, symbolically marked the end of the suburbs, and the start of the regions; besides, the first *regional products* (Gâtinais honey, rabbit *rillettes*) had made their appearance. In short, this motorway service station refused to choose sides, and Jasselin didn't like that too much. However, he took a chocolate brownie to accompany his coffee, and they chose a place to sit among the hundred or so empty tables.

An opening gambit was necessary, and Jasselin coughed several times. 'You know . . .' he finally ventured, 'I'm very grateful you agreed to accompany me. You were not at all obligated to.'

'I find it normal to help the police,' Jed replied seriously.

'Oh, well . . .' Jasselin smiled, without managing to elicit from Jed an analogous reaction. 'I'm delighted by that, of course, but few of our fellow citizens think like you.'

'I believe in evil,' continued Jed in the same tone. 'I believe in guilt, and punishment.'

Jasselin's jaw dropped; he had in no way foreseen that the conversation would take this turn.

'Do you believe in the exemplary nature of sentences?' he suggested, encouragingly. An old waitress passing her mop between the tables approached them, shooting hostile stares. She seemed not only exhausted and despondent, but full of animosity towards the world in general, and twisted her mop in her bucket exactly as if that was what the world meant for her: a dubious surface covered with various dirty stains.

'I don't know,' replied Jed after some time. 'In truth, I've never asked myself that question. The sentences appear just to me because they are normal and necessary, because it's normal that the guilty man receives a punishment, so that balance is re-established, because it's necessary that evil should be punished. Why? Don't you believe they are?' he went on, slightly aggressively on seeing that Jasselin was remaining silent. 'Well, it's your profession.'

Jasselin got himself back together to explain to him that no, that was the work of the *judge*, assisted by a *jury*. This guy, he thought, would be pitiless on a jury. There's the *separation of powers*, he stressed, it's one of the bases of our constitution. Jed quickly nodded to show that he had understood, but that for him it seemed a mere detail. Jasselin considered starting a debate on the death penalty, for no precise reason, just for the pleasure of conversation, but then gave up; he had undoubtedly a lot of trouble making sense of this guy. Between them, silence fell again.

'I've also accompanied you,' Jed finally said, 'for other reasons, more personal ones. I want Houellebecq's murderer to be found, and punished. It's very important to me.'

'Yet, you weren't especially close.'

Jed uttered a sort of painful groan, and Jasselin understood that he had unintentionally touched a sensitive area. An almost obese man, dressed in a dull grey suit, passed a few metres from them, carrying a plate of chips. He looked like a technical sales representative who was nearing the end of the line. Before sitting down, he put his hand on his chest for a few moments, as if he was expecting an imminent cardiac arrest.

'The world is mediocre,' Jed finally said. 'And the person who committed this murder has increased the mediocrity in this world.'

37

On arriving in Souppes (for that was the name of the village where
the writer had lived out his last days), they thought, at almost the
same instant, that nothing had changed. Nothing, of course, had
any reason to change; the village remained stuck in its rural perfec-
tion for tourist consumption. It would remain this way for centuries
to come, with the discreet addition of a few elements of creature
comforts like Internet connections and car parks. But it could
remain so only if an intelligent species was there to look after it,
to protect it from the aggression of the elements, and the destruc-
tive voracity of plants.

The village was as deserted as ever, peacefully and as if structur-
ally deserted; it was exactly what the world would look like, thought
Jed, after the explosion of an intergalactic neutron bomb. The aliens
could penetrate the tranquil and restored streets of the small town,
and delight in its measured beauty. They would even possess a
rudimentary aesthetic sensibility; they would rapidly understand
the necessity of maintenance, and would carry out the necessary
restorations; this hypothesis was both reassuring and plausible.

Jasselin gently parked his Mercedes in front of the farm building.
Jed got out and, struck by the cold, suddenly remembered his first
visit, the dog which leapt and gambolled to greet him; he imagined
the head of the decapitated dog, the head of its decapitated master
as well, became aware of the horror of the crime and for a few
minutes regretted he had come; but then he came to his senses. He
wanted to be useful, all his life he had wanted to be useful and,
ever since he became rich, the desire had become even stronger.
Here, now, he had the opportunity to be useful in some way. It was
undeniable. He could help in the capture and elimination of a killer,
and could also help this discouraged and morose old policeman

currently standing beside him, looking slightly worried, while he remained in the winter light, motionless, trying to control his breath.

They had worked remarkably well to clean the crime scene, Jasselin thought on entering the living room, and he imagined his colleagues picking up, one by one, the scattered fragments of flesh. There were not even traces of blood on the carpet, just here and there a few faded and worn stains. Apart from that, the house hadn't changed at all; he recognised perfectly the arrangement of the furniture. He sat down on a sofa, forcing himself not to look at Jed. You had to leave the witness in peace, you had to respect his spontaneity, not obstruct the emotions, the intuitions which could come to him. You had to put yourself entirely at his service so that he would be, in his turn, at yours.

In fact, Jed had headed in the direction of a bedroom, and was preparing to visit the whole house. Jasselin regretted not having taken Ferber with him: he had a sensibility, he was a *policeman with a sensibility*, he would have known how to deal with an artist – while he himself was just an ordinary policeman, old and passionately attached to his ageing partner and his impotent little dog.

Jed continued to come and go between the rooms, regularly returning to the living room, burying himself in contemplation of the bookshelves, whose content astonished and impressed him even more than during his first visit. Then he stopped in front of Jasselin, who started and leapt up.

However, Jed's posture had nothing worrying about it; he stood upright, hands crossed behind his back, like a schoolboy preparing to recite his lesson.

'My painting is missing,' he finally said.

'Your painting? What painting?' Jasselin asked feverishly while being aware that he should have known, that he should *normally* have known, that he was no longer in complete control of his faculties. Shivers went through him; maybe he had a cold coming on, or worse.

'The painting I made of him. That I offered as a gift. It's no longer here.'

Jasselin took some time to analyse the information; the cogs of his brain were turning slowly and he felt more and more ill. He was dead tired, this case was taking it all out of him and he needed an incredible amount of time to ask the essential question, the only one worth asking: 'Was it worth any money?'

'Yes, quite a lot,' replied Jed.

'How much?'

Jed thought for a few seconds before saying: 'At this moment, my value is going up a little, not too quickly. In my view, nine hundred thousand euros.'

'What? . . . What did you say?' he almost screamed.

'Nine hundred thousand euros.'

Jasselin fell back into the sofa and remained motionless, prostrate, mumbling incomprehensible words from time to time.

'Have I helped you?' Jed asked hesitantly.

'The case is solved.' His voice betrayed discouragement, an awful sadness. 'There have already been murders for fifty thousand, ten thousand, sometimes one thousand euros. Well, nine hundred thousand euros . . .'

They left for Paris soon afterwards. Jasselin asked Jed if he could drive, as he didn't feel very well. They stopped at the same motorway service station on the way back. For no apparent reason, a white-and-red cordon isolated several tables – perhaps the obese salesman from earlier had finally succumbed to a heart attack. Jed again ordered coffee; Jasselin wanted some spirits, but they didn't sell any. He ended up discovering a bottle of red wine in the section for regional products, but they didn't have a corkscrew. He went to the toilets and entered a cubicle; with a sharp blow, he broke the neck of the bottle on the edge of the toilet seat, then returned to the cafeteria, holding his broken bottle; a little wine had spattered his shirt. All that had taken some time. Jed had got up and was daydreaming in front of the mixed salads; he finally opted for a Cheddar–turkey duo and a Sprite. Jasselin had served himself a first glass, which he downed in one swallow; slightly cheered up, he was now, more slowly, finishing his second. 'You're making me hungry,' he said. He went off to buy a wrap of Provençal flavours, and served himself a third glass of wine. At the same instant, a group of Spanish pre-teens got out of a bus and came into the cafeteria speaking very loudly; the girls were overexcited, shrieking, their hormone levels must have been incredibly high. The group was probably on a school trip, they must have visited the Louvre, Beaubourg, that sort of thing. Jasselin shuddered at the thought that he could, at that time, be the father of a similar pre-teen.

'You said the case is solved,' remarked Jed. 'But you haven't found the murderer.'

Jasselin then explained to him that the theft of artworks was a very specific domain, that was dealt with by a specialised organisation, the Central Office for the Struggle Against the Traffic in Artworks and Cultural Goods. Of course, they would still be in charge of the investigation – after all it was a murder – but it was from that Office, now, that you had to expect significant advances. Very few people knew where to find the artworks when they belonged to a private collector, and even fewer had the means to treat themselves to a painting worth a million euros; that amounted to perhaps ten thousand people globally.

'I suppose you can give a precise description of the painting.'

'Obviously; I have all the photos you want.'

His painting was immediately going to be identified in the database of stolen artworks, whose consultation was obligatory for any transaction beyond fifty thousand euros; and because the penalties for non-respect of this obligation were heavy, he added, the resale of stolen artworks had become more and more difficult. Disguising this theft as a ritual crime had in fact been an ingenious idea, and without Jed's intervention they would still be going nowhere. But now things were going to take another turn. Sooner or later, the painting was going to reappear on the market, and they would have no difficulty tracing the culprits.

'But you don't seem particularly satisfied,' remarked Jed.

'That's true,' Jasselin agreed as he finished his bottle. At the start, this case seemed particularly atrocious, but original. You could imagine you were dealing with a crime of passion, a fit of religious madness, various things. It was quite depressing to fall back in the end on the most widespread, universal criminal motivation: money. He was going to mark, next year, his thirtieth anniversary in the police. How many times, in that career, had he dealt with a crime which was not motivated by money? He could count them on the fingers of one hand. In a sense this was reassuring, it proved that absolute evil was rare in human beings. But that evening, without knowing why, he found this particularly sad.

38

His boiler had survived Houellebecq, Jed thought on returning home, looking at the machine which welcomed him with an insidious roar, like a vicious beast.

It had also survived his father, he would speculate a few days later. It was already 17 December, Christmas was only a week away, and he still had no news of the old man and decided to phone the manageress of the retirement home. She informed him that his father had left for Zurich the week before, without giving any precise return date. Her voice did not betray any particular concern, and Jed suddenly became aware that Zurich was not only the operations base of an association which euthanised old people, but also a place of residence for rich, even very rich people – among the richest people in the world. Many of its residents must have had family, or relations, who lived in Zurich; a trip to Zurich by one of them could only appear perfectly normal to her. He hung up, discouraged, and reserved a ticket on Swiss Airlines for the following day.

While waiting for the departure of his flight in the immense, sinister, and itself quite lethal lounge in Roissy 2, he suddenly wondered what he was going to do in Zurich. His father had already been dead, obviously, for several days, his ashes already floating on the waters of Lake Zurich. By searching on the Internet, he had learned that Koestler (it was the name of the group of euthanisers) was being sued by a local ecology association. Not because of its activities – on the contrary, the ecologists in question rejoiced at the existence of Koestler, and even declared themselves *in complete support of its struggle* – but because the quantity of ashes and human bones which it was dumping in the lake was in their view excessive, and had the disadvantage of favouring a species of Brazilian carp, recently arrived in Europe, to the detriment of char, and more generally the local fish.

Jed could have chosen one of the palaces standing on the banks of the lake, the Widder or the Baur au Lac, but felt he would have difficulty bearing such excessive luxury. He took the safe option of a hotel near the airport, vast and functional, situated on the territory of the commune of Glattbrugg. Besides, it was itself quite expensive, and seemed very comfortable. But did cheap uncomfortable hotels even exist in Switzerland?

He arrived at about ten in the evening. It was freezing cold but his bedroom was cosy and welcoming, despite the sinister facade of the establishment. The hotel restaurant had just closed; he studied the room-service menu for some time before realising that he wasn't hungry, that he in fact felt incapable of ingesting anything. For a moment he considered watching a porn movie, but fell asleep after managing to work out the pay per view.

The following day, on waking, the surroundings were bathed in a white mist. The planes couldn't take off, the receptionist told him, and the airport was paralysed. He went to the breakfast bar, but only managed to swallow a coffee and half a *pain au lait*. After studying his map for some time – it was complex; the association was also in a suburb of Zurich, but a different one – then gave up and decided to take a taxi. The taxi driver knew the street well; Jed had forgotten to note the number, but he assured him that it was a short street. It was close to the train stop at Schwerzenbach, he informed him, and, besides, it followed the railway line. Jed felt uneasy at the thought that the driver probably saw him as a *candidate for suicide*. However, the man – a thickset fifty-something who spoke English with a thick Swiss-German accent – occasionally sent him dirty-minded and complicit looks which sat badly with the idea of a *dignified death*. He finally understood when the taxi stopped, at the bottom of the street, in front of an enormous, neo-Babylonian building, whose entrance was adorned with very kitsch erotic frescos, a threadbare red carpet and potted palm trees, and which was clearly a brothel. Jed felt deeply reassured at having been associated with the idea of a brothel rather than that of an establishment devoted to euthanasia; he paid, giving a big tip, and waited for the driver to turn round before going further up the street. The Koestler association boasted, in peak periods, of satisfying the demands of one hundred clients every day. It was in no way certain that the Babylon FKK Relax-Oase could boast of a comparable attendance, despite the fact that its opening hours were longer – Koestler was essentially open in office hours, with a late opening until nine on Wednesdays – and the considerable efforts at decoration – of dubious taste, that's true, – which had been put aside for the brothel. Koestler on the other hand – and Jed realised this on arriving in front of the building, about fifty metres further on – had its headquarters in a building of white concrete, of irreproachable banality, very Le Corbusier in its girder and pole structure opening up the facade and, with the absence of decorative embellishment, a building basically identical to the thousands of white concrete buildings that characterised semi-residential suburbs across the globe. A sole difference remained the quality of the concrete, and there you could be sure: Swiss concrete was incomparably superior to Polish, Indonesian or Malagasy concrete. No irregularity, no fissure came to tarnish the facade, and that was probably twenty years after its construction. He was sure his father would have made this remark to himself, even hours before dying.

Just as he was about to ring the bell, two men dressed in cotton jackets and trousers came out carrying a pale-coloured wooden coffin – a light, bottom-of-the-range model, probably made of chipboard – which they placed in a Peugeot Partner van parked in front of the building. Without paying any attention to Jed they went back in immediately, leaving the doors of the van wide open, and came out a minute later, carrying a second coffin, identical to the previous one, which they in turn put in the van. They had blocked the shutting mechanism of the doors to facilitate their work. That confirmed it: the Babylon FKK Relax-Oase hardly buzzed with such activity. The market value of suffering and death had become superior to that of pleasure and sex, Jed thought, and it was probably for this reason that Damien Hirst had, a few years earlier, replaced Jeff Koons at the top of the art market. It's true that he had botched the painting which was meant to retrace this event, and that he hadn't even managed to finish it, but this painting remained imaginable, and someone else could make it – though no doubt it would have required a better painter. Yet no painting seemed to him capable of expressing clearly the difference of economic dynamism between these two businesses, situated only a few dozen metres from each other, on the banal and rather sad street which followed a railway line in the eastern suburbs of Zurich.

Just then, a third coffin was loaded into the van. Without waiting for the fourth, Jed entered the building, and went up a few steps to a landing where there were three doors. He pushed the one on the right marked *Wartesaal*, and went into a waiting room with cream-coloured walls and dull plastic furniture – similar, in fact, to the one in which he had waited at the Quai des Orfèvres, except that this time there was no *unbeatable view of the Pont des Arts*, and the windows only opened onto an anonymous residential suburb. The loudspeakers fixed at the top of the walls played an ambient music that was certainly sad, but to which could also be given the adjective *dignified* – it was probably by Barber.

The five people gathered there were undoubtedly *candidates for suicide*, but it was difficult to characterise them any further. Their very age was quite indiscernible, anywhere between fifty and seventy years old – therefore not very old; when he came, his father had probably been the *senior member of his class*. One of them, with his white moustache and rubicond complexion, was manifestly an Englishman; but the others, even from the point of view of nationality, were difficult to place. An emaciated man, with a Latin physique, a brownish-yellow complexion and terribly gaunt cheeks – the only one, in fact, who seemed to be suffering from a serious illness – was avidly reading (he had briefly looked up when Jed entered, then had immediately plunged back into his book) a

Spanish edition of the adventures of Spirou; he surely came from some South American country.

Jed hesitated, then finally chose to address a woman aged about sixty who looked like a typical Allgäu housewife, and who gave the impression of possessing extraordinary skills in the domain of knitting. She informed him that there was, in fact, a reception room, that he had to go back out onto the landing and take the door on the left.

Nothing was marked, but Jed pushed the door on the left. A girl who was decorative but nothing more (there were certainly better ones at the Babylon FKK Relax-Oase, he thought) was sitting behind the counter, laboriously filling in a crossword puzzle. Jed explained to her his request, which seemed to shock her: members of the family didn't come after the death, she replied. Sometimes before, never after. '*Sometimes before . . . Never after . . .*' she repeated several times in English, chewing laboriously on her words. This retard was beginning to get on his nerves. He raised his voice, explaining again that he hadn't been able to come before, that he wanted absolutely to see someone from the management, and that he had the right to see his father's file. The word *right* seemed to impress her; with obvious reluctance, she picked up her phone. A few minutes later, a woman aged about forty, dressed in a light-coloured suit, entered the room. She had consulted the file; in fact, his father had turned up on the morning of Monday 10 December and the procedure had gone 'perfectly normally', she added.

He must have arrived on the Sunday evening, the 9th, Jed thought. Where had he spent his last night? Had he treated himself to the Baur au Lac? He hoped so, without believing it. He was certain in any case that he had *settled the bill on leaving*, and that he had left *none of his belongings behind*.

He insisted again, imploring her. He had been travelling when this happened, he claimed, he hadn't been able to be there, but now he wanted to know more, know all the details about his father's last moments. The woman, visibly annoyed, finally gave in and invited him to come with her. He followed her down a dark corridor that was cluttered with metal filing cabinets, before entering her luminous and functional office, which overlooked some sort of public park.

'Here is your father's file,' she said, handing him a slim folder. The word *file* seemed a bit exaggerated: there was only a single page, with Swiss German writing on both sides.

'I don't understand a word . . . I'll have to get it translated.'

'But what do you want, exactly?' Her calm was breaking up with every minute. 'I'm telling you that everything is in order!'

'There was a medical examination, I suppose?'

'Of course.' According to what Jed had been able to read in reports, the medical examination boiled down to taking blood pressure and asking a few vague questions, a sort of *job interview*, only with the difference being that everyone succeeded, and everything was systematically sorted out in less than ten minutes.

'We act in perfect accordance with Swiss law,' said the woman, more and more glacially.

'What happened to the body?'

'Well, like the immense majority of our clients, your father had opted for cremation. We therefore acted according to his wishes; then we scattered his ashes in the open air.'

So that was it, thought Jed; his father now served as food for the Brazilian carp of Zurichsee.

The woman took back the file, obviously thinking their conversation was over, and got up to put it away in the filing cabinet. Jed stood up as well, approached and slapped her violently. She made a stifled moan, but didn't have the time to consider a riposte. He moved on to a violent uppercut to the chin, followed by a series of sharp cuffs. While she wavered on her feet, trying to get her breath back, he stepped back so as to run and kick her with all his strength at the level of her solar plexus. At this she collapsed to the ground, striking a metal corner of the desk as she fell; there was a loud cracking sound. The spine must have taken a blow, thought Jed. He leaned over her; she was groggy, breathing with difficulty, but she was breathing.

He walked rapidly to the exit, more or less fearing that someone would raise the alarm, but the receptionist hardly looked up from her crossword; it's true that the struggle had made little noise. The station was only two hundred metres away. When he entered, a train stopped on one of the platforms. He got in without buying a ticket, wasn't checked and got off at Zurich Central Station.

On arriving at the hotel, he realised that this bout of violence had put him in a good mood. It was the first time in his life that he'd used physical violence against someone; and that had made him hungry. He dined with great appetite, on a raclette of Grisons meat and mountain ham, which he washed down with an excellent red wine from the Valais.

The following morning, nice weather had returned to Zurich, and a fine layer of snow covered the ground. He went to the airport, more or less expecting to be arrested at passport control, but nothing of the sort happened. And in the following days, he didn't receive any news. It was funny they'd decided against making a complaint; probably they didn't want to attract attention to their activities in any way. There was probably some truth, he thought, to the accusations spread on the Internet concerning the personal enrichment of members of the association. A euthanasia was charged at an average rate of five thousand euros, when the lethal dose of sodium pentobarbital came to twenty euros, and a bottom-of-the-range cremation doubtless not much more. In a booming market, where Switzerland had a virtual monopoly, they were, indeed, going to *make a killing*.

His excitement quickly subsided, into a wave of deep sorrow, that he knew was definitive. Three days after his return, for the first time in his life, he would spend Christmas Eve alone. It would be the same on New Year's Eve. And, in the days that followed, he was also alone.

Epilogue

A few months later, Jasselin retired. It was, if truth be told, the normal time to do so, but up until then he had always thought he would ask for an extension of at least a year or two. The Houellebecq case had seriously shaken him; the confidence he felt in himself, in his ability to do his job, had crumbled. No one had held this against him; on the contrary, he had been nominated *in extremis* to the rank of detective chief inspector; he wouldn't do the job, but his pension would be increased slightly. A farewell party had been planned – a big one at that. The whole crime squad was invited, and the chief of police would make a speech. In short, he was leaving *honourably*. This was clearly intended to make him know that he had been, if you considered the whole of his career, a good policemen. And it's true, he thought he had been, most of the time, an honourable policeman, or at least an obstinate policeman, and obstinacy is perhaps the only human quality that matters at the end of the day, not only in the profession of the policeman but in many professions. At least in any that have something to do with the notion of *truth*.

A few days after his effective departure he invited Ferber to lunch in a small restaurant on the place Dauphine. It was Monday 29 April, and many people had taken a long weekend; Paris was very quiet and in the restaurant there were only a few tourist couples. Spring had truly arrived, the buds had opened, and particles of dust and pollen danced in the light. They had sat down at a table on the terrace, and ordered two pastis before the meal.

'You know,' he said when the waiter put their glasses down in front of them, 'I really fucked up this case, from start to finish. If the other guy hadn't noticed the painting was missing, we'd still be floundering.'

'Don't be too hard on yourself; after all, it was your idea to take him there.'

'No, Christian,' Jasselin replied softly. 'You've forgotten, but it was you who had the idea.'

'I'm too old,' he went on a little later. 'I'm simply too old for this job. The brain gets stiff with the years, like all the rest; even quicker than anything else, it seems to me. Man wasn't built to live for eighty or a hundred years; at most thirty-five or forty, like in prehistoric times. There are organs that resist – remarkably, even – and others which fall to bits slowly – slowly or quickly.'

'What do you plan to do?' asked Ferber, trying to change the subject. 'Are you staying in Paris?'

'No, I'm going to move to Brittany. Into the house where my parents lived before coming up to Paris.' There was, in fact, quite a lot of work to be done on the house before they could consider moving in. It was surprising, Jasselin thought, to think of all those people belonging to a recent, and even very recent past – his own parents – who had lived a large part of their life in conditions of comfort which today seemed unacceptable: no bath or shower, no really effective heating system. Anyway, Hélène had to work up to the close of the academic year; their move could realistically take place only at the end of the summer. He didn't at all like DIY, he told Ferber, but gardening, yes, he promised himself real joys cultivating his vegetable patch.

'And then,' he said with half a smile, 'I'm going to read detective novels. I've almost never done it during my working life, so now I'm going to start. But I don't want to read the American ones, and I have the impression there's mainly just those. Do you have a Frenchman you can recommend?'

'Jonquet,' Ferber immediately replied. 'Thierry Jonquet. In France he's the best, in my opinion.'

Jasselin wrote the name down in his notebook when the waiter brought his sole meunière. The restaurant was good; they spoke little but he felt happy to be with Ferber one last time, and he was grateful he didn't drone on about the possibility of seeing each other again and keeping in contact. He was going to move to the provinces and Ferber would stay in Paris. He was going to become a good policeman, a very good policeman. He would probably be promoted to captain by the end of the year, commander a little later, and then inspector; but in reality they would never see each other again.

They lingered in this restaurant; all the tourists had left. Jasselin finished his dessert – a charlotte with marron glacé. A ray of sunshine passing between the plane trees lit up the square splendidly.

'Christian . . .' he said after a moment's hesitation, and to his own surprise he found that his voice quavered a little. 'I'd like you to promise me one thing: don't drop the Houellebecq case. I know it doesn't really depend on you now, but I'd like you to keep in regular touch with people from the Central Office for the Struggle Against the Traffic in Artworks and Cultural Goods, and alert me when they've found something.'

Ferber nodded his head and promised.

As the months passed and no trace of the painting appeared in the usual networks, it became clearer and clearer that the murderer wasn't a professional thief but a collector who'd acted alone without any intention of being separated from the object. It was the worst possible scenario, and Ferber pursued his investigations in the direction of hospitals, widening them to private clinics – at least those that agreed to cooperate; the use of specialised surgical equipment remained their only serious lead.

The case was solved three years later, quite by accident. Patrolling the A8 motorway in the direction of Nice–Marseille, a squad of gendarmes tried to intercept a Porsche 911 Carrera that was going at 210 kph. The driver fled, and was only arrested near Fréjus. It turned out that it was a stolen car, that the man was drunk, and that he was *well known to the police*. Patrick Le Braouzec had been sentenced several times for banal and relatively minor offences – procuring, grievous bodily harm – but a persistent rumour ascribed to him the strange speciality of *insect trafficker*. There exist more than a million species of insects, and new ones are discovered every year, particularly in equatorial regions. Certain wealthy collectors are ready to pay large, sometimes very large, sums for a beautiful specimen of a rare species – preserved, or preferably alive. The capture and a fortiori export of these animals are subject to very strict rules, which Le Braouzec had up until now managed to get around; he had never been caught in the act, and justified his regular journeys to New Guinea, Sumatra, and Guyana by claiming to have a taste for the jungle and life in the wild. In fact, the man had the temperament of the adventurer, and showed real physical courage: without a guide, and sometimes for several weeks, he crossed some of the most dangerous jungles on the planet, carrying only a few provisions, a combat knife and water purification tablets.

This time, they discovered in the car's boot a stiff attaché case covered with supple leather and pierced with lots of air holes; the perforations were almost invisible, and at first glance the object could easily pass for an ordinary attaché case. Inside, however, separated by Plexiglas, there were about fifty insects among which the gendarmes immediately recognised a scolopendrid, a tarantula and a giant earwig; the others were only identified a few days later by the Natural History Museum in Nice. They then sent the list to an expert – in fact, the only French expert on this kind of criminal behaviour – who made a rapid estimate: at market prices, the whole package could be sold for around one hundred thousand euros.

Le Braouzec owned up. He was having a dispute with one of his clients – a surgeon from Cannes – about the payment for a previous delivery. He had agreed to return and negotiate with the extra specimens. The discussion had turned nasty and he'd hit the man, who'd fallen head first onto a marble coffee table. Le Braouzec thought he was dead. 'It was an accident,' he said in his defence, 'I had no intention of killing him.' He'd panicked, and instead of calling a taxi to return home, as he'd done on the way there, he'd stolen his victim's car. Thus, his criminal career ended as it had begun: in stupidity and violence.

It was the regional crime department at Nice who went to the villa of Adolphe Petissaud, the practitioner in Cannes. He lived in the avenue de la Californie, overlooking the town, and owned 80 per cent of shares in his own clinic, specialising in male reconstructive and plastic surgery. He lived alone. Obviously he was a man of means: the lawn and the swimming pool were impeccably maintained, there were easily ten bedrooms there.

The rooms on the ground floor and upstairs told them almost nothing. It was the classical, predictable living space of a hedonistic and not very refined upper-class man who now lay on the living-room carpet, with a smashed skull in a pool of blood. Le Braouzec had probably told the truth: you were dealing with a business discussion that had, quite stupidly, turned out badly; no premeditation could be held against him. However, he would, most probably, be given at least ten years.

That said, the basement had a real surprise in store for them. They were almost all hardened, experienced policemen; the Nice region has long been known for its high crime rate, and has become even more violent with the appearance of the Russian mafia; but neither Commander Bardèche, who was heading the team, nor any of his men had ever seen anything remotely like this.

The four walls of the room, which was twenty metres by ten, were almost entirely covered with glass shelves two metres high. Regularly arranged inside these shelves, lit by spotlights, stood monstrous human chimera. Genitalia were grafted into torsos, and minuscule arms of foetuses prolonged noses, forming sorts of elephant trunks. Other compositions were magmas of human limbs, attached, intermingled and sutured, surrounding grimacing heads. They had no idea how such creations had been preserved, but the representations were unbearably realistic; the slashed and often enucleated faces were frozen in atrocious rictuses of pain, crowns of dried blood surrounded the amputations. Petissaud was a serious pervert, who carried out his perversion to an unusual level; there must have been accomplices, a traffic in corpses, and probably also of foetuses, that was going to mean a long investigation, thought Bardèche at the same time as one of his deputies, a young brigadier who'd just joined the team, fainted and fell slowly, gracefully, like a cut flower, onto the floor a few metres in front of him.

He also thought, fleetingly, that this was excellent news for Le Braouzec: a good lawyer would have no problem exploiting the facts, depicting the monstrous character of the victim. That would certainly influence the jury's decision.

The centre of the room was filled by an immense light table, about five metres by ten. Inside it, separated by transparent walls,

moved hundreds of insects, grouped by species. Accidentally acti-
vating a switch placed on the edge of the table, one of the
policemen triggered the opening of a wall: about ten tarantulas
rushed on their hairy legs into the neighbouring compartment
and started to tear to pieces the insects occupying it – big red
centipedes. So, that's how Petissaud spent his evenings, instead of
enjoying himself, like the majority of his colleagues, in anodyne
orgies with Slavic prostitutes, he took himself for God, quite
simply, and he acted with these populations of insects like God
did with human populations.

Things probably would have stayed as they were without the
intervention of Le Guern, a young Breton brigadier, recently transferred to Nice, and whom Bardèche was particularly delighted to
have taken into his team. Before joining the police, Le Guern had
done two years of study at the Beaux-Arts de Rennes, and he
recognised a small charcoal drawing hanging on the wall as a sketch
by Francis Bacon. In fact, four artworks were arranged in the cellar,
almost exactly at the four corners of the room. In addition to the
Bacon sketch, there were two plastinations by von Hagens – two
works which themselves were quite repellent. Finally, there was a
canvas which Le Guern thought he recognised as the last known
work by Jed Martin, *Michel Houellebecq, Writer*.

Back at the police station, Bardèche immediately consulted the
stolen artworks database: Le Guern had been right, on all counts.
The two plastinations had apparently been acquired completely
legally; the sketch by Bacon had, however, been stolen, about ten
years before, from a museum in Chicago. The thieves had been
arrested a few years previously, and had been noteworthy for their
systematic refusal to give the names of their buyers, which was
quite rare in this milieu. It was a drawing of modest format,
acquired at a time when Bacon's market rating was in slight decline,
and Petissaud had no doubt paid less than the market price. It was
the ratio that was normally used. For a man of his level of income
it was a big item of expenditure, but still possible. Bardèche was,
however, terrified by the values now attained by the works of Jed

Martin; even at half price, the surgeon would never have had the means to purchase a canvas of this stature.

He immediately phoned the Central Office for the Struggle Against the Traffic in Artworks and Cultural Goods, where his call triggered considerable agitation: this was, quite simply, the biggest case they'd had on their hands in the last five years. As the value of Jed Martin increased in vertiginous proportions, they expected the canvas to reappear, imminently, on the market; but that didn't happen, which left them more and more perplexed.

There was another positive point for Le Braouzec, thought Bardèche: he leaves with a case of insects valued at one hundred thousand euros, and a Porsche that was scarcely worth more, while leaving behind a painting valued at twelve million euros. That's what denoted panic, improvisation, random crime: a good lawyer would have no problem pointing that out, even if the adventurer probably hadn't been aware of the fortune he had in his grasp.

A quarter of an hour later the director of the Central Office phoned him in person, to warmly congratulate him and give him the mobile and office numbers of Commander Ferber, who was in charge of the crime squad investigation.

He immediately called him. It was just after nine, but he was still in his office, which he was about to leave. He too seemed deeply relieved by the news; he was beginning to think that they would never succeed; he thought, an unsolved case is like an old wound; he added, half joking, it never leaves you completely at peace – well, he supposed Bardèche would know that.

Yes, Bardèche knew that; before hanging up he promised to send him a succinct report the following day.

Late the following morning, Ferber received an email summarising their discoveries. The clinic of the doctor, Petissaud, was one of those which had replied to their queries, he remarked in passing; they admitted possessing a laser cutter, but asserted that the equipment was still on their premises. He found the letter: it was signed by Petissaud himself. They could have, he thought for a moment, been astonished that a clinic specialising in reconstructive plastic surgery would possess a machine for amputations; but, in truth, nothing about the name of the clinic indicated its specialty; and they'd received hundreds of responses. No, he concluded, they had no serious criticism to make of themselves in this affair. Before calling Jasselin at his home in Brittany, he lingered for a few moments on the physiognomy of the two murderers. Le Braouzec had the physique of a basic brute, without scruples, without any genuine cruelty either. He was an ordinary criminal, a criminal like those you meet every day. Petissaud was more surprising: quite handsome, tanned in a way you guessed was permament, he smiled at the lens, displaying an unabashed self-assurance. Basically, he had exactly the physique you associated with a cosmetic surgeon from Cannes living in the avenue de la Californie. Bardèche was right: he was the kind of guy who was, from time to time, caught in the nets of the vice squad, but never in those of the crime squad. Mankind is sometimes strange, he thought as he dialled the number; but unfortunately it was more often in the category of *strange and repugnant*, rarely in the category of *strange and admirable*. Yet he felt appeased, serene, and he knew that Jasselin would be even more so; it was only now that he could really *enjoy his retirement*. Even if it was in an indirect and abnormal way, the guilty man had been punished; balance had been re-established. The cut could now close.

In his last will and testament, Houellebecq's instructions were clear: if he were to die before Jed Martin, the painting should be returned to him. Ferber had no difficulty getting Jed on the phone: he was at home; no, he was not disturbing him. In reality, yes he was, a little bit, as Jed was watching an anthology of *DuckTales* on the Disney Channel, but he abstained from adding that.

This painting, which had already been mixed up in two murders, arrived at Jed's home without any particular precaution, in an ordinary police van. He put it on his easel, in the centre of the room, before returning to his usual occupations, which were for the moment rather quiet: he cleaned his lenses and did a bit of tidying up. His brain functioned more or less in slow motion, and it was only after a few days that he became aware that the painting *bothered* him, that he felt ill at ease in its presence. It wasn't only the smell of blood which seemed to float around it, as it floats around certain famous jewels, and objects in general which have unleashed human passions; it was above all Houellebecq's eyes, whose blazing expressiveness seemed to him incongrous, abnormal, now that the author was dead and he had seen spadefuls of earth fall one by one on his coffin, in the middle of Montparnasse cemetery. Even if he no longer managed to bear it, it was without question a good painting – the impression of life given by the writer was stupefying, false modesty would have been ridiculous. But from there to it being worth twelve million euros was another matter, one he had always refused to give an opinion on, just once saying to a particularly insistent journalist: 'You mustn't look for meaning in something that has none,' thus echoing, without being fully aware of it, the conclusion to Wittgenstein's *Tractatus*: 'What we cannot speak about we must pass over in silence.'

★   ★   ★

He phoned Franz that very evening to explain to him what had happened, and his intention to put *Michel Houellebecq, Writer* on the market.

On arriving at Chez Claude, in the rue du Château-des-Rentiers, he had the clear and irrefutable sensation that it was the last time he was going into the establishment; he also knew that it was to be his last meeting with Franz. The latter, slumped in his chair, was sitting at his usual place in front of a glass of red wine; he had aged a lot, as if great worries had befallen him. Sure, he had made a lot of money, but he had to tell himself that by waiting for a few more years he could have made ten times more; and no doubt he had also made *investments*, an unavoidable source of problems. More generally, he seemed to have difficulty living with his new wealth, as is often the case with people from poor backgrounds: wealth only makes happy those who have always known a certain material comfort, who are prepared for it from childhood; when it befalls someone who has had a difficult start in life, the first feeling that invades him, which he occasionally manages to fight off, albeit temporarily, before it returns to submerge him completely, is quite simply *fear*. Jed, for his part, born into a well-off background, and having known success very quickly, easily accepted having a credit of fourteen million euros in his current account. He wasn't even seriously bothered by his banker. Since the last financial crisis, far worse than that of 2008, which bankrupted Crédit Suisse, and the Royal Bank of Scotland, not to mention lots of other less important establishments, bankers were *keeping their heads down*. That was the least you could say. Certainly, they held in reserve the sales patter that their training had conditioned them to serve up; but when you indicated to them that you were interested in none of their investment products, they gave up immediately, uttered a resigned sigh, quietly put away the file they had prepared, and almost said sorry; only one last remnant of professional pride stopped them from proposing a savings account remunerated at 0.45 per cent. More generally, you were living in an ideologically strange period, where everyone in Western Europe seemed persuaded that capitalism was doomed, and even doomed in the short term, that it was living through its very last years, without, however, the ultra-left parties managing to attract anyone beyond their usual clientele of spiteful masochists. A veil of ashes seemed to have spread over people's minds.

For a few minutes they discussed the art market, which was quite demented. Many experts had believed that the previous period of speculative frenzy would be followed by a calmer period, where the market would grow slowly, regularly, at a normal rhythm; some had even predicted that art would become a *safe investment*; they were mistaken. THERE ARE NO MORE SAFE INVESTMENTS, as the *Financial Times* had recently headlined an editorial; and speculation in the domain of art had become even more intense, more disorderly and more frenetic, with values set and revised in the twinkling of an eye, and the *ArtPrice* league table now drawn up on a weekly basis.

They took another glass of wine, then a third. 'I can find a buyer,' Franz finally said. 'Of course, that's going to take a bit of time. At the price you've reached, there are no longer many people left.'

Jed wasn't in a hurry, anyway. Their conversation slowed down, before stopping completely. They looked at each other, with almost apologetic expressions. 'We've known a few things . . . together,' Jed tried to say in one last effort, but his voice went silent before the end of the sentence. As he got up to leave, Franz told him: 'You'll have noticed that . . . I didn't ask you what you were doing.'

'I did notice.'

In fact, he was going around in circles. He was at such a loose end that, for a few weeks now, he had begun to speak to his boiler. And what was more worrying – he had become aware of this two days before – was that he now expected the boiler to answer him. The machine, it's true, produced more and more varied noises: groans, roars, loud bangs, whistles of varied tone and volume; you might expect it one day or another to reach articulated language. It was, when all was said and done, his oldest companion.

Six months later, Jed decided to move into his grandparents' old house in the Creuse. By doing so, he was uncomfortably aware of following the same path taken by Houellebecq a few years before. He repeatedly thought, in order to persuade himself, that there were important differences. Firstly, Houellebecq had moved to the Loiret from Ireland; the true break for him had happened before, when he had left Paris, the sociological centre of his activity as writer and of his friendships, one could at least suppose, for Ireland. The break that Jed was making, leaving the sociological centre of his artistic activity, was of the same order. In truth, he had already more or less carried it out. In the first months after he achieved international fame, he had agreed to participate in some biennales, attend *vernissages* and give numerous interviews – and even, once, to give a lecture, of which he had kept no memory whatsoever. Then he had cut down, had neglected to respond to the invitations and emails, and in less than two years had fallen back into this solitude that was oppressive, but in his eyes indispensable and rich, a bit like the nothingness 'rich in possibilities' of Buddhist thought. Except for the moment, that nothingness only engendered nothingness, and it was above all for that reason that he changed residence, in the hope of regaining that bizarre impulse which had pushed him in the past to add new objects, described as *artistic*, to the countless natural or artificial objects already present in the world. It was not, like Houellebecq, leaving in search of a hypothetical childhood state. Besides, he *hadn't* spent his childhood in the Creuse, except for a few summer holidays of which he had no precise memory, just that of an indefinite, brutal happiness.

Before leaving the Paris region he had a final task to accomplish, a difficult one, which he had put off for as long as possible. A few months earlier, he had concluded the sale of the house in Raincy with Alain Sémoun, a guy who wanted to move his business there. He'd made a fortune thanks to an Internet site for downloading welcome messages and wallpaper for mobile phones. That didn't look at all like an activity, it was rather simplistic, but he'd become, in the space of a few years, the world number one. He had signed exclusive contracts with numerous celebrities, and, for a modest sum, by going through his site, you could personalise your phone with the image and voice of Paris Hilton, Deborah Channel, Dmitry Medvedev, Puff Daddy and many others. He wanted to use the house as a headquarters – finding the library 'hyper-classy' – and build modern workshops in the park. According to him, Raincy had a 'crazy energy' he badly wanted to channel; that was his way of seeing things. Jed suspected he was overstating his interest in the *rough suburbs*, but he was a guy who could overstate the purchase of a six-pack of Volvic. Anyway, he had a considerable gift of the gab, and had scraped together the maximum of all the local or national subsidies available; he had almost ripped Jed off with the price of the transaction, but Jed had come to his senses, and the other man had ended up proposing a reasonable price. Jed obviously didn't need this money, but he would have thought it unworthy of father's memory to sell cheaply this place where he had tried to live; where he'd tried, if only for a few years, to build a *family life*.

A violent wind was blowing in from the east when he took the exit for Raincy. It was ten years since he'd last been there. The gate creaked a little, but opened without difficulty. The branches of the poplars and aspens waved against a dark grey sky. The trace of a path could still be made out between the clumps of grass and the bushes of nettles and thorns. He thought with a vague horror that it was there that he'd spent his first years, even his first months, and it was as if the envelopes of time were closing upon him with a dull thud; he was still young, he told himself, he'd only lived the first half of his decline.

The closed shutters, with their white slats, bore no trace of a break-in, and the armoured lock on the main door opened with astonishing ease. No doubt word had gone around in the neighbouring housing schemes that there was nothing left to steal in this house, and that it didn't even justify an attempt at burglary. That was accurate, as there was nothing – or nothing sellable. No recent electronic equipment; just heavy, unstylish furniture. His father had taken his mother's rare jewellery with him – to the retirement home in Boulogne, then that in Vésinet. The safe had been returned to Jed not long after his death who'd immediately put it on top of a wardrobe, while knowing that he would be better depositing it at the local bank; if not, sooner or later, he would come across it again, and that would inevitably lead him to sad thoughts, because if his father's life hadn't been very happy, what could be said about his mother's?

He easily recognised the arrangement of the furniture, the configuration of the rooms. This functional unit of human inhabitation, which could easily have accommodated ten people at the time of its greatest splendour, had only accommodated three – then two, then one, and in the end no one at all. He wondered for a few moments about the boiler. Never, during his childhood or adolescence, had he heard of problems with the boiler; and nor during his brief sojourns, as a young man, in his father's place, had it ever been an issue. Perhaps his father had acquired an exceptional boiler, a boiler 'with bronze feet, whose limbs are solid like the columns of the temple of Jerusalem', as the holy book describes the wise woman.

Doubtless on one of those deep leather sofas, protected by the cathedral stained-glass windows from the heat of a summer afternoon, he'd read of the adventures of Spirou and Fantasio, or the poems of Alfred de Musset. He then understood that he was going to have to act quickly, and went over to his father's office.

He easily found the portfolios, in the first cupboard he opened. There were about thirty of them, 50 cm by 80, covered with that kind of paper with sad black and green motifs which systematically covered portfolios in the previous century. They were fastened by black ribbons that were worn, close to breaking, and stuffed with hundreds of A2 sheets, which must have represented years of work. He took four of them under his arm, and opened the boot of his Audi.

When he was making his third trip, he noticed a tall black man who was observing him, on the other side of the street, as he talked on his mobile phone. He was an impressively built man, with a shaved head – he must have measured over one metre ninety and weighed a hundred kilos – but his features were juvenile. He couldn't have been older than sixteen. Jed supposed that Alain Sémoun was protecting his investment, thought for a moment of going to explain himself, but decided against it, hoping that the description of the black would enable Sémoun to recognise him. It had to be the case, because the other did nothing to interrupt him, and just watched until he finished loading his car.

He wandered around upstairs for a few more minutes without feeling anything precise, without even remembering anything, yet he knew that he would never return to this house which, anyway, was going to change a lot – that other moron was probably going to *break down some walls* and repaint everything white – but nothing happened, nothing managed to imprint itself on his mind. He walked in the limbo of an indefinite, oily sadness. On going out, he carefully closed the gate. The black had left. All of a sudden the wind stopped again, the branches of the poplars were immobile, there was a moment of total silence. He turned back, went into the rue de l'Égalité, and easily found the motorway exit.

Jed wasn't used to the elevations, plans and cuts by which architects indicate the specifications of the buildings they are designing; also, the first artistic representation he discovered, at the end of the first portfolio, gave him a shock. It in no way resembled a residential building, but rather a sort of neural network, where inhabitable cells were separated by long curved passages, covered or in the open air, which branched out in a star shape. The cells were of various dimensions, and rather circular or oval shaped – which surprised Jed; he would have imagined his father more attached to straight lines. Another striking point was the total absence of windows; on the other hand, the roofs were transparent. Thus, once they had returned home, the inhabitants of the housing scheme would no longer have any visual contact with the outside world – with the exception of the sky.

The second portfolio was devoted to detailed views of the interior of the homes. What struck him first was the virtual absence of furniture – made possible by the systematic use of small variances in the level of the floor. Thus, sleeping zones were rectangular excavations, forty centimetres deep; you descended into your bed rather than getting up into it. Similarly, the bathtubs were big round basins, whose edge was situated at floor level. Jed wondered what materials his father had intended using; probably plastics, he concluded, no doubt polystyrenes, which through thermoforming could be adapted to almost any design.

At about nine in the evening, he heated up some lasagne in the microwave. He ate it slowly, washing it down with a bottle of cheap red wine. He wondered if his father had really believed that his projects could win financial backing, and somehow be turned into reality. At the beginning yes, no doubt, and this simple thought was already depressing, as it appeared obvious a posteriori that he had no chance. He did not seem, in any case, to have ever gone as far as the scale-model stage.

He finished the bottle of wine before plunging back into his father's projects, feeling that the exercise was going to be more and more depressing. In fact, no doubt with his successive failures, the architect Jean-Pierre Martin had made a headlong rush into the imaginary, multiplying the levels, the ramifications, the challenges to gravity, imagining, with no concern for feasibility or budget, crystalline and improbable citadels.

At about seven in the morning, Jed started on the content of the last portfolio. Day was dawning, still vaguely, on the place des Alpes; the weather promised to be grey, overcast, probably until evening. His father's last drawings did not look in any way like an inhabitable building, or at least one inhabitable by humans. Spiral staircases climbed vertiginously to the heavens, joining tenuous, translucent footbridges, which brought together irregular, lanceo-late buildings of blinding white, whose forms reminded you of certain cirrus clouds. Basically, Jed thought sadly on closing the dossier, his father had never stopped wanting to build houses for swallows.

Jed had no illusions about the welcome he would get from the inhabitants of his grandparents' village. He had noticed that while he was travelling through *la France profonde* with Olga, many years before: outside certain very touristy zones like the Provençal hinterland or the Dordogne, the inhabitants of rural zones are generally inhospitable, aggressive and stupid. If you wanted to avoid gratuitous assaults and trouble more generally in the course of your journey, it was preferable, from all points of view, not to *leave the beaten paths*. And this hostility, which was simply latent towards passing visitors, transformed into hate pure and simple when the latter acquired a residence. To the question of knowing when a stranger could be accepted in a French rural zone, the response was: *never*. In that they displayed no racism or xenophobia. For them, a Parisian was almost as much a stranger as a German from the North or a Senegalese; undoubtedly, they *did not like* strangers.

A laconic message from Franz had informed him that *Michel Houellebecq, Writer* had just been sold – to a Hindu mobile phone operator. Six million extra euros had therefore just been added to his bank account. Obviously the wealth of strangers – who paid for the acquisition of a property sums that they themselves could never have imagined getting together – was one of the main motives for the natives' resentment. In Jed's case, the fact that he was *an artist* further aggravated the situation further; his wealth had been acquired, in the eyes of a farmer in the Creuse, by dubious means, on the verge of swindlery. On the other hand, he hadn't bought his property, but *inherited* it – and some remembered him from the times he had stayed, for several summers, in the house of his grandmother. He was then already a wild, unsociable child; and he did nothing, on his arrival, to make himself appreciated – on the contrary.

The back of his grandparents' house looked onto a very big garden, of almost one hectare. At the time when they both lived there, it was entirely laid out as a vegetable garden – then, gradually, as the strength of his widowed grandmother declined, and she began a firstly resigned then impatient wait for death, the cultivated areas had shrunk, more and more vegetable patches had been abandoned, surrendered to the weeds. The back, which was unfenced, opened directly onto the wood of Grandmont – Jed remembered that once a doe pursued by hunters had found refuge in the garden. A few weeks after his arrival, he learned that a plot of fifty hectares, adjoining his own, and almost entirely wooded, was for sale; he bought it without hesitation.

Rapidly, word went around that a rather crazy Parisian was buying land at any price, and at the end of the year Jed found himself the owner of seven hundred hectares, all to himself. Undulating and uneven in places, his estate was almost completely covered with beeches, chestnut trees and oak; a pond fifty metres in diameter stretched out in the middle of it. He let the cold snaps pass, then had a three-metre-high metal lattice fence built, which closed it off entirely. On top of the barrier ran an electric wire powered by a low-tension generator. The voltage was insufficient to kill, but able to repel anyone who considered climbing it – it was the same, in fact, as the electric barriers used to dissuade herds of cows from leaving their meadows. In that way, it was perfectly within the limits of legality, as he pointed out to the gendarmes who came to visit him, twice, to express concern about the changes to the face of the canton. The mayor also came, and pointed out to him that by forbidding any right of passage to the hunters who had pursued deer and wild boar in these forests for generations, he was going to arouse considerable animosity. Jed listened to him intently, agreed that it was regrettable up to a point, but argued again that he was within the strict limits of the law. Soon after this conversation, he instructed a civil engineering business to build a road which crossed his domain, ending at a radio-controlled gate that opened directly onto the D50. From there, he was only three

kilometres from the entrance to the A20 motorway. He developed
the habit of doing his shopping at the Carrefour in Limoges, where
he was almost sure not to meet anyone from the village. He generally went there first thing on Tuesday mornings, at opening time,
having noticed that this was when there were the fewest customers.
He sometimes had the hypermarket all to himself – which seemed
to him to be quite a good approximation of happiness.

The civil engineering company also laid down, around the house,
a band of grey tarmac ten metres wide. In the house itself, however,
he changed nothing.

All these improvements had cost him a little more than eight million
euros. He did the calculation, and concluded that he had easily
enough left to live on until the end of his days – even supposing
he lived that long. His main expenditure, by far, would be the
wealth tax. There would be no income tax. He had no income,
and in no way intended producing artworks intended for sale again.

The years, as they say, passed.

One morning, listening by chance to the radio – he hadn't done
so for at least three years – Jed learned of the death of Frédéric
Beigbeder, at the age of seventy-one. He'd passed away in his residence on the Basque coast, surrounded, according to the station,
by 'the affection of his loved ones'. Jed had no trouble believing it.
There was truly in Beigbeder, as far as he could remember, something which could arouse affection, and, already, the existence of
'loved ones'; something which did not exist in Houellebecq, nor in
him: a sort of familiarity with life.

It was in this indirect manner, in some ways by cross-checking,
that he realised that he himself had just turned sixty. This was
surprising: he wasn't aware of having aged to this point. It's through
relations with others, and through their eyes, that you become
aware of your own ageing; you always have the tendency to see
yourself as somehow eternal. Certainly, his hair had gone white,

his face had become lined; but all of this had happened impercep-
tibly, without anything coming to confront him directly with images
of his youth. Jed was then struck by this incongruity: he who had
made, in the course of his artistic life, thousands of pictures did
not own a single photograph of himself. Nor had he ever thought
of making a self-portrait; never had he regarded himself, even
remotely worthwhile as an artistic subject.

For over ten years, the southern gate of his estate, the one opening
out onto the village, had not been activated; it opened, however,
without difficulty, and Jed again congratulated himself on having
called on the services of that company in Lyons which a former
colleague of his father's had recommended.

He had only a vague memory of Châtelus-le-Marcheix. It was,
as far as he could remember, a decrepit, ordinary little village in
rural France, and nothing more. But, after his first steps in the
streets of the small town, he was filled with amazement. First of
all, the village had grown a lot: there were at least twice, perhaps
three times as many houses. And these houses were attractive,
decorated with flowers, and built with a maniacal respect for the
traditional Limousin habitat. Everywhere on the main street, shop
windows were selling regional products and arts and crafts; over
one hundred metres he counted three cafes offering low-price
Internet connections. You would have thought you were in Koh
Phi Phi, or Saint-Paul-de-Vence, much more than in a rural village
of the Creuse.

Slightly dazed, he stopped in the main square, and recognised
the cafe facing the church. Or, rather recognised, the *site* of the
cafe. The interior, with its art nouveau lamps, its dark wood tables
with forged iron bases, and its leather seats, manifestly wanted to
conjure up the atmosphere of a Parisian cafe of the belle époque.
Each table was, however, equipped with a docking station for
laptops with 21-inch screens, plugs conforming to European and
American norms, and a leaflet explaining how to connect to the
network Creuse-Sat; the departmental council had financed the

launch of a geostationary satellite in order to improve the speed of Internet connections in the region, Jed learned on reading the leaflet. He ordered a Menetou-Salon rosé, which he drank pensively while thinking about these transformations. At this early hour, there were few people in the cafe. A Chinese family was finishing their *full Limousin breakfast*, offered at twenty-three euros a head, Jed noticed on looking at the menu. Closer to him, a hefty bearded man, his hair tied up in a ponytail, was absent-mindedly consulting his emails; he sent an intrigued look to Jed, frowned, hesitated about addressing him, then plunged back into his computer. Jed finished his glass of wine, went out, and stayed for a few minutes pensively at the wheel of his Audi electric SUV – he'd changed car three times over the last twenty years, but had remained faithful to the brand which had given him his first real joy as a driver.

During the weeks that followed, he gently explored, in small stages, without really leaving Limousin – apart from a brief passage through the Dordogne, and another even briefer one in the mountains of Rodez – this country, France, which was irrefutably his own. Obviously, France had changed a lot. He connected to the Internet, many times, had a few conversations with hoteliers, restaurant owners and other service providers (a garage owner in Périgueux, an escort girl from Limoges), and everything confirmed the first, astounding impression he had had on walking through Châtelus-le-Marcheix: yes, the country had changed, and changed profoundly. The traditional inhabitants of rural areas had almost completely disappeared. Incomers, from urban areas, had replaced them, motivated by a real appetite for business and, occasionally, by moderate and marketable ecological convictions. They had set about repopulating the *hinterland* – and this attempt, after many other fruitless attempts, based this time on a precise knowledge of the laws of the market, and on their lucid acceptance, had been a total success.

The first question Jed asked himself – displaying, in this way, typical artistic egocentrism – was whether his 'Series of Simple Professions', almost twenty years after he had conceived it, had kept its relevance. In fact, it hadn't entirely. *Maya Dubois, Assistant in Remote Maintenance* no longer had any *raison d'être*: remote maintenance was now 100 per cent outsourced – essentially to Indonesia and Brazil. *Aimée, Escort Girl*, however, kept all its relevance. Prostitution had even enjoyed, on the economic level, a genuine upturn, due to the persistence, in particular in South America and Russia, of a fantasy image of the *Parisienne*, as well as the tireless activities of immigrant women from West Africa. For the first time since the 1900s or 1910s, France had once again become a favourite destination for *sex tourism*. New professions, too, had appeared – or rather, old professions had come back into favour, such as wrought-iron work and brass-making; market gardens had also made a reappearance. In Jabreilles-les-Bordes, a village five kilometres from Jed's, a blacksmith had moved back in – the Creuse, with its network of well-tended paths, its forests and clearings, was admirably suited for horse riding.

More generally, France, on the economic level, was in good shape. Having become a mainly agricultural and tourist country, she had displayed remarkable robustness during the various crises which followed one another, almost without interruption, in the preceding twenty years. These crises had been increasingly violent, and burlesquely unpredictable – burlesque at least from the point of view of a mocking God, who might draw infinite amusement from financial convulsions that suddenly plunged into opulence, then famine, entities the size of Indonesia, Russia or Brazil: populations of hundreds of millions of people. Having scarcely anything to sell except *hôtels de charme*, perfumes and *rillettes* – what is called an *art de vivre* – France had had no difficulty confronting these vagaries. From one year to the next, the nationality of the clients changed, and that was all.

Back in Châtelus-le-Marcheix, Jed took up the habit of a daily walk, just before midday, through the streets of the village. He generally took an aperitif at the cafe on the square (which had, curiously, kept its old name of Bar des Sports) before returning home for lunch. He quickly realised that many of the incomers seemed to know him – or, at least, had heard of him – and looked upon him with no particular animosity. In fact, the new inhabitants of the rural areas in no way resembled their predecessors. It was not fate which had led them to do traditional basket-weaving, renovation of rural gîtes or cheese-making, but a business plan, a carefully weighed, rational economic choice. Educated, tolerant and affable, they cohabited easily with the foreigners present in their region – besides, they had reason to, since the latter constituted the core of their clientele. Most of the houses that their former owners from northern Europe no longer had the means to maintain had, in fact, been bought up. The Chinese certainly formed a rather closed community, but, if truth be told, no more, and even rather less so, than the English had done in the past – and at least they didn't impose the use of their own language. They displayed an excessive respect, almost a veneration, for *local customs* – that the incomers at first knew little about, but which they'd striven, by a sort of adaptive mimicry, to reproduce; thus there was seen a more or less decisive return to regional recipes, dances and even costumes. That said, it was certainly the Russians who formed the most appreciated clientele. Never would they have haggled over the price of an aperitif, or the rental of a 4x4. They spent with munificence, with largesse, faithful to an economics of the *potlatch* that had easily survived successive political regimes.

This new generation turned out to be more conservative and more respectful of money and social hierarchies than all those preceding it. More surprisingly, the birth rate had by this time actually risen in France, even without taking into account immigration, which, anyway, had fallen to almost zero since the disappearance of the last industrial jobs and the drastic reduction of social security cover imposed at the beginning of the 2020s. Making their way to the newly industrialised countries, African migrants now exposed themselves to a very perilous journey. Crossing the Indian Ocean and the South China Sea, their boats were frequently attacked by pirates, who stripped them of their last savings, when they didn't, purely and simply, throw them into the sea.

One morning, as he sipped a glass of Chablis, Jed was approached by the bearded man with the ponytail – one of the first inhabitants he'd noticed in the village. The latter, without knowing exactly his line of work, had identified him as an *artist*. He himself painted 'a little', he confessed, and offered to show him his work.

Formerly a mechanic at a garage in Courbevoie, he'd borrowed money to set up in the village, where he'd started a quad-bike rental business – fleetingly, Jed thought again of the Croat in the avenue Stephen-Pichon, and his sea scooters. Personally, this man's passion was for Harley-Davidsons, and for a quarter of an hour Jed had to put up with the description of a machine which had pride of place in his garage, and of the way in which, year after year, he'd customised it. That said, quads were in his view 'beautiful machines', which allowed 'fun rides'. And, on the maintenance level, he pointed out with common sense, it was, after all, less restrictive than a horse; well, let's say business was good. He had no reason to complain.

His paintings, manifestly inspired by *heroic fantasy*, mainly depicted a bearded ponytail warrior, who bestrode an impressive metal charger, visibly a space-opera interpretation of his Harley. Sometimes he was fighting tribes of slimy zombies, sometimes armies of military robots. Other canvases, figuring rather the *warrior's repose*, revealed a typically male imagination based on eager sluts, with avid lips, generally going about in pairs. In short, they were autofictions, imaginary self-portraits; his faulty painting technique unfortunately did not enable him to achieve the level of hyperrealism and brushstrokes classically required by *heroic fantasy*. All in all, Jed had rarely seen anything so ugly. He hunted for an appropriate comment for more than an hour, while the other man tirelessly took his paintings out of their boxes, and ended up mumbling that it was work of 'great visionary power'. He immediately added that he had kept no contact with the art world. Which was, in fact, the gospel truth.

The methodology of the work that occupied Jed Martin during the last thirty years of his life would have remained completely unknown to us if he hadn't, a few months before his death, agreed to give an interview to a young female journalist from *Art Press*. Although the interview takes up just over forty pages of the magazine, he speaks almost exclusively about the technical procedures used for the fabrication of those strange ideograms, now kept at the MoMA in Philadelphia, that are like nothing else in his previous work, nor, in fact, like anything known, and which, thirty years later, continue to arouse in visitors a sense of apprehension mixed with unease.

As for the meaning of this work which had occupied him during all the last part of his life, he refuses all comment. 'I want to give an account of the world . . . I want simply to *give an account of the world*,' he repeats for more than a page to the young journalist, who is paralysed by the situation, and turns out to be incapable of stopping this senile chatter, and this is perhaps for the best: the chatter of Jed Martin unfolds, senile and free, essentially concentrating on questions of diaphragm, amplitude of focusing and compatibility between softwares. It is a remarkable interview, where the young journalist 'let her subject speak', as was commented drily by *Le Monde*, who were dying of jealousy at having missed out on this exclusive, which led a few months later to her being appointed chief editor of their magazine – on the very day that Jed Martin's death was announced.

Even if he speaks at length about it over several pages, the camera equipment used by Jed had, in itself, nothing very remarkable about it: a Manfrotto tripod, a Panasonic semi-professional cameoscope – which he'd had for the exceptional luminosity of its sensor, allowing him to film in almost total darkness – and a hard disk of two teraoctets linked to the USB outlet of the cameoscope. For more than two years, every morning except Tuesday (always reserved for shopping), Jed Martin loaded this equipment into the boot of his Audi before driving along the private road he had built for himself, and which crossed his estate. It was scarcely possible to venture beyond this road: the grass, very high and dotted with thorn bushes, quickly led to a dense forest, with an impenetrable floor. The trace of paths through the forest had long been obliterated. The edges of the ponds, dotted with short grass which had difficulty growing on the spongy ground, remained the only more or less accessible area.

Although he had at his disposal an extensive range of lenses, he almost always used a Schneider Apo-Sinar, which had the astonishing particularity of opening to 1.9 while reaching a maximum focal length of 1200 mm in 24 × 26 equivalent. The choice of his subject 'responded to no pre-established strategy', he asserts, several times, to the journalist; he 'was simply following the spur of the moment'. In any case, he almost always used very high focal lengths, concentrating occasionally on a branch of a beech tree waving in the wind, sometimes on a tuft of grass, the top of a bush of nettles, or an area of loose and saturated earth between two puddles. Once the framing was done, he plugged the power supply of the cameoscope into the cigarette lighter socket, switched it on and walked back home, leaving the motor to run for several hours, sometimes during the rest of the day and even overnight – the capacity of the hard disk would have allowed him almost a week of continuous shooting.

The responses based on the appeal to the 'spur of the moment' are essentially disappointing for a general-interest magazine, and the young journalist, this time, tries to find out more: after all, she surmises, the shots done on a certain day were to influence the shots done on following days; a project had to be gradually elaborated and constructed. Not at all, maintains Martin: each morning, when he started the car, he had no idea what he intended to film;

every day, for him, was a new day. And this period of total uncertainty was to last, he adds, almost ten years.

He then treated the images obtained according to a method that belongs essentially to montage, even if it is a very particular form of montage, where he occasionally keeps only a few photograms out of three hours' shooting; but it is well and truly montage that enables him to achieve those moving plant tissues, with their carnivorous suppleness, peaceful and pitiless at the same time, which constitute without any doubt the most successful attempt, in Western art, at representing how plants see the world.

Jed Martin 'had forgotten' – that is, in any case, his assertion – what had pushed him, after about ten days uniquely devoted to filming vegetation, to return to the portrayal of industrial objects – first a mobile phone, then a computer keyboard, a desk lamp, and many other objects – that were very diverse at the beginning, before gradually he concentrated almost exclusively on those containing electronic components. His most impressive images remain undoubtedly those of computer motherboards on the scrapheap, which, filmed without any indication of scale, resemble strange futurist citadels. He filmed these objects in his cellar, against a neutral grey background destined to disappear after their insertion in videos. In order to accelerate the process of decomposition, he dowsed them with diluted sulphuric acid, which he bought in carboys – a preparation, he added, usually used for killing weeds. Then he also did a montage, sampling a few photograms separated by long intervals; the result is very different from a simple accelerated motion, in that the process of decomposition, instead of being continuous, takes place by levels, by sudden upheavals.

After fifteen years of shooting and montage, he now had at his disposal about three thousand modules, all of which were more or less strange, and of an average duration of three minutes. But his work only really began to develop when he went in search of double-exposure software. Used mainly in the early years of silent cinema, double exposure had almost completely disappeared from the productions of professional film-makers, as from those of amateur video-makers, even those who worked in the artistic field; it was considered to be a dated, outmoded special effect, due to its unashamedly self-proclaimed lack of realism. After a few days' searching, however, he ended up discovering a simple double-exposure freeware. He contacted its author, who lived in Illinois, and asked him if he would agree, for a fee, to develop for him a more complete version of his software. They struck a deal, and a few months later Jed Martin had exclusive use of a quite extraordinary tool, that had no equivalent on the market. Based on a principle quite similar to that of Photoshop layers, it allowed you to superimpose up to ninety-six videotapes, by setting for each of them the brightness, saturation and contrast; by making them, also, progressively pass to the foreground, or disappear in the depth of the image. It was this software that allowed him to obtain those long hypnotic shots where the industrial objects seem to drown, progressively submerged by the proliferation of layers of vegetation. Occasionally they give the impression of struggling, of trying to return to the surface; then they are swept away by a wave of grass and leaves and plunge back into a plant magma, at the same time as their surfaces fall apart, revealing microprocessors, batteries, and memory cards.

Jed's health was declining: he could no longer eat anything other than dairy products and sugary foods, and he began to suspect that he would, like his father, die of cancer of the digestive tract. Some examinations done at the hospital in Limoges confirmed this prognosis, but he refused to be treated, to begin radiotherapy or other heavy treatments, and just took comfort medication – that relieved his pains, which were particularly acute in the evening – and massive doses of sleeping pills. He made his last will and testament, leaving his fortune to various animal protection associations.

At around the same time, he began filming photographs of all the people he had known, from Geneviève to Olga, including Franz, Michel Houellebecq, his father, some other people too, in fact all those he had photographs of. He fixed them to a neutral grey waterproof canvas, and shot them just in front of his home, this time letting natural decay take its course. Subjected to the alternations of rain and sunlight, the photographs crinkled, rotted in places, then decomposed into fragments, and were totally destroyed in the space of a few weeks. More curiously, he acquired toy figurines, schematic representations of human beings, and subjected them to the same process. The figurines were more resilient, and, in order to accelerate their decomposition, he had to use again his carboys of acid. He now fed exclusively on liquids, and every evening a nurse came to give him an injection of morphine. But in the morning he felt better, and until his last day he could work for at least two or three hours.

It was thus that Jed Martin *took his leave* of an existence for which he'd never totally signed up. Some images now returned to him, and, curiously, while his erotic life had had nothing exceptional about it, they were above all images of women. Geneviève, sweet Geneviève, and poor Olga pursued him in his dreams. He found himself remembering Marthe Taillefer, who had revealed desire to him, on a balcony in Port-Grimaud, at the moment when, taking off her Lejaby bra, she had exposed her breasts. She was then fifteen, he thirteen. That very evening he had masturbated, in the toilet of the company flat that had been allocated to his father for overseeing the building site, and had been astonished to find so much pleasure in it. There returned to him other memories of supple breasts, agile tongues and tight vaginas. Come on, he hadn't had a bad life.

About thirty years before (and it is the only indication outside the strictly technical plan he gives in the interview to *Art Press*), Jed had made a trip to the Ruhrgebiet, where a big retrospective of his work was being organised. From Duisburg to Dortmund, from Bochum and Gelsenkirchen, most of the old steel factories had been transformed into places for exhibitions, shows, and concerts, at the same time as the local authorities tried to set up an *industrial tourism*, based on the re-creation of the working-class way of life at the beginning of the twentieth century. In fact, the whole region, with its blast furnaces, slag heaps, abandoned railway tracks where freight wagons rusted, its lines of identical and neat and tidy terraced houses, sometimes brightened up by allotments, was like a conservatory of the first industrial age in Europe. Jed had been impressed at the time by the menacing density of the forests that, after scarcely a century of inactivity, surrounded the factories. Only those which could be adapted to their new cultural vocation had been rehabilitated, while the others were gradually disintegrating. These industrial colossi, where once was concentrated the bulk of German productive capacity, were now rusted, half collapsed, and plants colonised the former workshops, creeping between ruins that they gradually covered with impenetrable jungle.

The work that occupied the last years of Jed Martin's life can thus be seen – and this is the first interpretation that springs to mind – as a nostalgic meditation on the end of the industrial age in Europe, and, more generally, on the perishable and transitory nature of any human industry. This interpretation is, however, inadequate when one tries to make sense of the unease that grips us on seeing those pathetic Playmobil-type little figurines, lost in the middle of an abstract and immense futurist city, a city which itself crumbles and falls apart then seems gradually to be scattered across the immense vegetation extending to infinity. That feeling of desolation, too, that takes hold of us as the portraits of the human beings who had accompanied Jed Martin through his earthly life fall apart under the impact of bad weather, then decompose and disappear, seeming in the last videos to make themselves the symbols of the generalised annihilation of the human species. They sink and seem for an instant to put up a struggle, before being suffocated by the superimposed layers of plants. Then everything becomes calm. There remains only the grass swaying in the wind. The triumph of vegetation is total.

Acknowledgements

I don't normally thank anyone, because I gather little information, very little in comparison with, say, an American author. But in this case I was impressed and intrigued by the police, and it seemed to me necessary to do a bit more.

This time, I therefore have the pleasure of thanking Teresa Cremisi, who took all the necessary steps, as well as the principal private secretary Henry Moreau and the police commander Pierre Dieppois, who gave me a kind welcome at the Quai des Orfèvres, and provided very useful information on their difficult profession.

It goes without saying that I felt free to modify the facts, and that the opinions expressed are exclusively those of the characters; in short, this is a work of fiction.

I also thank Wikipedia (http://fr.wikipedia.org) and its contributors whose entries I have occasionally used as a source of inspiration, notably those concerning the housefly, the town of Beauvais and Frédéric Nihous.